PENGUIN BOOKS

The Space Between Us

7000

D0275691

The Space Between Us

ANNA MCPARTLIN

PENGUIN BOOKS

PENGUIN BOOKS

Published by the Penguin Group
Penguin Books Ltd, 80 Strand, London WC2R ORL, England
Penguin Group (USA) Inc., 375 Hudson Street, New York, New York 10014, USA
Penguin Group (Canada), 90 Eglinton Avenue East, Suite 700, Toronto, Ontario, Canada M4P 2Y3
(a division of Pearson Penguin Canada Inc.)
Penguin Ireland, 25 St Stephen's Green, Dublin 2, Ireland
(a division of Penguin Books Ltd)
Penguin Group (Australia), 250 Camberwell Road, Camberwell, Victoria 3124, Australia
(a division of Pearson Australia Group Pty Ltd)
Penguin Books India Pvt Ltd, 11 Community Centre, Panchsheel Park, New Delhi – 110 017, India
Penguin Group (NZ), 67 Apollo Drive, Rosedale, Auckland 0632, New Zealand
(a division of Pearson New Zealand Ltd)
Penguin Books (South Africa) (Pty) Ltd, Block D, Rosebank Office Park,
181 Jan Smuts Avenue, Parktown North, Gauteng 2193, South Africa

Penguin Books Ltd, Registered Offices: 80 Strand, London WC2R ORL, England

www.penguin.com

First published in Ireland by Poolbeg Press 2011
Published in Penguin Books 2012
001

Copyright © Anna McPartlin, 2011, 2012
All rights reserved

The moral right of the author has been asserted

Set in 11/13 pt Dante MT Std
Typeset by Jouve (UK), Milton Keynes
Printed in Great Britain by Clays Ltd, St Ives plc

ISBN: 978-0-241-95013-5

www.greenpenguin.co.uk

Penguin Books is committed to a sustainable
future for our business, our readers and our
planet. This book is made from paper certified
by the Forest Stewardship Council.

ALWAYS LEARNING   PEARSON

To all my friends: this world would
be a sorry place without you

1. Introducing the one and only Eve Hayes

Dear Lily,

You've been away a week and it feels like a year! So, what's been happening on the home front? Well, not too much, really. You know the weirdo who works at the bowling alley? (The one who looks like Glenn Medeiros, not the one who picks his nose and eats it.) Well, he followed me from the chipper to the harbour and I could feel him behind me but I didn't let on until I realized that it was getting dark and there was no one else around. Then I turned on him and said, 'What do you want?' He pointed to his bike which was chained up just ahead of me and said, 'I want my bike.' MORTIFIED. Anyway, we got talking about music, he's an REM fan (yawn, isn't everyone?) and out of nowhere he said he liked me! Just like that. I said he was too short for me to like that way. Was that mean? You are my filter when it comes to social contact with plebs. He looked hurt but for God's sake I'm five foot eleven. What's he – about five foot six? We'd look so stupid together, plus there is that issue of him being weird. He said, and I'm not joking, 'We'll be the same height when we lie down!!!' Think about it, Lily . . . he's talking about sex! The cheek of him. So I mentioned his weirdness and he denied being weird. Instead he said he was different and being different was sexy. Can you believe it? I said yeah, maybe if being different is being fantastically good at something or being totally original and having some sort of vision, instead of getting a perm, wearing his sister's blouses and standing on street corners shouting out really bad poems. That really seemed to knock him. He wasn't pushed about the perm or the blouse comments but the poetry hit hard. I felt bad because he looked like I'd stuck a pin in him. I said sorry but he looked like he was about to start crying. Then he called me a stuck-up blonde bitch and stormed off. I sat on the wall and tried to eat my chips, which were now cold so I ended up giving most of them to a dog that had been licking another dog's shit on the beach. Then Gar, Declan and Paul arrived. Declan seems to be in an awful way without you. He was asking me if I'd heard from you. I said just that call you made from the phone box on Wed night and he said you'd rung him then too.

How is everything in Dingle? Is waitressing getting any better? Is the money good enough to stay? I really miss you. It's so lonely here without you. Gar keeps trying to get back with me and I've no intention but, and don't kill me, I did kiss him last night. It was stupid and I was a bit drunk and he was nice and told me my eyes were so green they shone like emeralds. I know – puke – but when you're drunk that kind of thing makes you feel amazing. Well, at least it made me feel amazing until we kissed and I realized I just don't want to go back there. I really like Gar as a friend but that's it. I made some stupid excuse that I had to go so now I have to face him and talk to him sober!

Do you think if the tips are good and you do well down there you can come home for August? I just can't believe this could be our last summer together and you're down there and I'm up here and it's so completely boring without you. I know your mother is broke but couldn't she ask your father for some money? How much does it cost to phone Greece to remind him he has a kid in Ireland who wants to go to college and needs help with the fees? It's not like he's been there for anything else in your life and I know it hurts. So sorry for bringing it up but it has to be said. He owes you.

I'm using my time to research. I spend a lot of my days in the library. The lads think I've lost it but I love the library. I've been reading about fashion through the ages and it's really interesting. Dad bought me a new and much better sewing machine to make

2

up for you leaving, and on Thursday I bought loads of oversized clothes in the charity shop so that I can rip them apart and start again. I wouldn't be caught dead in anything I've made to date – the material is way too naff – but it's something to do.

Clooney is never really home and when I do see him he's with a different girl every time. Dad seems amused by it. I'm not. He's changing and since he started in that stupid college radio he goes around the place like he's Bono or something. It's pathetic. The one he was with last night was a state. She had big wild black hair, like Kate Bush gone wrong, a million bangles, and her T-shirt hadn't been washed in about a year. They slept in his room because Dad was away. I wonder if Dad would be amused by that. It'll cost my bro! The next time he annoys me I'll charge him twenty quid for my silence. Anyway, she calls him my fluffy Cloudy!!! Can you believe it? It's sickening. Watched Young Guns 2 (with TV up loud) again last night. OK, so name who you'd go out with in order of preference: Emilio Estevez, Kiefer Sutherland, Lou Diamond Phillips, Christian Slater?

I'd go for

1. Emilio Estevez (really cute in a serious way)
2. Lou Diamond Phillips (exotic)
3. Kiefer Sutherland (I liked him in Lost Boys but in YG2 he was just there)
4. Christian Slater (does he really talk like that?)

Right, have to go, I'm pulling apart a size-sixteen pair of dungarees. Don't know what I'm going to make yet but I'm hoping for at least three pieces out of it.

MISS YOU, MISS YOU, LOVE YOU.

Your best friend,

Eve

PS Paul told me that Glenn Medeiros from the bowling alley (his real name is Ben Logan) writes those poems about his dead sister. Now I feel really bad. She died when she was ten. That's what that poem (the one he keeps repeating in the funny

voice) – 'Ten, Ten, Never Again' – is about. I still think it's weird.
I miss my mum but I don't make up poems about her death.

> *I was five, she was alive,*
> *I was seven, she was in heaven!*

PPS What's the weather like down there? It's been raining here
for three days solid. Sick of wet hair. Thinking about doing a
Sinéad O'Connor. So much for summer.

On 1 July 2010, twenty years after eighteen-year-old Eve Hayes had
sat down at her bedroom desk one rainy Sunday afternoon to
write a letter to her best friend Lily, a much older and wiser Eve sat
at that same old desk. It was raining just like it had been all those
years before. Eve's mind drifted back to that day, as it often did
when she felt sad or lonely. At the time a week had felt like an
entire year. She smiled at the memory of her desperation. She had
missed her pal so much that her heart hurt, and she'd walked
around like a zombie because she'd lost sleep engaging in all-night
conversations with Lily in her head. Eve would say something like
Hey, Lil, this time next year we'll . . . and Imaginary Lily would finish Eve's sentence . . . *be millionaires.* They were both big fans of
Only Fools and Horses and had the dialogue down. Eve would call
Lily a *plonker.* Imaginary Lily would call Eve *a saucy old git.* When
Eve got bored of basically calling herself names, she'd tell Imaginary Lily about her everyday happenings and annoyances, like, for
example, the morning she'd thought that her brother Clooney
had died on the toilet: he hadn't responded when she'd banged on
the door and sworn at him while considering whether it would be
better to pee in the kitchen sink or under the tree in the back garden. The sink had won. *Can you believe it, Lily? I peed in my own*
kitchen sink. I couldn't really do it in the garden because it's overlooked
by the Noonans' and we all know that Terry 'the Tourist' Noonan is a
perv with a set of binoculars and a second-hand Polaroid camera he car-
ries at all times. So not risking my rear end hanging on his wall!

Clooney had emerged from the bathroom ten minutes later, with a girl and a smug look on his face, while Eve had been up to her elbows in bleach and Fairy Liquid. She'd wanted to punch him but then eighteen-year-old Eve had often wanted to punch twenty-year-old Clooney. Instead she'd just screamed that she was straight telling Dad when he got home. He had laughed at her, and in her head when she told Imaginary Lily she had laughed too. Lily and Clooney were thick as thieves.

Back then, and on the advice of their guidance counsellor Mrs Moriarty, Lily had decided to go to medical school and become a GP. She liked the notion of being a doctor, and there was no way she was going to be a gynaecologist because she and Eve both agreed that fannies were disgusting. Besides, a GP practice was child-friendly and Lily had wanted to be a mother as far back as Eve could remember; they had been friends since they were in nappies. Lily had carried around a doll until she was ten. She called her Layla and treated her like a person. When Lily's teacher Mrs Marsh began to worry that Layla was some sort of psychological crutch for Lily, her mother put a stop to any more nonsense talk by giving the doll to charity. Lily cried for one week solid and Eve tried to soothe her by giving her friend her own precious monkey but, even as she handed Monkey over, she knew Layla was irreplaceable to Lily. And so, having confirmed that to be the case, she took Monkey home, cuddled him all night and promised she'd never let him go again.

Eve had always been determined to become a designer. She'd been sewing since she was twelve. She loved finding material, drawing patterns and making clothes. Also, she had the perfect model in Lily, who was tiny and petite and, no matter how unlikely the design or ensemble was, she would always wear Eve's creations.

As the years went by Eve's work improved. In the fifth year she won a design award and was commissioned to make four debs' outfits and a Communion dress for her dad's second cousin. Even before she'd received her Leaving Cert results, she had secured herself a place in St Martin's College of Design in London on the basis of her portfolio.

Lily was the cleverest girl in her class. She sailed through school and never had to work too hard, which meant she could take extra lessons in photography, art and piano. She was good at everything, even sewing, although she lacked Eve's flair.

'You're going to make it,' Lily would say to Eve.

'Yeah,' Eve would agree. 'Somewhere Coco Chanel's shitting herself.'

They both knew that Lily would study medicine at the university of her choosing. She based her first preference on where her boyfriend, Declan, wanted to go, which upset Eve: Lily had never talked about leaving Dublin to go to college but Declan favoured Cork. Eve thought that was an excuse: everyone knew that UCC was easier to get into than UCD. Lily would have sailed into UCD, Trinity or even the College of Surgeons but Declan would have to fight tooth and nail to get Cork. Lily insisted she was going to the same college as Declan, and pointed out that as Eve was going to London it was none of her business. *But still* . . .

It was an exciting time, full of promise, and the only real difference between the girls was that Lily was desperate to grow up while Eve was slow to embrace change. Twenty years ago, that summer was supposed to have been the last the girls spent together, but Lily needed to earn money for college: the only way she could do it was to go and work for her uncle in his restaurant 228 miles away. Eve often wondered in the years that followed what would have happened if she had followed Lily. *Would we still be friends?* She remembered the little mantra she'd say every night before she fell asleep. *Goodnight, Lily, I miss you, I miss you, I love you.* And conceded to herself that teenagers were mental.

The old desk looked out over her back garden and past it to the large old trees, the swing and Terry the Tourist's empty bedroom window. It had been years since she'd seen him. His family had moved after Leaving Cert but Eve's friend Gar had heard he was a press photographer in the UK, which made sense. Why take pictures of death in a war zone when you can look up some celebrity's dress outside the Ivy?

Absentmindedly, Eve traced the initials she'd spent a good hour or two carving into the table: BGML Ben 'Glenn Medeiros' Logan had come into Eve's life as Lily had left it. That summer twenty years ago Eve had fallen in love, made a huge mistake, told the truth, lost her best friend and grown up.

The old desk was the last of the furniture that would be taken by the movers. They were on a break, sitting at the back of their van eating sausage sandwiches from the local Centra shop. Eve had been left to roam around the house she'd grown up in one last time. She left her old bedroom and made her way downstairs. The red paint had faded, leaving intermittent vibrant squares on the parts of wall that had once been covered with family photos. They were all gone but Eve could see them as clearly now as if they were still there.

There had been one of her mother, father, Clooney, Eve and Lily. Eve, at two years old, was sitting on her father's shoulders. Her mother had her arms wrapped around four-year-old Clooney and Lily was holding Clooney's hand. It was summer and they were standing, freckled by the sun, under a blue sky and everyone except Eve was grinning. The oval shape had been home to a picture of Clooney and Eve hugging in their school uniforms on her first day at primary school. He was squeezing her tightly while Eve was battling to escape his bear-hug. The largest square had held the family portrait Eve's father had commissioned when her mother had become ill. The family sat in a line on the sofa in their best clothes, Mum at one end, Dad at the other, Clooney and Eve between them. She had been six, Clooney eight – Eve remembered the photographer getting annoyed because she refused to smile when he said, 'Cheese!'

'You can't help but smile when you say the word,' he had said.

'That doesn't make sense,' Eve told him.

'Why won't you smile?'

'I don't feel like it.'

'I can't take your picture if you don't.'

'Yes, you can. Just press the button.'

'It'll only be for a second. I assure you it won't break your face.'

'Why won't he just do it and go away, Mum?'

Her mother told the man that Eve loathed having her photo taken. 'We all have our pet hates,' she said.

'Look, love, I'm not asking the child to take over the controls of a plane or jump into the River Liffey. I'm just asking her to move the corners of her mouth up towards her eyes.'

Her father told Eve to smile in the voice that he always used when he meant business. The photographer poised the camera. Just as it clicked she stuck out her tongue. Clooney thought it was funny. Her father warned her to be good, but Eve was having none of it and her mother was tired so the photographer was asked to take another shot whether Eve was smiling or not. He did so: the others looked like they'd won the lottery and Eve looked like her dog had died.

The rest of the photos were pretty much the same, and from them, it would have been easy to think that Eve had grown up a miserable little girl, but the opposite was true. She was mostly delighted with life, herself and the world around her. The only time she stopped being delighted was when a camera was pointed in her direction. After her mother died that hardly ever happened because it turned out that her father hated the camera every bit as much as his daughter did. Every cloud . . .

Eve moved from room to room, memories floating in and out of her mind. Even though the kitchen had been refurbished, when she stood where the large table used to be and closed her eyes, she could smell her father's tomato-and-chilli sauce burning. She could see him standing over it, stirring vigorously and wearing a ladybird apron. He kept flinging pasta at the wall, insisting that when it stuck it was ready to eat.

'Kids, we have lift-off!' He spooned out the pasta and sauce.

Clooney, Eve and Lily had sat down and started to eat. Her dad had been taking apart an old radio he'd found in a skip and eating his dinner at the same time. Somehow he'd fixed it while he was clearing his plate. Eve's father had always done his best but Eve had once overheard her aunt say to her uncle Rory: 'God love them, those kids would eat fried maggots if their daddy served them with a smile.' And poor Lily, well, she'd thought the sun, moon and stars shone out of Eve's dad. He was kind to her and she called him Danny, not just because that was his name but because it sounded like 'Daddy'. Eve had copied her friend so Dad became Danny to her too. There wasn't a memory in the house that Lily wasn't part of.

As she moved to the glass doors that led to the stone patio, she was humming 'Senza Una Donna', the old Paul Young and Zucchero song. Clooney had sung 'Scent of Madonna' to make Lily laugh and annoy Eve – Eve had been easy to annoy as a teenager.

> *Scent of Madonna,*
> *Gives me pain and some sorrow,*
> *Scent of Madonna,*
> *She'll still smell bad tomorrow!*

'Dick.'

'Evey, don't call your brother a dick!'

'Well, tell him to stop acting like one.'

'Clooney, stop annoying your sister.'

'I'm only singing.'

'No, you're doing my head in!' Eve said.

'It's hardly the end of the world, Evey.'

The back garden was overgrown, the old tree-house long gone, but the big old oak tree was still there. Eve leaned against it and looked at the house. She remembered her mother living in her bedroom for months before she died. Eve was allowed to visit once a day, and only for a few minutes near the end. She always brought Lily, who would stay silent and stroke Eve's mother's hand.

'How are you, Mum?'

'I'm fine,' she'd say, with a big smile.

'You don't look fine.'

'No.'

'You look weird.'

'Don't be scared.'

'I'm not scared, I'm sad.'

Eve's dad often tried to explain to her that saying everything that entered her head wasn't the best idea in the world, especially when it made her mother cry. She never had mastered the art of subtlety, she mused now.

She sat on the old wooden swing-set, which she and Lily had sat on nearly every dry day until they were twelve and too old for swings. After thirty years it should have been falling apart but her father had looked after it, and it was as much a part of the landscape as the big old trees. She started to swing a little, remembering their squeals when they had gone higher and higher until their feet were touching the sky.

'The one who swings highest gets a wish!' Eve would call.

Lily had freaked out every time: there were so many things she wanted that it was hard to make just one wish. 'I can't think!' she would squeal.

When they couldn't swing any higher, Lily would call at the top of her voice: 'I love you, Eve Hayes!'

'I love you, Lily Brennan!' Eve would scream back, and they'd giggle and kick their legs wildly.

It had been a long time since Eve had swung or indeed done anything with abandon, so she sat and stared at the ground in front of her, at the patch of grass where she'd lain on her back, with Lily at her side, battling with the sun to look up at her mother's window. They were doing that on the day she died, lying on the grass, talking about this and that. Suddenly there had been a commotion, adults coming and going, Eve's aunt crying, her uncle talking on the phone. Eve's father called Clooney – and then something happened: people stopped moving around the house and someone unseen in Eve's mother's room closed the curtains. Lily held Eve's hand and even though they were only six they knew that she was gone.

Eve shielded her eyes from the sun and looked up at the window. It was the only room she hadn't visited one last time. The pain was still too raw because her dad had died in it only nine months before.

He had died on an October morning after a short illness. He was sixty-two, and up to the day he was diagnosed with cancer he had been his usual happy, healthy, busy self. He was still working as an investment banker, still mad about boats and golf, and dating Jean, a woman in her mid-fifties. It was early days but they had a lot in common and he really liked her. He still travelled, and visited Eve in New York at least three times a year. On his last visit he had brought Jean, and they'd been in love. His back had been bothering him for a while, and he had been diagnosed with Type 2 diabetes a few years before. Initially he had managed to control the disease but recently his blood sugar had been all over the place. Finally, at Jean's insistence, he went to his GP. Two weeks later, on 16 August, he was diagnosed with terminal pancreatic cancer. It was Jean who phoned Eve in New York.

'Hello, Eve?'

'Yes, hello?'

'It's Jean McCormack . . . your father's friend.'

'Oh, Jean! Hello, how are you?'

'I'm well. Thank you. Thank you for asking.' She sounded weird and it didn't take a genius to work out she wasn't making a social call.

'What's wrong, Jean?'

'It's your dad, dear.' She sounded like she was trying not to cry.

'What about him?' Eve's heart-rate increased, her temperature rose and the blood that had previously been in her head rushed to her toes. She held on to her chair. *Get to the point, Jean, for Christ's sake.*

'He has cancer.'

'Oh, no.'

'In his pancreas.'

'Oh, no.'

'You need to come home, dear.'

'What about Clooney?'

'You need to get him to come home too.' She broke down then and cried.

Eve listened to herself comfort Jean. It was as though she was hearing strangers converse through a wall. 'All right, Jean, it'll be all right. I'll call Clooney and we'll come home and take care of him. He'll be fine because I have money and I can pay whatever it costs, so you just relax because I'll sort it. OK?'

'OK, dear,' she said. 'OK.' But she had known that no amount of money could save Eve's father. She was doing the only thing that could be done: surrounding him with the people he loved and who loved him.

His health declined incredibly quickly, so the last two months of his life had been very special. Eve and Clooney hadn't lived in their childhood home since that summer of 1990. Their father didn't want to be in hospital or a hospice so it made sense that they stay there with him during the short time he had left. Although Eve's money couldn't save him it could pay for the round-the-clock care he required.

Clooney arrived home two days after Eve. Despite his tan he looked grey and new lines were forming around his eyes. He got drunk that night and cried like a baby. Eve made lists of things that needed doing and got busy fitting the room in which her mother had died with all the conveniences necessary to ensure that her father was comfortable. Eve's father was usually cheerful, but every now and then when he thought he was alone he'd scream and sob. Eve had had to hold her brother back from his door. 'He needs this,' she'd said.

'He needs us,' he'd replied.

'When was the last time you were grateful for an audience while you cried?' she asked.

Their father loved having them with him, especially when he

wasn't in pain. Jean was there from beginning to end but never tried to take over. Eve and Clooney thought it was odd that she prayed silently, her fingers moving up and down her rosary beads, while sitting at their father's bedside.

'You know my dad's agnostic?' Eve said to her one day.

'Yes, dear, I do.'

'And yet you pray.'

'I know. Selfish, isn't it?'

'I've lost you.'

'Well, I'm praying for me.'

'Oh.'

'And you? Are you an agnostic too?'

'Until the Virgin Mary, a jolly Buddha, Allah or Brahman come to sit on the end of my bed and tell me any different,' Eve said.

'It'll be hard to let him go,' Jean said. 'I pray for him because it makes me feel better, and I pray for me that when he's gone I'll have the strength to go on.'

'You will,' Eve said, with the confidence that came from experience, even though the thought of losing her father made her heart ache.

'What about you?' Jean asked.

'People live and then they die,' Eve said.

When they were alone Jean and Eve's dad flirted and laughed. She brought light into his darkened room and he wasn't the only Hayes grateful to her.

Eve and Clooney spent days in their father's room. He loved crosswords and watching re-runs of *Who Wants To Be A Millionaire?* Clooney would answer the questions, as though he knew what he was talking about, but more often than not he'd get the answer wrong, making the others laugh. On one occasion Chris Tarrant asked, 'Which legendary German scholar sold his soul to the devil?' He gave four names.

Eve looked at her dad and shrugged. He did the same.

'Tannhäuser,' Clooney said confidently.

It went to fifty:fifty. Faust and Tannhäuser were the two names left. Clooney looked at them and nodded smugly. The contestant picked Faust.

'Oops, you've just blown it.'

Chris Tarrant paused for what seemed an eternity before he smiled and announced that the contestant had just won £16,000.

Everyone celebrated except Clooney, who pretended to be put out by his dad's laughter.

'Faust. Damn it, Faust, of course.'

' "Of course", my rectum, you didn't have a clue!' Eve said.

'Fair enough,' he admitted, 'but if that was poker I would have won the hand.'

'Sap!' Eve said.

'Yeah, well, at least I'm not a Big Foot!' Clooney said, and laughed. Because of Eve's height she had been christened Big Foot by a boy called Eoin Shaw in her first class at primary school and it had caught on to the extent that she didn't rid herself of it until she moved into secondary school.

'Danny!' Eve appealed.

Her dad laughed and repeated, 'Big Foot,' under his breath. Then he recited the song the kids in Eve's class, all but Lily, used to sing. ' "Big Foot Hayes doesn't do Sundays. We go to Mass, she eats grass. Big Foot Hayes . . ." What was the end of it?'

'Danny!' Eve said again, but this time she smiled reluctantly.

Clooney thought about it for a second before raising his hand: ' "Big Foot Hayes blocks out sun rays." '

Eve's dad giggled. 'No future poet laureates in that bunch.'

Some afternoons they would play Monopoly together. Usually Eve won. Clooney suggested this was due to her cold, detached, industrialist Ming the Merciless personality.

'Ah, come on, Evey, don't take Shrewsbury Road! You always get it!' her dad said, when it looked like she was going to win again.

'Take comfort that it isn't worth what it used to be, Danny.'

'Just give it to him, Ming.'

'Can't do it, Clooney.'

'I'd be happy to part with Shannon Airport, Dad?' he offered.

His dad laughed. 'Of course you would, son.'

When he was still able for conversation they talked about everything and anything, except that he was dying. Jean took care of his will, discussed his funeral with him, and made notes of what he wanted. He had no truck with religion and didn't believe in an afterlife. He didn't look forward to kicking it up on a cloud in Heaven or fear burning in an eternal Hell. He wasn't expecting to see Eve's mum. Even as he grew worse and his pain became more difficult to manage, they continued to pretend that Clooney and Eve were staying for an extended visit and that all was well.

When he began to slip away from them, they finally let go of the pretence. As he battled for his last breath, Eve held his hand and whispered, 'It's OK to let go, Danny.' He squeezed her hand, closed his eyes and was gone.

Jean sat by the door with her head bowed, twisting her well-worn rosary beads. Clooney stood by the window facing out. Eve made notes of what she had to attend to.

Their father had wanted to keep the funeral simple, with a few words from Clooney and Eve, but if Eve didn't want to talk that was all right, because he knew what she was like. He wanted his old friend Lenny to play the guitar and sing a few Bob Dylan songs. Afterwards he wanted them to take his ashes out to sea on his beloved sail-boat and dump him ceremoniously in the waves.

'Is that legal?' Clooney had asked Jean.

'Who cares?' Eve said.

So that was exactly what they did. Eve had packed a picnic, including a bottle of expensive wine. She, Jean and Clooney stood on the deck, each lost in their memories. They made sure they knew which way the wind was blowing because he had been adamant that they shouldn't risk wearing or eating him. 'Wind direction is the key, Jean,' he had warned.

'Got it.'

'It's the key,' he repeated, before licking his finger and raising it into the air.

'Understood.'

'And don't throw the urn in.'

'Righto.'

'That's littering.'

'Indeed it is.'

'But don't keep the urn either.'

'Well, what would you like me to do with it?'

'Recycle it.'

'Okey-dokey.'

'I wish I had more time to love you, Jean,' he said, and smiled. 'I'm so very sorry about that.'

'Me too,' she said, allowing a tear to fall as she went on ticking off his list of requests.

When they had assessed the wind direction, Eve handed Clooney the urn and he tossed the ashes overboard. Eve poured three glasses of wine and they toasted him. Jean cried the whole way back, quietly and into a large hankie – she didn't want to make too much fuss. Clooney was silent and barely touched his drink. Eve had finished what was left in the bottle by the time they hit the harbour.

In the eleven months since her father's passing a lot had changed. It was time to leave the house and her childhood behind. She was looking forward to a new chapter in her life, a slower-paced one. It was time for Eve to stop and smell the roses.

She closed the dark-blue front door and walked down the short, tree-lined avenue. At the end, she turned to take one last look at the large white house covered with a pink-flowering creeper, and the big oak tree in the front garden. *Goodbye, old house . . . goodbye, childhood . . . goodbye, Mum . . . goodbye, Danny. You were amazing, we were lucky to have you both. I miss you. I love you. If I never see you again, thank you.* She didn't dally or shed a tear: her mother had taught her to keep her feelings to herself and that a lady always knows the right time to leave. She nodded to the guys in the van as they finished their lunch, then crossed the road, got into her car and drove away from the street where she'd grown up for what she believed to be the final time.

That morning Eve had spoken to Clooney briefly on the

phone. He was in some hellhole in Afghanistan, feeding orphans, and he didn't much care about the house sale.

'I need your bank details.'

'For what?'

'For the money from the sale of the house.'

'Just give my share to a cancer charity.'

'Please don't make it difficult.'

'I'm making it easy.'

'No. You're making it difficult. I'm not going to give away your money.'

'Please?'

'I'll set up an account in your name.'

'Does that mean I have to deal with tax?'

'You don't give away money because you don't want to deal with tax.'

'*You* don't. I do.' He changed the subject. 'You sound tired.'

'Of course I'm tired. I'm the one doing everything while you swan around Afghanistan.'

'People don't swan around war zones.'

'No. I suppose they don't,' she conceded.

'You must be happy to be home again.'

'Yeah,' she agreed, a little half heartedly. 'It's great.'

'Maybe I'll come and visit you soon,' he said.

'I won't hold my breath,' she said. 'A person has to be dying to get you home.' He didn't argue. Instead he ended the conversation by telling her to do what she wanted with the money. 'I don't need it, Eve, and I don't want it.'

Clooney had always been strange about money. Even as a kid, he had never wanted material things. He'd lived on his meagre expenses, banking his pay, for years. He had the life of a nomad without dependants. He fed the poor in the worst conditions known to man and didn't need a suit or a car to do that. Eve's brother, she thought, was the best person she knew at dealing with a crisis but the minute that crisis had passed he moved on because he wasn't needed.

Clooney had left home when he was twenty. In September 1990 he was due to start his third year in college. He was studying engineering and had secured himself a spot on college radio. He did a show with a girl called Vera Kilpatrick. They hosted an evening programme from Monday to Friday.

Clooney had never liked his name. Even though his parents had agreed to call him Matthew, his mum had changed her mind as soon as she saw him with one eye open resting in her arms. 'He's not a Matthew. He's a Clooney,' she'd said.

His father wasn't so sure he liked the idea but she was determined. 'It's Gaelic for "rogue". And this one is most definitely a rogue.'

Most people had never heard the name before and he was often asked to repeat and spell it – until 1994 when George Clooney played Dr Doug Ross on *ER*. Suddenly the whole Western world knew it, and on the rare Christmas when he was home the endless 'witty' comments made him miserable.

'Clooney? You fancy yourself.'

'Clooney, I need CPR. Stat.'

'Clooney? You're cute but not that cute.'

'Here, Clooney, you were a shit Batman.'

His dad joked that the reason he chose to live and work in third-world countries had nothing to do with altruism and everything to do with escaping the curse of the actor George Clooney.

In the late eighties and early nineties, a lot of DJs gave themselves stupid names and Clooney was no exception. Clooney Hayes became Cloudy Dayz and his sidekick Vera Kilpatrick was known as V Kill P. She'd play Kylie and Jason's 'Especially For You', he'd play Simple Minds' 'Belfast Child'. She'd play the Bangles' 'Eternal Flame' and he'd play Guns N' Roses' 'Paradise City'. Between their musical tug-of-war, they introduced their audience to sex and drugs and rock 'n' roll. They'd argue from the male and female perspective. They'd talk about anything, no holds barred, and they made a good team. They celebrated the 1988 decision to decriminalize homosexual acts between consenting adults by the European Court of Human Rights as a result of a case taken by David Norris against Ireland and its draconian laws. They canvassed to appeal the 1989 Supreme Court's ruling that prevented students providing leaflets and contact information on abortion services in the UK. They discussed the 1990 Criminal Law Amendment Act on rape and explained what the abolition of the marital exemption meant. They had great passion and chemistry and, although at the time Eve would not have admitted it, the show was pretty good.

Clooney could have gone into radio if he'd wanted to, and he would have made a fine engineer, but his bleeding heart claimed his future. He was fourteen when Bob Geldof's Live Aid changed the world. It had a massive impact on him. Millions were dying in the worst of circumstances, and long after the concert was over, the faces of the starving lived on in his head. When he was presented with an opportunity to join Peace Corps volunteers going to Africa, he abandoned his degree and left as soon as he'd had his vaccinations. In the intervening years he had worked with many non-governmental organizations across three continents; the two months with his dying father was the longest period Clooney had spent in Ireland since he was twenty.

Eve had left for St Martin's that same September in 1990. For the first year she studied for a BA Hons in Fashion, but when she realized she was not as talented as some of her peers, she changed to Jewellery Design and found her niche. The course lasted three years and, although she had enjoyed her time in London, when she graduated she took a job with a jewellery design house in Paris and lived there for three years. Eve wasn't much of a party girl. She was determined to succeed in her work and spent endless hours at her desk. She loved what she did, and eventually she felt she had learned enough to go to America to design her own line. She wanted to set up an international business. Life was good and she was content, until her dad died. Those precious two months had changed everything: she had slowed down and reconnected with her dad, her brother, her old friends and her home.

After a long silence of many years Eve had found many friends on Facebook. Her old teenage boyfriend Gar Lynch contacted her first, and then she got in touch with their mutual pal Paul Doyle. Gar had married Gina McCarthy, who was two years older than Eve. They had grown up around the corner from one another and had been friends until Eve was twelve when Gina had ended their friendship: Eve and Lily were too young for her now, she'd said, and slammed the door in their faces when they had come to ask if she wanted to play. Despite that, Eve had always liked Gina, and she was pleased to learn that Gar had ended up with her. Through Facebook she discovered they had two kids, two dogs, one cat and a boat. They had stayed in the same area because Gar couldn't think of any reason to move. 'Sea air, good schools, great restaurants, the best pub in Ireland and it's on the DART line. It's perfect here,' he'd said, via personal message.

She learned that, after college, Paul had moved to the UK but had returned home during the boom years. Despite a strained relationship with his parents he had stayed local too. Gar had explained that Paul had come out during his second year at Trinity College. Everyone had been surprised: he was a brilliant rugby player, hard as nails and always with girls. The lads thought he was a legend. Eve thought he was a major slut, a nice one, but the word was that if you wanted to retain any dignity or your virginity it was best to steer clear of Paul Doyle. She had been in London when he came out and missed all the drama. Later she heard from Gar and Gina that there had been plenty of it. Paul's father had gone on a bender for three days and nights, ending up in A&E with a split head and no memory of how it had happened. His mother had threatened to swallow an entire packet of sleeping pills only to be talked out of it by the local priest, who promised to pray that her son would escape eternal damnation. The priest had turned out to be a paedophile, which Mrs Doyle seemed to take better than her son's sexuality.

Paul had lived with a guy called Paddy for years and the first anyone knew of the relationship ending was his change of status on Facebook. He was great company but he never talked about his personal life, and in the three years since Paddy had vanished no one knew who Paul was with. One evening twelve months previously Eve had tried to extort information from him.

'No.'

'Ah, come on, tell me something.'

'No.'

'I need distraction.'

'No.'

'Why not?'

'Because I don't want to.'

'You're a crap gay.'

'You've no idea.' He smiled at her and changed the subject.

During her stay in Ireland she even caught up with Ben Logan. He'd contacted her through Facebook six months before her dad's diagnosis. She'd thought long and hard about whether or not to accept his friendship. She'd even polled some of her American friends.

'Never *ever* befriend an ex,' Debbie said.

'Absolutely befriend him – it's not like you've anything going on here,' Marsha countered.

'It's dangerous,' Debbie said.

'How is it dangerous?' Marsha said. 'He lives there, you live here, and it's just a little flirting on the net. God knows, she needs to do something.'

'So why can't she just buy a dress and go on a date?'

'I'm in the room,' Eve reminded them.

Despite Debbie's warning, curiosity won. Having procrastinated just enough to ensure that no one, especially Ben, thought she was too eager, she accepted his request and immediately trawled through his photos and updates. *Still short and still a total ride*. His hair was tight and he was tanned. *Oh, Ben, you'll always be Glenn Medeiros to me.* It was clear he went to the gym and his eyes still shone when he beamed into the camera lens. He owned a chain of organic supermarkets across Dublin, Wicklow, Galway and Cork. He was married to a woman named Fiona. From the photos it appeared that they went on lots of holidays and had no children. He messaged Eve a few hours after she'd accepted his friendship.

> Hey, Blondie, Didn't know if you'd accept, glad you did. Congrats on all your success. I always knew you'd do it although surprised you ended up in jewellery but then again I thought I was going to be a rock star and ended up in the food biz. How's life? Do you ever get home? Ben AKA Glenn M. XXX

She'd responded in a friendly way, congratulating him on his supermarket success and his marriage. She told him she hadn't been home in years, wished him well and politely signed off. After that they had made comments on one another's updates, tagged each other on photos from the past or funny YouTube videos, until Eve's dad got sick.

Eve was at home when he rang the house and asked if she wanted to meet for coffee. She'd spent most of that week running in and out of the hospital and setting up her dad's room at home. She hadn't contacted Gar or Paul so she was amazed that Ben had tracked her down. 'How did you know I was here?' she asked incredulously.

'I thought I saw you in Donnybrook so I decided to call.'

'I was nowhere near Donnybrook.'

'Well, then, it must be Fate,' he said. He still sounded like the boy she had loved and lost one summer twenty years ago.

Her heart skipped. *He's married, Eve, so just behave.*

They'd met for coffee near the hospital and even though she worried that it would begin awkwardly it didn't. They were as easy with each other as they always had been.

'So, posh supermarkets,' she said.

'So, cheap costume jewellery.'

'That's only a tiny part of the business and I prefer the term "affordable". And weren't you supposed to be a tortured poet turned rock star?'

'You were right and I was crap, but weren't you supposed to be the next Coco Chanel?'

'Things change.'

'But you haven't changed a bit.'

He'd looked at her approvingly and Eve's heart had skipped another beat.

Eve didn't melt easily. She wasn't conceited or vain, and she rarely felt beautiful, but she saw beauty in the strangest faces, and working in high-end fashion for many years hadn't changed that. To most of those close to her, though, Eve was beautiful. At five foot eleven, she was slim, with an athletic build, creamy skin, natural blonde hair and green eyes. Eve could have been a model if she hadn't despised cameras. She had cut her hair into a short crop in her early twenties and had worn a version of it ever since, not because it was trendy but because it was handy. She lived in jeans, vest tops and blazers and rarely wore makeup. She had never been girly; she didn't have millions of shoes, and the only piece of jewellery she wore was a gold disc around her neck with her mother's name on it. She had to watch her posture because on the rare occasions when she let herself go she slouched. When Eve looked in the mirror she didn't see what others saw. In fact, the only time she felt beautiful was when she saw herself through Ben Logan's eyes. Sitting in a coffee shop in Dublin, twenty years after they had split up, on the worst night of Eve's life, she blushed.

Since their reunion they had met regularly, at first for coffee, then lunch, then dinner, drinks at a bar, and when they slept together it was on the understanding that he loved his wife, she loved her life, and neither of them wanted anything from each other except a little distraction. They both knew that her time in Ireland was finite. They were absolutely confident that no one would get hurt.

Eve hadn't considered that her time at home and her father's death might change her, or that the life she'd built in America would no longer sustain her or, more importantly, that she would no longer be able to sustain *it*.

At first she denied that she wanted or needed a different life but, deep down, she knew she didn't want to be a captain of industry any more. She didn't want to design jewellery. She didn't want to promote or sell it. Her life had been so stressful for so long that she hadn't noticed she was a workaholic with little or no quality of life. It occurred to her that if she died no one would really notice and that scared her. *I'm so sick of being alone.*

Her board of directors were happy to buy her out. They had plans for the company that she had attempted to block so her change of heart was a dream come true. America had treated Eve very well but her hometown was calling. Six months after they had buried her father at sea, she moved back to Ireland, with two suitcases and a crate of books on design. *Clooney isn't the only one who travels light.* She also had a fat bank balance, which was something nobody else seemed to have in Ireland, two brownstone buildings and a penthouse apartment overlooking Central Park. Eve's accountant had been responsible for those purchases. She'd lived in the penthouse and rented out the brownstones. Clooney and Eve were different in many respects but they had one thing in common: neither was interested in accumulating things.

She rented an apartment overlooking the sea, ten minutes from where she had grown up. She joined a local gym and signed up for yoga classes.

She'd meet Gina for coffee but only when her kids were in school – Eve had never liked kids. As far as she was concerned they were noisy little people who constantly interrupted interesting conversations with banal comments like: 'Mum, Mum, Mum, Mum, Mum.'

'Mum is talking.'

'Mum, Mum, Mum, Mum, Mum.'

'*What?*'

'I, I, I am . . . I like cheese.'

Eve wouldn't pretend to like children because it was the acceptable thing to do and some people valued her honesty, although others did not. She hung around with the people who did. Happily, Gina had accepted Eve's position and was grateful for chat without childish interruptions.

Eve played golf with Gar and talked about the banking crisis, the consequences of an IMF deal and whether or not Ireland should burn bondholders. He was sure the country would recover but that it would take several years. He worked in exports so had one of the few relatively safe jobs, but he was considering moving his family to Australia.

'Whatever happened to this place?' she asked.

'We got greedy and messed it up,' he said sadly.

He didn't want to go but he was worried about mortgage increases, taxation and his children's future. His and Gina's pensions were all but gone. He wanted to live in a country where his kids had half a chance of getting a job when they grew up.

So typical – I get back and my pals leave.

She played tennis with Paul once a week. Afterwards they'd have dinner and sometimes they'd take a Sunday walk on the cliff. He didn't share Gar's concerns. He was resolutely positive about everything. It would be hard for a few years and then we'd right ourselves and be better than ever. Paul was an optimist but then he, like Eve, had no kids to worry about, and although he'd taken a heavy pay cut in the Justice Department, his four-bed semi-detached house was nearly paid for, he hadn't amassed personal debt during the boom years, and still had a few quid in the bank for a rainy day. Paul was not typical but he never had been.

One day as they walked along the cliff he pointed at the sea. 'You don't need to spend money to have a good time,' he said.

'Or to kill yourself,' she replied. She was referring to a local man in his forties who had jumped off the cliff the week before.

'You always have to bring things down.' He shook his head.

'Just keeping it real,' she said.

'It's not like you to think of the little people, Eve,' he said, and he was right. Eve was more often than not too wrapped up in her own world to notice the people around her.

'Maybe I'm finally growing up.'

'It's too late for that,' he said, and they walked on.

Paul was right. She often behaved like a spoilt madam because she was used to getting her own way, but when it came to Ben, she couldn't help but act like a teenager.

She had been home for a month before she contacted him again. Their affair had been based on Eve having an exit date, and before she had left it had been clear that his business was in trouble. Posh supermarkets didn't do well in a recession.

They met in another coffee shop, but this time he was drawn and fidgety. He was uncomfortable around Eve and it made her sad. She told him she only wanted to catch up, which eased the tension a little, but not completely. He had closed two shops, and if he couldn't turn things around in the other three, he faced bankruptcy. He couldn't afford to pay off the suppliers and close the shops. All he could hope to do was trade through but it was becoming more and more difficult and he was running out of ideas. He was a mess and she sympathized. He needed to focus on his business, restructure, negotiate with dying banks and prepare his wife for the possible loss of their livelihood. She told him she'd be there for him if he needed a friend. He thanked her and left.

After that they spoke on the phone a few times. Things were up and down. He found an investor but then the investor fell through. He had plans that were doable but only if he could secure credit. He was a fighter: he'd find a way. She listened to him and made suggestions. She offered to look at the books. He accepted, and she picked them up from his accountant. She spent a week making notes and working out how the business could survive. She thought she'd found a way of changing it to suit the climate so she left a message to talk to him about it. The plan would involve a big change she wasn't sure he was ready for, but it was nice to offer a solution. He didn't get back to her right away and she didn't want to press him.

Their relationship had changed. She accepted that. Besides, she was busy de-stressing – after all, that was why she'd walked out on her life. But there were days when she was so bored and lonely that she believed she'd made a huge mistake. Then she'd think of Lily. She'd rehash that summer all those years ago, who did and said what to whom and where it had all gone wrong. A combination of bad memories and regrets made her head hurt, so she'd lie down on her hard white sofa and look out of her floor-to-ceiling windows on to the sea her dad's ashes floated in. She'd stare at a passing ship moving slowly in the distance until she was sound asleep.

Naps were becoming Eve's new ritual. Her new life was all about relaxation yet she was still suffering from the anxiety that had plagued her since her dad had died. Her head often felt as if it was going to burst and the hole in her heart tore a little wider every day. She thought she might have a brain tumour or a heart problem so she saw a doctor.

'You're in perfect health.'

'Tell that to the pharmacist who practically accused me of painkiller addiction when I tried to buy my fourth box of Solpadeine in a month.'

'When did you last have an eye test?'

'Years ago.'

'Well, it's time for another.'

'What about the hole in my heart?'

'You don't have a hole in your heart.'

'Well, it certainly feels like I do.'

'Have you ever considered that you may be experiencing grief?'

'My symptoms are physical, not emotional.'

'You've lost your father, you've walked away from your business and life in New York, and you're starting again in an alien environment during a recession.'

'My father is dead almost a year. My business was my life in New York and I've no intention of starting anything here. Instead I'm enjoying a well-earned if slightly ahead-of-schedule retirement.'

'People can grieve for years, you know.'

'I'm not people. There's something wrong with me.'

She booked herself into a private hospital and had a battery of tests. She was checked from head to toe, inside and out and, other than a prescription for reading glasses, she was given a clean bill of health. *Stupid doctors, what the hell do they know?*

She spent a lot of time reading or on the Internet. Sometimes she'd stalk people she knew on Facebook. One day she tried to find Lily. She keyed her married and maiden names in, but she wasn't there. Even if she was, Eve probably wouldn't have done anything about it. There had been a moment at her father's funeral when she thought she saw Lily, but as the woman had drawn closer Eve had realized she was nothing like her old friend. Gar had mentioned Lily and her husband Declan once when Eve had first returned home. He'd told her that Declan was a heart surgeon and they had two kids, but he didn't know much else. They had gone to college in Cork and disappeared off the scene after that summer. Paul had heard that in recent years they'd moved to Killiney, which was only up the road, but were never seen around. Eve pretended she wasn't particularly interested but she was, and when she'd got home she'd Googled Declan Donovan. His private practice details and the hospital he was associated with came up a lot but otherwise nothing. There was a picture in which he looked older, of course, but otherwise the same. Eve had wanted to print it off and burn it, but that would have been childish so instead she gave the screen the fingers. *Screw you, Dicknose Donovan. I hope you die roaring.* She'd Googled Lily but found nothing. She wondered if Lily had ever Googled her or thought about her the way she thought about Lily. Probably not. After all, Lily had a full life with kids and a husband. Eve was pretty convinced that she couldn't have cared less if Eve lived or died.

After she'd left the removal men, Eve returned to her apartment, head pounding. She put two painkillers in a glass and poured water over them. She swished them around and didn't notice the water spill over the top of the glass until she slipped on it. *That's all I need. To be alone in this place with a broken leg.* When the tablets had dissolved, she drank them. She felt hot even though it wasn't a particularly warm day. The gleaming white porcelain tiles were cool under her feet. She rested the glass on the counter and sat on the floor in the lotus position. She stretched her arms over her head and leaned forward, resting her face on the tiles and hugging herself.

An hour later she was dancing around the kitchen, trying to shake off a particularly intense bout of pins and needles, when the phone rang. It was Ben and he sounded down. He'd had a massive fight with his wife and she'd stormed off to her mother's for the night. He wanted to come over. The headache had subsided, it was the first phone call she'd received in three days, she was lonely and bored and had missed him: she agreed enthusiastically. *Yipeeeeeee, Ben's coming!*

She took a long shower and dried her hair. She put on her lucky underwear, sprayed herself with perfume and put on one of her two dresses, a black jersey wrap that was comfortable and easy to take off. She really, really hoped that Ben wasn't wanting to discuss her business proposals but was looking for a little distraction.

If Eve could have known how things would turn out, she would have told Ben to chase after his wife. She'd have told him never to contact her again. She'd have hung up on him. But that had always been Eve's problem: she spent little time thinking of consequences.

2. Will the real Lily Donovan please stand up?

Dear Eve,

Holy moly, I can't believe you spoke to Glenn Medeiros! I laughed
hard when you asked him what he wanted and he pointed to his
bike. Still, it's curious that he just blurted out that he likes you.
I mean that takes real guts. I like that. He's been looking at you
for ages so it was obvious, but seriously, how ballsy do you have to
be just to come out with it, especially to a girl like you? And you
know what I mean by that. And yes, bringing up his perm, blouses
and bad poetry wasn't necessarily the best thing you could have
done but at least you didn't reduce him to tears so that's good. I'm
proud of you. Speaking of which I cannot believe that you kissed
Gar AGAIN – what is wrong with you? And yes, I promise I
won't give out although I'm itching to. I'm glad you've decided to
stay away from him for good and glory, and please do, regardless
of how many bottles of Ritz you've drunk. And when you're
breaking his heart please remember he's soft and he's still into you
so please DO NOT mention that you think he kisses like a goose
or whatever it is you say. Just tell him that you've thought about
it, and as you are going to London in September and he's going to
Dublin, you think you'd both be better off staying as friends and
leave it at that. Don't expand. OK?

Things are really improving here. I'm way happier than I was
when I arrived. The restaurant is lovely. The people are really cool.
It's always packed so the hours just fly by and the tips are really,
really good. I work six nights a week but it's only from 6 p.m. to
11.30 p.m. and then we all have a few drinks in the back kitchen.

There's a local late bar and a nightclub and they're both a great laugh. I've become really good friends with two of the staff around my age. Ellen is nineteen, she's just finished her first year in college in Cork and has so many stories. I know you're annoyed I'm following Declan there in the autumn but he's desperate to go to Cork, and Trinity would be awful without him and I seriously don't know why you care so much. You're going to be in London and now I'll know Ellen which is fantastic. Colm is seventeen – he's going into Leaving Cert next year. You'd love him – he's six foot four and built like a brick shithouse. He has dark hair and brown eyes and he's so funny. Honestly, I laugh all the time. He's a Gaelic footballer (don't make bogger jokes) but he's supposed to be very good at it.

You know me, I'm an early bird so I'm doing a lot of reading in the mornings. I borrowed Ned Linney's first-year biology, physics and chemistry books. Ned's the son of the woman who lives on the hill – the posh one that my mum cleans for? Well, he's a medical student (third year) and the books are OK, I'm getting through them. (I know I'm boring!) Aside from reading during the day, I meet Colm and Ellen for coffee at around eleven and then if it's a nice day we buy sandwiches and head down to the beach where we pretty much hang out all day. If it's dull or raining we go to Ellen's and listen to music and talk about this and that. And I know it's been raining up there a lot but down here it's mostly sunny, which is amazing. You should see me – I'm so dark my own mother wouldn't recognize me. By the way, have you seen her? I've tried to call a few times but she's never there.

Speaking of my colour and regarding my absent father, I would never ever ask him for a single penny. It's out of the question so please never ever bring it up again. Besides, I'm making really good money here but still, Eve, I have to stay for the whole summer. I need to make as much as I can and I know it's hard but there's nothing I can do about it. I'm really sorry. I do really miss you and I know you'd love Ellen and Colm and they would love you.

Look, there's one more thing and it's a bit sensitive. I know I promised I'd ring you once a week but I have only allotted so much money for the public phone and, well, Declan is suffering up there without me. He has begged me to phone him every day and he talks and talks and it's costing a fortune so I can't afford to call you too. So how about we stick to our letters? You write to me every Sunday and I'll write to you every Wednesday? I know it's not ideal and please don't give out about Declan – you know what he's like and I do love him so please understand.

OK, I'd better go. I'm in work soon and Colm is coming to collect me. Oh, that's another thing – please don't mention that I'm friends with Colm to Declan. I know it sounds strange and I'm sure he wouldn't mind but he's so upset I don't want him to think that there's anything going on because there's not and he's having a hard enough time with me being down here anyway so I don't want to make it worse for him. Thanks.

I miss you too and I love you and I promise we'll have many more summers together.

Lily XXXOOOXXXOOO

PS Be nice to Glenn Medeiros and DO NOT KISS GAR AGAIN.

PPS Forgot to answer you on Young Guns 2. Can't believe you'd go for Emilio Estevez first and Lou Diamond Phillips second – are you nuts? In fact my list is the direct opposite of yours.

1. Christian Slater (I love the way he talks)
2. Kiefer Sutherland (in brown leather, are you nuts???)
3. Lou Diamond Phillips (all right, but I wouldn't be running after him)
4. Emilio Estevez (he'll always be the weirdo Kirby Keger to me)

But that's probably a good thing – at least we'll never fight over men. XXX

Lily always woke at seven a.m. on the dot, regardless of the time she had fallen into bed. Seven a.m. struck and – *bing* – Lily Donovan was awake. She often tried to fight it but in the end her restless legs and busy brain won out and she rose to face the long day ahead. Lily's husband Declan said that Lily was keenly in tune with her body. He declared it to be a good thing but she disagreed. Sometimes she wished her brain and body could disengage for a short time. Even in sleep she was restless, which meant that more often than not her husband abandoned the bed in favour of the spare room. She liked it when he was gone and enjoyed every second of having the bed to herself, stretching out unencumbered and free.

On 1 July 2010 Lily woke up in a bad mood. She was fighting her mind and body and stubbornly keeping her eyes tightly shut and her breathing even.

Declan was walking around the room. The clock hit 7:01 and he started to whistle. 'I know you're awake,' he said.

'Asleep.'

'Awake.' He threw a cushion at her.

'Fine.'

She moved to stand and her insides ached. When he leaned over to kiss her she battled the urge to push him away. She didn't need to: he ruffled her hair and told her that her breath needed freshening. He continued whistling in the shower and while he dried himself off. She swung her feet out of the bed and threw her head back so that she could stare at the ceiling as she had the night before. *Morning, ceiling. Any new cracks? No? Good for you.*

The previous evening Declan had returned home in a good mood. He'd had no surgeries scheduled and, miracle of miracles, nothing unexpected had come in. He'd had time to catch up on paperwork and with patients' charts. He was energized and frisky. She knew it the second he walked in the door. He winked at her and was all over her while she was trying to put his dinner on the table. She didn't mind as it had been a while – and if he didn't initiate sex they didn't have it. That was for two reasons: 1. If he didn't initiate it he didn't want it and was turned off by her advances. 2. She hadn't particularly enjoyed sex in many years.

Lily figured it was an age thing. She and Declan had been

together so long it was bound to be boring and predictable, and when it wasn't it seemed so contrived. Sometimes when he was most turned on she was uncomfortable or it was sore. The previous night had been both uncomfortable and sore. He had secured her to the bed with some stupid handcuffs he'd been given as a joke Christmas present. The headboard was high and Lily was so short that she was dangling, which hurt her shoulders and wrists. Also, her head banged against the headboard as he thrust into her, and she felt as if he was tearing her inside out. She didn't complain because, if she had, one of two things would have happened: he would have banged the wall and stormed off, leaving her in the handcuffs until his huff had worn off (God knew how long that would have taken), or he'd have ignored her and kept going – at least when he did that he came quicker. The previous night she made all the sounds he expected to hear and, although it wasn't over as soon as she'd hoped for, she knew it would be a while before she had to endure that particular brand of passion again.

She got up and moved around, stretching her arms out in front of her. Her left shoulder was aching. *Damn it, I've pulled something.* Lily didn't have time for injury so she decided to ignore it in the hope that it would go away. She brushed her teeth, got into the shower and idly dreamt of drowning under it. Lily wasn't a negative person – in fact, she was known to all who loved her as Little Miss Sunshine. She arrived back into the bedroom in a towel in time to greet Declan, who appeared from their walk-in wardrobe fully dressed and smelling of her favourite aftershave. He was handsome when he wasn't ripping her apart.

'Hey, Lily, why don't we take a break this month? Maybe we could head to Paris or Rome. What do you think?'

'We're both too busy.'

'You're probably right. Maybe when things slow down.' He pulled her into him and kissed her. 'Last night was great.'

'Yeah, it was,' she agreed, and when she moved away he grabbed her arm to pull her back to him. She moaned a little.

'Are you all right?' he asked, filled with concern.

'I'm fine.' She pulled him close and kissed him deeply. 'Everything's fine.'

'Last night really was amazing,' he said again, grinning from ear to ear. 'I love it when you're bad.'

Yeah, well, I wish to hell you were any good. Lily smiled, wishing he'd shut up and go away. She had too much to do and was far too tired and sore to pretend her husband was anything other than, at best, mediocre in bed and, at worst, horrible. *Still, there's more to marriage than sex.*

In the kitchen, Lily's nineteen-year-old son Scott and her twelve-year-old daughter Daisy sat at the table with their father, drinking juice and waiting patiently to be served. Declan was reading the newspaper. Scott was staring into space and Daisy was practising her piano scales on the table. Lily wasn't sure why her children were up at seven thirty: Scott had just finished his college exams and Daisy was usually a late sleeper.

'What's this about?' she asked.

'I'm looking for a job,' Scott said.

'I'm going to practise for my piano recital. Are you coming, Dad?'

'When is it, Princess?' he asked.

'Tomorrow.' She pointed to the large circle on the calendar.

'We'll see,' he said. Everyone at the table knew it was unlikely so they moved on without a fuss.

'I'm impressed,' Lily said to Scott.

'Yeah, well, the early bird,' he said. 'Besides, every guy in my year is looking so the competition's fierce.'

'You'll get something,' Lily said.

'In this economy, you'll be lucky,' Declan said.

'Don't be so negative,' she said, smiling. 'Who could say no to that cute face?' She walked over to the oven and turned it on.

Declan put down his paper and rubbed his hands together. 'What do you fancy, kids? Omelettes? A mixed grill? How about Eggs Benedict? I think I'll have that.'

Scott wanted a mixed grill and Daisy wanted a plain omelette, so Lily got to work boiling the water for Declan's poached eggs, whisking eggs and pouring them into the frying-pan for Daisy and putting the various meats and puddings under the grill for her son. She was making Hollandaise sauce for the Eggs Benedict when Declan received a call from the hospital. It was an emergency case so he didn't have time for his breakfast. He left his paper on the table and picked up a piece of fruit from the bowl. 'Damn it, I was looking forward to that,' he said, before kissing her cheek.

He ran out of the door and Lily binned the sauce, then dished up the mixed grill and the omelette. She sat with them at the table and drank coffee while they ate. This had been her morning ritual for as long as she could remember. At some point after the kids were born Lily's meals had been reduced from three to two and sometimes one, depending on how busy she was.

'I was thinking maybe Granddad might let me work in his garage,' Scott said, when he was halfway through his breakfast.

'Oh, I don't know,' Lily said.

'Can't I ask?' He knew the answer, which was why he hadn't brought it up in front of his father.

'You know how your dad feels about his father.'

'It's a job and you heard him – they're hard to come by in this economy. I don't want to go to college without a cent in my pocket.'

'That won't happen.'

'He worked there when he was my age and I know Granddad would love to have me. It's only down the road in the car.'

'I've talked to your dad about a reasonable allowance,' she said.

'I don't want to rely on you for everything. Look, I know he doesn't get on with Granddad but I do.'

'And that's great.'

'So?'

'I'll talk to Dad.'

'Really?'

'Really.'

'Thanks, Mum.' He put down his knife and fork and headed up the stairs, taking off his T-shirt as he went.

Lily walked out of the kitchen and watched him go, her hands on her hips. 'I thought you were going out looking for a job,' she said.

'Well, let's see what Dad says about me working for Granddad first,' he said, grinning.

'You've already discussed this with your grandfather, haven't you?'

He nodded, then ran back to bed. She smiled to herself. Scott knew how to play both his parents but his mother especially. *You'd make a good politician, son. You're just about sneaky enough.*

Daisy was always a slow eater – even as a baby she'd taken hours to feed. She played with her food and nibbled tiny morsels but she'd never leave a plate with food on it. Everyone else in the family would be on dessert while she'd still be on her starter. It was just the way she was. Lily sat down with her daughter and poured herself a second cup of coffee. Between mouthfuls Daisy practised her invisible scales and hummed a little. Lily hummed along and mimicked her daughter's hands until they appeared to be playing the piece together.

'Perfect,' Lily said.

Daisy was very like her mother in that she demanded perfection from herself and didn't tolerate failure. She wasn't as naturally intelligent as Lily, or as gifted, but she had brains, talent and her father's drive, which more than compensated. She continued to pick at her omelette and told Lily a story about a boy in her class who had been mean to her and a few of her friends and was now in care. 'It's awful, isn't it, Mum?'

'Terrible.'

'He was horrible to Tess – he even threatened to pull down her tracksuit bottoms.'

'But he didn't. Did he?'

'No, but she was freaked and walked around holding them up all day.'

'He sounds like a nasty piece of work.'

'He is, but Tess says his father used to beat him.'

'That's no excuse.'

'He broke his arm once.'

'He could have broken his back – it still doesn't give him the right to go around pulling girls' tracksuits down.'

'OK. Take a chill pill, Mum.'

Lily laughed. ' "Chill pill"! Who do you think you are? The Fresh Princess of Bel Air?'

'I don't even know who that is,' Daisy said. She finished her omelette and handed her plate to her mother, who took it without comment.

Daisy got up and went into the dining room to play the piano for real and Lily got busy cleaning the kitchen. She knew she'd been obtuse about the poor boy who had gone into care. After all, he hadn't pulled down Tess's tracksuit and clearly he had a very difficult life, but she was sick of everyone making excuses for bad behaviour. Bad things happened to people every day and it was no excuse to become selfish or twisted, violent or sinister. Lily believed in turning a frown upside-down and she couldn't understand why others didn't do the same. Lily had always been that way, even though she had grown up with a woman who had resented her for being born.

Lily's mother, May, wasn't in the slightest bit maternal. She had never wanted children and Lily had been an unhappy mistake. May had been twenty-two and had had a good job in a bank in Dublin. She had loved it and was good at it, having been promoted twice since she'd started three years before. She'd gone on three sun holidays with bank friends before people from Ireland could afford to go to foreign destinations. She'd planned to make something of herself. She was a single, hardworking, fun-loving girl, who had met a Greek sailor in a bar in Dublin. He was on a month's leave and they'd spent every evening and weekend together. She didn't know she was pregnant until two months after he'd left. Although he'd promised to write he didn't, and her only means of tracking him down was through his ship's captain. She didn't have the option to terminate the pregnancy and her uptight, upright Catholic family disowned her. The bank dismissed her. The sailor chose to ignore his duty, and although she ended up corresponding with his mother, who sent money now and again in exchange for photos and letters on Lily's development, he never made any sincere effort to know his daughter. The exotic life Lily's mother had lived was over, and she couldn't look at her daughter's pretty face and see past that fact.

Lily had tried to please her mother from the moment she could walk, but nothing did the trick. 'Look, Mummy, look!'

'Go away, I'm busy.'

'But, Mummy!'

'Don't make me tell you twice.'

The first time Lily remembered her mother being happy or impressed was when she won an Irish-dancing contest. Then she had stood up and clapped, and afterwards Lily had heard her tell one of the other mothers that Lily was her daughter. Finally, after five years of trying, she had succeeded in pleasing her mother, and when that smile had lit her face, Lily was hooked. After that, failure was not an option, and because she was such a clever little thing good grades came easily, giving her the precious time she needed to notch up other achievements to please a woman who didn't much care. Lily's successes reminded her of the life she could have led instead of becoming a stigmatized low-paid single parent. She did try to be a good mother: Lily was always presented beautifully, ate well and, no matter how little money her mother had hidden in the shoebox in her wardrobe, always got to participate in everything she wanted to do. May wanted the world for her – she just couldn't disguise her pain that she had lost her own. She never told Lily that she'd tried to throw herself down a flight of stairs when she was four months gone or that she'd drunk a bottle of brandy in a hot bath at six months. Every now and then she'd mutter that Lily was most definitely a fighter, that was for sure, and she'd often mention her regret that she hadn't given Lily up for adoption.

'Don't think you wouldn't have been better off because you would,' she had said once, when she was drunk and distraught that yet another man had simply walked away from her. 'One day when you were older you'd have walked up to my door and thanked me, and I'd have welcomed you and we'd have talked about our perfect lives before saying goodbye.'

Now Lily scrubbed the counter until it gleamed. Then she moved on to strip the beds. It was the day before she returned to work – she worked one week on and one week off – so it was one of her busiest days: she had to ensure that the house was spotless and all the following week's dinners were made and frozen. Declan didn't like to eat past seven thirty in the evening and she didn't get in until just after eight. To be fair to him, she had always insisted on cooking from scratch and, depending on his taste that evening, he might have had to wait until ten for his dinner. That wouldn't have worked. In her head she made a list of ingredients necessary to feed her family for the week ahead. As a nurse she worked days, seven thirty a.m. to seven thirty p.m., so it was important that her house ran with military precision. Over the years she had managed to make it all work beautifully. Of course it was hard, but Lily had learned at an early age that nothing worthwhile was easy.

In the past, when the kids were younger, she and Declan had often rowed over her job. When he had finally passed all his exams and gone into residency in the Regional Hospital in Cork, he had approached her to give up her job at the Bons Secours. She had been supporting the family up to that point. It hadn't helped that Declan had hated Cork, and their time there was extended because he was forced to repeat two years of university. The first year he failed he blamed his young son's incessant crying and Lily's inability to soothe him. He was awake all night and studying all day and it was too much. She had tried her best to help, which had made him angrier.

'How can you help?' he'd roared one night, when he was studying for his first-year finals. Scott was only six weeks old and suffering from colic. She'd tried everything to soothe him but he'd just cried and cried. Declan was so exhausted and incapable of thinking straight that she'd tried to talk him into moving out of their little one-bedroom flat for the duration of the exams.

'Where the hell do you want me to go?' he shouted.

'Anywhere,' she said quietly.

'Are you trying to chase me out of my own home?'

'No,' she said, 'of course not. I just want you to be able to study. Couldn't you stay with one of the lads in your lectures?'

He was unreasonable and paranoid.

'So the baby's in and I'm out, is that it?' he'd said, gritting his teeth.

She decided to change tack. 'I'll do questions with you,' she offered, in a bid to curb his paranoia before it manifested itself as unbridled rage.

'Great,' he said. 'If there's a question on how to make beds I'll let you know.'

'I read a lot of the books on your course last summer,' she said, knowing it would piss him off, but after his comments belittling her nursing training she didn't much care. He had talked her out of medicine and into nursing for the sake of their family life. *Arsehole.* The baby had started to cry again just as he'd turned to say something else that would have been mean and vicious. He'd stopped in his tracks and listened with his hand to his ear.

'Why don't you focus on settling that child? Maybe you could read some books on that because, let's face it, motherhood certainly isn't coming naturally, is it?' he said.

'Nice! You're a prick, you know that?' she said. In her head she warned herself not to cry.

'I've got exams in a week, Lil! I can't remember my own name, never mind what the hell the parietal pleura is!' he yelled, throwing his book at the wall.

'Any chance you'd forget where we lived for a few days?' she'd said.

That was the first time he'd grabbed her by the hair and pushed her against the wall. He held her there tightly for a minute or two while he breathed in and out, perhaps attempting to calm himself. When he let her go she turned slowly to face him, terrified of what would come next, but he just looked at her strangely.

'You're destroying me,' he said, and walked out of the door.

Declan Donovan had always had a dramatic side to his personality. He probably would have made a good actor; he could certainly have played a convincing villain. Lily let the baby cry, poured a cup of coffee and sat at the kitchen table, afraid to pick up the cup because her hands were trembling. Her heart tightened in her chest and her eyes threatened to burn holes into her face. After a few minutes, she clasped her hands together and said to the wall, 'The parietal pleura is the name given to the cavity that surrounds the lungs, Dicknose.' It took a while for her heart-rate to settle and the trembling to stop but she didn't cry. Instead she smiled: 1. She knew what the parietal pleura was, and 2. Her only real friend, Eve, had nicknamed Declan 'Dicknose Donovan' the first time they'd met him. Now, for the first time, Lily had realized that her ex-best friend had been right. *You do have a dick of a nose.*

He passed the second year, and failed the third. He didn't have a crying baby to blame so instead he blamed his responsibilities as a young father and husband. Lily didn't pander to him that time. Having lived with him for three years, she had learned to pick her battles. She was working her nursing shifts and bringing up a two-year-old so she didn't have time for his bullshit. Instead she let him roar and scream and act the fool and when he later apologized and tried to make it up to her with dinner and flowers she accepted with good grace – what else could she do? Declan wouldn't accept her help, and he wasn't a good student, but when the drudgery of book-learning was behind him, he was quite brilliant from the practical point of view. After that third year he sailed through. His anger and frustration dissipated and life got better, although with every success he made Lily feel smaller.

'What the hell do you need to stay nursing for?'

'Because I like it and I'm good at it.'

'Oh, for God's sake, Lily, it's embarrassing.'

'Embarrassing?'

'You know what I mean,' he said.

'No, Declan, I really don't.'

'I'm a heart surgeon, for God's sake.'

'Congratulations.'

'Don't try to be smart, Lily, you know it's a turn-off.'

'Stay turned off for both our sakes.'

When she was pregnant with Daisy he was outraged that she wouldn't consider giving up her job following maternity leave.

'Look how easy it is for you to take care of the family when you're out of work,' he'd pointed out.

'If I'd wanted an easy life I'd have never married you, my darling,' she'd joked, in an attempt to get him off her back.

'You've always thought you were funnier than you actually are.'

'Why are you such an arsehole, Declan?'

'Don't push me, Lily.'

'*Or what?*'

Declan had never shoved her into a wall since that day when Scott was only six weeks old, but every now and then he was slightly rougher than he should have been. He'd push her out of his way instead of asking her to move. He'd hold her arm and squeeze it so tightly she thought it might snap. He once pulled her back into a room by her hair but he had instantly apologized. Lily wasn't a domestic-abuse victim: she just lived with a man who teetered on the edge of controlling a temper that rarely showed its face, but when it did it was safer to evacuate so that was what she did. After more than twenty years with him, she knew which buttons to press and which were off limits. Lily walked the line diligently.

She ripped the sheets off their bed and threw them into the laundry hamper. Using a stool, she pulled out the clean bedding from the top of the hot press. She started to cover the duvet but her shoulder hurt so she decided a hot bath might ease the pain.

She ran it and lay there, disappearing under the bubbles and enjoying the water jets. There were still beds to be made, shopping to
be got and an entire week's menu to be cooked but she didn't care.
She was enjoying half an hour off before she got back to work and
her kids began making demands. Lily was looking forward to
going back to work because a week at home was too long. She
preferred her time on the ward where she was truly needed,
people were grateful and time passed in the blink of an eye. She
loved helping people, no matter who was put in front of her or
what was wrong with them. Lily was capable, understanding and
fun, and she never failed to make someone feel better, happier and
more hopeful, no matter how scared or traumatized they were.

Lily Donovan was an excellent nurse. Her dream of becoming
a doctor had changed as soon as she'd said yes to marrying Declan. Even though she could have got through the course in her
sleep, Lily had realized early on that nursing was a calling and it
suited her caring, outgoing, perfectionist, kind, giving personality perfectly. It occurred to her that the only reason she was doing
medicine was to be with Declan and because kids with her out-
standing grades were encouraged in that direction. Before she'd
got straight As in her Intercert exams, at fourteen, she'd wanted
to be a beautician – and, if she was honest, it was still something
she was interested in. She was a slave to beauty magazines, loved
hair and makeup, and if she'd had her time again that was what
she would have gone into – beauty for fashion shoots. She had
never wanted to be a surgeon and was happy to leave the cutting
to her husband: he had a way with a knife but the bedside manner
of a brick. He might save a life but her care would make the early
days after an operation worth living, and she was proud of that.
Besides, her mother had warned her from an early age that as
soon as she turned eighteen she was on her own. University cost
money and medicine was a long course. If she became a nurse
her salary would kick in quicker and, anyway, children were her
real dream: doing medicine would mean she'd have to wait
longer for them than she cared to. It made perfect sense.

Lily had always yearned to be part of a family. When she was five she asked her mother if she would think about giving her a brother or sister.

'I'd rather be hit by a bus,' her mother said, and that was the end of the conversation.

Lily had met her father a few times. He had visited her twice in Ireland, and she had spent a month in Greece the summer she was sixteen, staying with her grandmother, who had very little English, her father's wife and their three children. He had left the navy and was a fisherman. He disappeared for days on end, and when he returned they spoke very little. It was a long month and at the end she was happy to leave and never return. She used to envy Eve, with a mother and father who loved each other and, most importantly, had wanted and loved Eve. She envied her having a brother as lovely, sweet, funny and cool as Clooney. She felt bad when Eve's mother became ill: perhaps she had caused it with her jealousy. *How come Eve gets a mum and dad who love her and a brilliant brother? Why not me?* Envy was a mortal sin and she prayed that God would save Mrs Hayes and not send Lily herself to Hell.

Lily's mother spent a lot of time talking about Hell. Everything she did, whether it was wash dishes or stub her toe, she offered up as penance for her sins. Lily had grown up in a very holy house. Her mother had fallen from grace by having her and she spent Lily's childhood trying to make up for her sin. She often told Lily that she had gone to three priests before she could find one who would baptize the baby. Lily never did find out if her mother was lying to make her feel bad: no one else seemed to have any difficulty in baptizing their illegitimate children.

'But I persisted to save your soul and what thanks do I get for it?' her mother would ask.

Lily didn't know what she wanted her to say.

She wasn't sure that her mother was a satisfactory example of a good person, but she loved her despite her failings. May wasn't all bad: she just didn't know how to be a mother. She wanted the best for Lily and didn't want her making the same mistakes as she had. She tried to be a good Catholic but she was good at bending the rules to suit her own needs. When Lily turned fifteen, she used her daughter's painful periods as an excuse to talk the local GP into putting her on the pill. She warned Lily against having sex, telling her it was a sin from which her soul might never recover, even though she knew that if Lily did engage in it she would do so to the detriment of her afterlife rather than her earthly future. She was proud, too, and occasionally, when Lily said something funny that made her laugh, she'd hug her tight. 'Thank you, sunshine,' she'd say. Lily might not have had a father who loved her, a mother who was grateful for her or a brother to play with but she had that. *Thank you, sunshine.*

Lily lost track of time and it was nearly ten thirty when she scrambled out of the bath. She tied up her hair, put on a pair of old leggings, a threadbare Ally McBeal T-shirt, an old housecoat and some fluffy slippers. She made up her marital bed, then went down the corridor to see whose bed she could strip. Scott was passed out cold so she made her way into Daisy's room. By the time she had finished, Scott was up and about. She got through his room quickly, without looking around too much for fear she'd find something she didn't like. Once the beds were done, she ran around vacuuming with the skill, speed and dexterity of an Olympian. Then she dusted and did the toilets. At one o'clock she fed the kids. Scott's friend Josh had arrived while she was dusting the banisters. She kept lunch simple, making ham and cheese paninis, with a little homemade coleslaw and relish. Daisy was still practising and wanted hers by the piano. Scott and Josh were in the sitting room on the PlayStation, which suited Lily fine.

'Thanks, Lily,' Josh said, grinning.

Lily was sorry she hadn't been stricter about her children's friends calling her Mrs Donovan when they were younger.

'You're welcome, Josh,' she said.

She started making a list and checked the store cupboard. Josh's grin had reminded her that she needed basil since Scott had eaten the entire plant for a bet when he and Josh had been out of their minds on weed although they had vehemently denied it.

'Crack is whack, Lily,' Josh had said.

'We're not talking about crack, though, are we, Josh? We're talking about weed.'

'Weed is . . .' He'd looked at her son, who was sitting on the kitchen counter munching basil.

'Free –' Scott said.

'– dom!' Josh finished, and they'd burst out laughing.

She'd sent them to Scott's room and turned to her husband, who shrugged his shoulders. 'They're just letting off steam,' he said. 'We all did it.'

'Yes, Declan, but we had the decency to do it behind our parents' backs. We can't be seen to support this type of behaviour and, besides, I *don't* support it and neither should you. There are plenty of studies that suggest cannabis isn't as benign as we'd like to think.'

Declan had laughed. 'Look at the nurse who knows everything!' And on that note the conversation was over.

Later she'd gone up to Scott's room to discuss the implications of smoking weed under his parents' roof, but before she could launch into her prepared speech Josh told her she was a prize-winning MILF and her son feigned puking. Then Josh hugged her and sniffed her hair. She'd left them, confused. Later she'd discovered that MILF meant Mum I'd Like to Fuck. Since then she had found it hard to look Josh, whose nappy she'd changed on more than one occasion, straight in the face.

The list was made and Lily was heading up the stairs to change into something suitable to wear outdoors when the bell rang. She answered, and it was Rachel from across the road. Rachel's face was frozen and she had a wild look in her eyes.

'Rachel?'

Rachel seemed to find her voice – she screamed straight into Lily's face.

'What's wrong?'

She screamed louder.

'Rachel, talk to me!'

She screamed even louder.

Lily shook her. '*Rachel!*'

The screaming was now so high-pitched that Lily could imagine random dogs around the country perking up their ears and Forrest Gumping their way towards their cul-de-sac.

Rachel turned, pointed and ran, still screaming, so Lily followed her to her house and there she found Nancy, Rachel's five-year-old daughter, lying on the patio in the backyard with an arrow sticking straight out of her eye. Rachel's scream seemed to increase by another full decibel, threatening to pierce all ears present.

'Rachel. Shut up. Do you hear me? *Shut up.*' Lily made a closing gesture with her hand.

Rachel stopped screaming. Instead she pointed to her daughter, who was starting to move a little.

'Well done. Now stay like that.' Lily put her fingers to her lips and Rachel nodded. Lily turned to Nancy. 'Hi, Nancy.'

'Hi, Lily, I think I have something in my eye,' the child said. She raised her hand to try to pull the arrow out.

Lily caught the hand in time to stop her, but she couldn't save Rachel: she passed out cold and hit her head on a plant pot.

'Oh, fudge cake!' Lily exclaimed. 'OK, Nancy, look at Lily.'

She didn't know how far the arrow had gone inside the child's head or if it had penetrated her brain. Nancy was talking and alert, which was positive. She wrestled with Lily, trying to free her hands so that she could take the arrow out.

'You can't do that, baby. Look at Lily. You cannot pull out the arrow. If you do you will blind yourself and you don't want to do that. OK?'

Nancy nodded.

'Are you with me, Nancy?'

'Yes.'

'Do you feel pain?'

'No.'

'Good girl. Now, I need to look at your mother and then I'm

going to call an ambulance but you have to stay lying down exactly as you are. OK?'

'OK.'

'You must not touch the arrow. OK?'

'OK.'

'Good girl. You're the best and bravest girl. Lily's here and I'm not leaving you. OK?'

'OK.'

Lily got up and went to Rachel, who was still out cold. Still watching Nancy, she placed her hand on Rachel's forehead and called to her. Her airway wasn't constricted but the back of her head was bleeding profusely. When Rachel came round, Lily kept her hand on her forehead and gently held her down. 'Rachel. Don't move. You've hit your head. Your breathing and colour are good. Do you feel any numbness?'

'No.'

'That's good too. I want you to stay where you are just in case, so don't move. OK.'

'OK.' Rachel grabbed Lily's hand. 'Nancy?'

'She'll be fine. Stay there.'

Lily ran to the house and grabbed the phone. Then she picked up a clean tea-towel and ran back outside. Both her patients were immobile. She phoned an ambulance, then wrapped the tea-towel tightly around Rachel's head. It was the best she could do in difficult circumstances. The two paramedics loaded Nancy and Rachel on board, but when Lily didn't get in with them, Nancy started to scream. She wanted her there. She reached out her hand and begged, 'Please, Lily, please, Lily, please, don't leave me!'

Lily looked down at her greyish-black leggings, the Ally McBeal T-shirt, the horrible housecoat and fluffy slippers. 'Fudge cake,' she said. She couldn't say no to a child with a ruddy arrow in her eye so she jumped aboard with no phone, a full shop to do and an entire week's worth of meals to cook.

Fudge cake was something Lily said instead of *fuck*, which she found quite aggressive and unnecessary. She sometimes said *fudging*. Every now and again she told someone that they could shine up their buttons with Brasso, emphasizing *shine*, *buttons* and *Brasso* in such a way that the statement became quite menacing. She also liked *bugger* or *bugger-balls* and sometimes she added a side of fries.

In the ambulance Rachel was clearly concussed. She was confused and babbling about leaving the keys in the car and asking Lily if she'd put the shopping away.

'Yes, you put it away.'

'Good, it's important to put the shopping away because Nero will eat everything in sight. Did you put the shopping away?'

'It's all in the presses.'

'Good, because there's a lot of frozen food there. Did you put the shopping away?' she asked the paramedic.

'Yip. It's all away, chicken.'

'Good. The last time Nero ate two M&S goat's-cheese tarts, half a packet of chocolate digestives and a roast duck. For days afterwards his farts would knock you sideways. Jim threw up. Did I put the shopping away?'

'All put away.'

When the paramedics had finished setting Nancy up, Lily held her hand and told the scared, sleepy little girl a story about a princess and a dragon. She was halfway through the story when Nancy asked where her eight-year-old brother Dylan was.

'I don't know, sweetheart. He wasn't at home.'

'Yes, he was. He's hiding down the garden.'

'Why would he do that?'

'Because he hit me in the eye with a bow and arrow.'

'Bugger-balls and a side of flaming fries!'

Rachel was too busy throwing up to react. They got to the hospital where Nancy was taken one way and Rachel the other. Lily went up to the third floor and found her friend Marion in the corridor wheeling the medicine trolley.

'What are you doing here? Thought you weren't in till tomorrow?' she said, taking in Lily's strange attire.

'I'm not. There's been an accident in a neighbour's place. A little girl and her mother. I need to use the phone.'

'I hope they're OK,' Marion said, and pottered away.

Lily phoned home. There was no answer so she phoned Scott's mobile. It rang out twice before he picked up.

'God, Mum. *What?*'

'Don't you dare *what* me – and pick up your fudging phone when I call you! There's been an accident in Rachel's and I need you to go across the road and hike over the wall into the back garden.'

'*What?*'

'I'm in the hospital with Rachel and Nancy. Dylan is hiding somewhere in the back garden.'

'So what am I supposed to do?'

'First, find him. The back door is on the latch. Bring him through the house or unlock the side gate and go out that way. Tell him his mother and sister will be fine and bring him to our place.'

'OK. But, Mum – *are* they OK?'

'Well, Rachel has a concussion and Nancy has an arrow in her eye.'

'Wow!'

'Yeah, wow. I have to go.'

'And, Mum?'

'What?'

'What's happening about dinner?'

'Don't annoy me, Scott.'

Lily sat with Rachel while Nancy was in surgery. Rachel received three staples to the back of her head. She was being observed for a brain injury but she was feeling a good deal better.

'Thank you so much, Lily. I'm so sorry I lost it.'

'No problem.'

She started to cry. 'Do you think she'll lose the eye?'

'I don't know,' Lily said honestly. In an attempt to lighten the moment, she added, 'But what's an eye between friends?'

Rachel wasn't listening. 'Oh, God almighty! Dylan!'

'It's OK – he's in my house with Scott and Daisy.'

'He didn't mean it.'

'I know.'

'I'm going to kill Jim. I told him not to buy a bow and arrow for an eight-year-old. He might as well have brought a gun into the house. I swear to God I'm going to get that bow and arrow and shove it so far up his arse he –'

The doctor treating her came in. Lily knew his face but couldn't put a name to it. He was just some kid out of college. He asked Rachel if it would be all right to examine her, and Lily went to check up on Nancy. She looked at the wall clock and registered that it was after four. She hadn't noticed time passing and she had so much to do. She walked into her husband's office and was leaving a message on his notepad about dinner when he came in.

'What the hell are you doing here dressed like that?'

'Well, that's a nice greeting!'

'You're wearing a pair of bunnies on your feet, that T-shirt is a disgrace and we both know you're far too skinny to wear leggings anywhere outside the house. In fact, I'd prefer it if you didn't wear them *in* the house, but I suppose that's an argument I lost years ago.'

'You know, Declan, sometimes I think you belong in a nuthouse. Did you consider for a second why I might be here dressed like this?'

Clearly he hadn't. His colour changed. He didn't say a word. He just waited for Lily to spit it out. She thought about letting him suffer but decided it was too cruel. As soon as he understood that a neighbour and her child had brought his wife to the hospital in that state he lost interest. She tried to talk to him about Nancy's eye but he reminded her that he was a heart man.

'You're more dick than heart surely, darling,' she said, smiling at him benignly.

'Not in the humour for your attempts to be funny.' Then he looked at his watch and said he hoped she'd managed to get to the shops. He'd been looking forward to chicken cacciatore all day.

'You are joking.'

'I never joke about dinner,' he said.

'Declan.'

'What?'

'Why don't you go and *shine* up your *buttons* with *Brasso*?'

'Will do as soon as you go home and make my dinner,' he said. She stood there.

'Seven thirty sharp,' he added.

He fixed his tie and eyed her before sitting down at his desk. He shook his head slowly, showing silent disapproval. He opened a file, which was Lily's cue to leave.

She walked out simmering because she had had the misfortune to marry an ignorant pig. She was so annoyed that she walked straight into Adam Wallace. He was the orthopaedic surgeon who worked on Lily's ward. He held her out in front of him and beamed at her. 'Lily, you never fail to dazzle me.'

'Ha-ha.'

'What's your story?'

She told him about Rachel and Nancy and, unlike her husband, he seemed concerned.

'I was going to get a coffee, join me,' he said.

It was at that point she realized she was light-headed from lack of food so she agreed. He drank his coffee, she tucked into a croissant and they talked about Nancy's injury and the possible prognosis. He complimented her on her quick thinking, which embarrassed her because she'd done nothing, really. They chatted until she realized time was ticking by and she had to check on Rachel before she went to the supermarket. Then she remembered what she was wearing. 'I can't go to the supermarket like this.'

'You look great.'

'That's a very kind lie.'

He laughed. 'A million women would kill to look like you do.'

'Just a million? I must be losing my touch.'

She walked away, smiling. Kind, sweet, sad Adam always cheered her up.

Nancy still wasn't out of surgery but Jim was with Rachel. It was clear he'd just had the face chewed off him. He looked contrite and terrified. Lily felt sorry for him. She hugged him, ignoring Rachel's glare. She said she had to go home and make dinner. If they wanted her to keep Dylan that night she'd be more than happy to. She asked Jim to call her as soon as Nancy came out of surgery and he promised he would.

She ran around Tesco like a hare. Luckily she didn't meet any-one she knew and, apart from the odd raised eyebrow here and there, no one seemed to notice her ridiculous garb.

It was after six when she made it home. Chicken cacciatore took between forty and fifty-five minutes to cook, never mind prepare, so she was hopeful that her inconsiderate husband would be late. Dylan started crying when he saw Lily so she hugged him tight, took him into the kitchen and told him about the cool staples in his mother's head.

'Oh,' he said, with a trembling lip, 'she won't like that.'

'Are you kidding me? How many people do you know with staples in their head?'

'None,' he said.

'Exactly,' she said. 'That's what makes it cool.'

He was eight, and eight-year-olds weren't as gullible as they had been when Lily was his age. He wasn't buying the cool-staples line.

'OK, so guess who's in trouble?' she said.

'Me,' he said, about to cry.

'Nope,' she said, shaking her head.

'Who, then?'

'Your dad.'

'Why?'

'Because he bought the bow and arrow.'

'Oh. Is he in big trouble?' His tone suggested he hoped the answer would be positive.

'Oh, yes.'

'Thanks, Lily,' he said, with a grin that told her he had cheered up considerably. He ran off to join Daisy and her friend Tess in the sitting room where they were watching TV.

Lily prepared the chicken cacciatore in record time. When it was in the oven she showered and changed for dinner. Declan liked her to change for dinner – he was old-fashioned that way. The kids were due to eat at six so by six forty-five they were starving. They always ate half an hour to an hour before their father and mostly they had a different menu but that night, due to time restrictions, they were all having the same thing.

'Ah, I hate chicken cacciatore!' Daisy grumbled. She plonked herself down at the table.

Tess sat in beside her, opposite Scott and Dylan, who were already eating.

'You do not hate it,' said Lily. 'You loved it as a baby.'

'Seriously, Mum. I'm twelve, not a moron.'

'Yeah, well, shove it down your neck or starve.'

Scott wolfed it, burped, said thanks and got up.

'Where are you going?' Lily asked.

'Do you really want to know?'

'I do now.'

'It involves nudity,' he said, chuckling.

'Get out,' she said, and when he'd gone she allowed herself a smile.

Dylan loved Lily's chicken cacciatore. 'Yum,' he kept saying. 'I wish you lived at our house.'

I wish I lived there too.

Tess was a huge fan of Lily's cooking. She often came for dinner because her mother worked late and her father had been off the scene for years. Lily took special care of her and always included Tess in everything the family did, so much so that even Daisy noticed and commented on it.

'Why is Tess coming to France with us?' she'd asked, the first year they took Tess away with them.

'Don't you want her?' Lily asked.

'Of course I do, but why is she coming?'

'Because she's your friend.'

'Cool! Can Josh, Cedric and Ethan come?' Scott said.

'No.'

'OK, just Josh.'

'No.'

'Why not? How come Tess gets to?'

'Because I said so.'

'So unfair,' he said, and walked out, slamming the door. It *was* unfair – but life was unfair, and nobody understood that better than Lily.

It was nice to have some grateful children in the house.

'Thanks so much, Lily. It was really lovely,' Tess said.

'You're welcome, sweetheart. How about you, Daisy?'

'I'm shoving it down, amn't I?'

'Yes, my angel, you are,' Lily said. Tess and Dylan laughed.

Declan arrived home at seven thirty. He was tired and grumpy because he had been delayed. He sat at the table and she served their dinner. 'I only have an hour. I have to go back to the hospital to check on a patient.'

'Fine.'

'You look nice,' he said.

'Thank you.' *Eat me.*

'Is that new?'

'No.' *Yes.*

'I don't remember seeing it before.'

'Really? Maybe you're suffering from early-onset dementia.' *Fingers crossed.*

He smiled. 'Oh, you're a riot today.'

He ate and left.

Lily cleaned up and put the plates into the dishwasher. *What a knob. It's not like this dress is coming out of your bank account, you tight bastard.*

Lily and Declan had never shared a bank account – well, except

56

when she was the sole earner. Lodged in Lily's account were her nurse's wages and the children's allowance and lodged in Declan's was the salary of a top heart surgeon. He paid the mortgage and utility bills, and she paid for the groceries, her needs and those of the children. Lily's kids had expensive tastes and for them she always tried to buy nothing but the best. When it came to shopping for herself, she went to second-hand designer stores or bought material. She might not have been a designer but she was handy with a sewing machine. The black dress was a recent purchase in an actual high-street shop. It was going out of business and, at 70 per cent off, everything had been priced to sell. She'd treated herself after a particularly brutal day and she wasn't going to let her husband, who had his suits custom-made by Louis Copeland, berate her for spending money on herself that should have gone on the kids. 'Well, don't come crying to me when Scott wants new trainers,' he would say.

'God, no, of course not. After all, you're only his father.'

'I've told you before, Lily, if you want to live off me give up your job.'

The conversation would descend into a row about the twice in twenty years when his dinner had been late to the table or why it was important for her to continue working, which would lead into an uncomfortable conversation about her need to be all things to all people and why she felt she had to flirt her way through life. This conversation would invariably end with him insulting her.

'I mean, a woman of your age. It's pathetic. The younger girls must laugh at you!' Or 'You're not half as cute as you act, Lily.'

They'd both shout and slam doors. He'd leave and cool off with his pals over a game of golf or bridge. She'd take a bath and talk herself out of crying. The truth was, she did try to be all things to all people. *So what? Why is that a bad thing? Why can't you just love me and let me be?*

When Lily had got married she was not quite nineteen years old. She cooked a little but not the way she felt a wife should. Of course, she had breezed through nursing school and although she attended classes in the first year, had never had to open a book. Instead of studying she took cooking lessons. Her teacher told her she had a flair for it so she took more lessons. Now she could have competed with any gourmet cook. She ran her kitchen like a hotel's, partly because her husband was so demanding and partly because she still wanted to be the perfect wife and mother.

She also attempted to excel as nurse and neighbour. Nursing was easy, but she had to work at her neighbouring skills. She could always be relied on to help anyone with anything, whether it was snaking out a drain, pinning up a hem or performing CPR, but she put some of her female neighbours' backs up. 'Little Miss Sunshine' wasn't always a compliment. Lily had a quick wit, she was game for a laugh, and she always got on easily with men, who all liked her – some a little too much. Petite, delicate Lily, with her shiny dark brown hair, brown eyes, soft lips and silky cappuccino skin, thanks to her absent Greek father, was always the belle of the ball. Every man in the room followed her with his eyes when she moved past; when she laughed, they laughed with her; when she spoke, they listened intently while fantasizing about what they would do to her if she'd only let them.

The women on the road noticed it, her husband noticed it, her fellow nurses noticed it, any woman she had ever tried to make a connection with after Eve noticed it, but Lily didn't. When she looked in the mirror she saw a thirty-eight-year-old woman who could have shopped in the children's department. She had twigs for legs, tiny breasts and big eyes. What Lily perceived as friendly banter, her husband and the rest of the world interpreted as flirting. It enraged him and estranged Lily from the other women on her road. She meant nothing by it: it was just who she was and how she related to people. Sometimes when her husband was disapproving, she'd see herself through his eyes. In a second she'd be reduced from his wife and the mother of his children to a flighty, insignificant, giddy, annoying, silly woman, who acted like one too. She'd feel less than a woman – just as she'd felt less than a daughter to her mother. Then she'd get a grip: so her mother was a bitch and she'd married a prick, she'd just have to soldier on. Lily loved her husband. He was the only man who really needed and wanted her. There were moments of great tenderness between them, and when he found her funny, which he often did, despite his comments to the contrary, his laughter lifted her to a place where her spirit soared.

Yes, Lily was the go-to person in times of trouble but the last person on the list when it came to coffee mornings or afternoon gossips. Lily wasn't good at gossip and she wasn't trusted around the ladies' men – anyway, who would they talk about if she was there? Lily was popular with her work colleagues but she had no real friends. As hard as she worked to please, deep down she felt like an outsider in her own life, and the niggling voice that had always told her she was an unlovable loser grew a little louder with each year that passed.

Lily was halfway through cooking meals for the week ahead when the phone rang. It was Jim. Nancy was out of surgery: the consultant was hopeful that he could save the eye, and there was no brain damage.

'Oh, Jim, I'm so pleased!'

'Honestly, Lily, I'm really grateful. Is there anything I can do for you?'

'I'm just glad she's OK.'

He sounded like he'd been crying. He was vulnerable and tired. 'Maybe a drink some time? You and me?' he said.

Is he coming on to me? No. Don't be stupid, Lily. Of course he's not.

'I don't think Declan would be too happy with that.'

'So don't tell him.'

Oh, no. This is uncomfortable.

'And Rachel, how is she?'

'Giving out.'

'She'll get over it.'

'Yeah, when I'm dead and buried and she's finished dancing on my grave,' he said. Lily laughed. 'Seriously, I know Declan's hard work too, so if you ever want to have a drink . . .' he said.

Oh, my God. Lily didn't respond. She knew her husband could appear aloof around the neighbours, and sometimes when he drank he got a little narky with her, especially if the other men in the room had been too complimentary. He liked to remind them he was boss and that she was his wife. She made light of it and, when she had to save face, she was smart and funny enough to defuse his annoyance and show them that she was a match for him. Jim was their first neighbour to comment on it and it stung.

'Dylan's fine,' she said. 'He's exhausted so I'll put him to bed, if that's all right.'

'It's fine. What time should I pick him up?'

'Well, I'll be gone by seven but Declan will be here until eight and Scott and Daisy will be here too, so whenever suits you.'

'Thanks.'

'You're welcome.'

'Lily?'

'Yes.'

Silence followed and she thought she heard him sniffle.

'Thanks again.'

'OK.' She hung up and went back to cooking a shepherd's pie, a lasagne, a lamb stew and a large pot of tomato and basil soup. It was after midnight when she stopped. She covered the dishes in clingfilm and left them on the counter. She fell asleep on the sofa while she was waiting for them to get cool enough to freeze them. She woke after two with a crick in her neck. She dished out the meals into plastic Tupperware tubs with Declan, Scott and Daisy's names on them and popped them into the freezer, stacking them so that they were easy to read. She fell into bed and was grateful that her husband was sound asleep. Her shoulder still ached but at least her crotch had cooled down. She heard Scott come in and could tell that he was drunk by how long it took him to get to the fridge. Too exhausted to deal with him, she closed her eyes and hoped he didn't burn the house down.

3. The strangest thing happened

Dear Lily,

I'm not even going to talk about how annoyed I am that Declan
is being such a dicknose, and I can't believe you're letting him
away with it. In fact, I'm really hurt. I'd call you if we could
arrange a time for you to be at the telephone box and, even
though I'm so monumentally pissed off with you, I'd still do
it – if, of course, Declan doesn't mind and you can spare five
minutes. Oh, and don't worry, I haven't said anything to
precious Declan about Colm or the other one (can't remember her
name and too pissed off to fish out your letter) but, seriously, if
you can't tell your boyfriend that you've made friends it's a bit
sad. I mean, what does he expect? Would he be happy if all you
did was work and moon over him? And don't answer that
because we both know what your answer will be and I also don't
want any excuses. As you said in your letter, you love him so
that's that. I just wish you loved me half as much (and no, not
being a lesbian about it) but where was he when you were bullied
in primary school? I was the one who pulled Megan Murphy's
hair out of her head and pinched her so hard she still has the
marks! (Which she showed me at the disco last Easter – they
were really small across her knuckles but seriously how bad is
that? MORTIFIED.) I was the one who carried you home and
put you in bed when you were so drunk you didn't even know
where you lived and I managed to do it unseen while your mother
was still in the sitting room doing a crossword. She would have
disowned you if she'd found you in that state. As a result of my
efforts, you got away with something that would have seriously

changed your life for the worse. I'm the one who's there for every little drama you have with Declan. I'm the one who picks up the pieces when you fight. I'm the one who's always on your side. I'm the one who wants nothing for you but happiness. I'm the one who really loves you and again not in a lesbian way. Although if I was a lesbian and you were my girlfriend, I wouldn't insist that you spend ALL of your money calling me because I may be a bitch but I'm not a selfish dicknose and that's all I have to say on the matter.

Now for my news – and you are not going to believe this. Gar, Dicknose, Paul and I went to the pub the other night and guess who was there with a brand new look? GLENN MEDEIROS!!!! He's cut off the horrible perm, and instead of one of those stupid-looking blousy shirts, he was wearing a Bruce Springsteen T-shirt and jeans and he looks really, really good. Like a different person. It's like a fairy godmother waved a magic wand over him. I had a drink with Gar and Paul (steadfastly ignoring Dicknose but, of course, he was too up his own bum to notice so don't worry about it) and then I went over to Glenn. He was sitting at the bar with two boys I don't know. I know it sounds stupid, bearing in mind up until very recently I thought he was a freak, but I was really nervous and every time I caught him looking at me before I went over (which was a lot) I pretended I hadn't but seriously you'd have to have been Helen Keller not to notice him. He'd never make it in the CIA, that's for sure. Anyway, every time I caught him looking at me my stomach flipped and flopped so much that I felt a little sick. (I SWEAR TO GOD.) So, I went up to him and of course I was trying to act cool so I kept it short and sweet because I knew if I said too much I might actually vomit. I walked up to him just like Tom Cruise walked up to Kelly McGillis in Top Gun. (Don't get me wrong, I still think that film is embarrassing but it's a good reference point.) He turned around from his friends to face me and he did look a bit smug but that was OK. He deserved to feel a little smug. I looked him up and down slowly and then I said, 'You're welcome,' and walked *off. His friends were in hysterics. I didn't look back but when I went over to our group Paul said he'd watched the whole thing and Glenn was grinning. Eve Hayes 15: Glenn Medeiros Love.*

Anyway, I went outside with Gar when he was having a smoke. (He still refuses to smoke inside in case Mr Duffy spots him and tells his father – what a baby!) And before I had a chance to say that I thought, because I was going to London and he was going to be in Dublin, we shouldn't get involved (exactly as you said) he told me that he was really into a girl from Bray. CAN YOU BELIEVE IT? I didn't know whether to be relieved or insulted. In the end I went with option 1. I wished him luck on getting together with her and he was actually really sweet about it. I'd had three bottles of Ritz by then and thought it might be a good idea to tell him not to peck, peck, peck her like a chicken (NOT A GOOSE) but then I remembered what you'd said and didn't say a word. When he went in I said I needed some air and stayed outside just to see if Glenn would notice. He was out like a hot snot. THRILLED. Of course he was mortified because I was sitting on the wall watching him run out and look up and down the street. He sat on the wall with me and when I called him Glenn he reminded me his name was Ben Logan. I told him that no matter how cute he was now he'd always be Glenn Medeiros to me. He laughed and focused on how cute I thought he was but I changed the subject and warned him that I'd find him most unattractive if he kept standing on corners saying those poems. (I know, don't freak out but I believe honesty is the best policy.) He didn't take it too badly. He said, 'Is it all right if I continue with my band?' I didn't even know he was in a band. I said it was fine as long as his band was a good deal better than his poetry. He told me they were and then out of nowhere he kissed me and I NEARLY DIED. He is an amazing kisser. I can't even describe it. And it was so romantic. The moon was out and even though we were in a car park I could see it glint off the sea in the distance. And the way he looked at me as he was moving in and out for kisses. Well, let's just say Glenn Medeiros is intense. We stayed outside for at least an hour. Paul came out to look for me, and when he saw us together, I asked him to say nothing to Gar and he gave me the thumbs-up. So I presume he's happy to say nothing to Gar, which is nice of him but then again he is a slut so there's probably some sort of slut code he's obeying. Either way I'm grateful. I've met Glenn twice since and I'm going to his gig in town on Saturday so I'll fill you in next Sunday – that is, if you don't give me a telephone number and time to call you so that we can actually talk. I know it's mad, and this time last week I thought he was weird, but I'm really into him. When he looks at me I feel like jelly, and I know there's a serious height difference but I really don't care. I've always said I'm not the kind of person who falls in love but, Lily, I think I could fall in love with him. He makes the world feel like a better place. I KNOW IT'S HORRIFYING. I'm seeing him tonight and I'm counting down the hours. It's pathetic but I can't wait.

Anyway, what other news do I have? Clooney dropped that yoke with the big hair. I think he's having a fling with V Kill P, which is pretty dangerous, bearing in mind I'm totally convinced she's a lesbian and if it doesn't work out it could mess up their radio show. Not a massive loss to the world but he can have any girl he wants so why does he have to be stupid about it? She's been hanging around the house a lot lately, and although they don't make it as obvious as he was with the yoke, they do seem to have got a little flirtier. She hasn't stayed over, but then again Dad is home, and I haven't caught them kissing all over the house, but then again V Kill P is way cooler than the yoke so she probably wouldn't be on for that. Watch this space.

I met Paul the other day and he was on his way into town to meet a girl. His rugby team are playing on Friday and I promised I'd go and watch. Maybe I'll get to meet her. He's in good form but he's nervous about the results and whether or not he'll get law. I told him not to worry, he'll fly through it, but he said he's not like you. He said you'll get medicine without breaking a sweat, but he'd had to work his balls off and even now he's not sure how he's done. I told him I had no doubt you'd both be in university doing your highfalutin subjects while I'll be in London behind a sewing machine. He laughed at that. He did say he wasn't entirely convinced that Dicknose would get medicine (even in Cork, never mind Trinity) either. (I promise I'll stop calling him that in my next letter. Just give me this one to vent – I think it's the least you can do under the circumstances.) I didn't say anything but it would be insane if you got medicine and Dicknose didn't.

Only a matter of weeks to go before we'll all know what lies ahead of us. Speaking of which I met Gina McCarthy in the coffee shop on Monday. She's home from college in Galway and she asked me if I'd like to join her so I did. She was talking about living there in the college accommodation, and the balls and the students' nights out and it all sounded amazing. So between your new friend down there having a blast in Cork, Gina loving Galway and Clooney living like a rock star, the reports on the college experience are all good. I just hope it's as good in London. Getting a little anxious but I'll be fine. I always am. Gina and I had a great time together and it reminded me of how much fun we had when we were younger and before she decided she was too old to hang around with us. She's working for her dad in the bar for the summer so we're meeting for coffee again tomorrow, and she's thinking about going into town to see Glenn's band on Saturday. (I'm going to have to stop calling him Glenn – I've got Gina at it now.)

Tell me more about your life. How is Colm? He sounds interesting and your type and, no, I'm not saying you should be with him but, having said that, it's not like you're married or anything so it mightn't be the end of the world either. Just a thought.

I have to go and beautify myself for Glenn. Talk soon I HOPE.
Your best friend,
Eve

PS Dicknose does really miss you and he's talking about you all the time – even Gar has a pain in his face listening to him.

PPS I DO LOVE YOU.

PPPS I cannot believe your taste is always the direct opposite of mine. Christian Slater first and Emilio last just isn't right but at least we will never fight over a boy.

Eve's unexpected date with Ben had pepped her up. She decided, as usual, to cook and nipped to the supermarket. She bought half the shop so that she had plenty of food to work with. She'd proved to herself long ago that she was far too impatient, mistrustful and possibly arrogant to follow recipes.

Four hours? That's ridiculous! I could be in another country in four hours. I'll see what it's like after two. What the hell is a fenugreek leaf? Screw it. Basil will work just as well.

She kept the menu plain and hearty but still managed to burn everything when she went online to search for a potato recipe and got caught up in a YouTube video and forgot she was cooking. As it turned out, Ben was more than an hour late so the apartment was cleaned and the smoke evacuated before he arrived. It was seven when she answered the door with takeaway leaflets in her hand. He walked in, wrapped his arms around her and lifted her up so that she was sitting on his hips with her legs curled around him. Before she knew it she was leaning against a wall and he was kissing her. He started stripping off her clothes, and then he carried her to the bedroom. They made it to the bed intact without having spoken one word. With Ben she felt safe and free, warm and beautiful. Eve could have looked into his brown eyes for ever. When he touched her she tingled, and when he held her and moved inside her she felt abandoned.

Eve enjoyed sex, and over the years she'd had many men – some she was simply attracted to, some she'd liked and a few she'd really liked – but there had only ever been one she'd thought she could love: Ben Logan. *You're just living in the past, Eve, because you just don't want to let go*, she'd tell herself, but her body wasn't listening.

They lay together facing one another, lost in their own little universe. He was tracing Eve's collarbone with his finger and she was cupping his cheek in her hand. She knew his world was collapsing. His wife was crying somewhere and what Eve and he had was a fantasy, merely his way of escaping the pressure cooker that had become his life and her way of escaping her head. She didn't talk business. She didn't say anything that would burst their bubble. Instead they lay in each other's arms, talking about the past as a means of avoiding the present.

'Call me Glenn,' he said.

'Glenn,' she said.

'I remember the first time you called me by my actual name,' he said.

'We were fooling around in a park,' she remembered, with a smile.

'It was the night I knew you were mine.'

She laughed. 'You always did have a head too big for your body.'

He pulled her into his arms. 'I loved you then, Blondie.'

Eve felt like crying so, instead of ruining the mood, she changed the subject.

'Gulliver Stood On My Son,' she said, and laughed.

'What?' Ben said, feigning disbelief. 'That was a great band name!'

'Yeah, it had Hall of Fame written all over it.' She giggled.

Ben loved to hear her giggle.

'I remember that gig where you went from "Long Way Back" to a rendition of "Nothing's Gonna Change My Love For You" as I walked into the club. It was so cheesy,' she said.

'It was funny,' he said.

'It was awful.'

'You loved it.'

'Yeah, I did.'

Ben had had to fight with the band all day to get them to do it. They were rehearsing in Billy's dad's garage when he'd floated the idea.

'No way,' Mark said, and put down his sticks.

'No fucking way,' Finbarr said, from behind his keyboard.

'I'd rather cut my knob off than do anything by Glenn Medeiros,' Billy said, taking his bass off and lighting a cigarette.

'Ah, come on, it's for my girlfriend,' he'd pleaded. It was the first time Ben had called Eve his girlfriend and he liked the sound of it.

'Rusty knife,' Billy said, pointing to a toolbox in his dad's garage. 'Knob.' He pointed to his penis.

'What about you, Tom?'

'Yeah, whatever.'

'Nice one.'

'No, no, no and fuck no,' Finbarr said.

Billy just kept pointing to his penis and making a snipping gesture. After a long discussion, they agreed on the basis that Ben would do all the gear after gigs for the rest of the summer. He was desperate for it to be spontaneous, and he knew Eve's bus wouldn't get her there until at least five minutes after they were already on stage so he had asked Terry the Tourist Noonan for a picture of her.

'I don't have one.'

'Liar.'

'I swear.'

'I saw you taking one the other day.'

'I was looking past her.'

'Give me the picture.'

'No.'

'Give me the picture or I'm going to report you for being a pervert.'

'I'm not a pervert.'

'Yeah, well, the guards don't know that and frankly neither do I.'

'Fine,' Terry had said, and he'd gone up to his room and brought down a collection. Eve at school. Eve on a bike. Eve lying out in her garden. Eve sitting by the harbour. In the one that was clearest she was leaning against a wall.

Ben took the picture from him. 'If I ever see you taking a picture of my girlfriend again I'll throw a bowling ball at your head and call it an accident,' he said.

Terry nodded. 'Fair enough,' he said.

Ben had given the picture to the guy at the door. As soon as Eve entered, he radioed the stage hand, who signalled to Mark on drums. He'd changed tempo, and by the time she was standing in the middle of the room, Ben was belting out the Glenn Medeiros classic to her as if she was the only girl in the room. He could still see her eyes lighting up, the smile that crossed her face, the way she'd hidden her face and then raised her hands in the air. She had loved it and it had been worth doing all the gear for the entire summer just for that moment.

'What are you thinking about?' she asked now, bringing him back to her.

'You,' he said.

'Sing me the song you wrote for me,' she said.

'No.'

'Ah, come on!'

'I'm not a singer any more.'

She pretended to sulk.

'I'll say it.'

'Oh, like those bad poems.'

'Exactly.'

'OK.'

> 'She's the one to avoid,
> strong, beautiful, a living android.
> She talks, I flinch, she makes me think.
> She chews me up and spits me out;
> she makes me scream, bleed and shout.
> This battle's lost but I'll return,
> when she is mine my war is won.'

Eve sang the chorus loudly and badly while punching an arm in the air.

> 'It's a long way back,
> you know I'll keep on coming,
> it's a long way back,
> without you I'm nothing.'

On cue, they burst into Glenn Medeiros's 'Nothing's Gonna Change My Love For You'.

'You'll always be Glenn Medeiros to me,' she said.

He seemed sad. 'I do love my wife.'

'I know.'

'But you're the one that got away.'

'No,' she said.

'Yes,' he said, nodding. 'That last night together I told you I loved you. You burst out laughing in my face and it was like I was being knifed.'

'I didn't mean it. I was nervous and drunk and scared.'

'Scared of what?'

'I don't know. You? Love? Leaving? I just wasn't ready.'

'Billy told me,' he said.

'I guessed,' she said.

'If I could do it again I'd know better.'

'I don't want to talk about it,' she said sternly, and he knew she meant it.

They'd never spoken about what had happened that night and they never would. They lay in silence. He held her hand. His eyes were full. She pursed her lips and he wiped away a stray tear. They stared at each other and engaged in a full conversation without saying one word.

Around ten they were hungry and neither of them wanted take-out. Eve rang a local bistro and was promised a table if they made it there for last orders at half ten. They jumped into the shower, got dressed and decided not to take a car so that they could have a little wine with dinner. They walked along the dirt road that led from Eve's apartment towards the village. It was quiet and dark. They were alone and wrapped up in one another. Every now and then they would stop in some little nook in the old stone wall that separated a farmer's field from the narrow road. He'd pull her to him and they'd kiss, hold on tight and kiss again.

'We'll miss our reservation,' she said.

'I wish we could just stop here and now in this moment for ever,' he said, stroking her cheek.

'Time to go,' she said, pulling him away from the wall. They began walking hand in hand down the road again. He was pensive and she could feel his thoughts slipping away from her and back to his wife. 'Don't leave me yet,' she said to him.

He smiled. 'I'm right here,' he said.

The car came towards them and Eve could see its lights. Suddenly her legs were buckling and Ben's hand was ripped from hers. She didn't black out, but it was all so surreal, like a pleasant dream morphing into a nightmare. One second she was looking at Ben, and the next she was sitting in the passenger seat of a car with her two broken legs poking out through the smashed windscreen. Her shoulder felt strange, and when she looked at it, it seemed to have disappeared. She couldn't move her arm. She looked back from her shoulder to her twisted legs and the road ahead and then to the drunken man who was driving. She smelt the stale odour of whiskey before she saw him. She had to focus hard to do that. He was weaving all over the road and her broken body rocked. He was mumbling to himself as though he was alone. *Where's Ben?* She tried to turn to look in the back seat to see if he was there but she couldn't move her body. *Where's Ben?* She tried to talk but she couldn't seem to connect mind and mouth. She tried desperately to find her voice and focused hard to be heard.

She heard herself whisper, 'Where's Ben?'

He didn't respond. Instead he turned on the radio. Eve's heart was beating so loudly it seemed to reverberate in her eardrums.

Still she felt no pain but, looking at her twisted legs resting on the bonnet of his car, she knew it was coming. She remembered what her yoga teacher had said about breathing and control, so she took a deep breath and then she let it go. In her head she said one word over and over. *Stop. Stop. Stop. Stop. Stop.* Until it finally reached her mouth in a whisper: 'Stop.'

He looked away from the road he was driving all over and towards Eve. He was angry. 'You wanted a lift, I gave you one,' he said.

She was confused. *Did we ask for a lift?* Once again she looked straight ahead just to confirm one more time that her broken limbs were hanging out of his missing windscreen.

'Ben?' she said.

'You were in the middle of the road!' he shouted at her, before wiping his nose on the sleeve of his woollen jumper. It was too dark and she couldn't make out its colour.

Lights flashed in front of them. The car swerved from left to right even though the driver seemed so focused on the road ahead. She wondered if he had noticed her broken limbs. On the steering wheel she saw the Nissan emblem. When they passed a streetlight or an oncoming car she could see that the bonnet was red, that he had a red beard and huge hands. On his left hand he wore a large gold Claddagh ring.

'Stop, stop, stop, stop, STOP!' she said, until the whisper became a shout.

He steadfastly ignored her, continuing to mumble while turning the sound on the radio up. She realized her right arm was undamaged so she could use it. She grabbed his jumper and pulled at it.

'*Please!*' she screamed. '*Stop!*' She couldn't think of or bring herself to say anything else.

'You wanted a lift!' he shouted at her. 'I'm giving you a lift. What more do you want?'

'To stop,' she said, in a voice and tone that sounded foreign to her.

'Fine,' he bellowed. 'Bloody women, never know what you want!'

He stopped the car in the middle of the road. He got out of the driver's seat, arguing with himself. He passed his smashed windscreen and her twisted legs and made his way to the passenger door. He opened it with a jerk and she felt herself falling. *Oh, God, he's going to drag me.* She steeled herself for the agony that was coming. He grabbed the arm that was missing its shoulder and pulled her. She screamed and begged, using only one word over and over. *'Please!'*

He let the arm with the missing shoulder go, took her by the back of her neck and pulled again. She felt the glass cut deep into her burning, pounding legs.

'Please.'

Her legs were so long that he had to twist her to get them through the hole in the windscreen. She saw them bend and felt another snap.

'Please.'

He had a good grip on her now and pulled from under her arms. He pushed on the place under her shoulder-blade where her shoulder now rested and for a moment she thought – hoped – she would die.

'Please.'

She felt her legs thud to the ground. He dropped her torso so that she was lying facing up at the stars. It was a clear night, beautiful, the same night that she had been with Ben, kissing against a wall like teenagers.

'Ben?' she said.

He ignored her. 'You wanted a lift,' he said, pointing at her.

She lay motionless.

'I gave you a lift,' he said, pointing to his car. Again he rubbed his nose.

She remained motionless.

'And it's the last lift you'll get from me,' he said, got into his car and disappeared, leaving Eve in the middle of the road.

She realized quickly that if she stayed there she'd be killed. She also knew that three limbs were badly damaged but she had one good arm. *You can do this, Eve. You're strong, remember? It's either pull yourself to the side of the road or become roadkill. Simple. No choice. Just do it.* Eve began to pull herself slowly towards the ditch at the side of the road. Every move was torture, every minute seemed like an hour, and she cried all the way. When she was on the verge she lay still, looking at the stars and praying that any car which could have killed her minutes before would now find her. *Where's Ben?*

She heard a car pass but the driver didn't see her, then another and another. She tried to wave with the one arm that still worked but she couldn't. She was so tired. *This is where I die. I hope you're OK, Ben. I'm so sorry about that night. It was my biggest and stupidest mistake. I think I love you. I think I've always loved you.* She closed her eyes and let go.

Big lights shone down on Eve and she heard voices before she could open her eyes. When she did, it was hard to focus on the faces looking down at her. She could hear a conversation but it was muffled – as though she was on the phone and the signal was bad. One of the faces she was trying to focus on was talking to her and with every blink he was becoming clearer. The other one was sticking her with something, which felt good. Suddenly it was as though the signal cleared.

'You're OK now, love. We've got you. Can you hear me?'

'Yes,' she said.

'Nice one,' he said, smiling down at her. He turned away. 'She's back with us, Brendan.'

Brendan said something that Eve couldn't make out.

'What's your name, love?' said the other.

'Eve,' she said.

'Well, Eve, we're going to move you now.' And the memories of her being dragged out of the car and crawling across the road flashed into her mind. Every nerve seemed to scream in preparation for pain like she'd never known.

'No,' she begged.

'It's OK,' he soothed her. 'You're in good hands. We won't let anything else bad happen. Isn't that right, Brendan?'

Another face appeared. 'That's right, Tony.'

Eve opened her eyes and focused on the white roof of the ambulance. She could feel that she was tied to a board. Although she couldn't see the wires and tubes she knew they were there. There was a mask over her mouth and she felt the cold crisp oxygen move in through her nose and warm breath escaping through her lips.

'There you are!' Tony said, removing the mask for a second. 'Back with us.'

'Yes.'

'Do you believe in God?' he asked.

'No.'

'Well, we were on the way to another accident when we saw you and that's a miracle in my book,' he said.

'Luck,' she said, and searched her mind because she knew she was forgetting something important. *Something, something, something.*

He laughed. 'Maybe,' he said, and moved to put the oxygen mask back on her face.

Another accident. She stopped him with her good arm.

'My boyfriend,' she said. Suddenly she was eighteen again and Ben was the boy she loved.

'Who's your boyfriend, love?' she heard him say.

'Glenn Medeiros,' she said, although in her head she was saying the words *Ben* and *Logan*.

He smiled at her. 'We'll do this pick-up and then we'll find Glenn.' And he placed the mask back over her mouth. She disappeared again.

When the ambulance stopped and the doors opened, Eve could hear people talking loudly and hurriedly.

'We did what we could.'

'We did our best.'

'Is he alive?'

'We weren't sure what to do.'

Eve knew it was Ben and she waited for what seemed like an eternity. *Come on, Ben. You can do it. You're strong too. You can do it. You can do anything and you'll be fine.* They loaded him into the ambulance. She couldn't see him.

'Is he OK?' she asked.

'Just worry about yourself, love,' Tony said.

'Is he OK?' she asked again.

'Just relax,' Tony said.

'*He's mine!*' she shouted. '*He's with me, he's mine!*'

'All right, OK, I understand, he's OK, relax now.'

And Eve disappeared for the final time on that journey.

In A&E she was alert again under glaring lights and surrounded by people. They were all busy and she was trying to work out if she was in pain or dead from the neck down. Someone lifted her arm and she heard herself scream. *Not dead from the neck down then. That's positive.* She was still secured to a body board and it was suffocating. Voices came and went.

'Hang in there, Eve.'

'Well done.'

'We're going to give you more pain meds – you're doing great.'

'OK, we're going to move you to X-ray.'

'Good girl.'

'I'll be in the other room and just outside. OK? Stay still. I know you will.'

'Well done. Now I'm going to take you back. It's OK, Eve, stop screaming, we're going to get you more pain meds.'

She saw the first detective at three a.m., according to the notes. He asked her if she could remember any details of the incident. He apologized immediately, and told her that if she didn't remember anything it was perfectly fine, he could talk to her another time. She didn't want him to go anywhere because she remembered so much and she wanted him to know it before she forgot an important detail or died.

'He was driving a red Nissan. I know it was a Nissan because I saw the emblem was on the steering wheel. He was taller than me and I'm five foot eleven, so maybe he was six foot one or two. He had red hair and a beard and when I say red I mean ginger. He had allergies, his nose was constantly running. He had big rough workman's hands. He was wearing a Claddagh ring and his breath stank of whiskey.' She was pleased that she had regained the ability to speak in sentences.

He was scribbling down everything she said. 'Hold on, I thought you were a pedestrian?'

'I was.'

'So how could you see the Nissan emblem on the steering wheel?'

'Because I landed in the passenger seat of the car. Through the front windscreen.'

His eyes widened in amazement but he didn't comment. He closed his notepad. 'Maybe we should talk again tomorrow.'

She knew there was something more.

I'm missing something, what is it?

'Something else,' she said. She focused for a minute or two.

The policeman stood up to leave.

'He was wearing a navy woollen jumper,' she said.

The detective smiled. 'If you were in that car it must have been pitch dark. How could you see the colour of his jumper?'

She held up her good arm and showed him her hand. 'Because the wool is stuck under my fingernails,' she said. He looked sideways at her, fascinated, before he took her hand in his and slowly removed the wisps from under her nails.

Then she asked him about Ben.

'I'll ask the doctors and get back to you.'

'When?' she said.

'Soon.'

'Now,' she said, as though she was in a position to make demands.

'Just a few more questions.'

'I don't know anything more. I helped you, help me.'

He agreed to find out. He disappeared. He didn't come back.

Eve went into shock officially at four thirty a.m. and disappeared for the final time on that horrific night.

Lily had the strangest dream: she was in a military aircraft carrier dressed in fatigues and going to war. She spent a few seconds looking at all the boys with her. They were talking among themselves. She wondered what the hell she was doing there. *This isn't a flower-arranging class.* Then she wondered if she was there because she was a nurse. *Damn it, why did I sign up for this?* There was a boy around Scott's age, maybe a little older, sitting beside her. He was pumped up and excited.

'Is this your first time?' he asked.

'Yeah. You?'

'Oh, yeah. I've been waiting to do this for a long time.'

'You're a kid. You don't know what a long time is,' she said.

'Whatever.' He smiled at her and rocked excitedly. She noticed the engines were getting louder, meaning they had to shout instead of speak. *I hate shouting.*

'I'm getting married,' he said.

'It's not all it's cracked up to be.'

'We're going to have a house and a dog and some kids and a rabbit,' he said, 'but first I'm going to kill some bad guys.'

'Get a rabbit or a dog. Do not get both.'

'Why not?'

'Because the dog will eat the rabbit. It's nature.'

'Nah, they'll love one another,' he said, and he was confident he was right.

'If they told you I was your enemy, would you kill me?' she asked.

'Who is they?'

78

'The people who've put us on this plane,' she said.
'No.'
'Why not?'
'Because you're a friendly.'
'But how do you know?'
'You look friendly,' he said.
'Not that friendly,' she said, took out a gun and shot him in the head.

She sat watching the blood tumble out of the hole in his face, mesmerized by his fixed stare. *All I wanted to do was join a flower-arranging class*.

Lily woke up in a cold sweat.

'Lily, are you OK?' Marion asked, after the change-over meeting. It was clear Lily hadn't been listening to a word about any of the patients she'd be taking charge of for the next twelve hours.

'I'm sorry, I didn't sleep very well.'

'You're pale. Would you like to lie down?'

'Are you nuts?' She almost laughed. 'We're short-staffed and overworked as it is.'

'Why do you keep pulling at your shoulder and guarding your chest?'

Lily hadn't noticed she was doing that. 'It's nothing – just my shoulder . . .' she said, as Adam walked in.

'Let me look at it,' he said.

She was embarrassed. 'No, it's fine, honestly.'

'She's been pulling at it since she got here. She's pale and off form too,' Marion said to him, as though Lily was a patient.

'I'm just tired,' she said.

'Follow me,' he said.

'Bugger-balls.'

'What was that?' he asked, smiling.

'Nothing.'

She followed him into his consultation room.

'Take off your top,' he said.

'In your dreams,' she said, in a tone that suggested that she was joking, yet they both knew her top wasn't coming off.

'I'm a doctor,' he said.

'Congratulations. Your mother must be so proud.'

Adam Wallace laughed. He was the closest thing Lily had to a real friend, and as long as she was clothed, she was at her most comfortable when she was with him. He was a forty-year-old man who had never married but had had his share of beautiful women over the years. The last had been called Caroline. She was a broker and seemed nice when Lily met her at various hospital events, dinners and charity balls. They had been together for four years. She had left when she realized he would never marry her. He was really down afterwards, and he and Lily had become friendly after a particularly boring charity dinner. Declan had been drunk and lording it over everyone at the table but Adam was vulnerable and sad. Declan had thought it was funny to suggest that Adam had paid off his latest beard, then wondered whether it would be cheaper for him just to come out – everyone knew he was gay anyway. That joke had gone down like a lead balloon, and when Lily had tried to make Declan sit down he'd pushed her, not forcefully but hard enough to cause embarrassment. She'd laughed it off and told him to pick on someone his own size.

Later Adam and Lily had met on the hotel balcony and she apologized for her husband's behaviour, explaining that he drank so rarely he couldn't hold the smallest amount with any dignity.

'It's no excuse,' he said. 'There are mean drunks and entertaining drunks. You married a mean one.'

She nodded. 'I married a sleeper. He'll have passed out by the time the band starts to play.'

'Can I ask you a personal question?'

'Depends.'

'Are you happy you married him?'

'I was eighteen.'

'Not an answer.'

'Happiness is a feeling, not a result.'

'How are you feeling tonight?' he asked earnestly.

'Tipsy,' she said, and grinned.

He had laughed, then become serious again. 'Why is getting married such a big deal to women?'

'Ah, Caroline,' she said.

He nodded.

'Why is *not* getting married such a big deal to you?' she asked.

He smiled. 'Good question.'

'And none of my business,' she had said, drained her glass and laid a hand on his shoulder. 'You might not marry but a man like you will never end up alone,' she said, and moved towards the balcony door.

He had called her back. 'One last question,' he said.

'OK.'

'If you could do it all again, would you still marry at eighteen?'

'Not a chance,' she said honestly, and walked away.

That was the night Adam Wallace had fallen for Lily Donovan.

Now he placed an arm round her shoulders. He was fiddling under her horrible pink nurse's tunic. 'You don't make life easy,' he said.

'Funny, that's what Declan says.'

'Declan doesn't know he's born. Do you play tennis or swim?'

'I like to swim when I get time.'

'When was the last time?'

'1991,' she said, smiling.

'Seriously,' he said.

'I don't do sports or exercise.'

He put his head to one side and looked at her quizzically. 'So how do you stay so slim?'

'I binge and purge.'

'I'm serious.'

'Honestly, I eat when I have time and I don't always have time.'

'Caroline lived on leaves and seeds and she weighed more than you do.'

'Can we get back to my shoulder?' she said, remembering she had to call in on Rachel and Nancy before she started her shift.

'OK,' he said, removing his hand from under her top. 'Try to move your arm inwards and across your chest. I'm going to provide a little resistance.'

She couldn't do it.

'OK. Try to rotate your arm inwards,' he said. He pressed on her chest. 'Is that painful?'

'No.'

'OK. It looks like you've done a bit of damage to the pectoralis major muscle – the connecting tendon seems inflamed. Do you know how it could have happened?'

'Not a clue,' she said innocently. *Flaming Declan and his S&M fantasies.*

Adam prescribed ibuprofen and told her to apply heat. If it didn't settle with rest, he ordered her to come back to him so that he could refer her to a physio.

'I know them all.' She laughed.

'Just come back to me and make sure you eat something today,' he said, feigning weariness.

She thanked him and left him to stare after her as she bounced down the hall like a teenager.

Lily walked into Nancy's room just as Jim was coming out with Dylan. It could have been awkward but Lily didn't do awkward. Instead she acted as though he hadn't pretty much propositioned her on the phone the previous night. 'Jim, how are you?'

'Good, thanks, better. Thanks so much for having Dylan last night. I picked him up after you'd left for work.'

'You're welcome,' she said, and bent down to Dylan. 'How are you doing, soldier?' The question reminded her of her dream. *All I wanted to do was join a flower-arranging class.*

'Nancy has a big plaster over her eye. She looks like a pirate,' he said.

Lily smiled. 'Cool.'

82

He agreed that it was indeed cool. He was clearly proud of the part he'd had to play in her new look.

Rachel came to the door. 'Well, are you going to sign the papers or are you going to stand in the doorway talking all day?' she said to Jim.

He sighed and left.

Lily pretended she hadn't noticed the tension and entered the room. 'Hi, Nancy, how are you feeling, darling?'

'Great,' she said, with a wide smile.

'That's good news.'

'She's a trouper,' Rachel said. 'We're so proud of her.'

'Well, I'm thrilled you're feeling better, Nancy,' Lily said. 'Now I must get back to work. See you soon.'

Nancy started to open one of three lucky bags.

Rachel took Lily aside. 'We really are so grateful,' she repeated unnecessarily. 'They think she's going to keep the sight but obviously there will be scarring on the eye. We don't know how much yet.'

'Try not to worry about it – it might be almost impossible to notice. Trust me, kids heal so much better and quicker than adults do.'

'You're right,' Rachel said, and nodded to herself.

'Dylan seems happier.'

'Dylan's lucky my father's in his grave because he would have taken a large stick to him.'

'Accidents happen,' Lily said, uncomfortable with the way the conversation was going. She wondered where the empathy Rachel had displayed the previous day had gone.

'Not if people act responsibly,' Rachel said.

'Jesus, Rachel, he's eight years old!' Lily said, and instantly regretted it when Rachel gave her a look to kill. It would have been clear to anyone looking in that Nancy was Rachel's mini-me and princess rolled into one. Lily felt sorry for Dylan. At least he had Jim, but Jim was always either working or, as Rachel often said, 'making a bollocks of it'.

Lily made her excuses and left them to it. Her first duty was to escort a patient who had been involved in a road-traffic accident to theatre. She arrived on the ward in time to meet Bob rolling the woman down the corridor.

'Ward Five?' she asked.

'Ward Five,' he confirmed.

She picked up the chart, smiled at the poor mangled woman lying on the trolley and walked alongside it towards the theatre.

Eve didn't remember waking but her eyes were open and her brain was half engaged. She was on a trolley looking at a white ceiling. Seeing was more difficult than it had been before she slept. When she closed her right eye she discovered that she couldn't see out of the left at all. She tried to work out if her eyelid was swollen or the eye gone. *My face? What's happened to my face?* The right eye leaked and speaking was difficult again. Eve's words seemed lodged in the back of her head and she was mentally trying to force them into her mouth, but she couldn't. She wondered if that was a result of drugs or head trauma. She couldn't seem to ask about her face so she tried to work out how it felt. It felt foreign. She tried to focus on the nurse but she was standing to her left so it was difficult.

They stopped at the lift and the nurse switched sides to tuck in the blanket covering her. 'Just waiting for the lift, we'll be there soon,' she said.

Eve's lips were bigger than she remembered; she started to purse them and they were swollen and sore. She ran her tongue over her teeth and they were all intact. *That's something.* She licked her lips, felt stitching and tasted blood. *Damn.* They moved into the lift. Her face seemed to roast when she hit the wall of heat and the smell of decay inside. She heard the button being pushed and she heard two women, who had stood aside to allow them in, talking beside her.

'I told Mike that if I wanted that kind of commitment I'd get pregnant but he just doesn't listen – he didn't even notice when I hinted heavily in the direction of an iPod.'

'What are you going to do?'

'I'm going to let him take care of it.'

'And he's OK with that?'

'Oh, he loves it.'

'So really he bought the dog for himself?'

'Exactly.'

'And you hate dogs.'

'Correct.'

'So now you've got a dog in your house that you don't like.'

'Well, I've had a man in my house that I don't like for two years so I might as well have a dog too.'

'Well, you're a better person than I am.'

'Not really. I stole his bank Link card and bought myself an iPod.'

The lift stopped and they got out. The nurse leaned over Eve and brushed a strand of bloody, matted hair off her forehead. 'Nearly there,' she said again, but Eve was somewhere else, thinking about Ben. *Where is he?*

The lift stopped and they were on the move again down a corridor. For some reason the pace had picked up: the lights on the ceiling seemed to be flashing past.

Suddenly and abruptly they stopped and she heard a man tell the nurse he'd see what was going on. Eve heard her push down the brake on the trolley with her foot and felt it jerk slightly.

'It shouldn't be too long now. I know it doesn't feel like it but you will be OK,' the nurse said.

Eve thought her voice sounded familiar, like a song she knew and could sing along to although she couldn't place the singer. Silence followed and her mind drifted back to Ben. *I saw him. He was with me.* She remembered that Ben had a wife and that she'd be worried for him. If they'd found his phone and called her she'd wonder what he was doing on that road. There were police involved. It would be hard for them to conceal the truth. Lying on the trolley, waiting to go into surgery, it dawned on Eve that her no-strings-attached secret affair that was never intended to hurt anyone could potentially devastate Ben, his wife and family.

The man returned and Eve's trolley started to move. The nurse quickened her step and took Eve's good hand in hers. Eve focused on her face. That was strange: she looked a lot like her old friend Lily. *Is that you, Lily? Can't be. Can it? It looks so like you. Your hair is different but if it is you then a bob suits you and you're still beautiful. That's nice. If it's her surely she'd recognize me – but maybe not, maybe I'm unrecognizable.*

They arrived at a door and the trolley stopped. Lily leaned down and smiled at her patient. 'Don't be scared. I know the guy who's operating and he's the best,' she said, and winked.

'Lily?' the woman whispered.

Lily looked at her patient. 'Yes?'

'Eve,' the woman said, pointing to her chest.

Oh, my God. Eve.

Lily covered her mouth.

'That bad,' Eve said.

'No,' Lily said, recovering. 'No, not that bad, Eve, not that bad at all.'

'I missed you,' Eve said.

'I missed you too,' Lily said. She felt like crying.

They reached the door to the theatre.

'Ben?' Eve said.

'Ben?' Lily repeated.

'Ben Logan.'

'Ben Glenn Medeiros Logan?' Lily asked in shock. *What the hell?*

'Please find him, Lily,' Eve said.

Lily nodded. 'I will,' she promised.

The theatre doors opened and Adam stood waiting in his scrubs. He waved at Lily. Bob pushed the bed through the door and Eve was gone.

4. Only the lonely

Dear Eve,

OK, I'm a bad friend. I feel horrible and I did try to call you twice last week after I sent the letter but there was no answer. Besides, I've got a question – are any of you Hayeses ever at home? And have you people ever heard of an answering machine? On Friday I walked to the phone box in the pouring rain (so much for it being mostly sunny here) and stood outside it for twenty-five minutes while the town gossip called every dog and duck she knows to fill them in on the exploits of a woman named Lucille Thomas who discovered her foreign boyfriend Benito kissing her brother in the back garden. Initially she was whispering but when I pushed my face up to the window in a bid to get her to hurry up, which obviously didn't work, she stopped whispering, and by the time she was on her fourth phone call, she was shouting because apparently the person at the end of the line was partially deaf. I think she saw my tan and thought I was a foreigner who couldn't speak English.

It's happening a lot here – when I go into the local news-agent's, to buy a Mars bar or something, the woman speaks slowly and shouts that the Mars will cost 45p. Colm was with me yesterday and he burst out laughing and spent the rest of the day speaking slowly and shouting at me. He had the whole kitchen staff at it by seven o'clock. Anyway, the point of that story is that I shouldn't have said I couldn't call you and I'm sorry I missed you, especially as by the time I got into the phone box

I was like a drowned rat. I'll try again later today or maybe tomorrow, it just depends on time.

And now to more important matters – you and Glenn Medeiros! I can't believe it. Not that you kissed but that you actually think you could have feelings for him – and that's not because he's not cute because even with the perm and the stupid blouses he was cute, but because you said you'd never fall in love and now after one kiss . . . It's just so unlike you but I am happy for you and I hope it's going well and that you haven't changed your mind about him since Sunday. And Gar with the girl from Bray is a turn-up for the books. I'm so happy that you were nice to him about it. He deserves to be happy and he's mooned over you long enough, so good for him and well done. I know it sounds condescending and I don't mean it to be but you really are changing for the better. I've just read that back and it is condescending – I'm sorry but you know what I mean, at least I hope you do.

Work is crazy busy and the craic is 90. We all get on so well and have such good fun and living away from home is a blast. Don't worry about London because you'll have such a good time. There's a great freedom that comes with living in a bedsit and away from parents. I thought I'd be lonely but I'm happy as a clam but then again I suppose Mum isn't around a lot anyway so it's not so different, and the fact that I don't have to cook is a real bonus. I get my real food in the restaurant and it's beautiful. In fact, I've decided that as soon as I get settled in Cork I'm going to do a cooking course at the weekends or evenings or something. Anyway, I have a coffee for breakfast. I buy a sandwich in one of the local cafés for lunch and then I have an amazing dinner at six when we open. Perfect.

Colm and Ellen are great. Ellen met a Spanish boy in the local pub. He's a chef in a hotel close by. He speaks perfect English and he's really nice. They are a nice couple, at least that's if they are a couple – at the moment they are seeing each other casually. Ellen just broke up with a boy in college and it was a bad break-up. She doesn't want to talk about it so I don't know the

88

details. Colm is really kind and we've been hanging around a lot lately because Ellen is off with her Spanish chef. He brought me to a GAA game and I met his friends and they all seem nice but a few of them were slagging him about me but he told them to shut up and that we were just friends and I had a boyfriend, so I feel better about things because I was starting to worry that we were spending too much time together and that maybe he thought something would happen. It's not really anything he has said or done, it's just a feeling. I'm probably mad. Declan says I have too high an opinion of myself – he's probably right.

It's not so strange that Paul mentioned to you that Declan mightn't get the points for medicine. Declan probably said something to him. He's really upset at the moment and I know you're annoyed at him but don't be. I was the one who decided to call him rather than you. Please be nice to him – he's having a really hard time. The other night on the phone he burst out crying because if he has to repeat his exams it will kill him. He's really worried about them. He's been poring over the exam papers since I left and second-guessing every answer he gave. I told him to relax and not to worry. He did well in the mocks. He'll be fine. I felt so sorry for him, he really is stressed out, and Gar is always in Bray (now I know why) and Paul is always slutting around in town, so he's really lonely. He mentioned he might come down to see me if his dad will give him some time off in the garage, but in the meantime please, please, please just be nice. He has noticed you ignoring him and he overheard you calling him Dicknose to Gina in the coffee shop – apparently, he was standing behind the coat rack waiting for a table and walked out before you could see him. He's wondering what he could have done to offend you and he's only pretending not to notice that you're pissed off because he doesn't want to get on the wrong side of you. So I'm begging you as my friend to make up with him. He could do with a shoulder to lean on.

How's Clooney these days? Are he and V Kill P still seeing one another? I was really shocked to hear that. I was so sure she was a lesbian. Although if anyone could change a girl's mind, he could, and I know you hate to hear me talking about Clooney like that but seriously he is one in a million.

I'm listening to a lot of the Beautiful South at the moment – they are one of Ellen's favourite bands and I love both their albums, Welcome to and Choke, and I think you'd really like them too. When I listen to 'Song For Whoever' I always think of you because it's clever. It makes me smile the way you do when you just say it like it is, no matter how blunt. I love that about you.

I'm glad you're hanging around with Gina again. Tell her I was asking for her. And I'm really glad you're seeing Glenn Medeiros and can't even tell you how happy I am that you might be in love because maybe now you'll get off my back about Declan – and now that I think about it I'm disgusted you'd even think that I'd do anything with Colm. Declan and I have been together two years! And even though everything is changing we are for ever, just like you will always be my best friend.

Now I have to go. Colm and I are going for a hike with Ellen and the Spanish chef. I can never remember his name – it's something like Oreo, like those American biscuits that Mary Walsh talked endlessly about when she came home from Florida last year. He's bringing a picnic basket.

I swear this living on your own stuff is easy-peasy. Did I tell you that there is an electricity meter in my bedsit? It's brilliant. I just have to fill it with 50ps and the electricity stays on and there's no bill at the end of the month. I just have to remember to have enough 50ps lying around and that's easy because I can keep them from my share of the tips so it's really handy.

Love you. And I'll try and call you again on Friday at around four p.m.

Lily XXXOOOXXXOOO

PS Top Gun is one of the best films of all time so stop slagging it off and I loved when you went up to GM and said, 'You're welcome' – that's so funny.

PPS Out of U2 who would you date first to last? I'd go for

1. *Larry Mullen*
2. *Bono*
3. *The Edge*
4. *Adam*

TRY AND BE THERE AT FOUR P.M. ON FRIDAY AND GIVE ME AT LEAST TILL FOUR THIRTY BEFORE LEAVING BECAUSE THAT GOSSIP COULD BE THERE AGAIN.

PPPS One last thing – I totally forgot to tell you about the fallout from the girl who found her Italian boyfriend kissing her brother. The brother has been kicked out of the house because the mother was with her and they both saw the kissing and apparently there was more going on than kissing. In fact, the gossip told the last caller that they had their hands firmly down each other's pants. Anyway, he's left town with the Italian and nobody knows where they went. I don't know the girl but apparently she's a fantastic singer and leads the church choir. I'm tempted to go to Mass just to look at her. That's another brilliant thing about living on my own – I don't have my mother making me go to Mass. Oh, and one last thing – I saw a man who looked just like Danny the other day and it reminded me to miss him. Tell him I said hi.

When Lily had recovered enough to start moving she ran down the hall, got into the lift and pressed the button for the ground floor. It seemed to take an eternity for the door to close. *Come on, come on, come on!* She ran to Admissions and waited impatiently while the receptionist gave a visiting couple directions to St Claire's Ward. *Come on, come on, come on!* When they moved out of her way she leaned in.

'I need to find a Ben Logan,' she said.

The receptionist typed in the name and shook her head.

'Nobody by that name here,' she said.

'Are you sure?'

'No Grogans.'

'It's Logan. L-O-G-A-N.'

'OK. Logan. Ah, yeah, here he is.'

'Where?' Lily asked.

'ICU.'

Lily nodded and walked away. When she was out of the receptionist's line of sight she started to run again. She didn't have time to wait for the lift, which was already going to be full, judging by the number of people waiting for it. *Bugger-balls and a side order of flaming fries!* She ran up the stairs two at a time and made it in two minutes flat.

Olivia Castle was on duty. She had transferred from Orthopaedics the previous year.

'Olivia,' Lily said, glad to see a friendly face.

'Hey, stranger, what has you visiting ICU?'

'Ben Logan,' she said.

'He's in Three. What's the connection?'

'None, really. I knew him years ago.'

'Oh.'

'Well?' Lily asked.

'He took a serious blow to the head.'

'How serious?'

'He's in a coma and on a ventilator.'

'Outlook?'

'Not good.'

'Oh.' Lily's heart sank. 'Is it OK if I go in for a second?'

'Go ahead. And, Lily, sorry about your friend.'

'Thanks.'

Lily walked into the room and instantly recognized Ben. He didn't have the facial injuries that Eve had. The back of his head had sustained the damage. He was surrounded by a wall of machines. Tubes poked out from under the bed linen, attached to various collection bags. Lily felt awkward standing there, as though she was the angel of doom. The room was stifling hot, the run up the stairs was the most exercise Lily had done in years, she hadn't slept well and had taken ibuprofen on an empty stomach. When she suddenly felt light-headed, she thought, *Fudge cake*, and promptly fainted. She picked herself up before anyone saw and sat on the chair with her head between her knees. *After all this time, Eve Hayes and Ben Logan.* What *is going on?*

Olivia appeared with a woman who was clearly distraught but silent. The woman stared at Lily. She lifted her head and immediately jumped up, risking fainting for a second time.

'Lily's an old friend of Ben's, Fiona,' Olivia explained, to the woman who was pale and trembling.

The woman redirected her gaze to Ben. He was dying in front of her but she was the one who looked like a ghost. Lily was acutely aware that she had no business being in the room.

'Really,' Fiona said, with eyes fixed on her husband. 'He never mentioned you.'

'It was a long time ago,' Lily said. 'I was more of a passing acquaintance.'

'Right,' she said. Olivia pulled out another chair and sat her down. She hesitated before taking his hand in hers. His knuckles were scuffed but, apart from the fact that the back of his head was caved in, he looked perfect.

'We had a fight,' she said.

'People fight,' Olivia said.

Lily remained silent. She waited for the appropriate moment to leave.

'It was a huge fight. I went to my mother's.'

'You're here now,' Olivia said.

'He's under a lot of pressure,' she said. 'Business is bad.' She touched the wedding band on his finger. 'I told him if he didn't get his act together I'd divorce him. I didn't mean it. I was just angry. He'd let things get so bad and didn't tell me, but he was only trying to protect me. I know that. I know he was doing everything he could to get out of the mess. I know he didn't want me to worry. He's my husband. I love him.' Tears of overwhelming sadness and regret fell freely.

'I'm sure he knows that,' Olivia said, putting her hand on Fiona's shoulder.

'I still don't know what really happened,' Fiona said. 'What was he doing there? It doesn't make any sense.'

Olivia handed her a tissue so that she could blow her nose.

'I don't understand,' Fiona added.

Lily couldn't bear it any more. She made her apologies and left the room. *Oh, Eve, what were you up to?*

She returned to her duties and watched the clock. One hour passed, then two, then three, then four. Declan appeared out of nowhere and nearly gave her a heart attack.

'I'm free for lunch if you're hungry,' he said.

'No. I can't,' she said.

'Why not?'

'I had to take some time earlier to get my shoulder sorted. I'm running behind.'

'What's wrong?' he asked, anxious.

'Adam had a look at it and it's fine – I'm taking ibuprofen,' she said, and began walking towards the lift, hoping he'd follow her. She wanted him as far away from her floor as possible in case Eve came back.

'What happened?' he asked.

'You,' she said, and he clasped her hand to stop her in her tracks.

'Me?'

'And your games,' she said. She smiled so that he knew she wasn't accusing him of anything untoward.

'Ah,' he said. 'The time has come to set aside such childish things.'

'Or buy a new headboard,' she said.

He laughed and kissed her in the corridor, and she knew their little flirtation would guarantee his good mood for the evening. *That's something.*

Another hour went by, and then another.

She saw Adam passing the ward when she was attending to Mrs Niven's catheter. She pulled the tube out so quickly that the poor woman squealed. 'I'm sorry – did that hurt?' she asked, craning to see where Adam was walking to.

'No pain, although I did worry I'd open my eyes to find my fanny in your hand, dear,' Mrs Niven said.

Lily smiled. 'It's just the suction,' she said, and waved her hand. 'You see? Fanny free!'

When Mrs Niven was settled and enjoying an episode of *Midsomer Murders*, Lily went to find Adam. He was in his office.

He stood up. 'Are you OK?'

'Not really,' she said.

He pulled the chair out for her and sat opposite. 'What's going on?' he asked.

'The woman you were operating on – Eve Hayes. How is she?'

'She's in Recovery. Everything went well.'

Lily nodded. 'How bad were her injuries?'

'Can I ask why you want to know?'

'We used to be close,' she said.

'Oh.'

'It was a long time ago but . . .'

'I understand. Well, the neck of her right fibula is fractured, she has a fractured left tibia and fibula, a fractured left shoulder. Her glenoid was sheared off the scapula with a fracture of her coracoid and acromion. She has a fracture to her left cheekbone and a laceration over the left side of her face running into the lower portable part of her nose.'

'Jesus,' she said, and burst into tears.

Her reaction was as shocking for her as it was for Adam. He got up and walked around his desk, sat on it and patted her shoulder. 'She'll be OK,' he said.

'I know – it was just shocking to see her like that,' she said, between sobs.

Adam didn't know where to place himself or what to do. He wanted to take her in his arms and cradle her like a baby but he thought that might be inappropriate so he continued to pat her, hoping she felt comforted rather than awkward.

'I'm really sorry,' she said, pulling herself together.

'Don't be.'

'It's been a long day.'

'I promise she'll be fine – I did some beautiful work in there,' he said, grinning.

'I've no doubt,' she said, and wiped away her last tear. 'How much longer in Recovery?'

He looked at his watch. 'She could be brought back any time now. She really did do well in surgery.'

Lily looked at her watch. It was just after six. Her shift finished at seven thirty. 'OK. Thanks, Adam.'

'You're welcome,' he said, rising from his desk.

She stood up and he hugged her. She smelt of orange blossoms and her hair was soft when he leaned his chin on her head for a second. She patted his back in a friendly gesture and he berated himself for his stupid crush on a married woman. *Get over it, Adam.* They parted.

Lily stood looking at him. 'One more thing,' she said.

'Anything.'

'Please don't mention Eve is here to Declan.'

'OK.'

'Thank you.'

'You're welcome.'

She moved to leave but turned back. 'And, Adam?'

'Yeah?'

'Thank you for not asking why.'

He nodded and she left the room.

Eve woke up in pain. Her left leg was particularly bad. *My shoulder's on fire. Am I dreaming? This is a really painful dream. Holy crap, what's happening?* Her throat felt as if she'd swallowed sandpaper and her lips were dry. When she licked the lower one she felt the stitches with her tongue. *Oh, now I remember.* In her good hand she held something that felt like a remote control. She searched with her fingers for the button but before she could find it a nurse took it from her.

'Are you in pain?' she asked.

'Bad.'

'OK.'

She pressed on something. In that moment the fire in Eve's shoulder seemed to engulf her entire body but just as suddenly it drifted away, and although she'd just woken she felt exhausted.

'There you go,' Lily said, and handed Eve what felt like another remote control. 'When it gets bad, press on it.'

Eve registered Lily's voice and the memory of meeting her at the theatre door flooded back. 'You,' she said.

'Me.'

'A nurse?'

'A nurse.'

'Good.'

'Everything went well, Eve. You're going to be fine.' Lily fixed her pillow.

'Where's Ben?' Eve said, battling the urge to sleep.

'He's on another floor.'

'How is he?' Eve said urgently, knowing she had only a little time before the drug took over and she disappeared.

'He's OK.'

Although twenty years had passed since she'd last seen Lily, and although she was doped up to high hell, Eve knew she was evading the truth. 'Your voice still rises an octave when you lie,' she said.

'OK,' Lily said. She took Eve's good hand. 'He's not so good, Eve.'

'How bad?' she asked, battling to stay alert.

'He's in a coma.'

'But he'll be OK,' Eve insisted.

'I don't know yet,' Lily said, and she was only half lying. He could still live and there was no need to tell Eve it would most likely be in a persistent vegetative state.

'Oh, God almighty, Lily, he has to be OK,' Eve said, beginning to slur. Big fat tears rolled down her face. Her head was as heavy as a bowling ball and her burning eyes sealed shut.

When she was asleep Lily wiped her old friend's wet face gently with a tissue.

The next time Eve woke it was to a rumpus. Lindsay Harrington in the bed opposite was a senile eighty-three-year-old who'd just had her hip reset following an accident in a park. She had mistaken a passing Bernese Mountain Dog called Prince for the pony she had had by the same name as a young girl. Her daughter had turned in time to see her mother attempt to mount the confused animal, which bolted, leaving Lindsay on the ground with a broken hip and talking about sending him to the sausage factory. Eve heard the voices of the nurses as they tried to restrain the old lady, who was shouting, 'Will you please let go! I have to find my handbag!'

Eve heard a nurse calmly telling her that she didn't have her handbag with her.

'Well, that's because it's been stolen! I'm surrounded by bloody peasants!'

'Nothing has been stolen, Mrs Harrington,' another nurse said. 'You have to stay still – you've just come out of theatre.'

'Oh, really?' Lindsay Harrington relaxed. 'I do love the theatre.'

One of the nurses must have pushed a button because Lindsay Harrington disappeared and Eve soon followed.

Lily was too tired to face dinner when she got home. She was pale with exhaustion so her husband took pity on her and ran her a bath. He helped her in and sat on the toilet, watching her as she sank into it.

'I haven't seen you this tired in years,' he said. 'Is it your shoulder?'

'It'll be fine.'

'I didn't mean to hurt you. You know that.'

'Of course I do.'

'Why don't you take the rest of the week off?'

'No,' she said, mild alarm in her voice.

'You're so desperate to get out of this house,' he said sadly. 'It's not like anyone will die without you.'

Lily had learned to ignore her husband's disregard for her work. 'I'm fine,' she said. 'It was a long day.'

'OK. I have something for you,' he said. He went into the bedroom and returned a minute later with a box.

Lily dried her hands with a towel and opened it to find a beautiful gold bangle inside. Declan didn't believe in a joint account but he was generous when buying his wife gifts. Lily often thought the reason she got away with second-hand and home-made clothes was because of the jewellery she wore with them. Declan had a habit of buying it when he felt bad about something. Her collection was extensive. 'It's beautiful,' she said.

'So are you,' he said, 'and I should say it more often.'

She sighed and took his hand in hers. With her heart in her mouth she seized the moment. 'I have a favour to ask,' she said.

'What?' he said, placing the bangle on her arm and admiring it.

'Scott wants to work in the garage with your dad this summer.'

Declan stopped gazing at the bangle and looked at his wife with a pained expression. 'I don't understand,' he said.

'They must have talked about it when he was here for dinner a couple of weeks ago.'

'And Scott wants to work in that garage?'

'Scott doesn't know the man you knew, Declan.'

Declan was lost for words. He didn't know what to think. His relationship with his father had always been horrendous. When Declan was growing up his father was a malevolent, violent drunk. He had chosen to discipline Declan in the way he had been disciplined as a young boy in a Christian Brothers boarding school outside Kildare. If Declan did anything his father considered to be breaking the rules, he would deliver him the worst and most brutal kind of beating. Declan had tried his hardest to be the best boy he could be but the rules changed depending on how much his father had had to drink. Mostly he damaged Declan just enough to terrify him but not enough to invite suspicion. The Christian Brothers had taught him well. Declan's father was a haunted, angry, bitter man. His mother was a quiet, distant woman who tended to live on another plane of existence, one that was sustained by prescription drugs and an unhealthy ability to disengage from reality. She had married a cold man and once when she'd had one too many glasses of wine she had admitted to her fifteen-year-old son, much to his embarrassment, that it was a miracle he was born because she could recall on one hand the amount of times they'd made love. She was her husband's housemaid and mother to his child, and although no one but the man himself could say if he had ever loved her, in the eighteen years they'd been together he had never once laid a violent hand on her. She turned away when her son was being disciplined, and pretended nothing was happening if her husband really lost it.

When Declan was thirteen he joined his friends Gar and Paul for a smoke behind the bike shed in the schoolyard. Their teacher caught them and duly reported their misbehaviour to their parents. Gar was grounded for a week. Paul was grounded for two weeks and made to go to Confession. Declan was punched in the stomach, stripped of all his clothes and locked into the coal-shed behind his house. With only straw to warm him, he was imprisoned there for twenty-four hours before his father freed him.

'Well, Smoky Joe, fancy a cigarette now, do you?' he had asked, and laughed as Declan made his way back to the house, blue with the cold. When he was fourteen his father kicked him so hard in the balls he had to wear a protective cup for two weeks. When he was sixteen he came home to find his father sitting at the dining-room table with a stick lying across it and Declan's report card in his hand. Declan had averaged B in all subjects, despite the usual D in Irish. The teacher said he could do better. That warranted a beating. He smelt the whiskey on his father's breath as he shouted, and when he grabbed the stick Declan punched him hard in the face. His father was shocked but still much stronger than his son. Declan received a broken collarbone and two cracked ribs. He sat in the hospital waiting area listening to his mother tell the receptionist that he'd been playing rugby, and when he was being patched up, the doctor relived his own glory days on the field.

'It's a hard game but worth it,' he said. 'It might feel like for ever but you'll be back on the field in no time.'

Declan was silent while his mother smiled and thanked the doctor. She told him what a promising rugby player Declan was and how proud she and his father were.

Afterwards he had called to see Lily. She was alone as per usual: her mother had taken a job working in a pub. She realized instantly what had happened and took him inside. They lay together in her bed and she held him while he cried like a baby. He never told anyone else what he went through at home but he told Lily everything, every beating, every humiliation. They were so alike in a lot of ways, both only children deprived of the parental love that was supposed to be bestowed naturally. They were both control freaks. In their early years together Lily would have said that the only thing that differentiated them was that, while she was emotionally neglected, she was never subjected to deliberate cruelty. In later years she realized that there was something else: she was a giver and her husband was a taker. He found strength in her acceptance, love and support of him and she found love in his dependence on her. They needed each other desperately. They fitted. They had their own little world that no one was privy to, not even Eve. She would never have understood and Declan would have killed himself if anyone had found out – God knew he'd been close to it before they had found each other.

Declan was desperate to go to university in Cork, not just because he wasn't sure he'd get the grades to follow Lily into Trinity: he wanted to go to Cork to get away from the house that he had nightmares about. Back then, Lily would have followed him to the moon to save him. When Declan got a place in Cork, he cut his ties with his parents and never returned to the house. The day after he left for college his mother moved out and went to her sister, who lived on a farm in Sligo. Although she and her son exchanged Christmas and Easter cards, she never accepted her complicity in Declan's maltreatment, and never apologized or tried to make it right. Their relationship had never progressed past those two cards each year.

Declan and Lily had been married for nine years, and Scott was eight years old, when his father knocked on the door. It was a Sunday and he shook his astounded son's hand, telling him he had found their address in the phone book and taken a chance on them being in. Lily was quite frightened, and Declan was stunned but ready for a fight. The strangest thing happened. The ogre who had made Declan's life such a misery sat in their kitchen and pleaded for his son's forgiveness. He had been sober for four years. He was in AA and Declan was the last person on his list with whom he wanted to make amends.

'I hurt you worse than anyone else,' he said.

'You were an animal,' Declan replied.

'Yes,' he admitted. He cried and tried to explain what had been done to him at his boarding school.

'I don't want to know. I don't care. It's no excuse,' Declan said, and his father didn't push it.

Lily often thought about that day and Declan telling his father that his torture at the hands of the Brothers was no excuse. She agreed with him. If only he could grasp that the same reasoning applied to his own behaviour. Of course he was nothing like his father. He would never lay a hand on his children and he battled with his demons every day. Lily knew that Declan did the best he could – she just wished he could do better.

After that day, Declan's father turned up often. When Declan realized that his father was serious about making a relationship with him and his family, and that he was utterly changed, he allowed him to visit once a month. They saw each other at Declan's home, where he was in control: that was the only way in which he could have the man back in his life. Declan's dad had been in counselling and he was in a group preparing a report on abuses by the clergy. He had admitted that his past was no excuse for his treatment of Declan. He had met many people who had suffered as he had and they had not turned into monsters. He was sorry and he meant it. Declan knew it but, even so, he could only just tolerate the man who worked tirelessly to become a part of his son's new life.

Scott had adored his grandfather from day one. He loved cars and trucks and racing bikes and was thrilled that his grandfather had his own garage. He loved to tinker and pull things apart. He liked the notion of building a car, and when he was sixteen his granddad, with his father's permission, bought him a car that needed work. Together they rebuilt its engine in Declan's garden and under his watchful eye. When the report on the abuses committed by the clergy finally came out in 2009 the whole country gasped at what the children under the control of the Church had endured. Declan read it from cover to cover and only then did he fully understand his father's past. They never spoke about it, but having read that report, he felt closer to his torturer. It was as though in some way they were kindred spirits. His father had been sexually abused, something he couldn't speak about – and Declan would never ask him to. Although their relationship remained fraught it had thawed considerably over the last year.

Before he had read that report, Declan would never have considered letting his son work in the garage that had been the scene of many beatings but now, sitting in his en-suite bathroom with his wife's hand in his, he found himself thinking more positively. 'He does love cars,' he said.

'And if anything did happen and I know it won't, but if it did it would be different,' she said.

'How's that?' Declan asked.

'Because he'd have you to come home to,' she said.

Declan's eyes filled and he squeezed her hand. 'I love you,' he said.

'I love you too.'

He didn't like to cry in front of his wife so he stifled a cough and left the bathroom.

And maybe it was because Lily was reminded of her husband's painful past, or that she had caught a glimpse of the boy she'd fallen in love with, or perhaps it was seeing her old friend battered and broken, or the ocean of grief she carried inside her – or maybe it was all of those things – but for the second time that day the tide she had tried to keep at bay rolled back in: she sat in the bath sobbing quietly until she was empty and cold.

Eve woke up twice more during the night. The first time she was screaming, having dreamed she was on a rack, her arms and legs being torn apart. She heard her shoulders dislocate and saw the Ginger Monster throw her legs into an old wicker basket. She was wet and sweating profusely. Her heart was racing and she was begging him to stop, repeating that she was sorry.

A nurse came running into the room. 'It's all right,' she said, in a soothing voice, before she pressed the button. The fire ripped through Eve and she became still, warm and heavy.

The ceiling disappeared, revealing a perfect navy-blue night sky complete with dazzling diamond stars and a pearl-coloured half moon. She was back on the road, leaning against the old stone wall separating a farmer's field from the passing traffic. Ben was eighteen again and wearing his Bruce Springsteen T-shirt. He was sitting on the wall and she was standing between his legs, kissing his face and holding him close.

'I wish we could just stop here and live in this moment for ever,' he said, stroking her cheek.

'We can,' she said. She hugged him tight, whispering in his ear that everything was going to be fine.

The second time she woke that night a nurse was standing over her fiddling with one of the tubes attached to her. She felt groggy and sick, but the sharp pain she'd experienced earlier had dulled and she knew where she was.

'What time is it?' she asked.

'It's just after three,' the nurse said.

'Where's Lily?'

'She's at home. She'll be back on shift in the morning.'

'OK.'

'Can I get you anything?'

'Ben,' Eve said, and drifted back to sleep.

Lily arrived into work early and checked in on Eve. She was asleep and comfortable. *Long may it last.* Post-operative day two was often the worst. *Hang in there, Eve.* She asked the other nurses to call her when Eve woke, then got to work. As it turned out Eve waited until late morning, when Lily was at the bottom of her bed reading her chart, before she opened her eyes.

'Good morning,' Lily said. 'You had a good night.'

'Clearly we have different ideas on what constitutes a good night.'

'Good to see you're coming back to us.' Lily smiled.

'Ben?'

Lily's heart sank. She'd dropped by the ICU on her way to her ward and he had not had a good night. 'The same,' she said.

'Can I see him?'

'No, Eve. Impossible.'

'Because of his wife,' Eve said, in a tone that suggested resignation. 'Does she know?' she asked, alarmed at the notion of the woman he married freaking out trying to find him.

'She's with him,' Lily confirmed.

Eve sighed with relief. 'I don't belong there.'

'Not to mention that you've two broken legs, a mangled shoulder and you've had enough hardware installed to give the Terminator a run for his money. You're going nowhere.'

'But mostly I don't belong,' Eve said.

Lily remained silent.

'How long?' Eve said, pointing to the damage to her body.

'Weeks,' Lily said vaguely.

'How many weeks?'

'Everyone heals in their own time. I can't answer that.'

'Ballpark.'

'Still pushy, I see.'

'Please.'

'Your shoulder is the worst injury. Adam basically rebuilt it and they might have to go back in. If they do, it will be in another month or so. Your right leg is in a cast for about eight weeks, your left leg will take at least that and you'll need physio.'

'What about my face?' Eve asked.

'Well, you look a state now but you'll heal as good as new.'

'Thank you.'

'You're welcome.' Lily sat down and pulled her chair close to the bed. 'I found your phone. It was in your jacket pocket. I could call Danny for you.'

'He died.'

Lily's face fell and tears filled her eyes. It was as though she had been punched in the gut. When Eve and Lily had parted company all those years ago, Lily had lost more than her best friend: she had lost the man who had been the closest thing she'd ever had to a father, and Clooney too. 'Oh, Eve, I'm so sorry.'

'Thanks.'

'If I'd known . . .' Lily trailed off because she hadn't known, and even if she had, would she have had the guts to turn up to his funeral? *Maybe – after all, it was Danny.*

Lily fell silent. Eve saw the pain in her face. She understood it. Lily had loved Danny just as she had. A vision of her father swinging tiny Lily around and Lily screaming, 'Faster, Danny, faster!' popped into her head.

'How about Clooney?' Lily said, after a few minutes.

'He's in Afghanistan.'

'What the hell is he doing there?' Lily asked, alarmed.

'Feeding people,' Eve said.

Lily nodded. *Of course he is.* 'Have you a husband or children?' she asked.

'No.'

'Who do I contact?'

'No one,' Eve said, as she drifted into sleep.

'Eve.'

'What?'

'You can't go through this alone.'

'Of course I can,' Eve said. She closed her eyes.

When Lily was sure she was asleep she opened the locker, pulled out Eve's phone and went out into the corridor. She scanned through the contacts and found Clooney's name. She paused for a second or two before hitting the call button. Clooney's phone went to voicemail. She took a deep breath and waited for the beep.

'Hi, Clooney, this is Lily Donovan – I used to be Lily Brennan. Eve's friend? I'm ringing because she's been in a serious car accident. It's not fatal and she's going to be fine so please don't worry, but she's badly hurt. She's going to need help. She's here in St Martin's Hospital. Ward Five on the third floor. I hope you get this and I hope you can come. OK. 'Bye.'

She switched off the phone and went to put it back in Eve's locker. Her heart was racing. She didn't know if she had done the right thing or not. She was filled with anxiety because although she had no right to interfere Eve needed someone and, although they were on good terms and it was nice to see her, their friendship had died a long time ago and that someone could not be her. Lily was Eve's nurse and she didn't have room in her life or the energy to be anything more. *I wish I could but I just can't, Eve.*

Eve was throwing her guts up the next time Lily returned to the ward. Lily took over from Marion while Eve cried with the pain the vomiting caused her injuries. Eventually, spent and dizzy, she lay back and stared at the ceiling. It swirled and the figure '8' kept appearing and disappearing. She blinked and a rabbit jumped through the top circle of the '8' before burrowing into the bottom circle with his little button tail twitching.

Lily returned with Adam in time to hear Eve singing 'Bright

Eyes' and waving her good arm at the ceiling. 'When we were kids we saw *Watership Down* eight times,' Lily told him.

Adam smiled and went to Eve. 'Hi, Eve, I'm Adam. I'm your surgeon.'

'There's a bunny on the ceiling.'

'Hallucinations,' Adam said to Lily, and made an invisible tick in the air.

'Lily says you're good. Are you good, Adam?' Eve asked.

Adam laughed. 'Yes, I'm good, Eve,' he said. 'I'm just going to check you for rash, OK?' He pulled down the sheet and peered at her extremities. Then Lily helped remove her paper nightgown so that he could examine her body. She was free from rash. Lily made a mental note to buy her some nightclothes. *Please come home, Clooney.*

'Are you experiencing any tightness in your chest or difficulty breathing?' Adam asked.

'No. I'm experiencing rabbits,' she said, pointing to the ceiling.

'No unusual swelling in your hands and feet?' he said, after examining them gently.

'So this is what doing drugs is like,' Eve said. 'I'm not sure I like it.'

'How about a headache?'

'Always have a headache. Life is one big headache.'

When he had confirmed that she wasn't experiencing any dangerous side effects, he prescribed an anti-nausea injection, which Lily gave her as soon as he left the room.

'What time is it?' Eve asked, for the third time in two hours.

'It's four o'clock.'

'How many bags and tubes are coming out of me?'

'Well, you have a bowel bag and a bladder bag. You have a tube in your knee with a bottle attached to collect pus and the same for your shoulder. You have a drip in your right arm.' She lifted Eve's good arm. 'And this is a cannula – it means we can inject the drugs straight in here.'

'So I just lie here, wee and crap myself and watch for rabbits.'

'For today. Tomorrow will be better, I promise.'

Before Lily left, she dampened Eve's lips with ice chips, trying to avoid the cut.

'Any news on Ben?'

'When there's news I'll tell you,' Lily said, keeping her voice even.

'OK.'

At seven, before the change-over meeting, Lily called to see Eve for the last time that day. She was distressed and calling out in her sleep. Lily waited until she had settled before joining the meeting.

Lily jogged around the shopping centre. It was an unscheduled trip and, as fast as she went about her business, she was still going to be late home. Her phone was out of juice and she knew that her delay would worry Declan. When he was anxious he became angry. She hoped he was still at the hospital.

When she got home, her heart sank when she saw his car in the driveway. *Bugger-balls.*

'I tried to call you four times,' he said, opening the front door as though he'd been watching for her through the glass.

'Sorry, my phone packed up.' She wasn't in the mood for an inquisition just because she'd dared to veer two hours off schedule.

'Where were you?'

'I got delayed.'

'Where?'

'Are you the police?' She was annoyed by the limitations he set. *Jesus Christ, just let me breathe.*

'Answer the question, Lily.'

'Oh, for God's sake, Declan, I was in the shopping centre. Are you happy?'

'What were you doing there?'

'I was looking for trainers for Scott,' she said, putting her meal into the microwave.

'So where are they?'

'I couldn't find any worth buying,' she said, leaning against the wall.

'You might have been dead.'

But they both knew that Declan's first thought was never injury and always infidelity. He was obsessed, even though she'd never given him any reason to be. He'd say it was her fault that he was as he was because she flirted with every man she met. Lily felt terribly aggrieved by that because in all the years she'd been married she'd never even dreamed of straying, even when things had been at their worst.

'Does dead on my feet count?' she asked, attempting to lighten the mood. She opened the microwave, took out her food and put it on a plate. Then she sat at the table, keenly aware that her husband was looming over her, silent. 'Anything on the box?' she asked, hoping she could turn the tide.

'No,' he said, sitting opposite her.

She started to eat. 'Where are the kids?' she said.

'Scott's out. Daisy's in the sitting room.'

'How was your day?'

'Fine – until I thought my wife was dead.'

'What do you want me to say, Declan?'

'That you'll never put me through that again.'

'Oh, for the love of God, I'm two hours late!'

Declan nodded. Then he picked up her plate and flung it at the kitchen wall. It smashed and food flew everywhere. 'Two hours is a lifetime,' he said, and walked out of the room.

Lily sat at the kitchen table, resting her head in her hands for a few minutes. Then she cleaned up the mess. She wondered what Eve would say – *I told you so? What did you expect? How could you pick that dicknose over me? Why didn't you give me a chance to explain myself? Why didn't you trust me? Everything could have been so different.* Maybe Eve had been right about Declan, but Eve didn't know him the way Lily did. *Then again . . .*

She was cleaning the wall when Daisy appeared.

'What happened?' Daisy asked.

'I dropped my dinner,' Lily said.

'Dad was really worried about you.'

'Yeah, he told me.'

'You didn't ask me how my recital went.'

'Oh, fudge cake! That was yesterday. I'm so sorry, Daisy.'

'It's OK.'

'How did you do?'

'I rocked it,' she said, smiling.

'Did you tape it?'

'Of course.'

'So why don't I make us some tea and you pull out some brownies and we'll watch it together?'

'Cool.'

Lily sat with her arm around her daughter, drinking tea and eating a brownie for dinner, watching Daisy play her piece perfectly. She thought about Eve being alone in the world. She thought about the nightdresses, underwear, perfume and creams she had bought for her that were stashed in the boot of the car. She thought about her husband's jealousy and temper. She wondered how long she could keep Eve's presence in the hospital from him, and feared what would happen if and when he found out.

5. The things we do and don't say

Sunday, 15 July 1990

Dear Lily,

I am so, so, so, so sorry that I wasn't there to take your phone call on Friday. I really did try to make it home but I was in town with Ben (I'm calling him by his name now because he's officially my boyfriend – more on that later) and his band rehearsal ran really late but Clooney said he picked up and you talked for about half an hour. What's that about? I thought you had no money for phone calls??? I asked him how you were and he said fine. I asked for your news but he just said you had no news. So what did you both talk about for that length of time? We haven't talked for five minutes since you left. Anyway, I'm not going to complain because I should have been there but I can't seem to get a word out of him unless he's annoying me.

Where do I start with my news? Ah, well, Ben is an AMAZ-ING singer and guitar player. His band is so cool. There are five of them, Ben on vocals and acoustic guitar, Billy on bass, Mark on drums, Finbarr on keyboards and Tom on lead guitar. They're called Gulliver Stood On My Son and they're going to be as big as U2. The gig was brilliant last night. The band were already playing when Ben got on stage and he took the mike and screamed out that they were Gulliver Stood On My Son and he was Ben fucking Logan and the crowd roared and cheered. He says the F-word because it's rock 'n' roll and it always gets the crowd going. And in the spirit of friendship and feeling bad for being overheard calling Declan Dicknose, I did apologize and asked him to the gig. I went up to him in the bar and said, 'Listen, I've been missing Lily and taking it out on you because she calls you all the time and she won't call me.' He was actually very nice about it. He said that he was glad it was that because he was really worried he had done something to offend me and he'd hate to do that, and then he bought me a drink. I made sure to buy him one back but it's the thought that counts. Declan came to the gig with Gar, who brought the girl from Bray. She's really nice – she's just going into Leaving Cert in September, the poor cow. It's all ahead of her.

Anyway, back to the gig. The band on before Gulliver Stood On My Son were called Bricking It and it was a good name for them because they were shit. I actually got quite stressed because, even though the rehearsal had been good, I thought, what if they get so nervous they're shit too? It would be written all over my face, and I'd be doing him no favours just saying yeah you were brilliant when clearly they weren't brilliant but it didn't matter because they were brilliant. They blew the roof off the place. I swear I was so excited and high I felt like crying. It was really weird and so unlike me.

I don't know, Lily, I look in the mirror and I don't recognize myself any more. Oh, don't freak out but I've cut my hair – it's in a bob now. I'm feeling and thinking so differently and it's so weird. And don't say I'm growing up or maturing or something else condescending. In a few weeks it feels like everything has completely changed and there's a part of me that wishes everything would just slow down a bit because I'm getting a little dizzy.

Declan and Gar were really impressed by the band. Afterwards we all had drinks together in the bar a few doors down from the venue. You'd really like Ben's band. Billy is twenty-one and he's an electrician by day. He has a thick Dublin accent and he's really funny. He's always making jokes. He calls Ben Bono's Bollocks. HILARIOUS. Mark is twenty – he's the quiet one but he's kind and really clever. His head is always stuck in a book and it's usually one I've never heard of but no doubt you'd know them all. He's in college doing Arts. He's still not sure what he wants to do besides the band. Finbarr looks really like your *neighbour's dad, well, a younger version – he's doing history, he has horn-rimmed glasses but he's cute with a quiff. Tom is nineteen, the same age as Ben, and he's Ben's cousin. He lived in France for years, his mother is French and he speaks French fluently. They seemed to get on well with Declan and Gar.*

    Ben and I left them drinking together in a pub and we walked around Grafton Street and Stephen's Green, and then he showed me a gap in the wall and I followed him into the park. It was really dark and a bit freaky, to be honest. I said if he knew about the gap, loads of others did, and some of them could be perverts, rapists, murderers and junkies. He said I had a way of ruining a perfectly romantic gesture and I told him I didn't do romance. We found cover and talked for ages. He told me that his parents own the bowling alley. I didn't know that, did you? And that other weird boy that works there, the one who eats his own snot, well, he's the son of a friend of the family and he was perfect until he was twelve and then one day he started seizing and now he's a bit brain-damaged. It's awful, isn't it? I said, 'Still, brain-damaged or not, you'd have to have always had a taste for snot to eat it.' He wasn't too happy with me saying that so we changed the subject. He told me that even though he likes college and marketing is OK he really just wants to sing and play the guitar. I told him I had no doubt that's what he was meant for. He was happy then. We kissed and kissed and kissed until my face was sore and my chin was raw. He slipped his hand under my blouse and I didn't even feel him doing it until it felt good, if that makes any sense. Not like poor Gar who nearly ripped my nipple off. And then he started moving south and I held his hand and said, 'NO WAY, not in a park, who do you think I am????' He said, 'I'm really sorry, I just got carried away and I really like you.' I felt bad then so I gave him a hand job because he didn't seem to mind the fact that we were sitting under a bush. Oh, and on our way out I found a stack of porn in plastic bags about two feet from where we were messing around, proving my point about perverts, rapists, murderers and junkies.

On the way to the bus stop he asked me if I was a virgin! Can you believe him? He really does have a nerve. I said it was none of his business and he stopped right then and there and grabbed me and pushed me against the railings. OK, when I read that back it sounds like he attacked me but it wasn't like that at all, it was sexy – and I hate to say it but he was firm but tender. (PUKING AS I'M WRITING.) He looked at me straight in the eyes and I couldn't escape his stare even though I tried because I was embarrassed (ME EMBARRASSED? IT'S UNBELIEV-ABLE) and he told me that it did matter because he was my boyfriend and he didn't care either way but it was an important detail! I nearly died. I mean, it's so personal and I hadn't really considered that we were going out but then I suppose we are and I want to be his girlfriend and I wish you were here because you're so much better than me at feelings. I feel like I want to run away but then I look at him and I want to stay and I'm scared. I know it sounds really stupid but I am. I don't get close to people. Aside from you, who knows me? Clooney a little bit, but that's just because he lives with me – and now when I think about it he doesn't really know me. I mean, I don't talk to him the way I do with you. Arrgh, it's so frustrating!!!! I just want to talk to you. I mean, what if he gets to know me and he doesn't like me any more? What if by the time he works out that he doesn't like me I like him so much that I'll want to die when he leaves? That's what was so great about Gar. He was nice and a distraction but if he'd decided to leave I wouldn't have cared. That was a real plus in our relationship.

Anyway, back to the night by the railings. I turned the question around on him and of course he isn't a virgin, he's a nineteen-year-old college rocker! So I told him the truth. I said that Gar and I had tried but it hadn't worked. He laughed, which annoyed me so I walked on. He caught up and apologized and asked what I meant. I told him that we were in my room and I'd thought that Danny and Clooney would be out all evening. Gar was nervous and first the condom took ages because Gar was

all fingers and thumbs and then when he got going it was like
I was being poked in all the wrong places and he was getting
frustrated so I asked if I could help but he said no – and then
we heard the door and it was Clooney and he was shouting
Danny's name and my name, and just as Gar was finally pointed
in the right direction Clooney came stamping up the stairs. Gar
jumped up and out of the bed and that was pretty much the
end of it. I didn't tell Ben that I'd been pretty much turned off
after that and broken it off with Gar. I still feel a bit mean for
not giving him a second chance but I was afraid he'd arrive with
a potholing helmet and a car jack. Ben said thanks for telling
him and I said, 'You're welcome,' and then he said, 'You won't
have to worry about that happening with me.' COCKY OR
WHAT? I told him he needn't get any big ideas. I had no plans
to be with him like that in the near future. He just smiled and
said, 'The best things are never planned.' I told him for a short
boy he really does have a big head. He just laughed. Anyway
I've been thinking about it since and I'm going to go for it with
him. I mean, so far so good, and let's face it, I'm eighteen and
I don't want to go to London a virgin. That would be a nightmare. I'll wait another week or so and see how it goes but that's
the decision made. I know you probably think I'm rushing into
it. I've only known him a few weeks etc but not everyone meets
their soul mate when they're sixteen and you've been doing it
for over a year so I'm really falling behind here. I need to get
going.

Oh, and V Kill P is a lesbian. Apparently she and Clooney are
just friends and they've been spending more time together because
she's just split up with her girlfriend and he's sworn off girls
since Bushy Head started stalking him. I'm not joking. He told
Danny and me the other night over dinner that she's everywhere
he goes. She's always at the radio station he's interning in. (He's
a runner as opposed to host which is a big comedown but it's a
nice place to work and it's only for the summer so he's happy
enough.) She's at the coffee shop he has lunch in and the bar he

drinks in. Danny told him that aside from the station he has to change his haunts. Clooney's really upset but Danny says change is better than rest so it would do Clooney good, and if he sees her in the new places he'll have to go to the guards. Clooney didn't want to do that. He said the whole place will be laughing at him but Danny said, 'Let them laugh, she's clearly not stable.' I agreed having met her – her hair alone confirms she's definitely nuts. Anyway, Clooney is hoping that making some changes will be enough to stop her, and I told him not to worry because he has a lesbian bodyguard. Danny and I thought that was really funny but Clooney failed to see the joke. Instead he stormed out and we didn't see him after that.

I met Gina for a drink. She's at a loose end because a lot of her friends went to the States to work in New Jersey for the summer. I asked her why she didn't go and she said she stayed to be with her boyfriend who then broke up with her when he got a chance to go to Germany with friends. I got a part-time job in Murray's coffee shop so she comes in when it's quiet and we catch up. She's going to come out for a drink with Declan, Gar, Paul and me on Friday. I'm going to meet Ben afterwards because he's working in the bowling alley late.

Speaking of Paul, we're not seeing much of him. I went to his rugby game with the lads but his new girl wasn't there and after the game he chatted for five minutes and said he'd catch up with us later but he disappeared. I did run into him yesterday and we had a quick coffee. He was quiet and I asked him if he was OK and he said he had a lot on his mind. I thought he was still worried about his exam results but he said he wasn't and what will be will be. He's resigned to repeating if he has to. He asked me about Ben and I told him I really like him and he was really pleased for me. I asked him not to say anything to Gar but he told me that Gar would be fine and I should do what I want to do. He's right. I don't know why I'm being such a sap about it. I asked him to come to Ben's next gig and he said he'd try. So I hope he does. Before he left he told me out of nowhere that I was beautiful and I deserved to be with who I wanted to be with. I know it's NUTS. I don't know what he'd been smoking or taking but it was really nice and I was embarrassed so I just said thanks, you too.

Oh, did I tell you Clooney is going camping with some friends? I think it's to get away from Bushy Head but guess where they're going? Yeah, he's going to be heading to your neck of the woods. Don't know how big or small that town is but you might bump into him.

Right, I'm going. I bought a size-20 linen dress and I'm going to see what I can make out of it. I hope you're still having a good time and Colm hasn't tried anything yet because he will, I'd put money on it.

I'd love you to try to call me again this Friday at four. I promise I'll be there. Ben's working and I'm not meeting the lads until eight.

Miss you, love you,

Eve

PS My list isn't exactly the opposite of yours which makes a nice change.

1. Adam (because he's the coolest)
2. Bono (because he's the singer)
3. Larry (because The Edge looks like someone's dad)
4. The Edge (because who wants to be with someone's dad?)

PPS I know all I did was talk about myself (what's new?) but I just really needed to vent and I am looking forward to hearing your news.

And one last thing, I really am falling in love with Ben. TERRIFIED.

On day three, for the first time since the accident, Eve felt somewhat alert. The amount of morphine that was being pumped into her was being reduced, and although she was sore and uncomfortable she felt brighter. Her morning started with a bed-bath, which Lily gave her. She arrived with towels, fresh linen, toothbrush and paste, lotions and swabs, and placed them on the over-bed table. When she went off to fill a basin with warm water, Eve saw that Lindsay Harrington had been joined by a woman in her seventies.

'Who's that?' the woman said.

'I'll be with you in a minute, Anne.'

'Is that you, Abby?'

'No, Anne, it's Lily. Abby is off today. I'm just with another patient – I'll be with you in a while.'

'OK, chicken. Not to worry. Is that girl any better, chicken?'

'Yes, Anne, she's much better,' Lily said, appearing by Eve's side with the basin of water.

'Oh, good, she was crying a lot last night. She's a noisy thing.'

Lily smiled at Eve. 'Yes, Anne, she is.' She pulled the curtains around Eve's bed.

Lindsay Harrington shouted at Anne, 'She's not the only noisy thing!'

'Jump off a building!' said Anne. 'Do you remember what a roof is?'

'Peasant,' Lindsay Harrington mumbled, but loud enough for all to hear.

Lily raised her eyebrows and Eve grinned. She braced herself when Lily pressed the button to raise the bed.

'It's OK,' Lily said, taking the side rail down. 'I've got you.' She put on her gloves and placed a towel on Eve's chest.

She brushed Eve's teeth, being careful to avoid the stitches in her mouth. The fluoride burned, and Eve sighed with relief when Lily offered her water to rinse with.

'I'm going to take off that paper gown and place a bath blanket on you, OK?'

'OK.'

Lily gently tore away the gown. Eve was covered from head to toe with yellow, blue and purple bruising. Her left leg and shoulder were brown with the iodine used to sterilize them for the operations. Caked blood spilled out over the bandages. Lily placed the blanket on Eve. 'We're going to take our time,' she said.

As terrified as Eve was she couldn't help but smile. 'Who's this *we* you're talking about?'

'Sorry, force of habit,' Lily said, squeezing water from the face-cloth before she gently washed Eve's face, careful to remove all the blood without dragging on the stitches.

Eve flinched once or twice but, although her eye and lip were still very swollen, when her face was clean she looked more like herself.

'Do you want to see?' Lily said.

'I don't know. Do I?'

'I promise it'll get better,' Lily said. She passed Eve a hand mirror.

Eve lifted it up and looked at her face. 'Holy crap,' she said.

'It's not that bad.'

'Easy for you to say,' Eve said, dropping the mirror. 'You still look like that beautiful teenager I used to know.'

It was the first time either of them had acknowledged that they had not been friends in a very long time.

Lily took the mirror from her. 'Trust me, she's long gone,' she said.

'Nah,' Eve said. 'She's still in there somewhere.'

'What about you, Eve? Are you still that girl?' She hadn't been able to disguise the edge in her voice.

'No, not exactly, you'll be happy to hear, but no one really changes that much – we are what we are.'

Lily agreed. 'So, sleeping with a married man?' she said.

Eve laughed a little. 'Not my best self . . .'

'I read that you had a life in America.'

Ah, she has *Googled me.* 'I did. It consisted of work and nothing else. I got tired.'

'And Ben Logan?' Lily asked.

Eve's eyes filled and Lily was sorry she'd brought the subject up.

'I tried to go back in time. It didn't work.' That ended the conversation.

Eve's shoulder was the biggest problem. She cried as Lily cleaned it because, no matter how gentle she was, the slightest touch felt like a knife going into it. When Eve was finally clean and lying naked under the bath blanket, Lily placed the bags of stuff she'd bought in the shopping centre on the chair. She pulled out three nightdresses, two soft woollen shawls and some cotton underwear.

'You shouldn't have,' Eve said.

'I'm not going to leave you dressed in paper. Danny would kill me,' Lily said, as though she was doing it for him rather than the woman in front of her.

'Thank you,' Eve said. She was battling the urge to cry again.

Eve's left arm was pretty much immovable so Lily had bought nightdresses three sizes too big. She cut the narrow straps of one so that she could slip it over Eve without moving her shoulder or arm. She pulled it up under Eve's frozen arm and tied the straps at the back of her neck.

'Ingenious,' Eve said.

'Ah, wait, there's more,' Lily said, and took out two nappy pins. 'It'll look so much better when it's fitted.' She gathered the extra material and pinned it at both sides. She stood back and surveyed her handiwork. 'Lovely,' she said. 'Would you like a wrap?' She held up a nice one in charcoal.

Eve nodded and Lily placed it around her shoulders.

'I'm really grateful,' Eve said, as Lily spritzed her with perfume.

'Glad to do it,' she said, and opened the curtains just as Clooney entered the ward.

'Clooney!' Eve said, clearly shocked, and it was clear to Lily from the look on Clooney's face that he was experiencing the same emotion.

'Eve, what happened to you?'

'What are you doing here?' she said, and she was crying again, not because she was in pain this time but because she was so happy to see her brother.

He bent to kiss her forehead, then pulled up a chair and sat down. 'As if I wouldn't come,' he said.

'I must be dying!' she joked.

'Well, if you are, it looks painful.'

Eve looked at Lily. 'You shouldn't have but thank you,' she said.

Clooney turned to Lily and smiled a wide smile. She smiled back, then left them alone.

Clooney turned back to his sister. 'Of course she should have. She's your old friend and I'm your brother,' he said.

Eve gazed into his haunted eyes and was glad he was out of Afghanistan even if it had taken her near-death to get him home.

Clooney had picked up Lily's message the previous evening. He had been in meetings all day and his phone had been on silent. His driver was talking about a bombing that had taken place earlier that day. A woman had approached some American soldiers and blown herself up. Clearly the intention had been to take out the soldiers but for some reason the bomb hadn't ignited properly, and while she'd managed to rip herself apart they were simply thrown clear. They were lucky, she was not. She didn't die on impact, instead she bled out slowly on the street. The soldiers and passers-by kept clear in case of a secondary detonation so, rumour ran, her only company on her journey towards Paradise had been a stray dog that licked up the blood before cocking his leg. Inured to such stories, Clooney was tired from a day of endless frustrating meetings so he wasn't particularly focused on what his driver was saying.

Clooney had been feeling restless for a while. Like Eve, his childhood in Ireland had instilled in him the need for change, but unlike his sister he was familiar with that sensation: he never stayed in one place or did one job for too long. He had been in Afghanistan for two years and was sick of security checks, minders, restrictions, dust and death. He dreamed of an exotic climate, lush trees, white sands, blue sky and sea. He dreamed of rest and silence. He was tired of arguing about funding and distribution channels. It was incredibly hard on the soul to watch war destroy lives and livelihoods, reducing good people to beggars and thieves. Before his father died he had witnessed two American contractors being kidnapped. Their car had been turned over by a roadside bomb, men had appeared from thin air and the scrambling security team had been shot on sight. Clooney's car was three behind the targeted vehicle. As his driver manoeuvred to get them out of the area Clooney had turned to look out of the back window and had seen the injured men being dragged into a waiting van. It sped off, the dust rose and the men were gone. Clooney had known he had been in no danger but the incident had had a huge impact on him, especially when one of the men was later beheaded. Over the years he had become accustomed to being cautious but he had never before experienced real fear, no matter how hairy the situation he had found himself in. That event had acted like an injection of poison that was slowly spreading through his system. It stole his sleep, which was ageing him. *I don't want to be here any more.*

Clooney had been establishing an exit plan since he'd returned after his father's funeral, and part of that plan was to say goodbye to Stephanie, an American journalist who lived in the same hotel. Her room was down the corridor from his. They had been seeing one another on and off for more than a year. It was casual – she would disappear for days and weeks with George, her ever-ready cameraman, chasing stories. When she was away for more than a month, he'd thought she might have gone home, but it turned out she'd followed a story into Pakistan. He liked her a lot – she was ballsy and fun – but, as a woman, she had no business being there. Then again, the same could be said for him and every other expat in the building. Stephanie came from a large family of boys and a military background – generations of her family had fought in wars around the world. She had been born to be one of the guys and seemed comfortable in chaos, far more so than Clooney, who'd started off his career replacing shacks with houses by day, then getting drunk and jumping into swimming pools at night.

One evening he'd got back to his room and was having supper there alone when Stephanie knocked on the door. She'd been Missing In Action for over a week. He let her in and she kissed him.

'How did it go?' he asked.

'A bust.'

'Sorry.'

She hunched her shoulders. 'Shit happens.'

She kissed him again and he pushed her gently away.

'Exhausted?' she said. His red-rimmed, steel-blue eyes were watering.

'I feel like I've been hit by a car,' he said.

'Me too. Why don't I run us a bath and we can lie down in it for a while before we hit the hay and lie down some more?'

'Sounds good.'

Stephanie went into the bathroom and turned on the tap. At first it spluttered and Clooney heard the pipes groaning. Then, as if someone had given the system a good kick, it powered up and the hot water flowed freely. The tiles around the bath were cracked and broken. It was still an almost pretty room even though its best years were behind it. The bath was discoloured, yellow in some places and black in others. The mirror over the washbasin was cracked from corner to corner and held together only by its thick golden frame. The hotel had once been one of the most beautiful in Kabul but, as with everything else, its splendour had been eroded by war. When it was filled, Clooney slipped in and she sat between his legs, leaning back on him. The bath was deep and long enough for both of them so they often unwound in it, usually with a gin and tonic but not that night. Clooney wrapped his arms around her and held her tight.

'Anything happen out there?' he asked her, as he always did.

'Nope. All fine,' she said, as she always did.

Clooney never knew whether or not to believe her because she was a risk-taker, arrogant and dangerous, and if he'd allowed himself to care for her he would have gone insane worrying about the endless horrible things that might happen to her. *Please don't die here, Steph.* 'There's more to life than war,' he said.

'This again?'

'I'm going soon.'

'You've been saying that for a while.'

'Just finishing this project and going,' he said. 'You should think about getting out too.'

'Nah. This is where I should be.'

'Don't you want something else for yourself?'

'What, like a marriage, house and kids? Is that what you want?'

'Hell, no,' he said. 'I was thinking more of a hammock, a cold beer and a blow-job.'

She laughed. 'That's a pervert's holiday, not a life.'

'It's better than this.'

She turned and looked at his tired face. 'I don't know,' she said, 'this is pretty nice.' She kissed him and slid further down into the warm water.

He stroked her arm. 'There's less than two weeks left.'

'And you're sure?'

'Yeah.'

'Where will you go?'

'I was thinking about the Galapagos Islands, maybe hang out in a beach hut for a while, then head into South America and take it from there.'

'Will you look for work?'

'No,' he said. 'No work.'

'All play. Good for you.'

Clooney never lined anything up when he finished a contract

but there was always something when he wanted it, usually a major catastrophe. He worked best as an emergency-response co-ordinator. He had led many teams into disaster areas and in some cases they were the first international responders so Clooney had witnessed the worst destruction and devastation that nature was capable of. He had also seen at first hand the strength of the human spirit, the best as well as the worst in people, and had experienced the best and worst of times. He celebrated the incredible highs when a life was saved in extraordinary circumstances or because of extraordinary risks taken. He wallowed in the lows when a three-year-old girl starved to death because a food and medicine truck had broken down only a few miles away. He remembered every name and face of those he'd helped to save and those for whom his help had come too late. In the early days he'd work a six-month or yearly contract, then take a month or six off. During that time he'd stay on a beach in a place where he could live like a king on a tiny budget. Of course, Clooney's idea of living like a king was different from that of most others. All he needed was sand under his toes, the sun in the sky, blue sea stretching out in front of him, a beer and some food. It had occurred to him recently that, although he had been moving around, he had been working constantly since 2004. He had landed in Indonesia two days after the 2004 tsunami. In 2005 he had left the country to lead a team in New Orleans following Hurricane Katrina. In 2006 he returned to Indonesia and was based in Java following a powerful earthquake. He'd stayed there until 2008 when he'd been approached to carry out a food programme in Afghanistan.

Clooney had been used to death and destruction but Afghanistan was his first war zone, and he swore to himself it would be his last. However depressing and horrifying the loss of thousands was to nature, Clooney couldn't comprehend man slaughtering man. He lived by a simple ethos. The wrath of nature is inescapable; the wrath of man is avoidable. Clooney was about peace and love. A tree-hugger at heart, he didn't belong in Afghanistan. The things he'd seen were slowly turning him into someone he'd never wished to be. He was becoming colder and more removed with each day that passed. *How can I give a shit about people who want me dead? And why wouldn't they? We've blown up your business, now have a sandwich and a nice day.* Clooney was long overdue a break.

Those few months in Ireland with his father had been hard. Clooney was used to seeing the worst the world had to offer, yet when his father had died, his designer-penthouse-dwelling sister had been made of sterner stuff. Clooney had watched two parents die in that house, and when the funeral was over he had thought about hightailing it to an exotic beach. A sense of duty prevented him bailing out on his work commitments.

Now he had just about finished and was counting the days. He'd miss Stephanie as he knew she would miss him, although they were both confident that in each other they had found respite rather than enduring love and companionship. They were far too different for that. He was way too much of a hippie for her, and she was a get-the-job-done, camera-toting military brat. They enjoyed one another but saying goodbye wouldn't be difficult.

He'd noticed a burn on the back of her thigh when she was getting out of the bath. 'What happened?' he asked.

'Nothing,' she said.

He followed her into the room. She put on a light cotton shirt and got under the covers. He threw on a pair of boxers and joined her in bed. 'I don't want you to die here,' he said.

'It's as good as any place.' She kissed him and fell asleep as soon as her head hit the pillow.

He'd lain awake for another three hours before he'd dropped off, and then it was only for an hour or two. Upon waking he'd discovered Stephanie had left. He checked his phone and heard that his sister had been seriously injured. Stephanie had left early. He packed and left a message for her, saying goodbye, at Reception. He handed over his duties to a colleague and left Afghanistan without looking back.

*

Clooney gazed at Eve, taking in the damage the Ginger Monster had done. She sighed.

'You look like you've been in a war,' he said.

'Well, the traffic was murder,' she said, but Ben was constantly on her mind so her smile didn't make it to her eyes. 'It's good to see you.'

'I would have preferred to meet on a beach.'

'Me too,' she agreed. 'Remember Bali?'

'How could I forget?'

'We should have done that more,' she said.

'You were always working.'

'Those days are over.'

'So we'll do it again.'

'Now *you*'re always working.'

'I'm finished,' he said. 'There were only two weeks left on that contract. Jerry's going to wrap it up. I'm done.'

'I'm glad. War doesn't suit you.'

'You're right.'

'And so to a beach?'

'As soon as you can come with me.'

'You don't have to do this, Clooney.'

'I know.'

'But it's really good to see you.'

'Back at ya,' he said. 'Now tell me everything.'

Clooney was the only person to whom Eve had confided that she had been seeing Ben when she was last home, and he'd warned her of the dangers of sleeping with a married man, especially one who claimed to be happy. She had never involved Paul, Gar or Gina in their secret. They didn't need to know and, if Clooney hadn't caught her getting out of Ben's car around the corner from her house, she wouldn't have told him either. Ben was Eve's shameful secret. She didn't need to fear Hell to embrace morality. She knew their affair was wrong. It worried her and it mattered to her.

Clooney was a lot more easy-going than his sister when it

came to ethics. 'As long as no one gets hurt it's nice to see you have a little fun,' he had said.

'If it feels wrong, it is wrong,' their father used to say, and even when it had felt right it had felt wrong. Eve was a very matter-of-fact person and always had been. She didn't like sneaking around; it didn't excite her. She abhorred the treachery involved in their seeing one another. The only thing that kept her going back was his eyes when he looked at her. Since she'd returned to Ireland, she'd told herself their relationship had changed and she was only trying to help with his failing business. Then they'd had sex and were hit by a car. Eve may not have believed in divine intervention but she did accept the possibility that the universe was telling them something. *If it feels wrong, it is wrong.*

Eve spent the next hour telling Clooney of how she had sold her business, come home and helped Ben, and how their liaison had culminated in the accident. She cried when she told him that Ben was on another floor in a coma with his wife by his bed. She begged him to find out how Ben was because she was sure Lily was hiding the extent of his injuries from her. He promised he would. She gave him the keys to her apartment and told him to stay there. It had been four days since she'd been home so she warned him not to eat the dairy products in the fridge and that he'd have to pick up the knickers that Ben had ripped off her in the hall.

Clooney had travelled through the night and he hadn't slept. Eve insisted that he go home.

'I don't want to leave you,' he said.

'You smell.'

He laughed. 'OK. I'll go.'

'Good.'

He kissed her forehead and left.

Lindsay Harrington was first to speak. 'Who's that handsome man?' she asked.

'My brother.'

'Do you think he'd go out with me?'

Anne piped up from behind her book, 'If he was deaf, dumb and blind maybe you might have a chance, chicken.'

'Tell him that my curfew is ten o'clock and he'll have to speak to my father,' Lindsay said.

'Of course,' Eve replied.

Anne sighed heavily. She had no time for the demented. 'She shouldn't be here. She belongs in the nuthouse,' she said.

There was an empty bed beside Eve. A nurse she didn't recognize came in and started to make it up.

'Are we getting another roommate, chicken?' Anne asked.

'Yes, she'll be joining you soon.'

'I hope she's a young one. We need to bring down the average age in here.' She pointed to Eve. 'That poor girl must think she's been taken to an old folks' home.'

Eve laughed a little.

'I'm afraid you're out of luck, Anne,' said the nurse. 'Beth is seventy-five.'

'Another hip?' Anne said.

'Another hip.'

'Is she nuts?' Anne asked, glancing at Lindsay, whose eyes were open though she didn't appear to be listening.

'No, Anne, she's not.'

'Well, that's something, chicken,' Anne said to Eve, who smiled in acknowledgement.

Anne Murray was seventy-two years old. She'd broken her hip when she'd tripped on her grandson's toy train that he'd left on the stairs. 'It was lucky I didn't break my neck,' she had told Eve, 'and I'm not even going to tell you how close I came to putting my head through the glass window at the bottom of the stairs. The pup!'

'I have two Labrador puppies, Simple and Simon,' Lindsay piped up. 'Simple chases his own tail until he gets so dizzy he falls on his side. Then he rolls on to his back and waits for me to rub him. My daddy says that when I'm old enough I can take him for walks. Simon doesn't like to walk. He's very lazy. Daddy says he was born an old man.'

'Oh, Christ, she's off again!' Anne said.

Lindsay would soon be celebrating her eighty-fourth birthday and her father had died thirty years before. There were moments of lucidity, when she was sometimes rude and abrasive, and others when she was sad and tearful but when she was lost in times gone by Eve found her quite sweet. Anne referred to Lindsay as a pain in the hole.

When Beth was wheeled in she was moaning, and cried out when they moved her on to her bed. She was riddled with arthritis – Eve saw that one hand was so badly affected it was like a claw. When the nurse left, Anne shouted to her that she'd be all right. She told her to settle down and sleep – it was the best thing for it. The woman disappeared soon after that.

Eve turned on her little TV for the first time. She watched some news. When the dinner lady came around she was hungry for the first time since the accident. The dinner lady cut up her food for her and she ate some salad with a slice of brown bread. She drank a cup of tea and felt almost human again.

Clooney had managed to track Lily down before he left the hospital. She was busy but gave him five minutes in the visitors' room. 'I just wanted to say thanks for getting in touch,' he said. 'It's really good to see you.' They gave one another an awkward hug. 'I often wondered what happened between you two,' he said.

'You were never one to beat around the bush.'

'Eve would never tell me.'

'It was all a long time ago.'

'You were so close.'

'We were kids.'

'And it had nothing to do with me?'

'No.' She shook her head.

'Good,' he said.

After that they talked about Eve's prognosis and recovery time. When Clooney asked about Ben, Lily explained that it was looking increasingly unlikely that he would make it. Clooney wanted to tell Eve the truth, but Lily said, 'She's not well enough.'

'She's stronger than she looks.'

'I disagree,' she said. 'Not when it comes to this.'

'She'll never forgive me if I lie.'

'So blame me.'

'I just wish she could say goodbye,' he said. As someone who had said goodbye to two parents and had witnessed hundreds and possibly thousands of people lose and mourn loved ones, Clooney knew how important that last goodbye was.

'He's a married man, Clooney,' she said.

'I know.'

'And, besides, she's still bedridden.'

'She's on that bed with wheels.'

She shook her head. 'He has a wife,' she said.

Lily called in to Eve just before she left for the evening. 'Do you need anything?'

'No, thanks,' Eve said, keenly aware that it was a flying visit and that since Clooney had walked in she had seen a lot less of Lily. *She's pulling away – but of course she is. Silly to think we could actually be friends again after all this time.*

'OK, then,' Lily said. 'See you tomorrow.'

'Lily.'

'Yes.'

'Thanks again.'

'You're welcome,' Lily said, and she was gone.

Adam called in after Abby had given her something to relax her. 'How are you doing, Eve?'

'I'm OK.'

'Good.'

'Can I ask you a question?' she said.

'Of course.'

'Am I ever going to be back to the way I was?'

'Yes . . .'

'But?'

'It's going to take a lot of work.'

'When do I start?'

'Give it another few days.'

'It's going to hurt,' she said.

'Yes, it will.'

'Life's a bitch.'

'And then you're dumped by one,' he said.

She grinned. 'Can I ask you something else?' she asked.

'Of course.'

'Do you know Lily's husband?'

'Yes,' he said tentatively.

'Is he still an arsehole?'

Adam couldn't help but smile. 'No comment,' he said.

'Understood.'

The taxi stopped outside Eve's apartment block. Clooney real-ized he'd forgotten to get cash.

'Damn it. You don't by any chance take Afghani, do you?'

'Is that some sort of hash?'

'No.'

'Pity.'

Clooney laughed. 'It's good to be home,' he said, and asked to be taken to an ATM.

A few minutes later he had his money and he was getting back into the cab when someone called his name.

'Clooney?'

It was Paul.

He shook Clooney's hand. 'Welcome home. Eve didn't men-tion you were coming back.'

It was clear Paul had no idea of what had happened to Eve, and when Clooney explained he was home because of her acci-dent, Paul joined him in the cab to hear the rest of the story.

Clooney let them into Eve's home, swiftly picked up her knick-ers from the floor and binned them before Paul saw them. In fact, he was too stunned by the story Clooney had told to notice much at all.

Clooney opened the fridge and found beer. He offered one to Paul who took it gratefully. It was a nice warm evening so they sat on the balcony looking out to sea while Clooney explained Eve's relationship with Ben.

'And she accuses me of being a dark horse,' Paul said, stunned that chatty, open Eve had wanted to keep it secret from him. He was also surprised to hear that Lily was nursing her. 'I thought she'd done medicine,' he said. 'Jesus, she had the best exam results in the school.'

'Nobody knows who they are at eighteen,' Clooney said. 'She's a nurse, wife and mother. She seems perfectly happy.'

'I'd heard she married Declan but I haven't seen either of them since they left for Cork. They just seemed to cut everyone off,' he said. 'Did Eve ever tell you what happened between her and Lily?'

'No. You?'

'No. It's a mystery.'

'All in the past now. Lily's being really good to her.'

'Lily Brennan's back on the scene?'

'Lily Donovan now, and she's still a beauty.'

Paul smiled. 'Eve Hayes and Lily Brennan were the best-looking girls in our school and I wasn't with either of them.'

Clooney laughed. 'I heard you had your pick of the girls back then. Little did they know you preferred boys.'

Paul smiled but didn't respond. Instead he focused on how attractive Clooney was. His blond hair had silver highlights and he'd be grey soon. His face was brown and battered but that lent character to rather than detracting from his looks. His steel-blue eyes were still as piercing as they were when he was young but somehow sadder. He had been a beautiful boy but he was even more handsome as a man.

'Did you meet Declan?' Paul asked, after a minute or two.

'No. To be honest, I wouldn't know him if I did.'

'We were so close in school, at least I thought we were, but then he left for Cork and I was going through my own shit. Gar tried to keep in touch with him but he never responded. I heard rumours, years later, about his dad, but I don't know – his father always seemed like a nice guy to me.'

'I know one thing,' Clooney said. 'Eve hates him, and Eve doesn't hate without good reason.'

'I can't believe she was with Ben Logan.'

'Poor guy.'

'His poor wife. Losing your husband is bad enough, never mind finding out he was having an affair.'

That was not something Clooney had considered. 'Maybe she doesn't have to know.'

'Eve is the only witness to the incident that has either brain-damaged or killed her husband. Why was he there? Why were they together?'

'Jesus, that's all she needs.'

Paul called Gar as soon as he got home. He told him about Eve's accident, her terrible injuries, the fact that she was with Ben Logan when it had occurred, that he was in a coma with his wife by his bedside and that Lily Brennan was nursing Eve. Gar put him on speaker so that Gina could hear. The conversation was a series of shocks.

Eve could have died. Ben Logan was dying. Lily was a fucking nurse. They agreed that they would visit Eve together the next evening. Gina was hoping to see Lily but Paul told them she worked days only. 'Damn it,' she said. 'I wonder what she looks like now.'

'Still a beauty,' Paul confirmed, confident in Clooney's assessment.

'And poor Eve!' Gina said.

'He said she's in an awful way but she'll recover.'

'Why didn't she call us?' Gina said.

'She didn't even call Clooney. Lily did.'

'Lily Brennan,' she said. 'Whatever happened with those two?'

'No one knows.'

Gar was silent, taking it all in. His wife turned to him. 'What do you think?' she asked.

'Whatever happened with all of us?' he said.

Declan had been Gar's best friend, or that was what he'd thought when they were growing up. When Declan had left for Cork and cut off all communication, Gar had been very hurt. He didn't understand why Declan had done that. When they were kids he'd never questioned Declan's explanations of his injuries. He'd heard rumours after Declan's mother disappeared but he'd never believed them. He had known his friend's dad – he had been Gar's family's mechanic – and he'd always seemed a lovely man. He had wondered why Declan and Lily had chosen to cut themselves off from their hometown and the people who cared about them. He wondered, too, what he could have done to deserve to be dismissed in such a cruel manner. He had grown up believing he would be Declan's best man at his wedding and Declan would reciprocate. He hadn't even been invited to the ceremony when Declan had married a year after he'd left, and had only learned of the wedding eight years later when Declan's father mentioned it while Gar was picking up his car after a service. He was too angry to ask questions. He didn't want to know. He didn't care. He felt bad for Eve, and of course he would visit her, but the thought of seeing Lily or, God forbid, Declan . . . *Fuck them both.*

Paul was freaked that Eve had been in hospital alone for four days and hadn't felt she could call him. He understood that their friendship had only recently been rekindled and he also understood her need for privacy – if anyone understood that, he did. He didn't care that she hadn't confided in him about Ben but he did care that she had nearly died and he wouldn't have known if he hadn't bumped into her brother at the ATM. *I thought we were friends.* As recently as the drink after their last game of tennis, he had considered confiding in her. Paul gave little of himself away but that night she had pushed and pushed. *All the while she was screwing Ben Logan on the sly, the cheeky bitch!* The game had been robust and they had enjoyed it. He had won but only by a point. She had noticed a cute guy at the bar and mentioned him, but Paul wasn't keen.

'He's too short.'

'Nothing wrong with short,' she'd said.

It all makes sense now – bloody Ben Logan.

'Are you seeing anyone?' she'd asked, for the hundredth time, and this time he had considered telling her but once again he balked. *Too many questions to answer.*

Paul had spent his childhood in a house where you grew up to be a hard worker and got married, with kids and mortgage. When he was young he knew he was different, but for a long time he couldn't work out why. He loved girls; he was tall, handsome and in a winning rugby team so he had his pick. He went outside his hometown, not because he was looking for beards as everyone had suspected when he came out, but because the only girl he was interested in was Lily and she was with his friend. Eve was beautiful but he had never felt that way about her. He could have married Lily. That night he had wanted to tell Eve he had been sexually attracted to all those girls back in the day, and the only reason he'd come out was because, although he'd great sex with them and with many boys, he could take or leave them all until he'd met Paddy and fallen head over heels in love.

Paddy was the one, as far as he was concerned. They had met at a club and the first moment he'd seen him he'd known. *I love you.* Paddy had long hair. He was broad, dark and, basically, the male version of Lily. He had her softness, openness and kindness. He was beautiful to look at and had the soul of a saint. He was funny, positive, free-thinking, inspirational and, most importantly, he knew who he was. Paul had never worked out who *he* was, but when he fell for Paddy, he was finally sure of himself. Paddy was a proudly open gay man and he demanded that of his partner. Paul came out to his parents to ensure that his relationship with the man he loved survived. They had been upset, but he didn't care because he was in love and, as far as he was concerned, it was for ever and that meant he was gay. Except he still noticed a beautiful woman, her curves, her skin, her smell, her hair and the way she moved. He hadn't coveted one, no matter how beautiful, for a long time but he always noticed them. After he and Paddy had been together for a few years, Paul still loved Paddy but he no longer cared to share his bed. Paddy felt the same but because they shared a home, a dog and a life neither wanted to admit it. Until one Friday night when Paddy was away at a convention in Brighton for the weekend and Paul went to a pub in Dublin where he met a girl called Simone.

With her dark complexion, brown eyes and silky brunette hair, she was Paul's type from the start. She sat next to him sipping a beer and he watched her read an article in *Vanity Fair*. She was consumed by it, one moment smiling, the next shocked, then saddened. He could read every emotion on her face. He was intrigued. When she was ready to leave, she leaned down to grab the bag she'd left by her feet only to find that it was gone. She stood up and looked around disbelievingly. Paul had seen it and recognized it as a Mulberry only because Emma, the girl in the cubicle next to his at work, was a Mulberry fanatic: she had at least five and talked about them endlessly as though they were her pets. He hadn't noticed anyone slope in to steal it because he had been focused on the story playing across her face. When she realized it was gone she looked lost. He had stood up and asked her if he could help. She explained that her bag had been stolen and was embarrassed that she couldn't pay for her beer. Paul immediately offered to pay, then walked her to the police station to make her complaint. He insisted she use his phone to cancel her cards. Then he asked her if she wanted dinner. They had ended up in bed together at his apartment for the entire weekend.

Paddy had returned on the Monday. Paul had sat him down and told him he'd met someone. Paddy couldn't believe his ears, especially when Paul admitted it was a woman. He was devastated, and the betrayal was all the worse because it didn't involve a man. Paul was shattered by the pain he had caused. They had fought, screamed and cried – the most passionate they'd been in years. Before he had left Paddy and their dog Samba, he kissed them both and, grief-stricken, moved into a hotel. A week later he'd rented a house in his local town and a year later he bought it.

Simone had been a fixture ever since. She was a model, spending a lot of time abroad. She was based in London and they had met when she was spending time in Ireland on a shoot. Their weekend had been a one-off as far as both were concerned. She was returning to London and he was returning home, but something had changed during their two days together and she couldn't forget him so she called him as soon as she arrived in London. That first year they only saw each other a handful of times. He went to visit her in London twice, she came to Ireland twice and they met in Paris once. The second year she ended up doing more work in Ireland, and they spent a month together in Cuba. That was when it became serious. Paul realized he was in love when saying goodbye became impossible. He had considered moving to London but Simone was tiring of the model scene – at twenty-nine she was considered ancient and the jobs were drying up. In five years she had taken five courses. Styling: she didn't like it. Makeup: not for her. Hair: definitely not. Photography: boring. Then she did a dog-grooming course and loved it. She had been travelling to and from Ireland for months. She'd found the perfect location to set up her new business and she was moving in with Paul.

He just hadn't told his friends and family. As far as they were concerned he was gay. He had confided in Simone that he was bisexual when he'd first met her, mostly because he'd thought he'd never see her again. Simone hadn't made an issue of it – in fact, she'd admitted to having messed around with girls, although she'd never gone all the way. 'It just wasn't me,' she said. She understood why he hadn't introduced her to friends and family and didn't care when she was living abroad because their time together was precious. But now it was different: now she was coming to live with him and they were becoming a family.

The morning she had told him she suspected she was pregnant they were sitting in a hotel in London, enjoying breakfast in bed.

'The crumpets are really good,' she said.

'Aren't they?'

'I think I'm pregnant.'

A grin spread across his face. 'I'd really like that,' he said, dropping his crumpet.

'Me too,' she said.

They hugged and kissed, and when they parted he asked her to marry him.

'I'd love to,' she said, and that was it.

They bought a test in Boots, returned to the hotel and she peed on the stick. He waited anxiously, already behaving like an expectant father. The stick turned pink instantly. Simone was having Paul's baby, and when she held it up and shouted, 'Score!' he cried like one.

They planned a simple wedding to be held in their favourite hotel in Westport. Simone's family and friends had all met Paul. In fact, he had spent so much time in London in recent years that they were shocked when Paul and Simone announced that she was moving to Ireland and not the other way around. Paul had a good, high-paying, steady job and a large house in a beautiful spot while she was pretty much out of a job and broke. She did worry how Paul's friends and family would take the news and he worried even more. *How do you go back into the closet?*

Paul had been in his mid-twenties before he confronted his bisexuality. He went to the library to read about it, and when he couldn't find anything that explained to him who he was and what he wanted, he went to a sex counsellor who told him he was a three on the Kinsey Scale, which meant he was equally attracted to men and women. From his past behaviour she concluded he was an alternating bisexual, which meant that when a relationship with one sex ended he might find himself falling for someone of the other. That was exactly what had happened. He could have fallen for a guy just as easily but Paul Doyle realized that the sex didn't matter: it was the person he was attracted to who did.

In Simone he had found someone who accepted him for exactly who he was. She wasn't jealous, she wasn't possessive, she didn't care about his past, she didn't care that he got a hard-on for other men. He was with her and she was confident in *them*. Simone wasn't a worrier. She lived in the moment. 'When you're happy be grateful, not greedy,' she'd say. She understood his reticence about explaining himself to friends and family, especially as he'd made such a big deal about coming out.

He felt foolish and was worried his friends would think him a fool. As for his parents, although his father had come around in recent years, his relationship with his mother was extremely strained. They tolerated one another but she believed that all gay men and women were going to Hell in a hand-basket, and the only thing she could offer her son in terms of support was her prayers. Of course she'd see his marriage and fatherhood as a win. She'd claim the power of prayer had saved him from himself and eternal damnation. Simone laughed at the notion but then she hadn't met his mother.

'You can say I used to be a man if it makes you feel any better,' she said.

'If you weren't pregnant I probably would.'

'You're going to have to do it soon,' she'd said, when he was leaving her to return home for the final time without her.

'I will.'

Then he'd gone back to work and put it off and put it off because he didn't want to have to go house to house explaining himself. Paul was so private that the very idea made him feel nauseous. Now Eve was in a terrible state. She had been having an affair with Ben Logan – he, Gar and Gina would be visiting her the next night – and Lily was back on the scene. The heat was definitely off him so it was the perfect time and place to tell them he was going to be a father and invite them to the wedding.

Cheers, Eve. Hello, Lily.

6. If this is the end

Dear Eve,

I'm lying in my bed writing this to you. Had a really heavy night last night – we all ended up in the club and I don't even remember getting home. Colm dropped over at ten this morning with a few scones. He told me he'd brought me home (and, no, nothing happened) and said I was singing most of the way. We'd sat on the bridge for a while and talked. I told him about Declan and our lives at home and plans for Cork. (Don't remember any of that conversation!) Before he left he hugged me and told me that I had no idea how amazing I was and he hoped I would see it some day. I was embarrassed. I didn't know what to say. He said Declan was very lucky to have me and he hoped he knew it, which I thought was very cheeky, but because I couldn't remember what I'd said I wasn't able to answer him. He looked concerned (if that's the right word, maybe troubled would describe it better) and the vibe was weird. I feel a bit sad now and I don't know why. I hate this feeling. I should never have got so drunk. It's pathetic. I'm thinking of staying in bed all day. I have a stack of books I want to read. It's just me, my bed, music and books.

OK, to cheer myself up a bit here are my top two reasons why living on my own is amazing:

1. Independence
2. Peace

I can get up when I want. I can eat or not eat what I want. I

*can come and go as I please. I'm free! It's an amazing feeling.
There's no shouting, no fighting. I haven't been to Mass since I
got here and I was thinking about going to Confession when I
arrived just to confess having sex with Declan so I could promise
not to do it again (at least for the summer) but I got as far as the
church and didn't go in. I know. Can you believe it? My mother
was whispering in my ear, 'If you die in an accident, have a
clean pair of knickers and a pure soul,' but I ignored her – except
for the clean knickers. You'll be happy to hear that my Catholic
guilt is lifting even if it is only a little. I still bless myself when I
see a coffin and this morning after Colm left I couldn't help but
say a silent prayer that I hadn't made a complete fool of myself
last night, and if I had, that everyone else was drunk enough not
to remember. Of course Colm remembers. He's playing a match
today so he didn't want to drink too much. What did I say to
him? It's really annoying me. I don't want to ask. I'm hoping it
will start to come back to me.*

Top two reasons why living on my own is horrible:

1. Missing you
2. Missing you

*Oh, and apparently he carried me home from the bridge. He said
I fell asleep in his arms. I was really apologetic but he said I
shouldn't worry, it was no problem. In fact, I'm so small and
light he managed to stop off at the chipper for a burger with the
lads while I slept on his shoulder. I really am so embarrassed.
Thank God I was wearing jeans. I'm never drinking again. And
the weird thing is I don't even feel that hung-over but maybe
that's because I've gone back to bed. I don't know.*

*You should have seen this place the night I moved in. It was
disgusting. The kitchen was like a grease factory and I'm not
even going to talk about the bathroom because the memory alone
makes me want to gag. Now it's still a dump but it's a clean one.
I nearly lost a finger scrubbing the toilet but that's another story.
I was thinking that I could subsidize university by getting a*

cleaning job. It would be really handy. I could work my own hours and it's cash in hand. Medicine is a five-year course and we only start to get paid as interns in year six. Neither Declan nor I have financial backing and I'm really starting to worry about how we're going to live. Maybe I was talking about that last night. I don't know.

I've been thinking a lot about our future lately. Declan is really worried he won't get medicine. It's his dream and he says if he has to he'll repeat. I'd die if I ended up in Cork alone! And I know that everyone thinks I'll just swan into a place but honestly I don't know if I will, and when I think about not getting a place, instead of being upset I feel relieved. Isn't that weird? Of course I'd never say that to Declan because he's up the walls but five years is a long time. We'll be in our mid-twenties before we'll be able to earn a single penny and then we'll have huge loans to pay back. Apparently we can only get a loan in second year and Ellen says it will depend on how well we do in our first year exams. I haven't heard that before. Have you?

I was gutted when you weren't there the other day but it was nice to hear Clooney at the end of the phone. He told me all about the Bushy Head – it's awful for him. He did mention that he was thinking about heading down this way so I hope he does. It is beautiful here when the sun is shining. I can't wait to show him around and he's going to love the water sports. I told him where to find me so I can feed him if he needs feeding. Oh, I forgot to tell you the chef in the restaurant is showing me how to cook and I love it.

My mother's going back to Lourdes again with the Legion of Mary. I eventually managed to speak to her on the phone yesterday and the first thing she asked me was if I was going to Mass. I said that I was fine and thanks for asking. It made me laugh. She didn't like that because Mass is no laughing matter. She said she was going to pray for me and canvass others in her group to pray for me too because I'm going to need all the prayers I can get. She said my plan to live in sin will secure my place in

Hell. I was really pissed off. I haven't spoken to her in an age and all she could do was threaten me with damnation. She thinks I should go to Trinity and live at home and let Declan go down to Cork on his own. She says I'm too young to be tying myself to one boy. She actually said I'm too young to have a clue about life and love, this coming from a woman who has no one in her life. And, anyway, if I'm going to Hell for having sex or living with the boy I love then everyone I know is going to go to Hell, and Heaven will be full of priests, nuns and weird spinsters who talk to themselves and smell like cat wee. I think I'd prefer to be in the fire with friends rather than in the clouds with weirdos, speaking of which I'm really happy for you and Ben. He sounds very mature and cool. I think it's a good idea to have sex with him. He sounds like he knows what he's doing, which is a big bonus because it took Declan and me ages to get it right, and I think it makes a lot of sense to lose it before you go to London. Plus you don't have the burden of worrying about going to Hell so there's nothing stopping you.

Anyway, that's about it. Maybe I'll go for a sleep, don't feel like doing anything now. I really miss you and can't wait to hear more about you and Ben.

Lily XXXOOOXXX

PS I wonder where we'll both be in six years. It seems so far away. Like another lifetime.

Eve saw the hulking Ginger Monster with his navy-blue jumper on. He had his back to her and he was leaning over a woman on the rack. *Please, not me, please, not me.* She tried to look over his shoulder to see if it was her but he kept moving and concealing the person strapped to his contraption. She felt burning pain in her legs and her arm as though they were being pulled apart. *Oh, crap, it is me.* He raised his arm high in the air and moved a little to the left so that she could see Ben's wife Fiona tied to the rack. She was wearing the little white-and-navy-striped T-shirt and the pair of tight pretty shorts that she had worn on their last boating trip. Eve remembered the outfit from their Facebook photos. It was cute but not too cute, with clean lines, expensive but not ridiculous. She had flowing brunette hair and a warm, friendly face. She had boobs and hips, and her skin was glowing and tanned. She was relaxed, happy and healthy. *I bet she doesn't suffer one long headache.* Eve remembered studying the photograph and feeling jealous of the happy brunette, but now in her nightmare Fiona was screaming so loudly that Eve could feel herself trying to cover her ears but only with her good hand because the other three limbs were still being invisibly pulled apart. She found a button at the side of her temple and tried to press it, hoping the fire would come and engulf the pain but it didn't. The Ginger Monster plunged his fist into Fiona's chest and ripped out her heart. She watched it beat in his hand for a second or two before her eyes closed. He threw it into the same wicker basket that held Eve's rotting limbs.

She woke up in a sweat. It was after ten a.m. She was sorry that she'd insisted on Abby removing the catheter because she was desperate to pee and couldn't face having to perch on a bedpan. She was sore and groggy and the image of Fiona wouldn't fade. She briefly contemplated wetting herself – after all, she didn't have a shred of dignity left. Once she'd pooped into a bedpan after taking an hour to do it, bearing down and gnashing her teeth while a nurse popped her head in and out of the thin piece of fabric that separated her from three women of a certain age who had decided to act as cheerleaders.

'How we doing, chicken? Is the poop near the shoot yet?' Anne had said.

'Don't think about it, just let it happen,' Lindsay had added, in a moment of lucidity.

'I'd love to have one,' Beth had moaned. 'I'm backed up to high heaven here.'

Now Eve pressed the call button and asked Abby for a bedpan.

'Of course,' she said. 'How'd you sleep?'

'Awful.'

'She was screaming again,' Anne said to Abby.

'The nightmares will pass,' Abby said.

'Maybe,' Eve said.

Lily appeared in the doorway with the detective Eve had spoken to on the night of the accident. 'Detective James,' she said.

'Close,' he said. 'James Hickey.' He shook her functional hand.

Abby asked him to wait outside for a few minutes.

Lily waited with him. 'She won't be long,' she said. He nodded. 'She's an old friend.' He nodded. 'Any news on the person who did it?' she asked. He nodded. *OK, I'm starting to see a pattern here.* 'Good,' she said. 'Have you spoken to Ben's wife?' He nodded. *Enough with the nodding, just answer the question, sunshine!* 'Does she know about Eve? Please do something other than nodding,' she said. He looked at her and paused before he spoke, as though he was deciding whether to answer or tell her to mind her own business.

'She knows he was walking along a dark road with a woman on the evening of the accident,' he said.

'Has she asked about Eve?'

He nodded.

Ah, come on! 'And you've said?' she pressed.

'What I know,' he said.

'Which is?' Lily said.

He smiled, admiring her tenacity. 'Which is . . . nothing more than they were hit by a car with a drunk driver at approximately ten sixteen p.m. on the night of the first of July and that we have located and charged the man responsible.'

'So Ben's wife must have questions?'

'I'm sure she does,' he said.

Abby appeared in the hallway.

'Do you have to inform Eve of Ben's condition?' Lily asked the detective.

'Is there a reason to keep the truth from her?'

Lily shook her head. 'She's just been through a lot,' she said.

'You can go in,' Abby said.

He nodded and smiled at Lily as he left her.

Eve was raised in her bed so that she could look the detective in the eye. She was experiencing a dull throbbing pain in her limbs, as though they were hollow and under a great weight, liable to snap at any second. It was bad but it wasn't bad enough to press the button. Anyway, she'd noticed that the amounts of painkiller had been reduced. The relief wasn't as strong but neither were the nausea and grogginess. She wanted to be alert while making her statement. She needed to make sure she did it right. *I won't let you down, Ben.* Eve knew that the likelihood of Ben's recovery was dwindling with each day that passed. She knew that if he lived he had a wife by his bedside ready and willing to love and care for her husband. She knew that if he died that woman would be the one to lead the mourners grieving for him. She knew that if his affair was discovered everything he and his wife had had together would be tainted. *We didn't want to hurt anyone.* If he died Fiona would second-guess every word, deed and gesture, and he wouldn't be there to explain. *If I could do it all again.* Fiona would be tortured and haunted. *I won't let that happen, Ben.* She prepared herself to lie like she'd never lied before. *I just have to stay as close to the truth as I can. Everything will be fine.* She sipped her water because her lips and throat were dry and for some reason she felt scared she'd lose her voice. *This has to be right.*

The detective told her that they had found the man who had knocked her down. His name was Eamonn Colgan. He had fallen asleep while parked in his neighbour's driveway. Her blood was all over the car and, remarkably, her description of the man had been a perfect match down to his Claddagh ring and his navy jumper. He claimed he remembered nothing of the accident, but with his alcohol levels, her blood evidence and testimony they would get a conviction. He asked her for a follow-up statement and she was ready. She told him that she and Ben Logan were very old friends. *True.* She said that actually he had been her first love. *True.* She said that they had reconnected on Facebook a couple of years ago. *True*. She said that when she came home to be with her dying father they had met for coffee. *True*. She said that his business was in trouble. *True*. He was keeping the failure of that business from his wife. *True*. And that she was trying to help with the business. *True*. She said that she had just sold her own successful and profitable business in the USA. *True*. That she had money to invest if the right opportunity came along. *True*. That on the night they were knocked down she had agreed to buy into Ben's business. *False*. And that they were on their way to have dinner and celebrate their business arrangement. *False*. In fact, he was just about to call his wife to meet with his new partner and join in the celebration. *False*. Their relationship was strictly business. *False*. But she cared about him. *True*.

Although the detective was far more interested in confirming her recollection of what had happened after the car had struck her and verifying her astoundingly accurate account of the incident, he did remind her that she had described herself as Ben's girlfriend on the night in question. Eve didn't remember doing that and, although she was momentarily put on the back foot, she recovered quickly. She told him that at one point that night she had thought she was eighteen again. There were many fleeting moments of confusion. *True*. He did mention that she had originally identified him as Glenn Medeiros. Eve didn't remember that either but it made her laugh, then cry.

'I used to call him that when we were teenagers,' she said.

'After the singer?' he said.

She nodded.

'We were having a bit of the bet about that at the station,' he said.

'He had curls and dodgy dress sense back then,' she said, and her eyes leaked again.

'I understand,' he said.

'I can't stop reliving that night,' she said. *True*. 'I don't know why I'm crying,' she said. *Lie*.

She gathered her thoughts together. It was important to

maintain her performance. She imagined turning off a tap and the tears stopped flowing.

She asked him to make sure Ben's wife saw her statement as soon as it was appropriate. She didn't want her thinking anything untoward. Eve said she was conscious that the other woman's life must be difficult enough without having to worry about who her husband was with that night. 'I know what I'd be thinking if I was her,' she said.

He nodded and agreed an affair was one possible conclusion. She didn't know if he believed her story or not. It wasn't pertinent to him making a case against a drunk driver so maybe he didn't much mind. When he confirmed he would ensure that Fiona was given a copy of her statement, she asked as nonchalantly as she could how Ben was doing.

'I'm afraid he's not going to make it,' he said.

'Excuse me?' she said. Although she'd thought his death was possible, the confirmation sent a shock through her body.

'He was declared brain dead yesterday afternoon. The ventilator will be turned off tomorrow morning,' he said.

She nodded slowly. 'Oh,' she said, fighting the urge to scream.

'I'm sorry,' he said.

'Yes,' she said, and took a breath. 'So am I. His poor wife.' *Don't lose it. Don't lose it. Don't lose it.*

He thanked her for her time. He told her he'd be back with any follow-up questions, if necessary, and either way he'd be in touch. He left her sitting up in her bed, staring at the thin curtain surrounding her. *He's gone.* Tears collected. *He's gone.* Her eyes, nose and ears burned. *He's gone.* She blinked. *He's gone.* Tears fell. *He's gone.* Her nose ran. *He's gone.* Her heart ached. *He's gone.* Her stomach turned. *He's gone.* She pulled the blanket over her head with her good arm, burying herself under it, grieving alone, in stifling darkness. She pushed the button that operated her bed until she was lying flat; she allowed her hidden tears to pour out unseen and silent. *He's gone.*

*

Lily watched the detective walk down the corridor. He was in the lift before she left the nurses' station and went into Eve's ward. She walked over to the mummy lying in the bed, and when she saw the damp sheet over Eve's face and heard her muffled cries she slipped her hand under the blanket and held her friend's, as she had all those years ago on a sunny day in Eve's back garden. When Eve finally stopped crying, Lily took her hand out from under the blankets and walked away to give her time to recover.

Lily was busy. It was one of those days when she didn't seem to stop. It was four when she finally got to eat some lunch. Declan was just out of surgery so they grabbed something together. When she saw Ben's wife and his mother staring into the middle distance with untouched cups of coffee in front of them, her heart raced and she lowered her head, afraid that if either woman focused they'd spot the nurse who used to know Ben and who called in to check on him at least twice a day. They had become acquainted with her face and they'd even spoken once or twice. Ben's mother remembered Lily's because she had cleaned the house of a friend of hers. She asked after her. Lily replied that she was fine and that she'd moved to the UK many years ago. Mrs Logan had burst into tears. 'I think we're losing him,' she'd said, and she was right.

Ben Logan was all but lost. The decision to turn off the ventilator had been made soon after their conversation.

Lily worried for poor Fiona. Although Eve hadn't said as much, Lily knew she was sleeping with Ben. She couldn't bring herself to sympathize with Eve's pain the way she could have if he hadn't been married. She knew she was being judgemental, pious and puritanical but she couldn't help it. Ben's wife was about to lose her husband and, when he was in the ground, it was likely she'd discover his affair and he'd die all over again. Lily knew how that felt, wondering how and why and what she could or should have done to change something she had no control over. *Poor Fiona.* Every time she saw her weary face she felt worse for her. Eve had always done exactly what Eve wanted to do, and to Hell with what anyone thought, and this woman was about to pay the price. Of course she pitied Eve too, but she wanted to avoid any conversation about Ben because it would be hard to sympathize without seeing Fiona's face in her mind's eye. Lily kept her head down but she didn't need to worry – Fiona didn't see past the middle distance.

Declan was looking forward to the dinner party they were due to attend and that Lily had forgotten about. She had nothing to wear, she was tired and Alice Gibson, the host, had made her feelings about Lily very clear from the first time they had met. As far as Professor Alice Gibson was concerned, Lily was beneath her. She was a pretty little thing who bounced around the hospital in pink. Alice was an academic. She was not ugly but she was built like her blocky father; she carried a few extra pounds around her waist and she battled with a hairy chin. She didn't have time for small-talk or jokes or raising men's egos by laughing at the stupid comments they made after a few drinks. Alice Gibson was a serious woman, highly intelligent, and although she was fascinating when she was lecturing, she was a dreadful bore socially. When Lily revealed her own intellect to be more than Alice's match, Alice's indifference had turned into jealousy. She was a poor host, never failing to be rude.

'I really don't want to go,' Lily admitted, while picking at a wilted salad.

'We can't cancel on the day – it's rude.'

'That's rich,' Lily said.

Declan laughed. 'Alice did not spill wine on you on purpose.'

'Yes, she did. She's also stood on my toe twice, turned her back on me and excluded me from conversation at nearly every chance she's had.'

'She's just not socially gracious.'

'She's a bitch.'

'She's Rodney's wife and Rodney is my good friend so we're going and we're going to have a good time,' he said playfully.

Lily knew he was laying down the law.

'Fudge cake,' she said.

'And you should wear that gold bangle I bought you,' he said.
'I hope you don't mind if that's all I wear.' She sighed.

Alice would be dressed in something that would no doubt look dowdy and fuddy-duddy but it would be expensive. She tried to think of her limited wardrobe and what Alice hadn't seen before but couldn't come up with anything. *Bugger-balls.* She didn't have the money or time to shop so she decided to wear a simple red dress she'd worn countless times before. She didn't doubt that it would make Alice's night. She'd already commented on the fact that Lily seemed too attached to it, but Lily felt comfortable in it, it suited her and, importantly, it was clean.

She left Declan still eating and headed back to her ward. On the way she bumped into Adam. 'Have you been roped in to this dinner tonight?' he asked.

'Yeah. You?'

'She emailed to tell me she's sitting me beside Tracey Barber.'

'Who's Tracey Barber?'

'Apparently she's a political analyst and I'm going to love her,' he said.

She laughed. 'Well, if she's anything like Alice she'll be a real keeper.'

He chuckled. Adam had about as much time for Alice's pomposity as Lily did.

'I wonder what insult or injury she's lined up for me,' she said.

'We can only wait and see.'

'At least we have each other,' she said, and when he blushed, she pretended not to notice. *Whatever you're thinking, Adam, get over it. Please.*

Declan wouldn't be working over the weekend so he was looking forward to relaxing and having a few drinks. Lily could only hope that he'd fall asleep before saying or doing anything to embarrass her.

Clooney spent the day trying to raise his sister's spirits but it wasn't an easy task. It didn't help when he'd mentioned that he'd bumped into Paul and that the gang were planning to visit. She started to cry.

'I thought you'd be happy,' he said, confused.

'I'm exhausted, in agony, my bloody legs are broken and my shoulder is a mass of metal. My head hurts, my bloody eyes burn. Ben is . . . No, Clooney, I'm not happy.'

'Two bloodys in one sentence. That's serious. I'm sorry.'

She shook her head. 'No, *I*'m sorry. It's nice of them.'

'What can I do?'

'Bring Ben back to life.'

'I wish I could.'

'Not as much as I do.'

Lily appeared with the medicine trolley. She came to Eve last. 'Time for your heparin injection,' she said.

Eve had to have one every day – it was the only medication not administered through the cannula and it stung like a bee. Clooney looked away. He'd always hated injections. Lily rubbed the spot with an alcohol swab. 'Over.'

Just as she said that Fiona Logan walked through the door. Lily's heart nearly stopped. *Oh, fudging fudge cake.* She looked from Fiona to Eve. She seemed relaxed. *Shit, does she know who she is?*

Fiona approached the bed. 'Eve?'

'Fiona,' Eve said, and smiled.

Lily didn't know where to put herself. *What the hell . . .*

'Lily,' Fiona said.

Lily waved. *Did I just wave?*

'This is my brother Clooney,' Eve said, and Clooney stood up. Fiona put out her hand to shake his. 'Hi, I'm Fiona Logan.'

'Ben's wife?' he said, suddenly catching on.

'Yes,' she said.

'Oh, right,' he said, and clearly he was as uncomfortable as Lily, but Eve remained calm and cool.

Oh God, oh God, oh God, Lily thought. *Eve, be nice, be cool. I need to sit down. No, I need to get out of here. Oh God, I need to pee. Oh Christ, please don't break her.*

'Please sit down,' Eve said, indicating the chair her brother had just vacated.

Fiona sat. 'I'm sorry it took me so long to come here,' she said.

'I understand,' Eve said.

Have I just walked into an alternative universe? Lily thought. Clooney was silent and watching. Lily didn't know whether to stay or leave. She put the needle into a sharps bin and fixed the blankets on Eve. She eyed the blood-pressure pump. *Maybe I should go and come back.*

'I saw your statement,' Fiona said.

'Good,' Eve said. 'I was anxious you should know exactly what happened and how.'

'I appreciate that,' Fiona said, tears welling. 'I had wondered why he was there. I was thinking all sorts. I feel stupid now.'

'Don't,' Eve said.

Oh, you lying bitch, what did you say? Lily wanted to move but she couldn't – curiosity planted her feet to the floor.

'We're turning off the . . .' Fiona said, but she couldn't finish the sentence.

Eve nodded. 'I know,' she said. 'I'm so sorry.' She appeared calm and detached but not so detached as to be cold. She showed the exact amount of emotion you would for an old friend.

When did you get to be such a good liar? Lily thought.

'It's like a nightmare,' Fiona said.

'I wish there was something I could do,' Eve said.

'That night . . . was he really going to call me so that we could celebrate?' Fiona asked, and choked up.

'Yes. He had been working hard on a plan to salvage the business. I have a copy of all his accounts if you want it back.'

'No,' Fiona said. 'Thank you.'

Bloody hell, I've heard it all now, Lily thought.

Fiona stood up. 'This time tomorrow I'll be a widow. You'll help me put that bastard Eamonn Colgan away?'

'Oh, yeah,' she said.

Fiona left.

Clooney smiled at his sister. 'You did the right thing.'

Eve looked at Lily, who sighed and shook her head. 'The right thing,' she mumbled to herself and walked away. Clooney followed her, calling her name. She turned to face him on the corridor. 'You're judging her?' he asked.

'She had an affair with a married man and now she's lying about it. Don't get me wrong – I'm thrilled she did it for Fiona Logan's sake but, Christ, Clooney, it's a long way from doing the right thing.'

'I see,' he said. 'You're still perched on that high horse of yours.'

His words were like a slap in the face. Smarting, she replied in a manner most unlike her: 'Fuck you.' She stalked away.

At eight o'clock on the dot, Gina, Gar and Paul arrived into Eve's ward laden with cards, fruit baskets, flowers and sweets. Clooney was still there. Lily had gone home. Anne, Lindsay and Beth were wide awake and looking to interfere.

Gina gasped when she saw Eve. 'Jesus!'

Gar overcompensated for his wife's reaction. 'You look great, way better than we expected,' he said, and gave Gina a filthy look.

Paul dragged some chairs over and sat down. 'Hey, Scarface. Would you like one?' He held up a box of Roses.

Eve shook her head but smiled at him, grateful.

Gar and Gina sat on one side of the bed, Clooney and Paul on the other.

'It's nice to see she has people in her life,' Anne said. 'It looked for a while like she'd no one. Except the tall fella.'

'Are they for me?' Lindsay said to Paul, pointing at the Roses.

'No,' he said, and Anne laughed.

'How rude,' Lindsay mumbled.

'None for me, thanks,' Beth said, as though someone had offered her one. 'I still haven't been able to go.' She rubbed her stomach.

Gar laughed at the old dears' conversation. Gina was too

focused on Eve and what she had to say about the accident to listen.

Within minutes their own visitors arrived, filling the room. With their chatter in the background, Eve told her friends that she had been with Ben for business purposes.

Gina seemed disappointed. Clooney was quiet. Paul said nothing. He wasn't about to tell Eve that Clooney had spilled the beans on her affair the previous evening. He empathized with her decision to lie. It was for the greater good. It made sense. Eve wasn't a seasoned liar, she didn't make a habit of it: she preferred the truth but not at any cost.

The story of the accident was juicy enough to take Gina's mind off Ben, until Paul asked after him. Eve faltered. While she collected her thoughts Clooney answered on her behalf. He told them that the machine was being turned off the next day. They looked at Eve for a reaction. She gave none. She was somewhere else building another wall, one block, two blocks, three blocks, four.

'I have some news,' Paul said, in a timely bid to distract them from his friend, who needed saving. He went on to tell his open-mouthed pals that he was getting married and having a baby. Even Eve was momentarily pulled away from her wall. As briefly as he could, he told them he was in love with a beautiful woman called Simone.

'But you're gay,' Gar said.

'I'm bisexual.'

'But you said you were gay!' Gar said.

'I was wrong. I'm bisexual.'

'How could you be wrong? I don't . . . All this time? I'm . . .' Gar looked at his wife, who hunched her shoulders, and then at Clooney and Eve. 'I don't understand.'

'I don't know what to say.' Paul wasn't one to explain himself. He didn't have the tools or feel the necessity to do so. *It is what it is.*

'So why didn't you just say so before now?' Gar asked.

'Because he's nuts,' Eve said.

'Something like that.' Paul smiled at her. 'I was with Paddy for eight years.'

'I've heard it all now!' Gar looked from his missus to Eve to Clooney and back to Paul. 'You're my friend. How did I not know this?' He really didn't know what to make of what Paul had said. When they were younger Paul had been the guy he looked up to, the one who always had girls chasing him. He was discreet and never spoke about his conquests, but it was obvious that he was good with them and he had a rock star's choice. When he'd come out as gay, Gar couldn't understand it and it had messed with his head for a long time. *Was Paul ever with those girls? Was he with them just to save face? And if he was and he didn't like girls, how come he was so good at being with them?*

Gina had spent years trying to form a bond with Paul but he was a closed shop. He liked her, she was a nice woman, but she was his friend's wife, not his friend. Gina had initially been upset by this but eventually she had accepted Paul and his oddities. *He is what he is.*

'I stripped my top off in front of you,' Eve said.

Paul smiled. 'Yes, you did,' he said.

Clooney stayed silent. He didn't know Paul well enough to care whether he was gay or bisexual. He was just glad the conversation was distracting his sister. 'Congratulations,' he said, when everyone had fallen silent.

Paul thanked him.

The others followed suit.

'I can't wait to meet her,' Gina said.

'I can't believe you're going to be a father!' Gar said.

'Me neither.' Tears filled Paul's eyes and his friends basked in his happiness until he became uncomfortable and changed the subject.

He asked about Lily, and immediately Gina was re-engaged. 'What's she like?' she asked.

'The same,' Eve said.

'What's Declan like?' Gina prodded.

'I don't know. I haven't seen him,' Eve answered. *And I don't want to.*

'But he works here,' Gina said.

'Yeah.'

'Weird.'

'Not really.'

'Did she mention why they dumped us all?' Gar asked.

Eve had a good idea as to why they'd disappeared, at least she thought she did, but there could have been a million reasons. It was all so long ago. *The past is the past. Let it go.* She didn't answer Gar.

'Is she here?' Paul asked.

'Her shift finished two hours ago,' Clooney said, looking at his watch. They had been there more than an hour. 'Well, I guess we'd better go – it's been a long day for Eve.'

Eve thanked them for coming and Clooney accepted a lift home.

'They're a nice bunch, chicken,' Anne said, after all the visitors had been cleared out.

'Thanks, Anne.'

'Except for the freak. You know what they called people like him in my day?'

'No.'

'Greedy.'

'Oh.'

Lindsay was asleep and Beth watching TV.

'It takes all sorts,' Anne said.

'Yeah,' Eve agreed.

'Would you like a bonbon?'

'No, thanks.'

'I could call a nurse to drop one over to you?'

'I'm fine.'

'I'm sorry about your friend.'

'Which one?' Eve asked, wondering if she was talking about the dying man or the freak.

'The one you call out to in your sleep,' she said. When Eve started to cry, Anne kindly pretended not to notice.

Alice was as rude as Lily had predicted. Upon opening the door she stood back and surveyed Lily's outfit. 'Ah, you're looking great,' she said, with an air kiss, 'in the old favourite.'

Instead of being her usual congenial self, Lily replied with steel in her voice: 'Is that new?'

'Yes.'

'Well, if you take it off now you could still get a refund.' She walked past her without a second glance.

Adam handed her a glass of champagne. 'Nice,' he said.

'Not in the mood for this tonight.'

'I see that.'

Declan didn't pay any attention to the words spoken between his wife and his friend's wife. He was more interested in talking to Rodney. They were discussing the surgery they had been involved in together that day.

The group gathered in the lounge, waiting to be called into the dining room. Alice stayed in the kitchen, pretending to preside over the catering company she'd hired. In fact, she was fuming and double-checking herself in the mirror.

Usually at parties or events, and particularly in large rooms with new people, Declan would watch Lily from a distance. If he saw her conversing with an unknown man, he'd call her to him. 'Lily, can you stand by me, please?'

'What do you want?'

'My wife, if that's OK.'

If she disappeared for longer than five minutes he would chase her down. 'Lily, where the hell have you been?'

'In the toilet.'

'What were you up to? It doesn't take half an hour to go to the toilet.'

'It does if you're in a room full of women with only two loos. For Christ's sake, Declan!'

If she spoke to a man who clearly appreciated her, Declan would belittle her, even though it didn't always work out in his favour.

'Lily, I'm sure Greg is just being polite. Nobody finds gardening interesting.'

'Greg is a gardener, Declan.'

When attending Rodney's intimate gatherings, he usually ignored her.

Lily and Adam stood together by the piano. Declan would have been jealous if he hadn't decided long ago that Adam was gay, not because Adam had never married but because he had a *quality*. He couldn't explain it, he simply compared it to having the X factor. Declan liked to look at a beautiful woman. Adam liked to talk to her. Declan was well groomed. Adam was dapper. Declan was an ex-rugby player. Adam had spent his secondary-school years ballroom-dancing. Lily knew her husband was wrong about Adam but she encouraged his misconception because it was nice to have a male friend that Declan wasn't suspicious of. Over the years Adam had noticed that her husband's theory allowed him closer access to Lily so he didn't care to put him right, no matter how rude or obnoxious he became when drunk.

In the car on the way over Declan had laughed at the notion of Alice lining up a date for Adam. 'That's a waste of time,' he'd said.

Lily stayed silent. She was thinking about what Clooney had said. *'Still perched on your high horse'* – *what was that supposed to mean? He doesn't know me!* Yet it bugged her. She also wondered why she had reacted so badly when Eve had done everything she could to minimize the damage to Fiona. *After all, who the hell am I to come down on a lie? I spend my life lying. Who does the truth serve? No one. Eve has probably endured one of the worst days in her life and I was a stupid bitch. Damn it. What is wrong with me?*

'Alice just won't listen,' Declan went on. 'She's determined to marry him off.'

'She should mind her own business,' Lily said.

'Lily, I need you to be nice to Alice,' he said sharply.

'I will be.'

'You're in one of your moods,' he said.

This grated on her because he often intimated that they were linked to her fluctuating hormones. She ignored him. She was picturing Eve's face and the heartbreak that had been written all over it.

'I don't know why they insist on asking him over anyway,' Declan twittered on. 'It's not like he ever stays long. Probably off to the Phoenix Park to get himself some arse.' He looked at his wife for a reaction but she was lost in her thoughts.

Her mind had drifted back to when Eve was a teenager in love. *I think I'm falling in love, Lily. I'm scared, Lily. He makes the world feel like a better place. I wish it could always be like this.*

'What are you thinking about?' Declan asked.

'Nothing,' Lily said.

'Impossible. Tell me what you're thinking.'

'That I wish I was at home in a bath.' *I'm thinking of knocking you out as soon as we get home, creeping back to the hospital and taking my old friend to say goodbye to her teenage sweetheart.*

'You have a look in your eye,' he said.

'No, I don't.'

'You do.'

'Just drive the car, Declan.'

Now Adam and Lily talked pleasantries until Alice came in and introduced him to Tracey, being careful to turn her back on Lily and exclude her from their company. Adam grabbed Lily's hand and mentioned to Alice that she had inadvertently missed Lily from the introductions. She pretended it was an accident while Adam and Lily pretended they believed her. Tracey stood quietly, waiting to meet Lily. When the introductions were over, Alice left Tracey with Adam. Lily stayed put. Alice's look suggested she wanted to punch Lily in the face but she asked her to join her in the kitchen.

'I'm fine where I am, thanks,' Lily said.

Adam smiled and Tracey told her that she looked stunning in her red dress within Alice's earshot.

Tracey was nice. She was tall and a little horsy around the jaw, but she had pretty eyes, blonde hair and a great figure. She wasn't Adam's type but she had a good sense of humour, and if he had met her in a bar and Lily wasn't standing beside her, he might have slept with her.

Dinner was boring. Declan was slurring after two glasses of wine and the whiskey Rodney had insisted he drank as soon as he walked through the door. Rodney didn't seem to notice because he was too busy arguing politics with Tracey.

'You can say what you want about Fianna Fáil, but are the others going to do any different?' he asked. 'No!' He slapped the table with his hand.

'It's important for the electorate to show their contempt for the way in which business has been done. The only way to do that is by voting out the current regime,' she reasoned.

'Cut off one head and another grows,' he argued.

'They're all a bunch of thieving bastards!' Declan said. 'The French revolutionaries had the right idea. Off with their heads!' In his fervour, he waved his hand and knocked over his wine glass.

Alice jumped up and Declan apologized profusely while Rodney talked over him . . . and so the interminable night went on.

Adam met Lily in the kitchen. 'Is it late enough to leave?' he asked.

'Yeah, get going,' she said.

'What about you?'

'I'm stuck until Declan can't stand any more,' she said, looking at her watch. It was eleven o'clock.

'One more whiskey should do it,' he said. He poured another large glass, went into the sitting room where the others were seated and handed it to Declan.

'Oh, you're not trying to get me drunk enough to have your way with me, are you?' Declan asked him.

Rodney laughed but Alice was unimpressed. 'Don't be ridiculous, Declan,' she said, looking at Tracey. 'There's no need for that.'

'Apologies, Adam,' Declan said, clearly believing himself to be on a comedy roll. 'I know it's Rodney you fancy.'

Rodney laughed again, and Adam swore in his head that this would be the last time he accepted an invitation to eat with either of his colleagues. 'I think it's time for me to take my leave,' he said. 'Goodnight, all. Tracey, it was nice to meet you.'

''To meet you nice,' Declan said, doing his best impression of Bruce Forsyth, which was pretty bad.

Alice tutted. 'I'm sorry, Adam,' she said at the door. 'I could ask Tracey for her phone number for you?'

'I can get my own phone numbers, Alice,' he said, 'but thank you.' He waved at Lily, who had emerged from the downstairs cloakroom. 'Goodnight, Lily.'

'See you tomorrow, Adam,' she said.

Alice closed the door and turned to Lily. 'Maybe Tracey would have had a chance if you hadn't monopolized Adam.'

'Excuse me?'

'No. I won't. You think you're better than everyone else.'

'That's rich coming from you, Alice.'

'I see you with Adam,' Alice said. 'Your husband might be blind to it but I see.'

'You are an élitist, angry, arrogant bitch, Alice,' Lily said. She walked into the sitting room and grabbed her drunken husband's arm. *Where the hell is this coming from? God, Declan's going to kill me.* 'We're going.'

'What?' he asked, confused.

'Now,' she said.

'I do feel a little sick,' he said, as she hauled him into the car. He fell asleep on the drive home.

Lily was smarting. *How dare Alice Gibson? Who the hell does she think she is? As if. Why can't she mind her own damn business?* Lily had always known Adam wasn't gay for one reason only: the way he looked at her. She didn't actively encourage him. She never pretended to be available. He was a friend and a shoulder to cry on when things were difficult with Declan, but lately it had become increasingly obvious that Adam had feelings for her. She could pretend not to notice when others didn't, but Alice's words meant that the game she was playing with herself was over. Damn it. *Why do you have to look at me like that, Adam? I just need a friend.*

Declan was so drunk that Scott had to help her carry him from the car. She stripped him in a matter of minutes and he was snoring before the light was turned out.

Scott was watching a movie. It was one o'clock but Lily was sober and ready for action. She couldn't leave the house without Scott noticing – he'd hear the car in the driveway, plus technically she could do with his help. She went into the sitting room and reminded him that she had talked his father into allowing him to work with his grandfather from the following Monday.

'I know. Thanks.' He shrugged.

'I need your help,' she said.

'With what?'

'I need you to help me with a patient.'

'OK?'

'I'm asking you to help me for free, but if you do, I'm going to buy your silence with fifty euro,' she said, holding up the note she'd just stolen from Declan's trousers.

'Buy my silence? Why?'

'Because you can't tell your dad.'

'Is it legal?'

'Of course it's legal!'

Scott looked at the money. 'OK.'

They made it to the hospital in fifteen minutes. Scott followed Lily up to Eve's room. He waited in the corridor while she talked to another nurse for a few minutes. The nurse nodded and turned her back. He stood at the door while she woke Eve gently.

'Eve.'

She opened her eyes. 'Lily.'

'Hi,' she said, smiling.

'Hi.'

'I'm sorry for being a bitch earlier.'

'It's allowed.'

'How about we take a little trip?'

'Where?'

'To see Ben.'

'I'd really like that.'

Lily called Scott from the doorway. He pushed in the narrow trolley on to which he would help to slide Eve.

'This is my son, Scott,' she said.

Eve smiled at him. 'It's nice to meet you, Scott,' she said.

'Wow, you're in bits!' he said, and Eve agreed that she was.

'You should see the car,' she said.

Lily unhooked Eve from her drip. She and Scott untucked the sheet beneath her and used it to lift her from her bed to the trolley. 'Lift on three,' Lily commanded, and they did so. After a little negotiating they were on the way to the fourth floor. Lily had called ahead from the car, asking permission of the nurse in charge. She was waiting for them when they arrived in the corridor. 'Keep it quick,' she said.

'We will.'

Lily and Scott pushed Eve into Ben's room and positioned her by his side. The area was small and they could barely fit the narrow trolley beside his bed. When Lily squeezed her hand it was shaking. 'We'll be outside,' she said, and left her alone with him.

She couldn't touch him because they could only get her into the room with Ben to her left. She tried to reach with her right hand but she couldn't. He had colour in his cheeks and his chest moved up and down mechanically. She watched it and when she closed her eyes she could feel her head resting against it.

'I met Fiona,' she said. 'She seems lovely, which makes you a total dick for cheating on her, but you always said she was lovely, which makes me a total dick for being the one you cheated with.' She waited as though by some miracle he'd answer. 'She doesn't know. She'll never know. She's yours and you're hers, and I'm just a . . .' Tears rolled down her battered face. 'I'm just a lonely woman who wanted . . .' She stopped and placed one finger on her lips, as though to silence herself while she thought of the right thing to say. 'I'm just someone who loved you a long time ago.' The pain in her heart sharpened as though an invisible knife was twisting inside her. It threatened to take her breath away. 'I'm going to forget the past year, if you don't mind. I'm going to remember you back when you were mine. It was really such a short time but I want you to know it meant so much. You were my first real love but you know that. What you don't know is that you were my only real love, and if I had only known what I know now, I would have done everything differently that night, that stupid, stupid, stupid night. And when I dream of you I'm going to dream that we're back at Paul's party and you take me to the bottom of his garden, to the bench beside the pond with his mother's dead fish in it, and we'll kiss and hold each other, and when you tell me that you love me and that you want to come to London with me, I'll say I love you back, and we'll make plans to be together and it will be perfect. In my dreams I'll be your wife, and we'll never be by that wall on that night. There won't be a car coming and a drunk behind the wheel. There will be you and me and children and grandchildren and all the mushy stuff you said you wanted that night when you were only nineteen.' Eve dried her eyes with her wrap. 'I'm sorry I was such a fool.'

She stayed silent after that, allowing her tears to flow like a river, emptying the contents of her broken heart. She had never cried for anything or anyone the way she cried that night, and she wasn't sure if it was the fact that she'd almost lost her own life, or guilt, or love, or the morphine, but when they came to take her back to her ward she had never felt so scared, so sad or so numb. She couldn't touch him, she couldn't look back, all she could do was cling to her old friend's hand and sob. *It should have been me. It should have been me. It should have been me.*

'Oh, Lily, please take me back and place his hand in mine just for a minute!'

Once Eve was back in bed, Scott stood by the door and watched his mother placate her. She stroked her hair and soothed her with whispered words as she had done with him and his sister so many times over the years. He couldn't hear what was said but the woman quietened. Before Lily left her, Eve clung to her hand. Lily bent down and kissed her forehead, then said something that seemed to make her relax. Lily covered her up to her neck and tucked her in. She turned off her light and left her staring at the ceiling, silent and calm.

In the car on the way home Scott asked his mother what she'd said.

'Oh, nothing,' she said.

'Seriously, tell me.'

'I said I'd make it better,' she said.

Scott laughed. 'You'll make it better? The guy is a fucking organ donor!'

'Don't say "fucking". It really is vulgar,' she said, thinking of what she'd said to Clooney and regretting it.

'Sorry, fudging – but come on!'

'Remember when you were ten and your best friend in the whole world was moving to Kerry and you cried and cried and cried?'

'What was his name again?'

'Steven Maher.'

'Steven Maher! God, I must Facebook him.'

'Anyway, you were a lost soul and nothing either your dad or I could promise seemed to make it better. A new football didn't work, a trip to the zoo didn't work, a –'

'OK, Mum, I get it.'

'Well, it was only when he left and I held you in my arms and said I'd make it better that you quietened down.'

'Maybe I was just tired of crying.'

'Maybe, or maybe you knew that, no matter what it took, I would do everything in my power to make it better.'

'You're a mental case, Mum.'

'Cheers, son.'

Lily and Scott sat quietly in the car for the rest of the journey home. She was lost in times gone by and he was contemplating why the broken woman had to be kept secret from his dad. When Lily parked the car and they walked up to their front door, he turned to her.

'I'm sorry for your friend,' he said.

'She's just a patient,' Lily tried to lie.

'She's the girl from the photos you keep in the shoebox in your wardrobe,' he said, and handed her back the fifty-euro note. 'I don't know why you're lying or being weird but I promise I won't say a word.'

Lily should have been annoyed with her son for invading her privacy but she was too alarmed to be. 'You didn't read the letters, did you, Scott?' she said, trying hard to hide her fear.

'No. A girl from the last century bleating on about rubbish? I read about three lines and lost the will to live.'

If he noticed her sigh of relief, he didn't say anything.

She shoved the fifty euro into his shirt pocket. 'Take it. It's your father's, and if you ever rummage through my stuff again, I'll tell your next girlfriend that you used to take your winkie out in the supermarket and ask old ladies if they thought you were a big boy.'

'That never happened,' he said, horrified.

'Well, she won't know that so don't you dare use this against me in future negotiations,' she said.

'Mum, seriously, I don't have to negotiate any more. I'm nineteen.'

'Trust me, son, that's when the negotiation starts.'

Lily watched her son climb the stairs before she headed outside into the garden. A white half-moon hung in the black sky.

She walked to the swing-set that she insisted they buy for Daisy when she was five. It was a large metal structure with two swings, featuring one red seat and one purple. It had been rooted in foundations so that it could support an adult's weight. Lily and Daisy had spent countless summer days swinging together, but Daisy and her friends had abandoned it now. Lily still sat on the purple seat when she felt sad or playful or contemplative or was simply in search of solitude. Often when she couldn't sleep and it wasn't too cold she'd put on a coat over her nightdress, venture out and swing for a while, thinking about her dreams.

One morning when she woke up to snow she wrapped up warm and put her wellies on. She trudged to the back of the garden, cleared the seat and swung as high as she could. In her head she replayed the scene of her and Eve battling, swinging faster and faster and higher and higher until their feet were touching the sky.

'The one who swings highest gets a wish!' Eve said.

And Lily couldn't decide on a wish but it didn't matter because Eve's long legs assured her win.

'I love you, Eve Hayes.'

'I love you, Lily Brennan.'

Now she thought about the goodbye scene she had witnessed. She thought about Eve and how sad and sorry she had been. She thought about Ben. He'd never again see a red sky, never again dip his feet into a fast-flowing river or feel the touch of a loved one. He'd never smile or laugh or make a joke. He'd never shout or scream in joy or pain. He'd never cry or moan. No more pain or loss for Ben Logan because even as Eve had poured out her heart to him he was long gone.

Lily looked up into the night sky as she swung, attempting to touch the moon with the tips of her toes.

Where are you now, Ben? Are you reaching for the light or running from the darkness? Is Danny right? Are you simply gone or are the possibilities for you endless? Maybe you've moved on to another dimension or a parallel universe. Maybe you've shed your skin and you're about to receive a commendation for a completed mission. *If you knew you were set to leave this earth so soon, would you have done it all differently?*

Lily thought about the last question for a long time. *If I knew I was set to leave this earth soon, would I do it all differently?* The liar in Lily said, no, she wouldn't. She loved her children, her husband and her life . . . but recent events had awakened in her the young girl who had been silenced a long time ago. She had been the girl with the world at her feet and the one who had thrown it all away out of guilt, fear and the overwhelming need to be everything to everyone. That girl was whispering in Lily's ear, calling into question every choice she'd made and the kind of life she led. *Are you a wife or a glorified slave? Are you an equal or a subordinate? Are you loved as a woman or as a possession? Are you free? Are you happy? Are you all you can be? Do you love or pity your husband? Do you fear him? Why do you never say no? Is this it? For better or worse till death do you part? Are you lonely? Do you miss your friend? Do you understand what happened that night all those years ago? If you knew you were set to leave this earth soon, would you do it all differently?*

On the night before Ben Logan's family turned off his ventilator and his organs were harvested so that others could live, Lily Donovan sat on a swing in her garden and admitted to herself that, aside from her children, she regretted every decision she'd made. *I hate my life.*

7. And death shall have no dominion

Sunday, 22 July 1990

Lily, Lily, Lily,

We all know what happens when you drink too much. You get maudlin and that's all that's wrong with you. Stop over-thinking everything, and I know that's rich coming from me but you're just driving yourself crazy for no reason. You are the most intelligent person I know. You will sail through medical school. Six years might seem like a long time but it will fly by. When I close my eyes I can still see us playing on the swing-set and it feels like yesterday. As for your mother, we both know she is a mental case. She always has been and she always will be so anything she says has got to be taken with a pinch of salt, although having said that no one, not even a mental case, is wrong 100% of the time. I think she is right about not attaching yourself to one boy at your age. I'M SORRY, DON'T KILL ME. If you're really concerned about money why not go to Trinity and live at home? You could see Declan at weekends and holidays. Would that really be the end of the world?

OK, so my big news is that Ben and I have DONE IT and it was AMAZING. Danny was on a big golf day with his pals so I knew we wouldn't see him till the middle of the night and Clooney was in town with friends. I brought Ben into the house and he spent ages looking around. He's really nosy. He looked at all of the photos and took ages over them asking questions, the first being why I'm such a moody cow in pictures and how come you were in so many. He wanted to know about my mother and he asked loads of questions like what was our last conversation and did I remember the way she laughed or smelt, and it was

weird because I've never really had that conversation before.
I didn't want to have it because it's so depressing and I didn't
want the vibe to be depressing, I wanted it to be sexy but he
wouldn't let it go. He kept asking so I told him about our last day
out together as a family – do you remember it? You were there too.
We were six and Clooney was eight and we went to some park
reserve. I can't remember the name of it. Can you? There was a
lake and barbecues and we played in the water and Clooney and
Dad fished and Mum lay out in the sun. The car boot was open
and the radio was on. When she was cooking she was singing
along to the songs and I remember how beautiful she looked and
that I stood staring at her for such a long time, wishing I could be
just like her. I haven't thought about that day in years and then
suddenly it was all so clear in my head – you and me paddling
and sitting in the shallow water. You had a swimsuit with a duck
on it and mine had big pink polka dots. I dared you to lie straight
back and let a wave wash over you and you did it and nearly
coughed a lung up, and then you made me do it too for revenge
but the wave didn't cover my face like it did yours and you called
me fathead and we both thought it was really funny and she
warned us to be careful. Do you remember? You and Clooney
chased each other around the picnic area and made Danny run
with me on his shoulders. And then she collapsed just by the car.
One minute she was walking and then she disappeared and
someone passing noticed her and called to my dad. He had her in
his arms in no time and he rocked her back and forth like she was
a baby. Clooney started to cry. When you saw him cry you cried.
I don't think I did. I just stood there needing a wee but afraid to
move. That was the beginning of the end for her, that day in that
place I can't remember. I told Ben about the memory and
suddenly I was crying. ME CRYING???? He said that it's good
to cry every now and then, and maybe if I did I wouldn't be so
gloomy in photos. He laughed at his little joke and then he
dragged me upstairs to my room. He spent ages looking around
there. I had to stand in front of my knicker drawer in case he

tried to open it but he didn't. He sat at my desk and straight away he noticed that I'd carved BGML into it. He said, 'I'm already inscribed on your desk,' and I tried to laugh it off saying he was not. He said, 'Well, what does BGML stand for?' and I was trying to think so I delayed answering by saying, 'What do you think it stands for?' He smiled and said, 'Ben Glenn Medeiros Logan.' He's very quick – Gar could have been looking at that for years and not got it. I said, 'No, it stands for Don't Go Morning Light.' MORONIC I KNOW. He fell around the place laughing and kept repeating Don't Go Morning Light over and over and I went so red in the face I had to give up and say, 'Fine, it's you, don't let that head of yours get any bigger or it will topple off that little body.'

Then he lay down on my bed and he stared at me. I didn't know where to put myself so I decided just to go for it and lie down beside him, as in, you're not going to intimidate me, Ben Glenn Medeiros Logan. He put his arm around me and instead of kissing me he asked me to tell him another story. I didn't want to. I still wasn't the better of the first one. I asked him to tell me something, and he said he'd been expelled from boarding school for smoking and getting drunk when he was fourteen! He said there were four of them who used to sneak booze into the school in shampoo bottles and they'd pay the groundskeeper to buy them cigarettes. They had a key for one of the sheds and they'd get up out of bed around one a.m. and go to the shed and drink and smoke till around four. They got caught – they were being watched because they all kept falling asleep in class. He said his parents went insane and he was brought home and it was really bad for a while but then they'd just lost his sister to cancer and his mother was in an awful way anyway. He said he thinks about that time often because his mother spent most days crying, his dad was a zombie and he was so unhappy he felt sick. He said that he made a promise to himself he'd never ever feel that badly again. I told him that was a stupid thing to say, that no one can make promises like that. He laughed at me and said I was right but it would have been nice if I could have agreed to make him feel better. I said I didn't realize that was a requirement. He kissed me FINALLY and I've told you before he's way better than Gar but I mean by hundreds and thousands of miles. I took off his shirt and he took off mine and he has a really good body. Then he had my bra off and our tops were skin on skin and his chest was so warm and I could feel his heart beating and when I unbuttoned his trousers I could feel he was about to burst through them anyway, and then STUPID ANNOYING Clooney arrives home shouting out my name. I couldn't believe it. Ben didn't freak out like Gar had. He asked me if Clooney normally barged into my room and I said no so he just lay there smiling and he pressed his finger to my lips, and when I didn't answer Clooney the third time he called, he stopped calling and disappeared somewhere. And then Ben was inside me. JUST LIKE THAT. One minute he's lying beside me then he's on top and then INSIDE!!!!! No crowbar necessary. It was unbelievable and the first time hurt and there was some blood but not enough to freak me out. Before we got going Ben made me put a towel on the bed, which was good thinking, although I was in such a rush to get going I picked up Clooney's football towel, it's one of his favourites. I washed it immediately but I still feel bad about it. Anyway, we did it again another two times and we've done it about ten times since then and every time it gets better and better. I'm blushing just thinking about it. I'm totally in love with him and I couldn't be happier I waited to be with someone like him. That first time we lay together for ages and although I did feel sticky and was longing for a shower, when we talked and he held me in his arms I thought to myself, this is what it should be like. When I couldn't wait any longer he talked me into joining him in the shower. You should have seen us scurry along the landing like two mice trying to avoid Clooney. We got into the bathroom and locked it and got into the shower and washed one another which was again AMAZING. We were all soapy and it was all lovely and of course Clooney tried to open the door and suddenly he's

*calling my name and Ben is grinning and I'm having a heart
attack so I just try to put him off by calling out that I'm sick. He
wondered why I didn't answer him when he came in, and I told
him I didn't hear him and to go away I wasn't well. And then he
asks me if I have the shits because Terry the Tourist had the shits
and was hospitalized with dehydration the previous day. Ben
was trying not to laugh. I said that I had pains and asked him to
go away. Finally he left us alone. Couldn't believe I'd got away
with it. Now I know how Clooney feels when he's entertaining.
NOT GOOD. Anyway, the next day Ben called and I introduced
Clooney to Ben and Clooney asked if we wanted coffee. I said no
but Ben said, 'Yeah, that would be great!' PISSED OFF. So we
then spent the next hour listening to Clooney go on and on about
Bushy Head and how she's ruining his life. Ben was really
interested and asked loads of questions, and I just wanted to get
up the stairs. Then Clooney suggested that we watch a film
together and Ben agreed so we ended up watching The Terminator with my stupid brother. Later when I walked Ben out he said
we'd have plenty of time and we kissed at the door and I just
kept thinking, no, we don't have plenty of time, we have one
summer together. I'm going to London and as much as we want it
to work out I can't afford to come home until Christmas, which
means we would have been together for less time than we'd been
apart. So it didn't make sense to me wasting time watching the
stupid Terminator. We have to take every moment we have
together and make the most of it. I was going to say it to him but
I didn't because I didn't want to stop kissing and I can't just
make a point with Ben and move on – he always has to discuss it
until I'm sorry I brought it up in the first place. So Clooney left
yesterday and I'm thrilled because when Dad's at work Ben and
me have the place to ourselves and Dad's working on a big project
so he's going to be out a lot. It's bliss. Ben wanted me to go to his
house the other day but his mother would be there so I said we'd
be better going to mine. He asked me if I didn't want to meet his
mother and I said no not really and that seemed to hurt him,*

which I don't understand. I told him that mothers don't really like me and that he'd probably be better off keeping me to himself. He laughed at that but I'm serious. Your mother hates me, Gar's mother thinks I'm rude and Declan's mother ignores me. Then again she's so stuck up she ignores everyone.

Bushy Head was hanging around outside the house last night. I wanted to go out to her but Ben said he'd do it. He went outside and they sat on the wall and they were there for ages and I was looking out the window wondering what the hell they were talking about and then she just walked off. He came back in and told me that he'd explained to her that she was worth more than standing by a pole looking into the house of some guy who didn't care about her. I told him he should give up marketing and become a psychiatrist. He said he reads those books all the time. He got into them after his sister died and his mother was so depressed that they had her on suicide watch for a while. I didn't know that – he hadn't mentioned it before. It's very sad, and now I feel bad about not meeting her. Maybe I'll suggest going over soon. Anyway, I'm not sure his little talk worked because I saw Bushy Head again in the village today and I don't think she has any good reason to be there so we'll see.

How's Colm? Do you remember any more from that night?

Love you

Eve

PS Gar split up with his Bray girl. Don't know why but I'm meeting him and the lads on Tuesday night so I'll fill you in next Sunday. Paul was seen in town with a girl who looked like a supermodel and it turns out she is a model! Don't know any more than that – it was Declan who told me someone saw them and Paul is being really coy about it. SICKENING.

PPS Declan's fine. I'm being much nicer to him, you'll be happy to hear. He really misses you and he's doing a lot of overtime at his dad's garage to try to get money for college. I called down there the other night to ask him to Ben's next gig. I think I interrupted a fight with his dad but I might be wrong because his *dad was really nice to me and told me I could stay for a coffee if I wanted to. I said no but then Declan insisted. He must really miss you if he wanted me to hang around!!!! So I did and it was weird. You know the way we normally only really ever slag one another off? Well, instead of doing that we actually had a real conversation. We talked about the thirty-two-year-old woman who jumped off the cliff on Tuesday because her boyfriend left her and it was deep. I finally get what you see in him. (Ha-ha at last.)*

Ben Logan's funeral was a huge affair. Family, new friends, old friends, acquaintances, neighbours, work colleagues, staff, suppliers and even some creditors and competitors turned up. The church was packed to the rafters, forcing many to stand outside. It was a bright hot July day and between the hymns, speeches and the sermon, birds could be heard twittering loudly from the trees that lined the church grounds. Not one person had a bad word to say about him. Every second story that was told brought peals of laughter or tears of joy and desperate sadness. Ben Logan had been a blessing to all who knew him. He had been kind, considerate, caring, friendly and funny. He was a good and fair boss, a friendly neighbour, the kind of friend who stays in your life for ever even if you haven't seen him in a long while. The music was poignant, and when a young girl by the name of Rosy Carey sang Eric Clapton's 'Tears in Heaven', there wasn't a dry eye in the house. Ben's dad spoke about the son he had cherished and lost, focusing on how Ben after an initial flirtation with being a bad boy had turned into the boy his mummy could lean on after his sister had died tragically, aged ten. He knew in his heart that she'd be waiting on the other side to greet him and, quoting from the song, he was confident she'd know his name when she saw him in Heaven. He spoke about Ben's determination, his love of music and travel. He spoke about his beautiful wife Fiona and the happiness she had brought into his life. He talked about how generous Ben was, even managing to joke about Ben's organ donations.

'There will be five lucky recipients of Ben's organs . . . well, four – let's face it, his liver's a dud.'

The congregation laughed, thankful for the momentary pause in heartbreak.

At the graveyard a friend of the family played and sang Blink 182's 'I Miss You' as they put what remained of Ben into the ground.

Lily had squeezed into the back of the church, and in the graveyard she stood slightly apart from the crowd. She had no real business there. She had never spoken to Ben Logan when he was alive; he was just the boy from the bowling alley who couldn't seem to take his eyes off Eve. That relationship had begun and ended one summer when she was down the country so the only memories she'd formed of him were through the descriptions in Eve's letters. Those letters had been Lily's long-time lifeline with her old friend; she had kept every one in the shoebox her son had stuck his nose into, along with some pictures of them together when they were young and inseparable.

Fiona spotted her and thanked her for coming. She asked how Eve was and Lily told her that it would be a long road but she'd be fine. Fiona seemed happy to hear it. She had accepted Eve's story and Lily was happy now to play her part in the lie. Fiona asked Lily if she would like to join them in the hotel but Lily made her excuses and left. She would later report to Eve that he had been a very popular, good man who was loved and cherished and would be missed every day thereafter.

Eve knew that, despite the depth of her feeling for Ben, their time together should have remained in the past. Although her feelings for him were real, their relationship was not. She realized in the first few days when she was lying in hospital that she hadn't really known him. If she had gone to that funeral she would have been as much of a stranger to him as Lily was.

'Even the best people make mistakes,' Eve said, referring to Ben.

'Yes, they do,' Lily agreed.

'I was just so tired and lonely.'

'You don't have to be lonely any more,' Lily said.

In that moment Eve saw that Lily was her friend again. She waited until Lily had left the room, then raised her blanket to cry in peace.

'Is she crying again, Anne?'

'She is, Beth.'

'Jesus, I've never met one like her!'

'Just leave her be, chicken. There by the grace of God go I.'

Ben's old band mates had stayed on for the afters. Billy had travelled from America to be there. Tom, Ben's cousin, had travelled from France. Finbarr and Mark lived close by and they had remained close all those years. Theirs was a tragic and long-overdue reunion. They joined the rest of the mourners in a hotel in South Dublin where they drank and sang and told stories about a boy and man they knew, loved and would miss.

Fiona was on medication, as was Ben's mother, prescribed by the same woman, Ben's aunt Celia. She was a GP and a great believer in medicating during times of stress. 'After all, stress is the number-one killer after road accidents,' she said. Ben's dad looked at his sister as though she was insane. She didn't seem to notice that she'd said anything inappropriate, just crossed her arms over her substantial chest and pursed her lips. Lots of people were inappropriate in their attempts to comfort the mourners, who had sat for hours on end in the church shaking hands with a seemingly endless line of people who squeezed their swollen hands a little too hard in an effort to convey that they'd meant what they'd said.

'At least he didn't suffer,' Lorna O'Loughlin said. 'If he had suffered it would have been a desperate situation altogether.'

If Fiona hadn't been so altered by the drug, she might have asked how much more 'desperate' Lorna thought the situation could get. Her husband, who hadn't even turned forty, had been hit by a drunk driver – he was dead, his organs were gone and he was about to be buried in a fucking hole in the ground. But she didn't say any of that. Instead she nodded, and Lorna was delighted to have helped with her words of wisdom.

'Thank God he didn't see it coming,' Michael Hannon said to Ben's mother. *What the hell does that mean?* She hoped he'd move on quickly.

'It would have been worse if it was cancer,' a random person said. *Huh.*

'At least he died when he was still living,' another one said, winking as she squeezed Ben's dad's hand. *What in Christ's name?*

At the reception it was clear that Fiona hadn't eaten or slept properly in over a week and was fading. Ben's mother had just buried her second child and everyone who knew her was acutely aware that it would be a long time before she came back from losing him, if ever. She sat there quietly holding Fiona's hand. She didn't speak or drink tea or have a sandwich or a piece of cake. She just picked a spot on the wall and stared at it until she could go home or Celia gave her another little white pill. Ben had been his mother's rock. As his father had said in the church, Ben was the one she had leaned on. He had been her friend and confidant. There wasn't a week gone by when he hadn't visited his parents and, although he got on famously with his father, his mother was one of the true loves of Ben's life. She knew that, his wife knew it, and so did his friends and family. It was a running joke.

'Fiona, do you take Ben and his ma to be your lawful wedded husband?'

It was one of the things that had made Ben so likeable. For those who weren't quite as deeply in despair, Ben's funeral was the perfect celebration of his life. The drink flowed and the musicians played and laughter followed tears followed laughter.

All the while Billy sat watching the crowd lament his old friend and band mate. Billy had left Ireland for America when he'd won a J1 visa in some sort of lotto. His departure had put the last nail in the coffin of a band that had been struggling for a long time.

Initially his decision had been met with resentment but over the years his band mates had all come round. He had set up his own electrician business, and, while he might not have been Donald Trump, he employed thirty guys, lived in a nice house and could support his four kids comfortably. He had been the last band member Ben had reconnected with, again via Facebook. They had only been in touch for two years but during that time they had shared with each other the things that they didn't share with anyone else. Maybe this was because they had always had a special connection – it had made Billy's abandonment all the more terrible in those early days – or maybe it was because they weren't next door to each other so it was easier for Ben to tell Billy that his business was going under and that he was terrified he was falling in love with the girl who had broken his heart when he was nineteen. Billy had heard the extraordinary story of the accident and who had been involved. When it was relayed to him that Ben's dealings with Eve were purely professional, he remained silent. Ben had told him in a recent email that Eve had returned to Ireland but that they had agreed not to see one another. He wanted his marriage to work and was beating himself up about the affair the previous year. He had questioned everything about himself, his wife and life. *Why did I open this can of worms? Why did I think we could just be friends? How can I do this to Fiona? How can I do it to myself?*

Billy had been there in the aftermath of Eve all those years ago. He had been the friend to pick up the pieces. Ben had mourned Eve as though she had died. She had been so cruel and careless with his heart that she had all but destroyed him. If Billy's decision to move to America had been the final nail in the band's coffin, Ben's broken heart had been the first. Billy couldn't bring himself to dislike Eve, despite what she had done to his friend, because he had kept her secret all those years. It was only when he'd unburdened himself and told Ben about the day that followed their break-up that Ben, having punched him in the face, had decided to make contact with Eve again.

'OK, I deserved that,' Billy had said. 'Just don't do anything stupid.'

The first time Ben had had sex with Eve, and much later that evening when he was working at budgets on his computer, he saw that Billy was online and he messaged him.

Did a bad thing with Eve

Not going to pretend to be surprised

I love my wife

Apparently you love your dick more

When did you become Captain Judgement?

After I made the same mistake you did and lost my first wife, my first
house and my dog

When Eve had returned to Ireland and made contact with Ben he had nearly suffered heart failure and, even though she assured him that she did not expect them to take up from where they left off, he had known deep down that it was inevitable. He had contacted Billy online.

She's back

If you want your marriage to work stay away

Ben assured him he would but over the next while he did admit that they were in contact.

She's just giving me business advice I swear

I'll buy that when I sustain a head injury

I'm not saying I don't want her. I haven't met up because I don't want
to put temptation my way. All our dealings are via email

Keep it that way

That was the last session of instant messaging between the two men. Even as Billy had signed off with a warning, he had known that Ben wouldn't be able to help himself around Eve and it was just a matter of time before he'd see her. He had considered a number of scenarios that would bring about the end of Ben's affair and/or marriage but not one had come close to death.

The bar in the hotel was stuffed with mourners. Fiona, Ben's mother, father and brother were sitting in a corner. The two women were silent, while the men were talking to the stream of people still approaching to shake their hands. The old band members sat together in a corner reminiscing about the good old days when they'd dreamed of becoming rock stars. It was well into the night before one of them brought up the fact that Ben had been with Eve on the night he died.

'Of all the people to be with on that night,' Finbarr said.

Billy was very confident that he was the only one in the room whom Ben had confided in so he said nothing.

'Eve Hayes,' Tom said. 'She was a real beauty back in the day.'

'Seriously banged up now,' Mark said. 'Fiona said she was in an awful way.'

'Still can't believe she was going to step in and save the business,' Tom said. 'Still, Fiona saw the business plan Eve had sent on email and it was really impressive.'

'Well, that one could smell a profit a mile away. She made a killing on her own business,' Finbarr said.

Billy found it interesting that not one person seemed to question why Eve was helping Ben. Instead he listened to everyone talk about what a wonderful marriage his friend had had, what a good man he had been and how he had landed on his feet the day he had met Fiona.

When he walked over to Fiona to sit with her for a while she was pleasant, but worried that it was all too much for Ben's mother.

'Did you know the woman he was with?' she asked Billy.

'Vaguely,' he said. 'They were together for only a very short time when they were kids.'

'She was going to invest in the business, but I'd rather pay off our creditors and close the business down. We have good insurance. It would be a clean start. Do you think that's callous?'

Billy didn't know Fiona very well – he'd only met her once before when Ben and she had visited him and his family in Chicago while they were on a road trip. It was during that trip that Ben had unburdened himself about Eve.

'I don't think it's callous at all,' he said.

'Do you think Eve will be disappointed?'

Why is she asking me this? Does she suspect? Does she think I know something? Why ask me? Why would she care? 'I think she's a businesswoman who has had many deals scuppered for lesser reasons than an old friend's death,' he said.

Fiona's eyes leaked. 'I'm leaving here. I don't know where I'm going but I can't stay.'

Billy nodded. There wasn't much he could say. Ben's mother hadn't spoken once during his brief time sitting with her and when he addressed her she looked right through him as though he was invisible. There was no escape for her. Before Billy made a break for it, he told Fiona he'd miss his old friend greatly.

'If someone had told me I'd only have him for ten years I'd still have married him,' she said.

'I know he'd feel the same,' Billy said, and he wasn't lying, because aside from Ben's infatuation with Eve he remembered the guy who had come to Chicago, bounced out of an RV and introduced him to his beautiful wife. He was grinning, hugging her close. When she moved his eyes followed, and when she spoke he smiled. He couldn't keep his hands off her, much to Billy's second wife's annoyance. 'She's a person not a goddamn puppy!'

Billy surveyed the large room filled with people who Ben's life had touched. He accepted that today would be the true end of his friend Ben Logan. And despite Ben's feelings for a girl who had broken his heart when he was a teenager, she was now a forgotten footnote. Thanks to her lie, that was where she would remain. He bore his own guilt silently. If he had never mentioned Eve, and if he had kept secret the day they had spent together in A&E after Ben had run out on her, his friend wouldn't have contacted her and he wouldn't have been hit by that drunk – but he had deserved to know the truth and Eve deserved the truth to be told. Billy had been twenty-one and too young to know what to do for the best back then. Eve made him promise to keep their day together a secret. She had made a lot of sense when she told him that her relationship with Ben wouldn't survive London and that it was better to leave things as they were. She was trying to be brave and do the right thing, but if Billy could have had his time again he would have told Ben straight away, then maybe things would have turned out differently. *I'm sorry, old friend. RIP.*

During the second week of Eve's recovery Lily was off duty but used many excuses to come and go from the hospital. Her husband found her most attentive: she brought him packed lunches and dropped in to see if he needed any dry cleaning picked up.

'You could have phoned.'

'I was passing.'

She'd spend twenty minutes with her husband before heading down to her ward and spending an hour with Eve. It was a different dynamic when she came as a visitor. They talked about everything and anything, filling one another in on the years that they had missed. Clooney would show up most days and the three would talk about their happy childhood spent together – Lily, the missing Hayes, had come home. *Danny would have loved to see her again. If only I'd got knocked down last year*, Eve thought. An unspoken pact between the girls meant that they would never speak of the night that had cemented the end of their friendship, but other than that everything was on the table.

Lily told Eve about the birth of her kids. 'Horrifying. Hence only two kids and Daisy was a mistake. I cried for the first month.' She told Eve about her house and her need to have everything in its place. 'Scott thinks I have OCD.'

'He's right. When you were a kid you used to line up the towels on the rack like the psychopath in *Sleeping With the Enemy*.'

Lily told Eve about her job. 'I realized that Mrs Moriarty wanted me to be a doctor more than I did.'

'Who was Mrs Moriarty?'

'Our guidance counsellor.'

'I don't remember her.'

'That's because you knew exactly what you wanted to do and wouldn't take any guidance from anyone.'

'Oh, right. Well, you're an excellent nurse, probably the best nurse in the world.' She smiled when Lily raised her arms in the air and bowed. 'And you seem to like it. Do you?'

'Yeah,' Lily said. 'Nursing has been my escape.' As soon as she said it she knew she'd said the wrong thing. *Damn it.*

'Escape?'

'From the house, the kids and the neighbours, who use me when they want something but never remember to invite me to their coffee mornings – the usual,' she said, careful not to include her husband in the mix.

'Ah,' Eve said. 'That's because they're jealous bitches.'

Lily laughed again, pleased she'd dealt with her slip, but also because that was something the old Eve would have said. 'I hardly think that's the case,' she said.

'It's exactly the case,' Eve said. 'In most rooms you're probably the best-looking woman in there by a mile, with your tiny little frame, your lovely skin, big brown eyes and silky hair. You're heading for forty and you look fourteen. You're funny, sweet, kind, warm, intelligent and every middle-aged-woman-battling-the-bulge-and-trying-to-hold-on-to-her-husband's nightmare.'

'You're a middle-aged woman – how come I don't get on your nerves?'

'Because even with a face full of stitches I'm better-looking than you. I do have the personality of a storm trooper so you'd have me there but I have no man for you to rob – plus I know something they don't.'

'What's that?'

'You're loyal to the point of self-sacrifice.'

They were both silent for a minute or two. Then Eve resurrected the question about nursing.

'So, aside from escape and your sheer brilliance, is nursing where you want to be?'

'You know I always liked beauty. Hair and makeup, maybe for fashion shows and photography – that was the real dream if I hadn't been so dumb as not to follow it.'

'I remember *Girls' World*,' Eve said, 'and you insisted on doing my hair all the time.'

'You had such beautiful hair.'

'And it's not beautiful now?' Eve laughed.

'It's short.'

'So are you.'

Lily laughed. 'I used to do Daisy's all the time but she won't let me near her now.'

'God, now I think about it, when we were younger that was all you used to talk about. In fact, when my mother got sick you used to come over and insist on brushing her hair once a week. I talked about designing clothes and you'd talk about doing hair and makeup! Then it all changed. Why?'

'I got the best Intercert exam results the school had ever seen and Mrs Moriarty told me a girl with my intelligence should do more with my life, like medicine.'

'You were always open to suggestion.'

'And you certainly benefited from that,' Lily said, remembering the many times Eve had talked her into acts of insanity all in the name of fun.

'You never wanted to be a doctor – that was Declan's dream. You wanted to be a wife and mother and nursing was a good option. It kept you close to him and you could breeze through it and earn more quickly.'

'Exactly.'

'It used to make sense but now your kids are nearly grown-up.'

'Daisy's only twelve.'

'All I'm saying is, if it's still the dream why not go for it?'

'Because life's not that simple, Eve.'

'No one's saying it is. The right decisions are usually the hardest. I'm only suggesting a beauty course, not exiling yourself on an island.'

Lily was silent for a while, thinking about what Eve had said. *I could do it. I know I could. If I knew I was set to leave this earth soon, would I do it all differently?*

On another day Eve told Lily about her time in London, Paris and New York.

'Amazing?' Lily asked.

'Sometimes.'

'You must have met incredible people.'

'Ah, people are people.'

'Come on, tell me one fabulous thing.'

Eve thought about it for a minute and sighed. 'I had sex with a few movie stars, a rock star and a politician. He was a kinky one.'

'You are joking.'

'His wife videotaped it.'

'Ah, come on!'

'We watched it back afterwards over pizza and wine. They were a lovely couple, and it was a great night, but when they were drunk enough I recorded some talk show over it because my arse looked huge and nobody wants that.'

'Are you joking?' Lily asked.

'No. I swear.'

'Who was it?' Lily was nearly falling out of her chair she was leaning so far forward.

'Can't say.'

'Ah, come on!'

'Lean in.'

Lily leaned in.

Eve whispered a name.

Lily's jaw dropped. 'No fudging way!'

Eve nodded.

'I've heard it all now.'

Eve laughed. *You haven't even heard the half of it.*

Clooney would tell the girls stories about his time in exotic and troubled locations.

'Do you ever get tired of it?' Lily asked.

'All the time,' he admitted.

'Tell her about the plane crash,' Eve said.

'Ah. Now. What?' Lily said, bracing herself.

'We were flying in a six-seater turboprop plane and about to land just outside New Orleans. The plane came up short of the runway, we hit an embankment, lost the right wing and propeller, but luckily everyone survived. The worst injury was a broken leg.'

'Clooney didn't have so much as a scratch, and he helped three people out before the plane burst into flames,' Eve said.

'Of course you were the hero of the piece!' Lily said, smiling.

Clooney hunched. 'Like Eve said, I wasn't injured so if I'd stood around it would have made me a really big dick.'

'What's he saying about a big dick?' Beth shouted at Anne.

'Nothing. None of your business. Let him talk,' Anne said, and waved at Lily, Eve and Clooney, who nodded and waved back.

'Any news on my private room?' Eve whispered to Lily.

'I'm working on it,' she said.

Over the first three days of Eve's second week in hospital, the trio talked about their past, their present and their hopes for the future. Clooney and Eve were on the cusp of life-changing decisions. He talked about what he would do and where he would go, but Eve was vague, which wasn't like her. Lily listened, while fantasizing about making a drastic change in her own life.

When Eve was feeling really blue, Lily could walk through the door and cheer her up.

'Take your head out of your arse! Isn't that what you Americans say?'

'We both know I'm not American.'

'Really? Then what's with the twang?'

'I don't have a twang!'

'Oh yes you do!' Clooney agreed. Then he went on to slag off his sister for having some kind of Cockney accent when she was in London and a serious French lilt when she lived in Paris. Lily joined in, remembering how Eve had talked like she'd swallowed a bucket of spit the one summer they'd spent learning Irish on a small island off the coast of Cork.

No matter how sad or bad Eve felt, Clooney and Lily could make her laugh and, most importantly, laugh at herself.

In the middle of that second week Lindsay was moved into a care home.

'Goodbye to you all. Tell the blonde she's invited to my party, but the others can stay at home,' she said to the nurse, who was helping her into her wheelchair.

'Ah, blow it out your arse!' Anne said, as Lindsay waved from bed to bed as though she was the Queen and those around her were common folk standing behind barricades waving flags and hoping for a smile.

Anne went home a day later. She insisted on being wheeled up to Eve. She took her hand. 'You'll be all right, chicken,' she said. 'You have your brother and your friend. You're not alone any more.'

'Thanks, Anne.'

'And, chicken, don't make a habit of sleeping with married men – even if they don't die on you it leads to nothing but heartbreak.'

'OK.'

'And, chicken . . .'

'Yes, Anne?'

'Tell that bisexual I'm glad he picked the right team.'

'No intention of it, Anne,' she said.

Anne laughed and waved, and then she was gone, leaving Eve with Beth and two new women she didn't have time to get to know: a private room had become available and she was moved into it.

''Bye, Beth!' Eve said, as a nurse wheeled her away.

'Are you going home, love?' Beth asked.

'No, moving into a private room.'

'Oh, good! It would be a crime to let you go – you're still in an awful way.'

Eve had been in her new room for six days when the physio started on her shoulder. It was agonizing and would go on for the rest of her stay. Every day for forty minutes, simple stretching and resistance exercises became torture. Eve would count down the hours and minutes until the physiotherapist Mica came to her room. She'd take a deep breath and they'd begin. The pain was immense but after some coaching and cajoling she'd push through, often crying during the session. Mica was nice but stern, and took no prisoners.

'I know it hurts but if you want your shoulder to work again you've got to do this.'

'I don't. It's fine. One good arm will do.'

'Don't be ridiculous – now push against me.'

After physio was concluded Eve received two painkilling pills, the dread lifted and her day would begin. She'd read books, stare at daytime TV, sleep when she could, read more books and watch more TV. Visitors broke the monotony. Gina would come most days when the kids were in school. She brought little gifts of cheesecake, homemade banana bread and colourful cupcakes. Eve didn't eat cheesecake, banana bread or cupcakes when she wasn't confined to bed and feeling like a beached whale, certainly not when she was. The nurses appreciated them and looked forward to Gina's arrival. She talked about the kids, the price of things and general news. Occasionally she'd bring up Paul and his impending nuptials. Gar had taken the news of Paul's bisexuality badly. He couldn't understand why his friend had spent so much time lying to himself and others. Gar felt let down. He looked at Paul and saw a stranger. *All these years.* He thought about the things he had told Paul about himself and Gina and the things they got up to in the bedroom. He would never have done that if he hadn't believed Paul was on another bus. *Jesus Christ, he might have been imagining her and me and him. Ah, for fuck . . .* Gina was worried because Gar had been avoiding Paul and, aside from a few workmates who liked to play rugby every week in the summer, he didn't really have friends.

'He'll come around,' Eve had said, one particularly nice day when the sun was beating through the window and she was sweating like a pig. Her headaches were getting worse. *Nothing like being stuck in an overheated stuffy hospital to give a girl a headache.*

Lily ran in, having had lunch with her husband, and Gina nearly fell over in a bid to get up and hug her. Lily was happy to see Gina but she felt a little awkward that there was an elephant in the room and Gina wasn't as good at avoiding it as she and Eve had been.

'Where the hell did you go?' Gina asked.

'Ah, you know.'

'No, I don't know.'

'Cork, then here.'

'Why have you never come home?'

'Oh, we settled in Dalkey.'

'Yes, very posh, but only down the road so why have we not seen you?'

'Down the road might as well be America when you've got two kids,' Eve said helpfully.

Gina laughed. 'I hear that. I've got two as well – they're younger than yours. You must have had Scott straight away.'

Eve had told Gina all about Lily's children. Usually Eve didn't like people's stories about kids – as fascinating as they thought they were, they usually weren't – but Lily could always tell a good story and her kids seemed funny, if not a little spoilt. Lily agreed that she did get pregnant very early on, in fact she'd conceived on the honeymoon, but that had always been her plan so it was a very welcome development.

Gina wasn't letting go. 'I still don't understand why you never came home.'

'My mother preferred to visit us.'

'But it's your hometown.'

'Look, Inspector Clouseau, some people move and keep on moving,' Lily said.

'OK, OK,' Gina said, with her hands up. 'We just missed you, that's all.'

Lily had missed them too. She nipped in on the Friday evening when Declan was away at a conference in London. Paul, Clooney, Gina and Gar were there. Gar was subdued, having been made to visit by his wife. He didn't want to see Paul, and he couldn't have cared less about Lily, who'd abandoned him the first chance she'd got. Paul wasn't one for making a fuss. He pretended he didn't notice Gar's mood, which he figured he'd get over soon enough, and he'd never really minded about Lily and Declan's defection. *People do what they do.* He just got Lily a chair and told her it was good to see her. 'How's Declan?' he asked.

'Fine, thanks,' she said, and that was the end of that.

When she got up to leave, Clooney stood up with her.

When she left he waited a moment or two before he made his excuses, leaving Paul and Eve to fight over the remote control, and Gina and Gar to glower at one another. He caught up with Lily in the corridor. They walked to the lift together. 'Going down,' he said, pushing the button.

'You wish!' she joked, and he laughed.

They walked to the car park together and, just as they were about to part, he asked her if she wouldn't mind getting something to eat with him. Clooney knew that Declan was away, that Daisy and her friend were fed, that Scott was working late in his grandfather's garage and that she was going home to heated-up leftovers followed by washing and ironing.

'I'm sick of eating on my own,' he said.

'I don't know,' she said.

'Two old friends grabbing a bite to eat . . . please,' he said, and pouted. 'I'm so lonely.'

Lily had always been a sucker for a sad story. 'OK. I'm giving you an hour.'

'Is that an hour from now or from the time I order?'

She thought about it for a minute, then concluded that she'd take note of the time and decide later, depending on whether or not he was boring.

'I'm never boring,' he said.

'I'll be the judge of that,' she said, and he followed her to her car like a playful puppy.

Clooney was bored and he hated being bored. Paul was busy

planning a wedding and moving his fiancée to Ireland. Gar wasn't available to anyone, and of the friends Clooney had once had in Ireland none remained. V Kill P lived in London, his school mates had all moved abroad and his college friends lived around the country. He'd never stayed in Ireland longer than a week or two before his dad was diagnosed with cancer so he had never bothered staying in touch. When he'd returned last time, he was busy with his dad, busy with Eve, and with Eve came Gar, Gina and Paul. Now he was busy doing nothing most of the time but sitting on his sister's balcony. Clooney was more of an action guy than a profound thinker. He wasn't a reader. He had broken his ties with Stephanie and had finished his contract in Afghanistan. He wasn't going back there and wasn't sure where he would go next. Time would tell, and until then he would sit alone in an empty, modern, cold, unfamiliar apartment waiting for the appropriate times to visit his bored, moody, frustrated sister. *Tick tock tick tock tick tock tick tock.*

Lily pulled up outside a restaurant that she was unfamiliar with. It was on a main road and there seemed to be a lot of parking. They got out and she followed him inside. The place was quaint, old-style Italian, with gingham tablecloths, candles in red glassware and wood counters. The smell of tomato sauce and pizza hit them, and for the first time in a few days, Lily felt hungry. Since that night on the swing she had been deprived of sleep and off her food. Her mind was constantly racing. She'd been questioning everything about herself and her life, and things she hadn't noticed for years had started to become huge problems. Like earlier in the week at breakfast time.

'Mum, I'm thinking I'll have a spinach omelette. Dad, I'm working on a vintage BMW today,' Scott said.

'Year?' Declan said.

'It's an early V8.'

'Mum, I'm in the mood for pancakes but only if we have the proper syrup,' Daisy said.

'A 501?' Declan said to Scott, then glanced at his wife. 'Make mine a grill, easy on the pig, though. I have a morning meeting and I don't want to have bacon breath.'

'A 502,' Scott replied.

'Nice,' Declan said. 'I'll bet it's belonging to one of the Brownes. They made a ton of money exporting butter in the fifties through to the seventies. The father was a huge vintage-car enthusiast. I'm sure his sons have followed suit. I worked on some of those beauties myself back in the day. Oh, and, Lily, can you make sure the egg doesn't break? It was broken yesterday.'

No 'please'. No 'thank-you'. When the hell did I become a bloody dogsbody?

'I'm making a grill,' she'd said. 'You are all either in or out.'

Her family stopped what they were doing or saying around the table and looked up at her.

'You're joking. Right?' Scott said.

'Seriously not funny,' Daisy said.

'What's this?' Declan said.

'I'm not a chef. This is not a restaurant. Do you want a grill or not?'

The two kids looked at one another and then at their father. He mumbled something to them about her hormones, belittling her, as he so often did, and they laughed together.

For a long time Lily would have either let it go or made a joke, but that morning she had thrown the pan that was in her hand across the kitchen. It hit the wall and gouged out a piece of plaster. Declan and the kids were stunned.

'Kitchen's closed,' she said, and walked out of the room.

When her week's nursing was over and her week off had begun, she had faced a dilemma. She wanted to visit Eve, and see Clooney, Gar, Gina and even Paul – she hadn't clicked with him as well as Eve had in the past. She'd always thought he was too quiet, aloof, and she'd sometimes found him cold, but it was nice to be close to the people she'd grown up with and had been apart from for so many years. She couldn't tell Declan, not just because of his hatred of Eve but because he didn't like Lily to have friends of her own.

He didn't like her to stray off her daily routine. He had to know where she was at all times. Every day was the same if slightly different: there was a day planner on the fridge that was to be adhered to and it left little room for personal time. Lily hadn't really noticed that her life had been eaten up with responsibility and, although it had bugged her that her mobile phone was used as a tagging device by her husband, she had never felt truly trapped before. If she left it to ring more than five times, he questioned her.

'Where are you?'

'In the supermarket.'

'Why did it take you so long to answer?'

'For God's sake, Declan, I had to fish the phone out of my pocket.'

'Who are you with?'

'Buffy the Vampire Slayer. Would you like a word?'

'Don't get smart. You know I worry.'

Every time Declan questioned or harassed her about where she was or where she was going, what she was doing or who she was with, he told her it was because he worried. For too long she'd accepted his harassment as a symbol of his love, albeit an annoying one. But something was changing in Lily. For the first time in years, her eyes were open and she was looking at her life through a different lens, one that was not so rosy. *If I knew I was set to leave this earth soon, would I do it all differently?* Over the years she had helped Declan build her prison. She had become a wife and mother in the same year. When all her peers had been out drinking, carousing and expanding their minds with drugs or books she was breast-feeding, sleep-deprived, the woman behind the man who would some day become a heart surgeon.

In her determination to excel in everything she did and to fulfil Declan's dream of marrying a dedicated housewife, she became the best housewife she could be and that took time. Lily Donovan made Nigella Lawson look like a slacker. From early on she cooked different meals for her husband and kids. It had made sense when Scott was a baby and a fussy eater and Declan was a resident, working every hour God sent. Then Daisy had come along: she was another fussy eater who happened to have polar opposite tastes to her brother. At that stage it had been easier to feed the kids different food but at the same time. So at five every evening Lily's children had had their meal. She had cleared away their plates and reset the table so that when Declan called or texted to tell her he was leaving the hospital she could prepare a fresh meal for him. Declan liked two courses on weekdays and three at weekends. For a long time, when the kids were small and there was more housework, Lily and Declan couldn't afford a cleaner. When they could afford one Declan offered to pay, but Lily had a perfect routine, everything was in its place, her home was hers to control, and she didn't like the idea of having someone pick up after her family. She'd heard terrible stories from the neighbours about cleaners who had stolen from them or, worse, commented on a child's dirty underpants left on the floor. She didn't like the notion of anyone commenting on her children's underwear so, between cooking breakfasts, packing lunches and presiding over two sittings for dinner, she'd clean the house and do the garden, according to the requirements of each season. She'd run her kids to and from school, rugby, ballet, football, piano, friends' houses, parties, discos, bars, nightclubs and the pony club. Every moment of every day was accounted for and there was no room for her to deviate from that schedule.

In the early days and up until the mid-noughties, Lily had worked the night shift, which meant she always worked one week on and one off. On the weeks she worked, she'd be home for eight in the morning and meet Declan in the doorway on his way out. She'd rustle up breakfast and lunch for the kids and pack their bags. When they were gone she'd sleep for five hours. When she woke she'd clean, shop, garden, pick up the kids, ferry them around, feed them at five, and then prepare dinner for Declan. Her night shifts affected Declan's breakfast for two weeks out of every month. When her shifts changed to twelve-hour days, he was utterly horrified. She had set the bar so high that he couldn't see why she would let the perfect little world she'd created slide so that she could nurse ungrateful strangers. Declan got used to being able to read the planner on the fridge and know where his wife was at each and every moment and what she was doing. Over the years he'd slowly become more and more clingy and demanding of her time. Any deviation from her daily schedule caused him a kind of angst that left little room for rationality.

Lily had filled her days with so much work and responsibility, and she'd spent so many years making excuses for her husband's controlling nature and paranoia, that she hadn't allowed herself to look at her life for what it was. *A fudging prison sentence.* It became apparent to her when she was forced to plan her daily escape from her home and duties so she could go to a funeral or visit her old friend. And because she was undergoing an inner crisis and behaving erratically, one minute throwing pans across the kitchen and the next arriving in her husband's office with gourmet picnic baskets, Declan was confused. He didn't know that she was simply using him as an excuse to be in the hospital, but he did sense that something was up. He considered early menopause and, in case her madness wasn't medical, decided to keep a closer eye on her. His phone calls increased, which meant she often had to leave Eve's room to answer her phone and make up a plausible lie. With each day that passed it got harder. *Why can't you just give me five minutes' peace?* When he was forced to go to London for a weekend conference Lily was delighted: she was badly in need of respite. He had tried to talk her into going with him but she was steadfast in her refusal. He behaved like a spoilt child and she ignored him. When he realized he wasn't going to get his way, he demanded she come upstairs and perform her duty as his wife. He sometimes used sex as a weapon but only when he was really pissed off. If Lily was being dogmatic and/or defiant he would unzip his pants and tell her to suck him off. *Nothing like a woman on her knees sucking cock to put her in her place.*

He grabbed her by the back of her head and pushed himself into her. 'Deeper.'

How about I bite it off?

'Harder.'

Halfway up or at the neck or base?

'Come on, swallow it!'

I mean, what's the point in biting the tip off or even half of it when I could chow down on the whole lot. I'll swallow it all right – they'll have to cut me open to get it out.

When he was just about to come, he pulled her off him by her hair, threw her on to the bed and pounded into her as though he was drilling a hole in the earth's crust. When he was finished he rolled over and turned on the TV. She got up and showered. Before she left the room he told her that sometimes she was such a disappointment in bed it left a bad taste in his mouth. *You don't leave such a great taste yourself, Dicknose.*

Lily didn't care. She would be free of him for three whole days. The conferences on Friday and Saturday were intense, the evenings involving scheduled group fun, and Sunday was a golf day. Declan couldn't make calls during the conferences and previous years dictated that if he tried to ring his wife in the evening or on the golf course he would be forced to do so in front of a crowd. There was always one who would later make jokes about it. Lily's husband had treated her like an unpaid prostitute but he would be away for three days, and when she left him sulking in their bedroom she skipped down the corridor with a song in her heart. *Free Nelson Mandela, Mandela will be free. Oh, Nelson Mandela!*

Now, in the restaurant with Clooney, she placed her phone on the table in front of her. *Just in case.* She looked around the room for somewhere quiet where she could take a call after no more than five rings if she needed to. She saw an area that had been cordoned off. *That'll do at a pinch.*

'Are you scoping the place out?' Clooney asked, amused.

'Something like that.'

They looked at the menus. Clooney wanted pizza. 'It just smells so good.'

Lily favoured a pasta dish, something spicy with lots of chicken. Her body craved protein.

'When did you last have a meal?' Clooney asked, as he watched her inhale her dish.

'A few days, maybe a week,' she said, as a matter of fact.

'You've lost weight,' he said. 'You're skin and bone.' He picked up her hand and put his finger and thumb around her wrist. There was room for two more wrists in the circle his fingers created.

'Is that why you asked me to dinner? To feed me up?'

'No,' he said, 'my intentions were purely selfish.' He laid her hand back on the table. 'Are you OK?'

She could see he wasn't asking to be polite or because he couldn't think of anything else to say. She could see that he was concerned for her and had a genuine interest in how she was. Those steely eyes were looking straight through the lovely happy Lily façade and right into her soul. She was either going to avert her eyes and break contact long enough to form a lie or she was going to hold his stare and admit that she wasn't OK.

'I'm great,' she said, looking over his shoulder towards the window.

'Liar,' he said, and changed the subject. They began talking politics.

She noticed that when she spoke he actually listened, and even when they didn't agree he didn't dismiss her opinion or patronize her. They debated American foreign policy. She argued for pulling out of Iraq and Afghanistan and, much as it pained him, he argued against it.

'If you saw the damage done.'

When he argued it was with passion, but without inflated ego, and he wasn't vitriolic. It made a nice change. He was gentle and happy to be hanging out, exchanging ideas.

Lily made him laugh.

He liked her turn of phrase: 'I made a buggery-balls of it to be honest.'

He liked her sunny disposition: 'There's always something to be grateful for. Like shoes and the Stereophonics.'

He was especially enamoured of her penchant for innuendo or a good dirty joke. 'Did you hear the one about the horny pilot?'

'No.'

'As the plane began to descend towards the airport, the captain announced: "Ladies and gentlemen, this is your captain speaking, we are now arriving at Dublin airport. On behalf of the staff and crew, I'd like to thank all of you for flying with Aer Lingus. We hope you had a pleasant flight." He forgot to turn off the intercom. He turned to his co-pilot and said, "Christ, Bernard, I really shouldn't have eaten that curry before we took off. When we land I'm going to go to the hotel, take the biggest shit of my life and get a blow-job from Jenny, the new stewardess." The pilots laughed. Jenny, who was seeing to the passengers, darted towards the cockpit, tripped over an old lady's walking stick and landed on her back. The old lady looked down at her and said, "No need to rush, dear . . . he said he's going to have a shit first."'

Clooney laughed and Lily bit her lip the way she always did when she was pleased with herself. While she was talking and laughing, Lily had managed to finish her pasta. It was the first meal she hadn't just chased around with her fork in days. She marvelled at her empty plate.

'Want some dessert?' he asked. She was about to say yes when her phone rang. He saw the fear register in her eyes, the look of panic that crossed her face when she saw her husband's name on caller ID and realized that where they were sitting was no longer quiet but bustling with people. One ring and Lily registered the caller. Two rings and she knew the restaurant was too noisy to pick up in. Three rings and she was standing and looking around wildly. Four rings and she was running to the front door. Five rings and she picked up in the car park.

'Hello?' A large truck passed her on the main road. *Oh, God, why did I choose a restaurant on a main road? What kind of fool am I?*

'Where the hell are you?'

I could say I'm in the garden and a truck passed the wall, no, no. He'll ring the house to check up on me if he hasn't already.

'Can you hear me?'

Oh, fudge cake, bugger-balls, think, think, think . . . OK, OK, OK, *go old school, Lily.*

'Hello?' Lily said loudly.

'Yes, hello, can you hear me?' he said.

'Declan?' she said, as though she was straining to hear.

'I can hear you perfectly. Where are you?' He was clearly annoyed. Someone in the background was talking to him. 'Just give me a second, will you?' he said, to whoever had dared to address him while he was on detective duty.

'Declan? Declan?' Lily said. 'Oh, for God's sake!' She sighed and hung up. Then she turned off her phone. Her hands were shaking. *Don't be ridiculous, Lily, just calm down. You are not doing anything illegal. You are just having dinner with an old friend. Relax.*

She went back into the restaurant and sat down. She was still flushed and despite her pep-talk she was still trembling slightly.

'Does Declan normally have that effect or is it just that you're with me?' he asked.

Lily shook her head. 'We were having such a nice time, Clooney.'

He knew she wanted him to let it go so he pretended to do just that. *What the hell is going on?*

After surveying the menu they agreed that two coffees would be a healthier option than dessert. Lily felt a little sick having eaten more than she had in days and also because of the phone call she had handled so badly. *He's going to lose his mind.* Clooney knew that she was itching to go. Her entire demeanour had changed as soon as she had seen Declan's name light up on her phone. He had noticed that when she came to visit Eve she was constantly looking at her watch and she jumped every time a staff member walked into the room and made a reference to her being there, most especially when they mentioned her husband. Like the time when Marion had come in to take Eve's pulse.

'Hey, Lily, you here again? Declan must be taking advantage of this.'

'We're both way too busy to be fraternizing here . . . Besides, I have to go.'

'You've just got here.'

'Busy-busy. I'll see you soon.'

Or the time when Abby had come in to give Eve her heparin shot and noticed Lily sitting there.

'Lily, fantastic. I was going to mention the Heart Foundation Ball to Declan but I know you deal with the diary – can we put you down for two tickets?'

'Absolutely.'

'Great. I'll mention it to him when I see him later.'

'Oh, no, no, don't, it's fine. I'll just check our diary and get back to you.'

'Oh. OK.'

'I've got to go.' And she was gone.

Clooney wasn't the only one who had noticed it. Eve had too. 'Just leave it, Clooney, it's none of our business,' she'd warned.

He agreed but there was something about the way Lily was reacting that bugged him. *Is it fear?*

That question had been answered in the restaurant.

Clooney had ordered a taxi to pick him up during their coffee and as soon as it came they paid the bill – Lily insisted on going Dutch. They walked outside together. He leaned in to kiss her cheek and she backed away, alarmed.

'I'm sorry, I was just saying goodbye,' he said, embarrassed.

'I know. I'm sorry. I'm just tired,' she said. She hugged him and pulled away quickly. 'I can't go into the hospital tomorrow or Saturday so I'll see Eve when I'm back on days on Monday.'

'OK,' he said. 'I'll tell her.'

Lily watched him get into the taxi and drive away before she got into her car. She took her phone out of her pocket and put it on the seat beside her. It remained off. She exhaled, gripped the steering wheel and cried.

8. One day, one month, one year, one life

Dear Eve,

When you walked in on Declan and his dad arguing did you hear shouting or what? Was Declan acting weird? What did he say? I can't seem to get him on the phone the past few days. His father told me he was out but I know he was there because he always waits on my calls. Tell him I'll keep trying but please ask him to write to me if there's something wrong. OK? Thanks for being good to him. I knew if you gave him a chance (it only took two years) you'd like him. He is very deep and emotional. Please let him know I love him and miss him. I hope he's OK and I can't wait to see him when I get home.

I can't believe I've been here nearly one month already. Only another month to go and I'll be coming home and we'll all be preparing to go off to college. I know your course starts in early September but at least we'll have a few days together before you go. If it's sunny we should go up on the cliff together and bring a blanket and a picnic and we'll walk to the gap in the fence and head down the grassy slope that takes us to our special place. We can lie on our blanket looking out towards Wales and daydream about your life in London and mine in Cork. We can reminisce about all the good and bad days we had as kids.

Me getting my nose broken in basketball – bad
Me getting to know Declan as a result of that broken
nose – good

You stuck in bed for two months with glandular
fever – bad
Getting your first sewing machine and discovering
your love of design – good

So much has happened to us in the past eighteen years and most
of it has been shared experiences. It's amazing really when you
think about it. I remember it all, don't you? All that time we spent
on those two swings in your back garden daring each other to
touch the sun. The time you picked up Sarah Potter's dog
Franko's dog-doo and wrapped it in a Cadbury's wrapper and left
it on Terry the Tourist's gatepost and he picked it up and when
he realized what it was he wiped his hand on his jacket and
screamed like a girl. I wee'd myself laughing. When we snuck out
of our bedrooms in the middle of the night and met Gar and
Declan in the golf club and we stayed out most of the night. The
first time we ever drank together and you kept repeating, 'Follow,'
and bursting out laughing as though it was hilarious. These are
the memories that will keep us close when we are far away from
each other, these are the memories that keep you close to me now.

Well, I might as well admit it, you were right about Colm. He
tried to kiss me on Monday night so give yourself a big round of
applause. I'm really pissed off. I told him time and time again
that I only liked him as a friend, and after our conversation last
week I really thought he'd got me but he hadn't. There was a
bonfire in the woods at midnight so we left work together and
walked through the woods and as we were walking he started
acting weird. One minute we're happily talking about a funny
incident in the restaurant and the next minute he's telling me
that I'm making a mistake with Declan and I'm too young to be
thinking about settling down. I couldn't believe it. First I've never
said anything about settling down (that I can remember and it's
incredibly uncool to bring up something disclosed by a drunk
person who has admitted time and time again to memory loss),
and second, who is a sixteen-year-old to tell an eighteen-year-old

what's what? And please don't side with him. I know your views about life and love but you spend another two years with Ben and then talk to me about moving on. Anyway, I told him it was none of his business and he said it was because he was really into me and then he kissed me. One minute we're talking and the next his tongue is down my throat. I pushed him off and I was hopping mad. He apologized because he could see I was steaming but I really wasn't in the mood to hear it. He told me he'd never try it again and that he just thought that if we kissed I'd see that we could be good together. I've kept telling him over and over since I arrived that I only saw him as a friend and that I had a boyfriend, so how stupid does he have to be? And I know you saw it coming and you'll say, well, that's boys for you, but come on. I was nice to him, I liked him, he was my friend – does that mean I led him on? Because seriously, as we were getting close to the bonfire that's what he said. He walked off in a huff and I just didn't have the heart to go to the party so I came back here. My head was bursting with our argument, I kept thinking about it over and over and what I should have said and where it had all gone wrong. He hasn't really spoken to me since. Work is weird. He's being polite but he won't make eye contact and there's no laughing and messing around any more. Ellen noticed but she's staying out of it. Besides, she's really wrapped up in Orfeo. They spend most of their time together in his hotel accommodation when we're off, and when we're working the restaurant has got so busy that she's run off her feet as head waitress. So in one week our little gang seems to have fallen to pieces. It's sad and I'm sad. I wish I was home with you and Declan but it's only another month. I can do another month.

On the bright side Clooney arrived and he came to the restaurant yesterday. He's in great form and looking good. He must be lying out by the tent all day because he's the colour of Danny's old mahogany desk. His friends seem nice, Marty and Vince, but Vince's girlfriend Pauline seems a bit snobby. I met them for drinks after work last night and I was having a laugh with the boys and she was giving me daggers. She looks at me like I'm dog-doo on her shoe and she definitely doesn't share my sense of humour. It's really timely that Clooney is here, seeing as Colm isn't talking to me and Ellen is so busy shagging that she doesn't have time for anyone else. The minute her relationship gets serious she drops her friends.

I have a day off tomorrow so Clooney has asked me to go boating with them. I said I wouldn't go because of Pauline, but Clooney said not to mind her, she wasn't going because she hated the water. Then he announced to the lads that I was going with them and suddenly she wasn't afraid of the water at all and she's now going, which is painful because it's bad enough being in her company in a large bar, never mind a small boat. Clooney thinks it's hilarious and made that cat miaowing sound which I hate and it drives me mad. I only met her yesterday and in one day she decided she hated me. What a bitch.

I phoned my mother on Sunday. She's seeing someone!!!! Can you believe it? I can't really. I think she might be hallucinating. She says he's from the UK and he's over in Ireland for six months working on a thesis on (you've guessed it) religious devotion but here's the kicker – he's not a Catholic, it's a broad paper on all religions and their followers. He sounds like a smart guy and she says that what started off as a fight on the church grounds turned into lunch, then dinner and she's seeing him again. She sounded really giddy on the phone and it was nice to hear her in such good form. His name is Albert. I hope he sticks around for a while – it would be nice to see her happy.

OK, that's it. I'm off to see the wizard.

I love you and miss you and wish everyone was as easy to read as you and everyone just said it like it is like you do.

Lily

XXXXOOOOXXXX

PS I showed Colm a picture of you (before the fight) and he said you were a bang, which is country-speak for beautiful.

PPS I've learned how to make quiche so I'll make it for our picnic on the cliff. Remember that time we got stoned up there with Paul and Gar and you ran around singing 'The Sound Of Music?' Still laugh at that.

One last thing. Rate these horror films in order of preference: Friday The 13th, Fright Night, The Lost Boys, Nightmare on Elm Street.

Mine are as follows:

1. *The Lost Boys (because Corey Haim is so cute singing in the bath and I love the granddad: 'One thing about living in Santa Carla I never could stomach, all the damn vampires.')*
2. *Friday The 13th (because it was my first horror, I was staying over, your dad made sausage rolls and let us stay up watching it until after midnight)*
3. *Fright Night (I love vampires)*
4. *Nightmare on Elm Street (because it was amazing but it gave me nightmares for a whole month afterwards)*

XXXOOOXXX

Every morning started at five. Eve's dreams were often interrupted by the sound of buffing. The steady hum of the machine gliding across the floor outside her door would invade whatever reality she had created in her head. The first time it was during a particularly weird and vivid dream. The Ginger Monster's appearances weren't as spectacular as they had once been. Once in a while he was reduced to a drunk. When he appeared that morning it was only to dance on her grave. He was doing a jig and he was wearing Michael Flatley-type attire, which made her smile even as he hornpiped his way around her headstone and back in time for his big finish. What Eve found more disconcerting than the dancing drunk was the writing on her headstone:

Spinster? Really? Ah, come on. It would appear that even in REM sleep Eve identified herself as a businesswoman and bitch. She agreed that the world would be better off without her and a few billion others, due to overpopulation, but the word *spinster* really stuck in her craw. *I don't want to die single.* She was contemplating the words on her headstone when the Ginger Monster seemed to reboot. He faced forward, his arms tight by his side and his legs began to hop wildly. *All right, all right, I've seen the show.* It was then that she heard the steady hum in the background and turned in time to see a swarm of bees approaching. They moved through the blue sky, and as they did, they seemed to swallow it whole so that light became darkness. She pictured outlandishly large heads, on tiny bee bodies, with large open mouths that held nothing but two sharp teeth, darkness and death. *Huh, well, I'm already dead so . . .* She looked round to the Ginger Monster who was too busy attempting a two-hand reel by himself to notice the sky had disappeared down the gullets of the killer bees and that they were heading straight for him. The hum grew louder and louder until eventually he looked up and screamed so loudly that Eve had to cover her ears. She was waiting for him to disappear but instead she woke to see the face of the woman who had been buffing the floor.

'You were screaming, darling,' she said.

'Sorry.'

'Would you like me to get a nurse?'

'No, thanks.'

The woman left her to return to sleep. The floor-buffing had become a sort of alarm clock. The sound infiltrated her dreams. Sometimes her brain allowed her to recognize it as a signal to wake and recalibrate. *Oh, I'm not in the chocolate factory licking cherry wallpaper, I'm in a hospital bed, and that noise isn't the revving of the Wonka's wondrous boat it's that damned buffer. Oh, no, it's five o'clock!* One eye would open then both, to reveal that she was in the small room, with the white walls that she stared at every day and the tattered poster she knew by heart:

The Message Is the Same in Any Language!

Operite Ruke
Lavarsi le Mani
Lavese las Manos
Xin Hay Rura Tay

WASH YOUR HANDS

To her left was a large window with a sill wide enough to sit on comfortably. It looked out on to the staff car park. The habit had formed in the first few days: Eve would open one eye followed by the second, glance at the poster and read it, then look out of the window to see if any doctors or nurses were coming or going. If there was nothing to see she'd close her eyes. It was only then that she'd consider whether or not her body felt better or worse than the day before. Some days it didn't wake up for a minute or two after her brain. The first time she woke and couldn't feel a thing from the neck down, she panicked, but she quickly got used to the numbness and was grateful for it in lieu of the torturous pain she'd endured. On other days her body seemed to be waiting for the buffer to wake her: as soon as she opened one eye, the skin on her right leg began to crawl, and by the time her second eye was open the itch was so bad that she tore at the plaster hoping by some miracle that her fingers would break through so that she could scratch the healing wounds that lay beneath its solid surface. Sometimes her shoulder ached so badly that she considered what life would be like without her left arm. Can you amputate a shoulder? The dull pain in her left leg was bothersome but once it was covered with blankets, and as long as nobody leaned heavily on the bed or made any attempt to put anything near it, she felt comfortable enough.

On the weeks that Lily was working she'd wake up to her and a thermometer. 'Good morning, sunshine,' Lily would say.

'Morning, Lil.'

'How you feeling?'

'Bored, frustrated, sore, decrepit and insanely itchy.'

'Did Clooney bring you that cast-scratcher?'

'He found it online. They say that you can bend it as much as you want and it won't break.'

'And he broke it?'

'Didn't even get to scratch once.'

They'd talk while Lily worked but all too soon she'd have to move on to another patient.

'You're all good. I'll see you for your bed-bath later.'

Then she'd be gone and Eve would be truly awake. She'd read that stupid poster, look out of the window, then turn on the TV, watch some morning show where people were unreasonably happy about badly made clothes and ponder on the long day that stretched ahead. She wouldn't be able to relax until physio was over. The dread would kick in as soon as she'd been served breakfast because once that was over it would be less than an hour until Mica or the other physio, Norman, would come through the door and the torment would begin. At least Mica had a sense of humour.

'Come on, four more and you can punch me in the arm,' she'd say.

'Five more and I can punch you in the face.'

'Sorry, the face is too pretty.'

'I'll be the judge of that!'

Norman was serious, and although he was kinder, he wasn't any fun. Also when he moved her he'd insist on doing so after counting down in Irish – *a h-aon, a dó, a trí* – before each lift.

'Are you ready? *A h-aon, a dó, a trí!*'

Oh, just do it.

'OK, here we go. *A h-aon, a dó, a trí!*'

'That's very annoying,' she said one day. 'Do you know that?'

'I do now,' he said, but it didn't deter him when he moved her back into bed. 'Are you right? *A h-aon, a dó, a trí!*'

'Annoying bastard,' she mumbled.

He chose to ignore her.

Physiotherapy was over by eleven thirty. After that came lunch at twelve and once lunch was over Eve would watch the TV, the wall or the window until Clooney came in around two. He'd stay till about four and then, if Gina couldn't get in or if Lily was too busy to call or not working, she'd revert to watching the TV, the window or the wall. She read fashion magazines but even they became boring, and there weren't enough to keep her occupied.

Adam checked on Eve's progress most days. 'Can you move your arm for me?'

'No.'

'Excuse me?'

'If you wanted to see my arm move, you should have been here when *A h-aon, a dó, a trí* was here because that's torture time and you're two hours too late.'

'*A h-aon, a dó, a tri?*' he said, laughing.

'You know who I mean,' she said.

'I do. Come on, no resistance, just show me a little movement, please,' he said.

'God almighty,' she said, but she moved her arm and he was pleased.

'I don't think we'll have to go back in. It was touch and go but, because I'm a genius, *A h-aon, a dó, a trí* is persistent and you're a fighter, things are looking good.'

She had come to enjoy his little visits. Sometimes Lily was there too and the three of them sparred with each other like old friends.

'Is she still demanding to be taken to the toilet?' he asked Lily one day.

'She won't drop it, but it's too soon for her to go by herself.'

'I'm right here,' Eve said.

'How are her stools?' he asked, with a grin.

'Jesus Christ. Right, that's it, both of you, out!' Eve said.

Lily and Adam laughed, pleased with themselves and their childish toilet humour.

Not so funny when you're sitting on a bedpan and supporting your entire body weight with one arm, bastards!

'How much longer will I be in here?' Eve asked them one day.

'At least another month,' Adam said.

'No,' Eve said.

Adam looked at Lily and they grinned.

'Yes,' Adam said.

'Look, here's the deal. I'm giving you three more weeks to get me mobile. After that I'm leaving.'

'That's not a deal, that's an ultimatum,' Lily said.

'Really, Lily?'

'A deal suggests we get something back,' Adam said.

'OK, you make me better in three weeks and I'll buy you a new car, Lil, and I'll help you pick out a more suitable one, Adam.'

'What's wrong with my car?' Adam said.

'Nothing. It's just not you.'

'Oh, and you know me?'

'I know that you're tall and awkward, and no matter how far you shove the seat back you look like Sideshow Bob driving around in his little clown car.'

'Oh, it's so good to have her back!' Lily laughed.

Adam thought about what she'd said. 'Caroline talked me into buying that car,' he said.

'The ex you wouldn't marry?' Eve said.

Adam looked at Lily, who shrugged. 'She asked,' she said.

'Yes, the ex I wouldn't marry.'

'Are you holding on to it because you think she'll come back?'

'No.'

'So get rid of it and buy something you fit into,' she said. 'Even better, get me out of here.'

'Let's have you sitting on a toilet first and we'll see how we go from there,' he said.

As her facial wounds healed, she became more conscious of the way she looked and smelt. Clooney had been instructed to bring in her creams and perfumes but she still couldn't wear any normal clothes. Clooney added to her collection of shawls, all of which he bought in a light silk: Eve thought that if the Ginger Monster hadn't killed her, the heat in the hospital would. Her hair was a mess and needed cutting. She had Clooney contact her hairdresser, who came to her room. It was an ordeal but Nick was a total pro. Lily helped lift her into a wheelchair, then pushed her into the bathroom. Eve leaned as far as she could over the bath for him to wash it, guarding her damaged arm and praying it wouldn't knock against anything. He handled the shower head very carefully, but they both got soaked. Then she sat in her room while he cut and styled her hair. It was a sharp cut and she had lost weight so her face appeared strikingly angular.

'You could have been a model,' he said.

'You mean before I was ravaged?' she said with a smile.

'So you've a scar on your face. Harrison Ford has a scar and *hello?*'

The stitches were gone and her lip was back to its normal shape. That scar was on the inside so it couldn't be seen. The area around her eye was back to normal, aside from some light yellow bruising and an angry pink line that measured three centimetres across her left cheek.

'Do you think I should wear makeup?' she asked, pissed off that she faced the possibility of having to put it on every day for the rest of her life. *Just when I've retired. What a pain . . .*

'Not yet. You're still healing,' he said.

'I know but . . .'

'But what?' he said.

'Nothing,' she said.

'Are you interested in someone in here?'

'Oh, don't be ridiculous, Nick!'

'Oh, my God. You are!'

'I am not.'

'You're going red.'

'That's anger, frustration and the damned heat in this place.'

Nick had known Eve, years before, when they were both training in London. He had done the hair and makeup for a lot of her jewellery shoots at college. They were both equally ambitious, both Irish, and both workers. They had got on from the start and he was one of the few people she had missed when she left for Paris. When she had returned to Dublin the previous year she'd looked him up. In the years between he had become very successful in the UK before returning home to set up a high-end salon in Dublin. When he wasn't on photo shoots, fashion shows or working on ad campaigns, he was in his salon. He was an old and good friend but his time was limited as Eve's had once been. They didn't socialize but Nick knew her well enough to detect that she was hiding something now.

'OK, whatever you say,' he said.

'I just don't want to look like damaged goods.'

'You're not damaged goods.'

'I'm the definition of damaged goods,' she said.

Eve's window had become a source of fascination for her. She started to identify the faces and cars, timings and rituals of the hospital staff. There was a nurse she called Patty because she could never just get out of her car, lock it and walk inside. She'd get out, pat her handbag, lock the door, walk about two metres, pat her bag again, turn round and either reopen the car and get something or go back and check the door to ensure it was locked. Patty was a great source of distraction on the days she was working and it was better watching her than staring at a fly on the wall.

She'd watch Adam come and go. He always parked his silly car in the same spot. Doctors had designated parking – she had to pay closer attention to the nurses because they parked where they could and there were a few bays out of sight. Adam would get out of the car and lock it. He'd never check himself or fix his hair or double-check to see if the car was locked. He was just in and out, except when he met someone coming the other way, which was most days. He seemed to know more people in the hospital than anyone else – either that or he was just friendly or sat on more medical boards. He'd stop and talk, and Eve would wonder who the other person was and what they were talking about. Sometimes the conversations were short, sometimes a little longer. Eve saw him with Lily a couple of times. Lily was always harassed. She leaped out of her car and a couple of times it appeared that she had forgotten to lock it. Lily was a runner. She'd run from the car to the hospital and back. The only time she stopped was when she met Adam, who sauntered. He'd stop her and they'd talk for a minute or two before Lily ran in.

One morning when Eve was gazing outside she saw Declan Donovan for the first time in twenty years. He was parking his car and the top was down so she recognized him at once, but initially she didn't trust her eyes. The car was a Mercedes – she wasn't sure what class as she'd never been too interested in cars. Lily drove a Volkswagen Polo that was five years old and had a dent in its rear bumper – the result of Scott driving into a post on his first and last lesson with his mother, she had told Eve. The Merc was new and eye-catching. Even from a distance she could see the cream interior before Declan put up the top and got out. He shrugged into his suit jacket before he closed the door, then brushed it down and looked at himself to make sure it wasn't crumpled. *That is you, isn't it?* He strode confidently towards her. The closer he came to the doorway three floors under her, the surer she became. *Oh, God, yes, it is you!* Her heart-rate increased, her pulse shot up. *I feel sick. Oh, Eve, seriously? Puking is a tad over-dramatic, don't you think?* Apparently not: Eve puked over herself.

It was Lily who cleaned her up. 'What brought this on? Has Clooney been feeding you on the sly? You know you can only have hospital-sanctioned food.'

'No,' Eve said, but when she focused on Lily's question, she reconsidered. 'Well, yes, of course he has. I can't be expected to live on the slop I get in here – but I'm not sick, I'm fine.'

'Your pulse is elevated. Are you in pain?'

'No.'

'Headache?'

'I always have a headache.'

'That's not right. I'm going to call Adam.'

'Please don't.'

'I'm calling Adam.'

'Crap.'

Lily had confided in Eve that Adam was the only real friend she had had in many a long year and that she was worried he had developed feelings for her. She didn't want to lose him but she wasn't interested in him sexually, and wouldn't have been even if she wasn't married. Eve had known straight away that he wasn't to Lily's taste – she knew it because, even in her fragile state, he was most definitely to her own. He was tall and lean, not particularly broad but muscular. He had the body of a long-distance runner. He had a head of floppy brown hair that seemed to do its own thing. She wondered if he even had to brush it. Some days his eyes looked brown and other days they were green. She wondered if that had something to do with the light, the weather or his mood. He had a wide smile and good teeth. He dressed with flair – his suits were always a little different and stood out from the pinstripe, grey, black and navy brigade. His shirts were coloured or patterned, never white and never boring. He had fashion sense, which others saw as odd or, as in Declan's case, gay, but Eve approved. *Damn, I look like hell.*

Adam came about an hour later. Eve's pulse had steadied and she was no longer nauseous. He looked at her chart. Since she had moved into her room he had begun sitting down whenever he visited her, and as the time passed, his visits increased and so did the time he spent sitting by her bedside. Initially he gave Eve extra attention because she was Lily's mystery friend. He was loyal to Lily and he liked Eve being the secret he helped her keep from Declan. Adam couldn't stand Declan because he didn't like the way he treated Lily. *If I had a woman like her I'd treat her like a goddess.* After those first five or six days, when Eve had been so out of it that she was simply a set of healing bones, he began to like her. She was a smart mouth. She didn't suffer fools gladly. She wouldn't be talked down to. *No wonder she and Declan don't get on.*

'I don't like these headaches,' he said.

'So turn down the heat in this place,' she said.

'It's not that hot.'

'I could grow marijuana in here.'

He laughed. 'Tell me about the headaches.'

'Well,' she said, 'they're basically pains in my head.'

'I can see why you and Lily are such good friends. Do they affect one or both sides of your head?'

'Both.'

'Is the pain pulsating, or a pressure, or a tightening pain?'

'Pressure.'

'Would you describe it as moderate or severe?'

'Moderate.'

'On a scale of one to ten, assign numbers to moderate and severe.'

'Oh, for God's sake!'

'Just do it.'

'Moderate is a four or five and severe is nine or ten. My arm is usually around nine, my right leg zero, my left leg four to six and my head is three to seven, depending on the moment, minute or hour.'

'Do you feel nauseous?'

'Sometimes.' *A lot and especially when I see that prick Declan.*

'Are you sensitive to light and sound?'

'Sometimes.' *Like now.*

'Any stiff neck, confusion, double vision, weakness or numbness?'

'No.'

He asked another hundred questions and she answered no to all of them.

'Any changes in personality recently?'

'I curse more.'

'You curse more,' he said, nodding and smiling.

'Yeah, I'm not sure if it's because I'm back in Ireland or if it's because I'm crippled but the word "fuck" sounds so much better to me now than it did when I lived in the States.'

'That aside,' Adam said, 'I think you're suffering from chronic tension or daily persistent headaches. I could send you for some neurological testing to be sure. '

'No need. I got the all-clear recently and the headaches haven't changed since then.'

'I'm going to prescribe you something for them and then I'm going to open the window.'

'No.'

'Why?'

'There's a weird smell.'

He opened the window and put his face outside. He pulled back. 'There's no smell,' he said.

'It comes and goes.'

He leaned out. 'Well, there's a vent just below and to the left of you. It could be coming from that. I'll have Maintenance take a look.'

'OK.'

'And,' he said, 'I've been looking at a new car.'

'Good for you.'

'I'm thinking a BMW.'

'As long as you can fit in it, buy it,' she said.

He smiled. 'OK,' he said, and left her alone to stare out into the car park and admit to herself that she was attracted to Adam. Adam, who was not only her doctor – *Eve, the bloody great cliché!* – he was Lily's friend and clearly had a crush on her. Not to mention that Ben Logan wasn't even cold in the ground. *I don't love him or anything, Ben. I just like him. He's nice and you're dead and, besides, life is short. I don't want to die alone and you were never even mine. I miss you, though. I hope that if you're conscious, somewhere in the universe or beyond, it's a good place full of love, light and happiness and not a fucking hothouse where you spend day after day hovering on bedpans and looking at morning TV, walls and a car park.*

It was just after six when she watched Declan make his way to his car. Then she turned to the wall. The poster hadn't changed.

She turned on the TV. The news was on. Clooney would return at seven thirty with a new perfume. She had worn Chanel No. 5 all of her adult life but she couldn't stand the smell any more. She'd sent him to find something new so that she could wear it when Paul came with his fiancée, Simone. She didn't like meeting new people, her head hurt, she was pissed off that she liked Adam and that Lily's week off was starting and she'd made it clear she couldn't visit as much. Eve hadn't asked but she knew it was because of Declan. He had been playing on her mind, going so far as to take the Ginger Monster's place in some of her more disquieting dreams.

Days blended with little to define one from another. Eve's car-park watch now revolved around Declan. Once she witnessed Lily collide with him. It was at an odd time. Lily had forgotten something in her car and was heading towards it and Declan had just parked. It was after midday. Sometimes on a Tuesday or a Wednesday Declan didn't arrive to the hospital until after midday. Eve surmised he had consulting rooms elsewhere. Lily never really went to the car park in the middle of the day and it was unusual for her to forget something. When they met, Eve watched them talk to one another. They seemed distant but polite – that is, until Declan seemed to grab Lily's arm aggressively. Lily pulled away easily so he couldn't have hurt her but it upset Eve. She wanted to jump out of bed and yell out of the window, *Keep your hands off her!* But she couldn't walk, never mind jump, and it wasn't her business anyway. She did ask Lily about it but Lily brushed her off.

'Oh, he was just being playful. I wasn't in the mood.'

Eve knew she was lying, and Lily knew that Eve knew she was lying, and they left it at that.

When Clooney came later that evening it was the first thing she said to him.

'Do you think Declan's a wife-beater?'

'You mean, do I think Lily's a battered wife?'

'Same thing,' she said.

'No, it's not. I don't know Declan, I know Lily, and there's no way she'd put up with getting beaten.'

'Yeah. I suppose you're right,' she said, 'but then again I know Declan better than you do and I think he has it in him.'

After Eve had said that, Clooney confided in her about Lily's reaction to her husband's phone call the night they were having dinner.

'You had dinner together?' Eve said.

'Didn't Lily tell you?'

'No, she did not.'

'Probably too small a detail.'

Bullshit, she thought. *Now, Clooney is exactly Lily's type. If, of course, she wasn't a happily married woman.*

Eve became stronger. The first time she went to the toilet she was wheeled in, and although a nurse had to hold her, she pulled her own pants down and insisted on being left alone to do her business. It was only when she screamed, 'Oh, no, shit on my hand, shit on my hand!' that the nurse appeared.

When the sun was at its hottest Clooney began to take her into the hospital gardens and there they'd sit for hours, people-watching and enjoying the sun, the flowers, the smell of the grass and each other's company. Eve was finding inventive ways to make her one good arm work for her. Adam was still concerned about her headaches but her shoulder, he'd said, was making a remarkable recovery, and after the first two weeks of resistance she had come to an understanding with her physiotherapists. She worked tirelessly on her shoulder and her left leg. She spent more time out of bed and in her electric wheelchair. She zipped around the corridors, stopping to chat with Marion, Abby and all the other nurses she'd come to know. She steered clear of the canteen because Lily had mentioned once she was meeting Declan there and Eve was terrified of bumping into him. Clooney would bring in picnic supplies from her favourite deli and, when she wasn't feeling nauseous from the smell that nobody seemed able to do anything about, they'd eat outside on fine days and in the conservatory when it was wet. Her friends came and went, less often as the time went on but she still saw most of them twice a week.

Simone had been a revelation. Eve had never met Paddy, but Gina maintained he was very like Paul – quiet, closed off and sometimes cold. Gina suspected that Paddy hadn't liked her and Gar, and she was right. Paddy had had nothing against them – they just had nothing in common. Eve knew this because, in a rare candid moment, Paul had said as much. 'He would have liked you, though,' he'd added.

Simone, on the other hand, was an open book. Simone was beautiful to look at but there was a softness to her features that Eve hadn't seen in other models. She was extremely excited to meet Paul's friends, if a little disappointed that Gar hadn't made it. Gina produced a dreadful excuse and turned red. She always overcomplicated her lies, turning them into tall tales that had no beginning, middle or end. She'd start strong but end up mumbling, hoping someone would intervene and stop her. Paul did so by complimenting her on her dress. She blushed again, and Simone noticed. She hugged her and told her she was really pleased to meet her because Paul had spoken so highly of her. That shocked Gina, but Simone was either a much better liar or had been speaking the truth, and Gina chose to believe the latter. Simone did seem to know an awful lot about Paul's friends. Even Clooney was startled when she talked to him about the places he'd been and the work he did. Either she was a politician in a model's body with an eidetic memory or Paul had opened up to her more than he ever had with any of his friends over the many years he had known them. He seemed more relaxed around her – he touched her and leaned on her, laughed more easily and spoke more in longer sentences. It was interesting to watch. Meanwhile, Gina and Simone got on like a house on fire, destined to be friends for life. *Funny old world.*

Gar sometimes visited Eve at lunchtime. He'd sit and eat a panini or ciabatta roll and sip a takeaway coffee while she picked at her hospital food.

'It's not that bad,' he'd say.

'It's not that good either.'

'Want half my panini?'

'No, but thanks.'

Gar noticed the smallest improvements in Eve and he was very encouraging. He always made her feel better, reminding her that there was light at the end of the tunnel.

That's a light I'm not ready to see yet, buddy.

When she got bored she'd bring up Paul. 'Have you spoken to him yet?'

'Nothing to say.'

'That's a bit childish.'

'You think?'

'Yip.'

'I'm not even angry any more,' he said one day, 'just disappointed.'

'I understand. He's your friend, you thought you knew him.'

'Exactly. Gina says I'm making a big deal out of it.'

'I think he didn't know who he was for so long that, when he finally realized or accepted it, he felt silly – that, combined with a personality so private he doesn't tell himself his own secrets. It has nothing to do with how he sees you as a friend.'

Gar laughed. 'He was always like that even as a kid. I'd ask him how he did on a test and he'd say bad or good – he'd never give the actual mark. When we were teenagers he'd disappear and we'd never know where he was, until he'd just turn up. We all decided he had this amazing sex life, with girls from different towns and villages, but he never said a word.'

'Lily and I used to call him the virgin-taker.'

'Did he even have sex with any of those girls?'

'I've no idea,' Eve said. 'Probably not. Can you imagine if Paddy was the first person he had sex with?'

'Oh, that makes perfect sense. No wonder he fell in love.'

'You see? We're doing it again.'

They talked about Simone, that she seemed nice and Paul was happy, comfortable and different around her. Gar worried that Gina was getting too close. 'After all, they're not married yet and the way things are going he could run off with the priest next.'

Gar felt better when he was laughing about his friend, not because he enjoyed being cruel but because it was a release from feeling like a fool. He couldn't help but focus on all the time he and Paul had spent together over the years and, although he had confided in Paul, his friend had locked him out, like an unwanted visitor. He also wondered why he hadn't noticed this before. *Was it because I thought he was having sex with men and I just didn't want to know? What does that say about me? And why does it matter so much?* Also, it bothered Gar that Paul knew he was pissed off and had made no effort to approach or appease him.

'You know what he's like,' Eve echoed Gina's mantra.

'It's not good enough,' Gar said.

'He's not going to apologize for not telling you his business until he was ready to tell you his business, so get over it and be friends or get over it and don't,' she said one day, looking over his shoulder to see who was coming and going in the car park. She saw Declan pull into his spot and pointed. 'There's Declan.'

Gar nearly broke his neck turning round. When the car was parked and Declan was getting out, Gar got out of his seat and stood by the window staring down. Eve warned him not to get caught. They were a little excited, like two kids doing something they shouldn't. When he looked up and stared straight at the window, as though he felt someone looking at him, Gar spun round to face Eve. 'He's looking, he's looking, he's looking!'

He sat down and they laughed at their foolishness, sure that he hadn't really seen Gar and aware that Lily hadn't told him Eve was in the hospital.

Gar had stopped wondering a long time ago why Declan had walked away from his life and friends. 'Another one I didn't know,' he said.

That's for sure, Eve thought.

Lily met Gar a few times while she was working. She'd stop in and say hello. Gar had always liked Lily – she had a calming effect on Declan, who was highly strung and competitive, which made him a great rugby player but a bit of a hothead off the pitch. Lily could make him laugh at himself. He relaxed when she walked into any room. They were a good couple. Gar had been jealous of him back then. Declan and Paul were the stars on the pitch, Gar always lagging behind. Paul had any girl he wanted, or didn't want, and Declan had Lily.

When Gar had gone out with Eve, he thought he had finally matched up to the two boys, but Eve wasn't interested, and because Gar had had no confidence back then, he had supposed the problem was his. They made good friends but they had zero chemistry. She was beautiful and they had good fun as long as they weren't kissing because kissing Eve was like kissing a wall. It was only when he and Eve parted and he kissed other girls that he understood it wasn't him or her – just that Eve and Gar were never going to work. He was with her to compete with the lads and she was with him because he was one of the few boys who wasn't afraid to ask her out.

Poor Gar had never felt quite good enough and, if he was honest with himself, that was why Declan's desertion had caused him so much pain. *The first chance he has to get away from me, he does.* And why Paul's lie of omission hurt so much. *I'm a fill-in for Declan and clearly a pretty poor one.* Gina had done her best to rid Gar of his insecurities, but as hard as she worked at pointing out how great he was, there was always something in the back of his mind that told him he wasn't. He always looked at what other people had achieved and compared himself unfavourably.

To all who knew him, he seemed at ease with himself and content with his lot, and he was, for the most part. That was one of the reasons he and Gina hadn't gone crazy in the boom years and racked up ridiculous debt. When others were buying holiday homes abroad and bigger ones in Ireland, he was happy with his house. He didn't need a new car and he didn't like to go on holiday anywhere more than once. *What's the point in that?* But that didn't stop him placing greater worth in others than in himself because a little part of him had always hoped his life would be larger than it turned out to be. 'Just be content to be content,' Gina had counselled many times.

'What are you thinking about?' Eve asked, when he had slipped into silence for an awfully long time.

'You can't change people,' he said.

'No, you can't.'

'We are what we are,' he said.

'That's right.'

They had a few lunches together when they did very little talking and instead watched TV. He'd bring Eve a takeaway coffee and sometimes a slice of cake even though she'd told him not to. Clooney enjoyed it with afternoon tea.

Clooney and Lily became closer that month too. They'd find a place in the hall or a space in an old TV room to have a chat. They never discussed Declan or even the kids. They'd talk about everyday things over a coffee or a shared slice of cake that Gar had brought Eve or a muffin that Clooney would pick up in a coffee shop. Chocolate-chip was her favourite. Eve often slept for an hour in the afternoons and it was then that he and Lily would catch up. They were both relaxed in one another's company – they had grown up together, after all. They knew and cared about each other.

Clooney had forgotten how well she knew him.

'The sale of Danny's house fell through,' he said one day.

'Oh, no! I thought it was a done deal.'

'The guy lost his job just as they were about to draw down the loan.'

'Oh, the poor man!'

'I suppose so. To be honest, I was thinking, Screw him. Now I have to deal with the house.'

'I love that house.'

'Great. Do you want to buy it?'

'You and Eve are lucky, you find it easy to let go.'

'So do you,' he said. 'After all, you let us go.'

She nodded sadly. 'I didn't feel like I had a choice. It's not something I'm proud of.' *If I knew I was set to leave this earth soon, would I do it all differently?*

He didn't push it. He hated to see her sad so he changed the subject. 'Maybe we'll keep it. I might move back here some day,' he said.

'You're just saying that to avoid doing anything that involves money or solicitors – you wouldn't last a year here,' she said.

'How do you know that?'

'You used to give me your pocket money because thinking about what to spend it on would stress you out,' she said, giggling.

'Nah, I just wanted you to have it.'

'Don't worry,' she said. 'Eve will be back on her feet sooner than anyone thinks and she'll take over.'

'I'm counting on it,' he said. She squeezed his hand and left him to go back to work. Clooney watched her walk away. *If I had you, Lily, would I ever let you go?* Deep down he knew he would, but she'd make it hard.

In the month that passed after Declan returned from London, things in the Donovan household began to change dramatically. Initially he had sulked because of the phone incident, even though Lily had made a decent effort at lying. She told him she had gone for a walk and her phone had run out of juice. It was simple but plausible. It shouldn't have led to any further questions or drama, but of course it did.

'You never walk.'

'Because I never have time to walk.'

'Oh, I take up so much of your time that you can't go for a simple walk, is that what you're saying?'

'No, Declan, that's what *you're* saying. I'm saying I went for a walk.'

'I don't believe you.'

'I don't care,' she said.

'Excuse me?' he said.

'You heard me, Declan. I don't give a shit. I'm a grown woman, and if I want to leave my house and have a walk, I will, and you won't dictate to me what I can and can't do or where I can and can't go. Those days are over.'

She had never said anything like that to her husband before, primarily because she'd never admitted to herself that he had taken total control of her life.

Bugger-balls, bugger-balls, bugger-balls. What have I done? OK, just be calm, it's OK, it's fine. Everything is great, everything is lovely, and everything is fantastic. What am I doing? If I knew I was set to leave this earth soon, would I do it all differently? Jesus, Lily, stop saying that!

Declan had been with Lily since he was sixteen years old. He knew her inside and out, he had been party to every smile, laugh, cry, moan, whinge, every grimace, every lie and every truth for so many years. He knew Lily better than she knew herself. He had started to spot the changes in her during the days and weeks preceding his trip to London. She'd always had a smart mouth but she was becoming more cutting by the day. She wasn't as tolerant of his idiosyncrasies. He was a worrier, she knew that. He liked things in order. He liked routine. He liked to know where his wife was and who she was with. *Why the hell is that suddenly a crime?*

Not to mention that she liked routine, things in order, and she was the one who had instigated her own routines. It was Lily's planner on the fridge, not Declan's. He wasn't some sort of keeper, but he deserved to know her location at any given time. He was her husband. She was his wife. She had her duties and he had his.

Lately she had been remiss most of the time. She appeared bored when he talked and she didn't seem to notice when he was down. The last good chat they'd had together was when she was exhausted in the bath and he had presented her with the gold bangle. *What the hell does she want from me?* The night at Rodney's had been alarming. She would normally have made an effort to be pleasant but she had gone into that house looking for a fight. Alice had nearly died of mortification when Lily had told her to send her dress back. She wasn't used to Lily's sharp tongue, and Rodney had confided in him later that she had vowed never to have Lily in her house again. Rodney was Declan's only real friend and he had been disgusted that Lily had caused a rift. When he said so to her she was gleeful.

'Good. She can give it out but she can't take it.'

He was hurt that she was so pleased to have caused difficulty between him and Rodney. Of course they could see each other on the golf course or in any number of situations but warring wives would cause problems. She couldn't see how upset it made him or if she did she didn't care. *She's jealous, Lily. Why couldn't you just suck it up?*

Then she had thrown the pan at the wall and told her family the kitchen was closed. Now she did one breakfast each day and never asked him what it should be. One morning he had woken to a bowl of *porridge*. The kids hadn't even attempted to eat it. Again his wife hadn't seemed to care.

'Eat it or leave it,' she said, and left her family sitting there like stunned mullets.

'Is Mum having a breakdown?' Daisy had asked.

'No,' he'd said, 'she's just tired.'

'I'll grab something with Granddad,' Scott said, getting up. 'We usually take a break for a natter and a roll around ten anyway.'

Every time Declan's son said something that showed his relationship with his granddad was a world away from the pain he had endured, it was like a knife in Declan's chest. He put on a happy face for Scott, and Lily knew how much it hurt, but she didn't bring it up. She had divested him of her interest, care or consideration. Their sex life was worse than ever. Lily lay there like a cold fish. He hadn't tied her up because of her shoulder injury, but if he had, she'd have made him feel skeevy, not sexy. She was looking at him differently and she was pulling away. She wouldn't answer a straight question and, although she kept denying there was a problem, Declan wasn't a fool.

The first time he saw Clooney Declan had been in the canteen eating lunch with Rodney. He noticed him a few times before he recognized him. He was sitting alone in a chair directly opposite, staring straight out of the window. He was lost in his own world and Declan admired his physique – he was strong, broad, built for rugby. He wondered if he played the game. When he crossed the floor to refill his coffee mug he realized the man was familiar somehow. Declan wasn't sure if it was his eyes, face or gait that resonated but he couldn't concentrate on what Rodney was saying, and by the time he'd put a name to the face he'd had no idea what Rodney was talking about.

When Clooney had walked out of the canteen Declan had made his excuses and left Rodney to finish his lunch. Like a spy, he had followed Clooney to Lily's ward. She was off that week so his mission wouldn't be scuppered by an unwelcome encounter with his wife. Clooney disappeared into Room 8. He'd waited for the nurse to move away from her station and taken a look at the room list. Seeing Eve's name in black and white wasn't as shocking as he would have thought – seeing Clooney had softened the blow – but he felt uneasy and his hands were clammy. The hospital was suddenly too hot and stuffy. He needed air. He had gone outside and was grateful for a cool breeze. He had sat on a bench in the hospital gardens, thinking through the meaning of Eve's presence on his wife's ward. It certainly explained Lily's behaviour, her disappearances and her inability to tell him where she was or who she was with. The gourmet packed lunches every second week suddenly made sense. *She wasn't coming here for me, she was coming here for her.* The lies of omission and outright deceit were breathtaking. Lily hadn't seen Eve in twenty years but she was back, and Lily was hiding her from him. *Is it because you don't want to hurt me? Is it because I said I never wanted to see her again or hear her name spoken? Is it because you love me and you don't want to open that old can of worms? Or is it that you don't trust me? You want her back in your life. You remembered that you love her. Some friendships are for ever. Isn't that what you said to me when we were sixteen and your best friend did everything to break us up and you wouldn't choose? But eventually you did choose, Lily. You chose me. You should have told me.*

He had to work out what to do. *Say something or say nothing?* He decided to say nothing and just let it play out, but while he was doing so he'd tighten his grip on Lily. He wasn't going to let her slip away, not because of things that bitch Eve might be saying or doing. If he confronted her directly it could lead to an ugly discussion or a fight that he didn't want or need. Instead he'd make sure she was as busy as possible on her days off and keep a close eye on her when she was working.

Declan was unable to handle complex emotion. When sad, confused or troubled, his feelings usually developed into all-consuming anger. That was what had driven him to make his wife suck him off in such a disrespectful and brutal way the night before he'd left for London. Like his dad, Declan lashed out when he was hurt. *You did this to us, Lily.* But afterwards, lying alone in their bed, he had felt sick, sad, worried and sorry. *I'll make it up to you. I'll bring back something nice, Lily.* He tossed and turned all night because Eve was back and Lily was pulling away. *Oh, God, don't take her from me!*

When he returned home from London he rang her more often, and when she was in work he made more visits to her ward. He watched her try to hide her panic. *Just tell me, Lily.* He stood smiling as she squirmed, pretending he had no idea how his impromptu visits affected her. *This is killing you so just tell me, Lily.* On two occasions he had watched her sit in some cosy corner sharing cake with Clooney. He was far enough away to remain unseen but close enough to bear witness to the tenderness between them. That was when the anger and bitterness resurfaced. *You fucking slut.* When Declan was angry he became unreasonable and mean.

'You're getting fat,' he said, that evening.

'No, I'm not.'

He looked her up and down and sighed, then walked out of the room, leaving her to wonder what he was playing at.

On the weeks that she was home he'd fill every moment of every day with important jobs he needed doing, and when he ran out of things for her to do he'd offer her assistance to neighbours, like Rachel Lennon when she needed someone to look after Nancy, who was still recuperating from her eye surgery. *I'll just keep her busy until that bitch and her brother are out of our lives.*

'You told her what?' Lily had screamed.

'I told her you'd take Nancy Monday to Wednesday while she helps settle her mother into a care home,' he said calmly.

'You had no right.'

'Don't be ridiculous. The kid needs to be minded, you're home and Rachel was desperate.'

'Rachel hasn't bothered her arse speaking to me since the day I checked on Nancy in the hospital,' Lily said, seething.

Declan dismissed her, delighted that his encounter with Rachel Lennon over the recycling bins had paid off. *Let's see you go for your walks now.*

When he had time off, he'd return home, even if it was only for an hour. He'd check her phone for calls. He'd read her texts. He even went through the dirty-clothes hamper and checked her knickers to find traces of sexual excitement. He was single-minded in his mission. He would determine if Lily was cheating with her new best friend Clooney, and if she was, he'd destroy her.

The day Eve had watched Lily bump into Declan in the car park, he had seen her flirt with Clooney outside Eve's door. She had been too busy laughing to notice him.

'Where are you going?'

'My car.'

'Where are you going in your car?'

'I'm getting my lunch, which I left in the boot, if that's OK with you.'

'Since when do you bring in your own lunch?'

'Since my account is running low and I married a mean bastard.' Lily had begun to walk away and Declan grabbed her arm.

'What do you mean you've run out of money? Who did you spend it on?' he said.

She had spent it on Eve and now she was sorry she'd mentioned it. She had pulled her arm away. 'I don't ask you what you do with your millions and you've no business asking me what I do with my pittance,' she said, and went to her car.

He had stood frozen, not sure whether he should follow her and throttle her or take deep breaths and move away. He chose the latter option. He fixed himself, checked for wrinkles in his suit and walked inside, unaware that he, too, was being watched.

Lily was suffering a personal crisis. While on the one hand she was enjoying every moment she spent with Eve and Clooney, on the other something inside her had snapped. She was in flux, unable to see a way forward but sure there was no way back. The more crazily Declan behaved, the easier he made it for her to disengage. Every day that passed, every job he gave her, every cruel word he spoke chipped away at the pity and understanding that had kept her by his side all those years. Scott was a young adult, and at twelve Daisy was old enough to understand. *Wasn't she?* If she and Declan split up it would be hard on them, but if she stayed she might lose her mind. *Which is worse: divorced sane parents or married crazy ones?* She wished she could have carried on until Daisy turned eighteen but she couldn't. It was all too much. She couldn't play her part in the charade any more. She was suffering from severe anxiety, so much so that Adam had prescribed medication. She had made him promise not to tell anyone.

'What's going on?' he'd asked.

'Nothing,' she said.

'Don't tell me "nothing" and then ask me to prescribe.'

'I'm going through some things with Declan,' she said.

'I see.'

'I can't sleep.'

'And you're not eating.' He had looked at her thin frail body.

'Scraps here and there. It's hard to eat when your heart feels like it might explode.'

'Is there anything I can do?'

'You can prescribe and not say anything.'

He had written on his notepad and Lily had taken the two pieces of paper he handed her. He'd prescribed a week's supply of anti-depressants, and had scribbled down the name and phone number of a counsellor. 'She's very good,' he said.

'Thanks,' she said.

When the prescription had been filled, she'd binned the counsellor's name and didn't think about her again. *It would take one hell of a counsellor to sort my problems out.*

When she was away from work it was almost harder to keep going. She missed her daily chats with Eve – even if her friend did push her to the limit.

Eve would look her up and down. 'Something's wrong.'

'Nothing's wrong.'

'Not stupid.'

'Not wise either.'

Or:

'You look tired,' Eve would say.

'I am tired.'

'Is the fact that you're unhappy keeping you awake?'

'Mind your own business.'

Or on one occasion:

'Share my sandwich with me,' Eve said.

'No, thanks.'

'So you'll only eat cake with Clooney?' Eve had raised an eyebrow and grinned.

'It's not like that,' Lily said.

'Something's going on with you.'

'Eve. Please.'

'OK, OK,' Eve said, holding up her good hand, 'always in your own time, Lily B.'

'I'm Lily D.'

'Not to me.'

When she was at home she veered between snapping at Daisy and trying to make it up to her.

'Mum, can you find my black coat?'

'You're big enough and bold enough to look for it yourself,' she said. She was cleaning the toilet.

'Mum, will you listen to me play?' she said as Lily was leaving to go to the dry cleaner.

'Not now, Daisy.'

'Mum, when you've stopped vomiting can you make my breakfast?' she said, standing over her mother who was leaning on the toilet bowl.

'*Leave me alone!*' Lily screamed, and returned to vomiting the meagre contents of her stomach.

There were days when the child didn't even get a sentence out before she was dismissed.

'Mum.'

'Go away, Daisy.'

'But, Mum!'

'I mean it. Whatever it is, deal with it.'

The once attentive, patient, loving mother was turning into someone Daisy didn't recognize or even like very much. *Where's my mum gone?* Daisy didn't cry but her confused face was heart-breaking, and a remorseful Lily would attempt to make it up to her with gifts of her favourite sugary doughnuts, unwanted hugs and apologies. *I'm turning into Declan.*

Doing the various jobs kept her busy, and minding Nancy was an added complication to already stressful and busy days. Nancy was a dote but she liked to talk and rarely took a breath. Lily found it hard to cope with her while she was doing the washing, shopping, scrubbing and vacuuming.

'Lily, ma wha na ma wha na na.'

'*What?*' Lily shouted over the vacuum.

'Lily, ma wha na ma wha na na.'

'*What?*'

'Ma, wha, na ma wha na na.'

Lily turned off the vacuum cleaner. 'What?'

'I've seen *Pirates of the Caribbean: Dead Man's Chest* three times.'

'OK.' She turned the vacuum back on.

'Mah, Lily, it's man na na na.'

'*What?*'

'It's man man na na na.'

She turned off the vacuum cleaner again.

'What?'

'It's not scary.'

'Nancy.'

'Yes, Lily?'

'Can you leave me alone for approximately ten minutes?' she asked, through gritted teeth.

'OK,' Nancy said, 'and then we can do my eye drops.'

'Fine.'

It was after she had taken care of Nancy for three days, and somehow managed to do the laundry list of new jobs her husband had heaped upon her, that Nancy appeared one morning when Lily was in the garden.

'Hi, Lily.'

'Hi, Nancy, how's your eye?'

'Better.'

'It looks good. I bet it's nice to have the patch off.'

'It is. I miss it sometimes. What are you doing?'

'Gardening.'

'Why don't you come to my house for coffee, cakes and a chat?' Nancy said.

'I'm really busy, but thanks, Nancy.'

'But all the women are there.'

'What women?'

'The neighbours. Mum's made lots of cakes.'

Lily was stopped in her tracks. Rachel Lennon had used her to mind her daughter for three days, then invited the entire neighbourhood to a coffee morning and excluded her. In the past she would have been hurt but she would have put on a happy face and said nothing. Not any more. In her mind she pictured a scene straight out of *Desperate Housewives*. She'd rip off the dusty green apron she wore for gardening and march over to the Lennons' like a woman possessed. She'd make a grand entrance and say something smart, cutting and witty before telling Rachel to shine up her bloody buttons with Brasso. She'd embarrass Rachel Lennon in front of all the neighbours before making a grand exit.

'Yes, Nancy, I'd love to come. Thank you,' she said, dropping her shovel and walking towards the Lennons' house. Behind her, Nancy was talking about the Dolans' dog – it was some sort of YouTube star.

'He wears a hat and makes a bumping sound. It's very funny.'

The door was on the latch. Lily walked into the kitchen, which led to the garden where most of the women were sitting, including Rachel. They were chatting and laughing, but when they saw her they stopped. Rachel stood up and sheepishly greeted her. 'Lily? How are you?'

They weren't drinking coffee although there was some made –

they were quaffing wine before noon. They looked at her as though she was some sort of alien.

She gazed around at them. She had helped all of them in one way or another over the years, and they were all there enjoying themselves, having deliberately excluded her. She didn't feel smart or pithy any more. The hurt was overwhelming. *I bent over backwards to be friends with you people.* She tried to speak but words wouldn't come. *What have I ever done to any of you?* There was no witty line. Instead her eyes filled with tears and she stood in the middle of the Lennons' garden crying while the neighbours silently watched her.

Amy Fitzpatrick, a bleached-blonde Botox-riddled woman, was pressing her glass to her lips as though it was the only thing preventing her from commenting or maybe even laughing. She was forty-five years old, skinny and haggard, despite her beautician's attempts to make her look otherwise. She looked like she hadn't eaten since the mid-eighties and Lily had long suspected she was bulimic. She dressed in the same clothes as her twenty-year-old daughter and years of overdoing it on the tanning bed had left her with dark crêpy skin. She was as mean as a snake and had argued or battled with everyone there, yet she had been invited.

Naomi Smith, in her mid-thirties, had once been svelte and glamorous. She still knew how to dress but she'd let herself go as soon as she'd become pregnant with the first of her five children. She had a faceful of cake. She didn't know whether to chew or swallow so instead she let it melt in her mouth. She was still beautiful but her size, her investment in her children, and her husband's haunted look suggested her lady garden was closed for business. When she wasn't eating, cooking or baking she was droning on about her kids. She was the woman everyone avoided on a day like this when they wanted to get pissed yet she was still invited.

Sofia Harris was wearing sunglasses, looking at the floor and wrapping a napkin around her fingers tightly. She was tense and nervous at the best of times. In her late forties, she was the mother of IVF twins she found hard to manage. One of the babies had been born with a heart problem and she had spent the first two years of her little girl's life in and out of hospital. The twins were five, and the child was fine now but needed to be monitored. As a result Sofia was hyper-vigilant. She often leaned on Lily when things were tough and, as the only one actually drinking coffee at the coffee morning, she had the grace to be embarrassed. Sofia liked Lily and had often stood up for her with the other ladies but they had all agreed Lily wasn't a girl's girl and probably wouldn't come even if she was invited.

There were others, some smirking, some grimacing, some just staring in a kind of mild shock, a few Lily didn't know. Rachel's expression had changed: from registering surprise, it now showed discomfort.

'I think you should go,' Rachel said, and she was right.

Lily had no business there: she was an intruder, a crying one at that. *Eve was right. You are jealous bitches*. She found her feet and started to walk away but before she did she managed two words: 'No more.'

She left the women speechless. There wasn't a word said or a sound made as she walked through the Lennons' house to the front door. It was as though she'd left the women frozen in that painful moment. She met Nancy coming out of the toilet.

''Bye, Nancy.'

''Bye, Lily.'

Lily ruffled her hair. 'Be nice to your brother.'

'OK.'

Not sleeping was the worst part of 'the snap', watching darkness turn to light, hearing the alarm go off and putting her two feet on the floor with that dreadful burning sensation in her eyes, a heavy head and a palpitating heart. Some days the only thing she ate was half a slice of cake or a muffin with Clooney. He had a calming, relaxing effect on her – he was like the human equivalent of lavender. He noticed her weight loss and the circles around her eyes, as did Eve. She challenged her numerous times but Lily tried to sidestep her questions.

'Are you trying to make me look fat?' Eve had said jokingly, the first time she noticed Lily's rail-thin physique.

'Ha-ha.'

'What's going on?'

'Same ol', same ol',' Lily said, in the sing-song voice she used when she was trying to avoid confrontation.

'You don't eat when you're stressed,' Eve said. 'You lost over a stone before the Intercert exams and Mrs Connolly thought you were anorexic. Turns out you were just a big fat worry-wart swot.'

'You've caught me out. Mrs Connolly was right.'

'It's him, isn't it?'

'No,' Lily said firmly.

'You're a liar,' Eve said, and Lily walked out.

Clooney attempted to approach her in a gentler fashion. They were sitting together in the conservatory. Lily was so tired and so suffocated by her husband's tightening of the reins that she had become a little careless about being seen sharing coffee and cake with him. He broke the slice in two and handed her a piece. She smiled, looked at it and sighed. She ate it slowly and tried not to gag. She was constantly on the verge of tears. Her happy façade was crumbling. Clooney watched her hand shake and, instead of questioning her, pulled her gently into his arms. He kissed the top of her head and told her to go to sleep. She laid her head on his lap and there she slept for twenty minutes.

9. The rocky path to freedom

Lil,

Hate to say I told you so but Colm was always going to try it on with you. No matter what you said or did he was after you from the start. I could smell it from the page. Just read that back and it looks weird but you know what I mean. As for Ellen and her Spanish cookie, I hate girls like that. The minute they get serious with a boy they disappear. Gina's older sister Helen is like that – she not only ditches her friends, she ditches her family. Gina told me on the QT so don't say anything but Helen's last boyfriend beat her up really badly and locked her in the house, and when her dad went over to sort him out she took the boyfriend's side. WHAT A MENTAL CASE. Anyway, he ended up leaving her and now she's at home but Gina says she's like a ghost. She doesn't really do or say much, she just lies around the house. I said she should be checked for a brain injury because I read something about it in a magazine. She said she was checked again and again. Don't say anything but she spent some time in the nuthouse after she tried to kill herself when he left. The poor girl, she must be a sadomasochist.

Well, at least you have Clooney and his friends, and Colm will get over it, so don't worry about him. Tell my brother I said hi and the house is quiet without him. It's amazing to have the bathroom pretty much to myself. Dad is gone so early in the morning and it means I can relax in the shower. I can't wait to live on my own. Having said that, I'm going to be in college accommodation sharing with a bunch of God knows who for a couple of years, which will probably be worse than sharing a

bathroom with Dad and Clooney – at least they're both really
clean. London is getting closer and I'm nervous. I've been sewing
up a storm. Gina asked me to make her a dress for her sister's
(not the nutter, can't remember her name, the one who's ancient)
kid's Confirmation. She bought some beautiful material. I made
her a cream mid-length dress and she loves it and it really does
suit her. I'm really happy with it but other than that I'm in pretty
bad humour. Ben's stupid grandmother had a stupid stroke and
she lives in stupid Cavan. He's been there since Monday evening.
She's ninety-two and apparently she's on the way out so the
family have to stay there until she pops her clogs. She's been
breathing her last for seven days now and I wish she'd just hurry
up and die. I know it sounds harsh but she's managed ninety-two
years on this planet and I'm with her grandson one month and
she decides to die and worse than that die slowly in CAVAN. If
she was doing it down the road at least I could still see him. I
really miss him. I miss him so much my bones hurt and I feel like
crying all the time. I know. SAP. I keep thinking about the way
he looks, smells and feels. I have a T-shirt of his that he left here
last week. He was wearing it under a jumper and he forgot to put
it on after we had the most amazing sex (more on that when I see
you). Anyway, I put it in a drawer and every now and then I take
it out and sniff it. Next thing I'll be put into a nuthouse like
Helen. Every day that goes by and his grandmother doesn't die is
another day I don't get to see Ben, and the worst of it is even if
she does die today right at this minute I still won't see him until
at least Wednesday because of the stupid funeral. He phoned me
last night and I asked him if he could say goodbye and come
home and then go down when she dies, which I think is a very
reasonable request, but he said absolutely no way was he leaving
his mother. We had a bit of a fight then because I'm not sensitive
enough. I told him he knows who I am and I am what I am. I'm
not going to pretend that the death of a ninety-two-year-old
woman he doesn't really know is sad, especially as she's been
demented for years, which means even if she did once know him

she wouldn't remember him, and probably doesn't even know or care that he's there. ARRRGH!!!! It's so frustrating. He said his mother is really upset and when I asked why he hung up the phone. He did call me back later but he was really pissed off with me even though I apologized. He said I could be very cold. I said I preferred the word practical. He said I can call it what I want but it worried him. I said there was no need to worry – I'm not going to turn into a psycho and kill his family, although I could see myself putting a pillow over his granny's face. Does that make me evil or expedient? Anyway, it was our first fight and afterwards when he rang back for the third time he said he was sorry and he knew I was odd when he fell for me and he loved me and I told him I loved him too on the stupid phone.

God, I miss him so much it actually makes me want to vomit and it makes me feel really bad for being so horrid to you all this time about Declan. Finally I know what you mean and every stupid love song I ever hated has meaning and makes me ache. I actually started to cry in the café the other morning when the Smiths' 'There Is A Light That Never Goes Out' came on the radio. Remember how I used to think it was fatalistic bullshit? Well, suddenly the image of being hit by a bus or a truck with Ben by my side seemed plausibly heavenly and when I say I cried, I bawled – big fat tears. Terry the Tourist's mother was in having tea and scones with some English pal of hers, a very proper lady called Vera, and they both came over and comforted me, thinking someone had died, which is ironic because if Ben's 'old bat' granny would actually die then I'd get Ben back and I wouldn't have to be crying at stupid songs on the stupid radio.

Declan is fine. I don't really remember how he was that day after the fight with his dad, maybe a bit quiet, but then we had that conversation and he seemed fine. Why are you freaking out about it? I fight with Danny all the time and God knows you fight with your mother. It's what teenagers and parents do, Lily!

I haven't really got a lot of news. Paul is never around and Gar is seeing another new girl, again from Bray, and Declan told me it's the other girl's friend and that's why they broke up. He decided he preferred her friend and her friend went off with him happily. Can you believe it? Gar's a big stud in Bray. It's weird, he seems way more confident and happier. We're getting on really well when he's around. He called into the coffee shop the other day and he was in great form. He says his new girlfriend is amazing in bed and I said EXCUSE ME as if he was trying to intimate that I wasn't but he apologized and said he didn't mean it like that and he was just happy that things were working out for us both, which I thought was really nice. I'll miss Gar when I'm in London. He's a good friend. He said he's going to help me move some of my designs from my bedroom to the garage. I can't even get into my wardrobe there's so much stuff there, and Clooney's not here and Danny mumbles about a sore back every time I mention it. I told him I'd make dinner. I hope he likes beans on toast.

I've been spending a lot of time with Declan in the past few days. I have my lunch hour at three in the coffee shop and he has his at three too so we sit on the side of the street and eat sandwiches together. He said he hasn't heard from you and he's really worried. I told you you were probably busy but when I mentioned that Clooney was down there he got a bit shirty. I told him to relax – you'd swear Clooney had headed down there to ravish you the way Declan was acting. I explained, just in case he was thinking anything weird, that Clooney might as well be your older brother, and I told Declan that you loved him and would never do anything to hurt him, and I even mentioned that I had tried to get you to leave him a number of times and you wouldn't. First he got really annoyed and then he laughed, saying I was weird. I prefer the word honest. WHATEVER. Anyway, he seemed to calm down. Jesus, Lily, you really need to call him because he's up to ninety about it. Other than that he's fine, not as uptight about his results as he was. He said he's just going to hope for the best and if he doesn't get in he's going to freak out then, which is a much better plan than freaking out now. It's weird that Declan and I are working two shops away from one another and spending time together. I really didn't know him before, Lily, and I still think he's arrogant, has a pole up his arse and he's way too intense, but for the first time I see what you see in him. He's kind. I mentioned I thought a certain bolt looked brilliant and I could use it in my designs, and since then he's been collecting odd-looking scrap metals for me and he has a really good eye. He gave me so many bits and pieces that I ended up making a necklace with some of them and some wire and a woman stopped me on the street and asked me where I bought it. He's going to keep giving me bits he thinks might work in clothes or jewellery. I swear there is a bolt that I know would make a cool ring. I just have to think about how to do it. And he's funny, he's very dry, it's like he talks and you either think what a dick or you realize he's joking and laugh. The other day he said I'd be a great seamstress! I nearly punched him in the face until I realized he wasn't trying to put me down, he just didn't know what a designer is. I explained and he was nice about it although I'm not sure he gets it. If it's not medicine or law he seems a little lost. His dad passed us on the street the other day when we were sitting there and he was drunk as a skunk – he dragged me up off the pavement and started dancing around with me. He was just messing but Declan got really annoyed. He pushed his dad off me and his dad pushed him back, then pointed at him and laughed. There was some big match on so his dad went off with a friend to do a little more celebrating and gave Declan the rest of the day off but when he left Declan kept working. He's hilarious. What a swot!

It's been a really quiet week, boring to be honest. I really miss you. Gina says hi. She hasn't really been around – she's working late nights and spending most of the day in bed, which is a pain. Tell Clooney that Danny and me miss his spag bol and don't worry about Colm, it'll blow over soon – look at me and Gar, two months ago we weren't even talking.

Love

A very bored Eve

Oh and my top four are as follows:

1. *Friday The 13th* (for the same reason as you. Remember halfway through it Clooney jumped up behind you and said boo and you lifted out of the seat and started crying? Priceless)
2. *Nightmare on Elm Street* (because I'm not a baby)
3. *Fright Night* (if it had been my choice it wouldn't be in my top four – I'd pick *Psycho* or *When a Stranger Calls*. Vampires are retarded)
4. *The Lost Boys* (I love it but it's a comedy not a horror)

The more complex Declan's emotions, the more irritable and irrational he became. His wife was cheating on him with her old best friend and her brother. Those two had nearly destroyed Declan and Lily's relationship in 1990 and she was hiding her new friendship with them from him. He should have said something. He should have told her he knew about Eve and sat her down and asked why she would keep Eve's presence a secret or why she had handled the situation as she had. He should have been kind and understanding and spoken to her about how and what she felt on seeing her old friends again. He should have sympathized and empathized. After all, twenty years had passed and twenty years is a long time. He had built a life with her and they had two children together, which counted for something. He should have gone to see Eve and made it right with her. He should have shaken Clooney's hand and let bygones be bygones. *We all make mistakes.* Of course, his stubbornness, vanity and paranoia prevented him doing any of it. There had been a time in Declan's life when he had trusted Lily with every thought in his head, every hidden secret, every fear and shame. Then he had been a deeply traumatized, lonely boy, desperate to escape a life of misery. When his father had tortured him and his mother ignored him he had gained strength from Lily's love. He had believed in her and trusted her completely. She had broken that trust only once and that was enough to ensure he never fully trusted her again. He had sworn he'd forgiven her and had begged her forgiveness, but he was a liar. Not only did he not forgive her sins, he blamed her for any sins he'd committed as a result of her breaking his trust because if she hadn't . . . he wouldn't have . . . *It could have all been so different. Fucking Eve and Clooney Hayes! If I thought I could get away with it I'd have them both killed.*

If Declan had been another kind of man he would have taken his wife in his arms, told her he loved her and asked if she was happy. If she wasn't, what could he do to make a difference? It might have worked. Lily might have opened up and told him she needed space to breathe; she was sick of feeling like a slave to him and the kids. She wanted their sex life to be more about love than service. She wanted him to consider her feelings and to stop treating her and the rest of the world like his enemy. But you can't change just because a person asks you to. Maybe that was why Declan didn't confront his wife. Maybe he knew that she would use it as an excuse to try to change him and the way they lived when he liked life as it was. He didn't want anything to change. He didn't know how to change. It wasn't possible and, anyway, who was Lily to tell him he needed to change? She had spent eighteen years calling him paranoid, and maybe sometimes she had been right, but this time he wasn't paranoid: he was right. Declan didn't say anything to his wife because even though a tiny part of him was whispering, *You'll lose her*, the bigger part, the egotistical, arrogant, paranoid and angry part, was screaming, *She's making a fool of you so sort the bitch out and end this!*

Every day that passed, every look between them, every word unspoken, every lie he elicited from her lips cemented his fury and fuelled his thirst for justice. Declan Donovan was bubbling and it was only a matter of time before he reached boiling point. Then all hell would break loose and Lily would suffer his wrath but it would be over. Never once, as paranoid as Declan Donovan was, did he think his wife would walk away. *I won't let her.*

*

When the cast on Eve's right leg came off, it was a cause for a mini-celebration. Lily brought a little cake with a candle, which she made Eve blow out before she wrapped it up so that she and Clooney could eat it later. Eve's shoulder was improving every day and it meant that she could start to walk with crutches. Her shoulder ached but she was determined and her first attempt at walking – aborted after six steps and a dizzy spell – was considered a resounding success. The first day she didn't have to be lifted in and out of bed brought tears of joy, not least because she wouldn't have to listen to Norman say, '*A h-aon, a dó, a trí*. It's the little things.'

Her first real bath felt as though she was submerged in what the religious would call Heaven. Her first shower, although she was forced to sit down and was accompanied by a nurse called Monica, was truly blissful. The water tumbled down on her and it felt like she was in a tropical storm. *Remember, Ben, when I told you about my time in Kenya with Clooney? This is what it felt like.* She often talked to Ben even though he wasn't listening. She just liked to say his name. Sometimes she'd give out to him, like when her bowels refused to co-operate and she was stuck on the loo for an hour looking at the poster on the door that had a picture of a brown sack with 'biohazard' written on it and two syringes. It read: 'Reminder: Dispose of Hazards properly.' *I'm trying Ben. I am trying. I feel like I'm pushing out a baby here. By the way, I'm sorry you never got to be a dad. I think you would have been a good one.* Sometimes she'd tell him about Adam. *He's nice, Ben, he's kind and he laughs when I talk. Sometimes when I'm attempting humour, sometimes when I'm deadly serious. I entertain him. I like it.* When she had been worked hard by her physiotherapist and she was sweating, hurting and exhausted, she'd fall into her clean white hard bed, close her eyes and talk to him about what could have been. *I should have offered to bail you out. I should have invested in you instead of screwing you so I guess I screwed you twice. You could have saved your business so your and Fiona's lives would have returned to normal. Where are you now, Ben? Are you somewhere or nowhere? Was being unplugged your full stop? Did you know it was happening? Did you hear them cry? Did you call out in your head for more time or were you happy to let go? Are you gone? It should have been me, it should have been me, it should have been me. I'm sorry, Ben. I'm sorry for being weak and stupid and selfish and I know you are too.*

When she opened her eyes after an hour or two of sleep she'd focus on the poster in her room.

The Message Is the Same
in Any Language!

Operite Ruke
Lavarsi le Mani
Lavese las Manos
Xin Hay Rura Tay

WASH YOUR HANDS

Then she'd turn to the window. *Ah, there you are, Patty.* She'd check the time and she'd turn on the TV. *It's two o'clock and that's Ellen time. Ben, did you ever watch Ellen? She rocks.* For someone who never watched TV, Eve had a new-found respect for the medium. She watched shows she'd never seen before, like American cop shows: *Bones – funny*; and *Criminal Minds – freaky.* She liked hospital shows, like *Grey's Anatomy* and *House*, mostly because she could identify with the people in the beds, but her absolute favourite were the chat shows. They were a revelation, and even though she didn't know some of the guests, the hosts themselves were the stars. People like Ellen, Graham Norton, Piers Morgan and Conan O'Brien became Eve's new friends.

Adam called in most days to sit and chat, and even though she'd threatened not to speak to him when he refused to discharge her on her original deadline, she had forgiven him and they had become close.

'What are you doing later?' she asked one day, after *Ellen* and before *Coronation Street*.

'I'm going on a date,' he said.

'Blind or with someone you actually know and like?'

'Blind.'

'What do you know about her?'

'She's forty-five, divorced, two kids and owns her own bakery.'

'OK, so she's older, has children who will no doubt hate you, and she sells fatty food. Sounds like a dream come true. What does she look like?'

'I told you it's a blind date.'

'So you haven't even seen a picture?'

'No.'

'Then don't bother going,' she said.

'Why not?' he asked, laughing.

'Attraction is based on looks and if you don't like the way she looks, no matter how nice she is, an hour spent making small-talk won't make a difference.'

'That sounds shallow,' he said.

'I prefer *accurate* and, besides, I know you like them pretty.'

'What's that supposed to mean?'

'Lily,' she said, and smiled. 'You have a thing for her. Don't worry, most men do.'

Adam blushed, and stuttered, 'I – I – I –'

'Here's the thing. Even if Lily wasn't unhappily married, and we both know she is, you're not her type.'

Adam gasped, shocked that Eve could be so blunt. 'How do you know that?' he said, attempting to sound merely interested rather than concerned.

'Because you're my type. We always had opposite tastes in men and still do.'

'I'm your type?'

'Most definitely. You see, Lily likes her men square and broad. She likes the V-neck-jumper-and-deckshoe-wearing guy with a stripy shirt for good measure. She likes the average bear and you are not the average bear, and I like that about you.'

'I'm touched.'

'No, you're not – you're sad because you know I'm right about Lily. She's never looked at you in that way. There's no sexual tension between you, and even though you could look at her all day, she doesn't see you as anything more than her friend.'

'You're right,' he admitted.

'Do you like the way I look?' Eve asked. 'Don't be afraid to tell the truth. If I'm not your type I can take it.'

'I'm your doctor,' he said, feeling a mixture of sadness and discomfort.

'You won't be for ever, so answer me.'

'You're beautiful,' he said.

'So when I get out of here, take me on a date.'

'I can't, Eve,' he said.

'You could if you wanted to. Life's too short, Adam, and we could have some fun,' she shrugged, 'so you can't blame a girl for asking.'

'I'm your doctor,' he repeated, and moved to leave.

'Adam,' Eve said, 'whatever happens or doesn't happen with us, be Lily's friend. She doesn't have many and she counts on you. Don't hang in there hoping it will turn into something else because it won't. She's never going to love you like that because if it were possible she'd love you now. Don't hold it against her.'

He thanked her and didn't come to see her again for three days.

Hey, Ben, did I tell you? I really messed up with Adam.

Lily spent August avoiding her husband as much as possible. He was making life extremely difficult, turning up in any and all places at the most inopportune moments. It had got so bad that the only time she felt safe from him was when he was in surgery, so she did a little spying of her own, keeping tabs on when it was safe to share her coffee or lunch break with Clooney.

Lily knew she was falling in love with Clooney. She knew that, even though they weren't having sex, she was cheating on her husband and that with every look, glance, touch and tender moment she and Clooney shared she moved further away from him. She tried to pretend to herself that it was simply friendship and that Clooney was like family, but she knew and he knew that there was something between them. They were playing a dangerous game, and it was exciting and fun, and Lily hadn't felt so alive in a very long time. But she was a wife and a mother, and Clooney was the kind of man who came into a woman's life, made her feel special for a while, then left. He had never promised to be anything else. He wasn't a liar – like his sister he shot from the hip. He never made promises he couldn't keep. They talked about what he would do and where he would go after Eve had made a full recovery. He never said he'd stay, and Lily never even intimated that she'd like him to. Every day they could, they would sit together and drink each other in, both living on the tiny touches that mean so much when you're falling hopelessly in love. They lived in the moment, as Eve and Ben had once done, because in the moment there was no husband or kids or guilt or faraway countries calling – there was only Lily and Clooney, electrically charged and fizzing around one another.

Eve would have had to be blind not to see what was happening but she said nothing. She would not interfere. She had done that once before and it had cost her dearly.

August was passing quickly and Eve was getting stronger every day. Lily worried about a future that didn't include her caring for Eve and spending time with Clooney. She couldn't imagine life returning to the way it had been. *I was so unhappy for so long.* When Lily wasn't lost in Clooney, when she returned to the real world, the guilt she felt was so immense it threatened to choke her. She was down to a ridiculously low weight; she suffered from stress headaches and a kidney infection that wouldn't go away. Although she was sleeping, she had dizzy spells. She knew she couldn't go on like that. She spent days and nights thinking about the effect a break-up would have on the kids. Her whole adult life had been about her kids, she had dedicated herself to them – she had lost her youth to taking care of them – and although she had been taken for granted and had allowed herself to be treated as a second-class citizen in her own house, she had few regrets: motherhood was her greatest pleasure and achievement. But she had been dying slowly for many years, so miserable it hadn't seemed to matter – until suddenly she had seen light and hope, and the possibility of a better future. Clooney was not the answer – he'd never stay – but the way he made her feel had ignited in her the spirit to fight for a better life. *I deserve better*.

One afternoon she joined Eve and Clooney in the gardens. Eve was in her wheelchair but determined to use her crutches so Lily and Clooney walked with her, wobbling and cursing, between them. Declan was involved in a long surgery so Lily didn't feel the need to be careful. She was just enjoying an August day with some old friends. It was innocent and she was happy. She had an hour for lunch. They spent half of it walking Eve around, and when she was exhausted but determined to make her own way up to her room in the electronically powered wheelchair, with her crutches lying across her lap, they stayed behind. Lily hadn't been feeling well all day. She was used to getting on with things no matter how poorly she felt, but her back was killing her, the antibiotics she was taking for the kidney infection still weren't working and she was battling waves of nausea. Clooney placed his jacket on his lap and she lay there while he stroked her hair and they reminisced about Danny. She had loved him so much she filled up and he wiped away her tears.

'He loved you too,' he said.

When the hour was over she stood up quickly – a little too quickly: she fainted. She came round in Clooney's arms.

'You should see a doctor,' he said.

'Handy that I'm here then,' she said, smiling.

'You need to take care of yourself,' he said.

'I will,' she lied.

He hugged her tightly and she held on as long as she could.

'You can't go on like this,' he whispered in her ear. 'We can't go on like this.'

When he was sure she was OK and she was steady on her feet, she told him that she'd see him later and left him sitting on the grass to think about what they were playing at.

He didn't see the guy with the camera photographing their every move. He hadn't noticed him on any day over the previous month – he was used to seeing the same faces every day and they tended to blur into the background. He sat in the garden for another few minutes before returning to Eve. When he passed the guy on a bench taking a picture of the fountain, he commented on the camera. The guy smiled and nodded, and Clooney walked on, unaware that evidence was being gathered and that Lily was in danger.

When Adam returned to Eve's room after the three-day sabbatical, he did so rather sheepishly.

'Well?' she said.

'Well what?'

'How did your date go?' she asked.

He relaxed, sat down and told her. 'You were right,' he said.

'She was ugly.'

'No,' he said, 'just not my type.'

'When can I get out of here?'

'Well, you're doing great so, all going well, maybe next week.'

'And then you'll ask me out.'

He shook his head but he was smiling, and she knew he was considering her proposal. They remained silent for a minute or so, both quite content to be still in one another's company.

Eve looked at him. He was so busy thinking she could almost see the mouse run on the wheel. 'What are you thinking?' she asked.

'That Lily is falling for your brother.'

'Oh, you spotted that.'

'Hard to miss.'

'It is when you're interested,' she said.

'I can't just switch it off.'

'I know.'

'Do you think she'll leave Declan?' he said.

'I don't know.'

'Does he love her?'

'Clooney?' she asked.

He nodded.

'I think he's always loved her,' she answered, 'but Clooney's a rolling stone. He might be what Lily wants but he'll never be what she needs.'

'Why do you like me, Eve?'

'You're kind, gentle, you have a great laugh, a good sense of humour, you're accomplished but you aren't defined by what you do. You're sexy, athletic, warm, and I think you'd be really good in the sack. Speaking of which, when do you think I'll be match fit?'

He laughed. 'You're a very interesting woman.'

'OK, well, that's a start.'

'I had a dream about you the other night,' he said.

'Good or bad?'

'Good – very good.'

She grinned. 'Now you're talking!'

It was a Friday night. Clooney met Gar and Paul for a drink in the local pub. Gar had forgiven Paul, who had called up to his house and asked him to be his best man. Paul didn't acknowledge his friend's anger, disappointment and frustration. He had simply told him he wanted him to be his best man and promised that he had no more secrets. 'What you see is what you get,' he said.

'Finally.'

Paul smirked. 'It was a long time coming.'

'All you had to do was be honest about who you are.'

'It's easy when you know but it took me a long time to work it out.'

'You were always a bit slow,' Gar said.

'So will you be my best man?'

'Yeah, of course I will.'

Paul pulled him into a hug and they slapped each other on the back. No more conversation necessary.

It was seven weeks to the wedding and Paul had spent the day picking out menus and registering for gifts. He wanted a quick drink and wasn't in the mood to talk. He switched into listening mode, allowing Clooney and Gar to entertain him with their argument on whether or not Brian O'Driscoll was the greatest rugby player in the world or whether he was just a good rugby player from Ireland. That argument lasted a good half-hour. Every now and again they would look to him to add his comment but he remained silent and pensive. They talked about soccer and the matches that would be played the following day. They made a bet as to who would win in a game between Manchester United and Liverpool. They talked about weapons of mass destruction, the fall of Communism, ethnic cleansing, Kim Kardashian and wave energy. Paul remained quiet throughout.

Eventually Clooney remarked on Paul's silence. 'You haven't said two words.'

'Tired of talking, been talking all day, can't talk any more,' he said.

'He does this,' Gar said.

'If you're so tired, why did you come out?' Clooney asked.

'Because if I stay home Simone will want to keep talking,' he said.

Gar burst out laughing. 'Welcome to living with a woman!'

'You can't help who you fall in love with,' Paul said, 'but if I could it would be a man.'

Paul was going through a transitionary period in his life and he was happy but also fearful. Everything was changing so fast and he hoped he was fit for the challenge. *What kind of husband will I be? What kind of father? Will this woman be enough for me? More importantly, will I be enough for her?* Introducing her to his family had been scary. Predictably, his mother had reacted with joy and praised God for putting her son back on the path towards Heaven. It had sickened him. She had fawned over Simone as though she had been sent directly by God in answer to a mother's prayers. Over dinner, Simone had told the story of how they had met. His father had carried on eating quietly as she spoke, Paul's brother and his wife were not quite sure what to think, and his mother had interrupted every second sentence to thank God.

'We were in a pub in town,' she said.

'The power of prayer,' Paul's mother said.

'We just started talking and I don't know – something clicked.'

'And that's the power of prayer!' she said again, slapping the table.

'I knew straight away,' Simone said, and she smiled at him.

But Paul wasn't in the mood for smiling. He was in the mood for fighting. He wanted to hurt his mother the way she had hurt him every time she'd insisted he needed to be saved. *How fucking dare you? You're the reason I hated myself till I was twenty-six. You're the reason I thought about killing myself every day I lived in your house. You're the reason I've spent so many years hiding I don't know how to stop. The power of prayer! If prayer had any power you would have been hit by a bus.*

Simone could see him smarting and she could feel his pain. She turned to his mother and smiled sweetly. 'We're going to aim to be faithful, but at the end of the day he's always going to yearn for a bit of cock and sure that's only natural,' she said.

Paul's mother's mouth had fallen open. She'd dropped her fork and looked around her as though she was hearing things. Paul's brother Alan had burst out laughing and his wife joined in. Paul had just sat grinning. 'I love you,' he said to Simone.

'I love you too,' she said, and kissed him, 'exactly as you are.' His mother had been rendered dumb.

Paul's father had said nothing. He had reacted badly to Paul's coming out but over the years he had grown used to having a gay son. Now he was bisexual, getting married and having a baby. It

258

was all a bit much. He had read a few pamphlets but they'd raised more questions. *Christ, I'd need to do a degree in this bloody thing.* He didn't know how to feel or what to say so he kept quiet. Paul was like his dad in that respect: when in doubt he'd say nothing and hope it would all work out.

'Do you think Eve will be able to dance at my wedding?' Paul asked Clooney, over his fourth pint.

'Maybe.'

'Why? Do you want to make sure there's someone worse than you on the dance floor?' Gar asked.

'Something like that,' Paul said. He might not have been one to talk about his emotions but he felt things intensely. He had been rocked by Eve's accident and the possibility that he might lose her. With Eve he could quietly be himself. She accepted him as he was, heterosexual, gay, bisexual, quiet, secretive. Eve allowed people to be who they were and she either liked them or didn't. She was the polar opposite of him and he found her open nature, strength and confidence comforting. Her searing honesty and her devil-may-care attitude inspired him. He was a sentimental old sod behind his calm demeanour. Eve's near-miss had reminded him that, in Simone and the baby, he had love and security and he was terrified it would all go away. *What if I don't deserve this? What if they're taken from me? What if I fail them?* He had nightmares, seeing Eve dying on the ground, seeing Simone beside her and the baby covered with blood. When he had woken up screaming, Simone was beside him to soothe him and talk him down.

One afternoon when they were alone together, he told Eve about the nightmares. It was the first time he'd really opened up to her about anything personal. If she realized it was a major step forward in their relationship, she didn't make a fuss about it.

'Perfectly normal to be anxious,' she said.

'I'm scared I'll let them down,' he said.

'Why?'

'Because . . .'

'Because what?'

'You know why.'

'Can I be honest?' she said.

'You're always honest.'

'I know, but I'm asking permission because what I have to say is harsh.'

'OK,' he said tentatively.

'You don't think you're good enough because you were raised by an ignorant phobic woman who told you every day of your life that because you liked men there was something wrong with you. You need to realize that you're a better, stronger person than your mother and you need to stop torturing yourself.'

'OK,' he said, smiling. 'That wasn't so harsh.'

'I'm not finished. You're like me – we're selfish, restless people. We do what we want to do when we want to do it, we get bored easily and we put ourselves first. Let's face it, we're both adult baby arseholes, and in your case, it's time to put others before yourself and that's scary.'

He laughed. 'I can do that. Simone makes it easy.'

'Good,' she said. 'Then you'll be fine.'

'What about you? Are you going to grow out of being an adult baby arsehole?'

'No,' she said.

'Fair enough.'

Gar and Paul were watching snooker on the TV over the bar and Clooney was lost in his own world, thinking about Lily. He was worried. She was fading away in front of his eyes. She spent her life running around after people and taking care of everyone but herself. He wanted to wrap her up in cotton wool and care for her. He couldn't stop thinking about her, and every time he did he battled the urge to run to her house and save her from the man she should never have married. Clooney didn't know Declan but he did know that Eve hated him, and that he was the reason the girls hadn't spoken for twenty years. He was also aware that Lily was at a crossroads. She would choose either Declan or herself. Clooney had been there the last time she had faced that decision and she had chosen Declan. *Who's it going to be, Lily?*

While Clooney was sitting in the pub with Gar and Paul, Lily's crisis came to a head.

Scott's car had broken down and his grandfather was keeping it in the garage. Lily had said she'd pick him up and it was after seven when she got there. Scott and his granddad were happy, both under cars with the radio on. Lily hadn't been into the garage since she was a young girl. The place was exactly the same but the vibe had changed. Scott rolled out from under his car as did his granddad. They were two peas in a pod, happily covered with grease, sharing a rag to wipe their hands, talking easily with one another. It was a different world from the bleak place she remembered. She said no to a coffee and was anxious to leave.

Scott's grandfather smiled at her. 'It's nice to see you back in here,' he said.

'Thank you, Mr Donovan,' she said.

'How many times? It's Jack.'

Lily would never be comfortable using her husband's father's first name because for so long he had been Mr Donovan, the ogre she dared not speak to.

'I Ie'd make a serious mechanic,' he said of Scott, 'but I suppose his dad wouldn't like that.'

'I'm sure he'll be happy with whatever Scott chooses,' she said.

'Doubtful,' Scott said, and he and his granddad grinned at one another. 'Dad's too much of a snob.'

'Your father is what your grandfather made him!' Lily snapped. She was uncomfortable with her son and his grandfather making fun of Declan. *How dare you? You destroyed him. It's your fault he's broken. It's your fault I've been trying to fix him since I was sixteen. It's your fault he never had a real chance.* Suddenly Lily was crying.

Scott and Jack glanced at one another awkwardly, neither

knowing what to say. She dried her eyes and ordered her son into the car. He said goodbye to his granddad.

Lily was quiet on the drive home.

'Is everything all right with you and Dad, Mum?'

'Why do you ask?'

'Because you're both acting like freaks.'

'No,' she said. 'It's not.'

'Well, whatever's going on, I think he's going to try to make it up to you tonight.'

'What makes you say that?'

'He's given me fifty euro to go to the movies and Daisy's staying with Tess.'

'Oh,' Lily said, half happy they would finally have the space to talk and half panic-stricken by what needed to be said. 'I'll drop you at Josh's, then?'

'Yeah. Mum?'

'Yeah?'

'How's your friend?'

'She's good,' she said, smiling. 'She's good and cranky, which means she's getting back to herself.'

'I'm glad,' he said.

She pulled up outside Josh's house and he got out. 'Good luck with Dad,' he said, and ran into the house.

He'd seen his parents fight before, and they'd been sulking for weeks. *Tonight there'll be a big row, then Mum will give in, and by the following weekend she'll have some nice new jewellery.* He didn't expect his life to change for ever that night but more often than not the biggest changes come unexpectedly.

Declan had met with his PI as soon as his surgery was over. The guy had been waiting for him in his office. The pictures of Lily and Clooney were on his desk. He opened the folder and saw his wife with her head on another man's lap. He clenched his teeth and flicked through the other pictures. They were smiling at one another, hugging, touching, sharing food, looking at one another the way lovers do. He sat at his desk, staring at the colour pictures of Lily and Clooney falling in love.

'Have they slept together?' he asked, in a calm detached manner, which suggested to the man he had hired that he didn't care either way.

'Not on my watch,' the guy said. 'Your wife is a very busy woman. The only time I see her sit and take a breath is with him.'

'I didn't ask you if she sat.'

He flicked back to the picture of Lily with her head on Clooney's lap. He had his hands in her hair.

He wrote a cheque and told the guy to go. He left, and Declan sat in his office, swallowing hard, battling the urge to get up and tear the place apart. He practised breathing in and out and focused on being calm but he couldn't contain himself. His blood rushed to his head, his ears burned, and his heart-rate was through the roof. He felt like he was on fire. Awash with adrenalin, he stood up and turned the table over, smashing his computer screen. He flung his chair against the wall, shattering the glass frame that held his professional certificate. He kicked the brains of the computer around the room, and when there was nothing left to break, he kicked a hole in his door. When the place was wrecked he picked up his folder of photos and exited, telling his stunned secretary to get someone to clear up the mess.

Lily got home a little after eight. The house was in darkness. Declan's car was in the drive but when she called his name he didn't respond. She took off her coat and hung it up. She walked up the stairs and turned on the landing light. She went into her bathroom, had a shower, dried herself and put on a comfortable pair of trousers and a soft wool top. Then she went downstairs. She thought he might be sulking somewhere, maybe in the sitting room or his office, but they were in darkness too. The kitchen was empty. Perhaps he was canvassing the neighbours to see if they could use her services or maybe he had gone for a run. He had been running a lot in the recent past. She didn't care. She wanted everything to be over but she had no idea how to begin the conversation that would lead to the end of the marriage. *I just can't do it any more.* She was scared, too, that he'd throw her against a wall or, worse, that he'd throw himself off a cliff. He had manipulated her with that threat on many occasions: *I would die without you. I swear to God, Lily, if you walk out that door I'll cut my damn wrists.* She was going to ask him to leave and he would lose it. He'd scream and shout and cry and roar, and then maybe he'd beg and threaten but she intended to hold firm. *Please just go. Let me breathe. Let me be. I'm so tired.* He'd ask her what had changed and the answer would be 'Nothing', and that was the problem.

But, of course, that was a lie. Everything had changed. She'd reconnected with her old friend, she'd realized how short life was and she was falling in love with another man. She felt silly and bad and wrong and selfish, and doing anything for herself felt so alien she wasn't sure that she could go through with it. *What if he does cry and beg and wail and plead? Could I really let him go, knowing what he's been through? What do I say when he brings up the kids? What if they hate me for breaking up their family? What if he says no? Do I leave? Where do the kids go? Do they come with me? Do we even have a place to go? No. He'll have to go. God knows, he can afford it. What if he falls apart? I'm so tired of feeling sick with guilt and wishing every hour and day away. Why doesn't he come home so we can end this? Where the hell are you, Declan?*

When it was clear he wasn't coming home, she undressed, put on her nightdress and got into bed. *I don't understand.*

She didn't hear him come in. She woke with his hand clamped over her mouth and nose and he was moving inside her. Her arms were over her head and he was holding her wrists in place with one hand. She heard her shoulder pop and felt a nauseating pain. She could smell the booze. She was rammed into the headboard, her neck was strained, she couldn't breathe and her insides seemed to be tearing. He was vicious and violent, and as he attacked her, he warned her to shut her dirty mouth. She struggled to breathe and there was a moment before she bit his fingers, which were jammed into her lips, when she thought she might suffocate. She managed a quick breath before he repositioned his hand – now it bore down on her face so heavily she thought her nose and cheekbones might snap. He flipped her over on her stomach and pushed her face into the pillow. Then pain cut into her back passage.

'Do you like that, you fucking whore?' he said.

She passed out.

When she came round her lip was split and bleeding, she had a severe headache, her shoulder was dislocated and her anus was torn and bleeding. She got up slowly to the sounds of him taking a shower. On the bed she saw a folder. It was open, and pictures of her and Clooney were strewn across the bed. Some of them had spunk on them, others had her blood. She realized her husband was going nowhere, that there would be no talking or negotiation. She knew that if she didn't get out, she'd either walk down to the kitchen, select the sharpest carving knife and plunge it deep into his heart, or he would rape and torture her again. She put on her flip-flops and a pair of knickers lined with a panty pad to absorb the blood. Then she walked out of her bedroom and down the stairs. She took her coat from the hanger in the hallway and, with her good arm, slung it over her shoulders to conceal the blood on her nightie. She picked up her handbag, opened the front door and walked outside.

She got into her car slowly and carefully. She drove to Eve's place. She'd never been there before but she knew the apartment block. She had never taken Clooney's phone number because there was no reason she could think of to ask for it and, anyway, she had been scared that Declan would find it on her phone. She saw the building on the cliff as she turned up the narrow dirt road that Ben Logan had been killed on two months before. She drove up to the block and parked. She got out slowly and painfully.

Once she'd rehung the coat over her shoulders, she held it

together tightly with her fist and walked to the main door. She looked on the panel and every name was there bar Eve's. However, if Eve was going to live in an apartment it would be the penthouse. She pressed the button. When nobody answered, she pressed it again, and this time she held it down.

Clooney woke up, answered the bell, heard her voice and buzzed the apartment-block door open. Then he waited for the lift, bouncing up and down and resting his hands on the door, willing it to open. When it did, he saw that she was bruised and bleeding and that her arm hung at an odd angle.

'He raped me,' she said. 'He called me a whore and then he raped me.'

Clooney brought her inside silently. She didn't seem to know whether she wanted to sit or stand or lie down. Clooney knelt so that she was looking down at him. He took her hand. 'You're safe now,' he said, and her eyes leaked tears on to her sore face. She sobbed, her lip bled again and he stood up, held her cheek against his and whispered that he had her, she was safe and there was no going back. When she was calm he asked her if he could look at her arm.

'It's dislocated,' she said.

'I know. We're going to need to pop it back in.'

'You know how?' she asked.

He nodded. 'I've dislocated this baby four times,' he said, pointing to his left shoulder.

He took her arm and very slowly rotated it until it hit a thirty-five-degree angle. The pain, he knew, would be immense, and she screamed as the joint slid back into place. She sighed and rotated it slowly.

'It's OK?' he said.

She nodded, and plonked herself on the floor. She bent her knees and hugged them tight. He sat beside her, and when she held out her hand to him, he took her in his arms. When she cried, he rocked her there on the floor. When she fell asleep he car-

266

ried her to bed. It was when he placed her under the covers that he saw the blood on the back of her nightdress. Clooney lay, watching her sleep, and thought of all the things he wanted to do to Declan. He wanted to drive to his house and burn it down with him in it, or pull him into the street and beat him to within an inch of his life, or run him over with his car or just punch him in his face. He wanted the world to know what Declan had done, to walk around the hospital and his neighbourhood with a megaphone, shouting it out. He wanted to see him stand in front of a judge and be sent down. He was angry and raw. And then a question occurred to him: *Has he done this before?*

The next morning Lily woke to a running bath and breakfast being cooked. Eve's robe was on the bed and she put it on quickly to hide the blood. She walked into the kitchen and Clooney pointed to the sofa. When she was settled with a rug over her, he placed a tray with a small plate of scrambled eggs on her lap.

'Eat.'

'Can't.'

'Three bites, not all at once, take your time,' he said, 'but please, three bites.'

He served himself and sat down opposite her. She was playing with her food, moving it around the way she had done when they were kids. He took the fork, put the smallest piece of egg on it and fed it to her. He watched her swallow and smiled.

'There's a bath in there ready for you but we have to talk about whether or not you want to press charges before you get into it.'

She shook her head. 'He's the father of my children,' she said.

'And last night he violently raped you.'

'I can't.'

'You know I won't make you do anything you don't want to but, Lily, this should be recorded.'

She was crying again – silent fat tears that just kept coming, burning tracks into her face, creeping down her neck and soaking the collar of her nightdress. Clooney stood up and hugged her.

'I'm sorry,' she said.

'Don't be,' he soothed. 'You don't have anything to be sorry about.'

'I can't,' she said.

'OK, OK,' he said.

After that he asked her if it would be all right to take some photos of her face. She agreed. He brought her into the bathroom, and when she wanted to undress, he left her alone, got some of Eve's things for her, then walked in backwards and put them on the chair next to the bath.

'We'll buy something that fits when you feel a little better,' he said.

Then he picked up her nightdress and took it out of the room. When he walked into the kitchen, he looked at the blood and semen stains, folded it, wrapped it in clingfilm and put it into a bag.

When she was washed and dressed in clothes that were far too big for her, he insisted she had her shoulder properly looked at. She agreed to see Adam, so Clooney rang him, told him what had happened and asked him to come to Eve's place. Adam arrived within an hour. He examined her shoulder and her face. She wouldn't let anyone near her below and he didn't press her, on the condition that she saw a gynaecologist later. He was a bone man and, in any case, she'd been through enough. She found walking hard – she was in such bad shape that he was shaken to the core. He put her back into bed and gave her something to help her sleep.

'You can't say anything,' she said, as he was leaving the room.

'Everything will be OK.' He closed the door.

He joined Clooney in the kitchen. Clooney poured him a coffee and the two men sat in silence, neither knowing what to say or do.

After a while Adam scratched his head. 'We should report it,' he said.

'We can't.'

'We have to change her mind.'

268

'I've kept the nightdress. It's got his semen and her blood on it.'

'Jesus Christ,' Adam said. 'I always knew Declan was an arse-hole but this is something else.'

The two men fell silent again, their minds busy running through macho scenarios in which they slew the demon and saved the damsel in distress, but the damage had been done and they were powerless to act without her consent. Even if either of them had been the type to go to Declan's house or place of work to punch him or kick him or hit him with a baseball bat until he needed to be hospitalized, it would only have caused Lily more pain and her children distress. If they said something and Lily didn't back their story, Declan was the kind of prick who would sue for defamation and both men knew, regardless of the evidence Clooney had kept, that Lily would never file a report. She had said so herself – Declan was the father of her children: she would never allow them to think that their father was capable of such an unspeakable act. She wouldn't do it to them. Both men felt frustrated and impotent. Lily had told Clooney about the photos, which meant that Declan was building a case against her for infidelity.

'But you haven't been together?' Adam said to Clooney.

'No.'

'You want to be?'

Clooney sighed. 'I fell in love with Lily when I was fourteen and she was only twelve.'

'And you were never together?' Adam said.

'One summer a long time ago,' Clooney said, 'and I ended up driving her back to him.'

'I'm sorry.'

'We always wanted different things. She wanted a family. I wanted adventure. She wanted a home. I prefer a tent on a beach. All she ever wanted was some stability. I couldn't give her that.'

'And now?'

'I think I'm always going to be the guy who leaves,' Clooney said. 'Can't help loving her, though.'

They resumed musing, each man working out a separate strategy to get Lily back into her home and get Declan out. They concluded it was impossible. If Lily didn't threaten to charge him he'd have no reason to leave. In fact, Adam was absolutely sure he'd revel in his small victory. If Lily left him, he'd make damn sure she left with nothing.

'We could bluff?' Adam said.

Clooney perked up.

'We could say that she was going to press charges if he didn't get out,' Adam went on, as Lily walked into the room.

Clooney wondered how long she had been listening. She sat on the sofa and hugged a cushion. 'He won't believe you. He knows I'll put the kids first. He'll play with you and then he'll raise the stakes. He'll call me names and tell you I like it rough, and he'll hope that one of you punches him so he can call the guards. If you don't, he'll tell you to get out of his office because, you see, Declan doesn't think he's done anything wrong. You can't scare someone who believes they have justice on their side.' She was calm and even-toned. She knew the man she had married. 'Thank you for trying to help me, though,' she said. She smiled. 'I'm going to be fine,' she said. 'I always am.'

That day, Clooney didn't make it into the hospital to see Eve. Instead he lay in her large bed with Lily in his arms.

Early that evening Lily remembered Daisy was waiting to be picked up. She phoned Tess's mother and confirmed that it was OK for Daisy to stay another night. The woman offered to put Daisy on the phone but Lily said no. She wasn't ready to attempt to explain herself to a twelve-year-old.

Afterwards she talked to Scott and made sure he was all right. 'The old man had a serious hangover this morning,' Scott said.

'Scott, I'm leaving your father,' she said.

'What?'

'I'm going to ask a solicitor to send him a letter asking him to leave the house but if he refuses I can't go back. I have no money.

I don't know where I'll be living so you and Daisy might have to stay with him for a while until I get settled.'

'You sound like you're crying. Are you crying, Mum?'

'I'm fine,' she lied. 'I'm sorry.'

'It'll blow over,' he said.

'No, Scott, it won't.'

'You can't leave him,' he said, as though her previous words had just sunk in.

'I have to.'

'You need to come home,' he said, in a voice that reminded her of Declan.

'Don't speak to me like that,' she said.

'Why are you doing this?'

'Because I have to.'

He called her a bitch and told her she was ruining everyone's lives. Then he hung up.

She bit her split lip, and Clooney presented her with more food he wanted her to eat.

'Kids,' he said, putting a small piece of fish, baby potatoes and some steamed vegetables in front of her. 'Selfish little bastards, aren't they?'

It was her first real smile. She picked up the fork, put some food into her mouth, chewed and swallowed.

Later that night, facing Clooney in bed, consumed by exhaustion but battling to stay awake, she smiled a little 'I'm almost free,' she whispered.

He kissed the top of her head and cupped her beautiful fragile face in his hands. 'Yes, you are,' he said. 'Now go to sleep.'

10. The blame game

Lil?

Hello?

Where are you? It's been two weeks and not a word. Have you forgotten all about us? Declan is freaking out. I've never seen him so upset. He says you haven't called, and when I told him you hadn't written, he lost it. He had a massive row with his dad because his dad won't give him time off to go down there after you. I was there! I went into the garage to have lunch and collect my odds and ends to make some jewellery (I've even sold a few pieces in the café!) and he asked me if I'd heard anything and I said no and he said you hadn't called, and then he started to bite at his fingers the way he does when he looks like he wants to start crying, and then his dad came in and said something shitty about me being there but he did it in a mumble so I couldn't actually hear what it was but just loud enough so I knew he was unimpressed with me being there. Declan said to him he needed time off to go away and his dad just laughed, and Declan walked right up to him and I swear it looked like he was going to punch his father in the face and then his father squared up to Declan and it looked like he was going to punch Declan in the face, and I was thinking holy shit but anyway I think they remembered they weren't animals, or that I was there or something, but they both backed away from one another. I told Declan I'd come back for lunch later but didn't return. I thought it best to give him some room to cool down. He was really angry and it wasn't pleasant to be around.

Anyway, I went back the next day to see how he was and I

was running really low on those small fiddly bolts that make such lovely bracelets. Can't wait for you to see the stuff! I'm using Gina's dad's old kiln now too. I've a few pieces put by for you but meantime Barry Douglas wants a necklace for his girlfriend – as if he has one but, imaginary girlfriend or not, he's a paying customer – and Rebecca Kelly is looking for a pair of earrings. I don't charge much which is probably part of the charm but still, between me making the stuff and Declan finding the materials, we could have a nice little business going. Oh, and don't worry, I haven't forgotten about that dress you wanted made for the debs' ball. I picked up the pattern last week while I was in town and the material is my present to you. I hope you like it when it's finished. I can't wait to see you in it.

Back to the story. I went to the garage to see Declan and pick up my bits. I waited until I saw his father pass the coffee shop – he never works past four. I brought in some leftover cake that would have gone off or into the bin and a sandwich for him but he was too agitated to eat. He said that his dad wouldn't let him go down the country and he was holding his wages. I couldn't believe it. Can you? Declan was kicking things around and acting like a caged animal, one minute calm the next throwing such a tantrum that if I wasn't so busy ducking from a box of screws hitting the wall it would have been laughable. I mean, I understand his frustration but he is so dramatic. Anyway, I managed to calm him down. I told him if he needed to borrow money I'd give it to him – it's the least I could do bearing in mind I've earned about two hundred quid selling jewellery made from scraps he found. His humour changed completely, he picked me up and twirled me around and told me I was the best friend in the world. It was nice to see him so happy. I told him I should get Terry the Tourist to take a photo just so that we could all have a record of it. Anyway, his mother's birthday is late next week and it's a big one – she's forty – so he has to stay here for that but afterwards he's on the way down to you. He says he'll leave his dad a note. I can only imagine what it will say.

Seriously, please write. I know it's probably got really busy in the restaurant and the weather's good and you're probably friends with Colm again and Clooney's there with his pals but I'm up here all alone – well, not all alone but it feels like that. I was so bored last Wednesday I went to see Ghost with Danny. It was brilliant. You should see it if there is a cinema down there. Is there a cinema down there?

Finally Ben's granny died last Friday. She had been anointed four times, which is weird considering that if you believe in that stuff surely once should do the trick. Anyway the funeral was on Monday so Ben didn't get back until Tuesday. It was so great to see him. He looked tired and he needed to cut his hair but other than that he is so handsome. I'd forgotten how handsome he is. He walked into the coffee shop and I swear my heart skipped a beat and my insides fizzed a little. I love that feeling, don't you? Although it plays havoc with my appetite and you know I love my food. We had the best night ever on Friday night. Ben rented a hotel room in town. I told Danny I was going in to a gig and we stayed there from five o'clock in the evening until last bus. It was a small hotel that had the worst wallpaper I've ever seen and it smelt of smoke but the sheets were clean and the bed was big. We had such a good time. He really makes me laugh when I'm with him and I know it's stupid to say but I really feel beautiful and when he touches me – arrrgh! But it got me thinking and suddenly I felt really sad. I didn't tell him because I didn't want him to feel sad too but I've only got three weeks left before I leave for London. He forgets my course starts a whole month before everyone else's. I remind him but I don't think he wants to remember that. I think he wants to pretend and that's OK. I understand that. I wish I could pretend but I have to get ready, I have to focus, this is my lifelong dream. He fell asleep for a while and I lay there looking at him and I cried because even though I was inches away I missed him already. I thought my heart was going to split down the middle. I felt genuine pain so I went into the bathroom and I cried there. When he woke up I was in the bath and he joined me and I felt better but still it's constantly on my mind. Three weeks, Lil, that's all we have left. It makes me want to puke just thinking about it. Do you remember when we were sitting in Paul's dad's car and Roy Orbison came on the radio singing 'Love Hurts' and I said it was the worst song in the world? Well, it's still in the Top 10 shit songs of all time but finally I get it when I think about getting on that plane and leaving home, my dad, Clooney, you, the lads. I think it'll be OK, we'll write and see each other at Christmas, and I won't be in London for ever and I'm sad and lonely but I know I'll be fine. When I think about leaving Ben I think I actually might die. It's so stupid and dramatic and pathetic because I've known him for such a short time but the thought of losing him takes my breath away. I don't like it. This is not where I wanted to be this summer but even so (the last two weeks aside and Ben's stupid gran RIP) this is the best summer I've ever had. Three weeks left. Are you even going to be home in time to say goodbye? Please write to me. I miss you.

 Eve

CAN YOU BELIEVE OUR RESULTS ARE OUT TOMOR-ROW!!!!!!!!!

When Lily went to collect Daisy she was gone: Declan had picked her up. When she went to Jack Donovan's garage she found him there alone. Declan had asked Scott to stay at home to mind his sister.

'He's been busy,' Lily said.

'Is Scott right? Are you leaving Declan?' he asked.

'Yes.'

'For another man?' His question was without malice or judgement.

'For myself,' she said.

'Is he like I was?' he asked, and looked at her straight in the face. His eyes felt like a tractor beam locked on hers and she couldn't escape his look.

'No and yes, probably. He's never touched the kids.'

'You?'

'Once or twice,' she said, breaking away from his stare.

'I never touched his mother,' he said, in a whisper, while wiping grease from his hands with an old tea-towel.

He pointed to two battered chairs that he and Scott sat on to share their lunch.

'You said the other night that he is what I made him,' he said.

She remembered saying it.

'I put my hands up. I was a terrible father and I did terrible things, but at some point Declan has to take responsibility for who he is and for what he's done.'

'Suddenly you're the Dalai Lama,' she said, shaking her head. 'I remember the various states he was in when you'd finished with him. I remember the marks and the bruises and the crying. I've listened to him scream your name in his dreams and, yeah, you're right, we are more than our past and it's not a good enough excuse. But sometimes when he's at his most vicious, paranoid and bullish, I look at him and I see you as clear as if you were standing in front of me. He's your son, Mr Donovan. He is what you made him, genetically and socially. Maybe you're not the narcissist or the bully you used to be, or maybe you're just a different kind, and even if you've changed utterly through the AA or finding God or peace or purpose, I'm glad for you, but don't think we'll ever be allies because we won't.'

She got to her feet and brushed herself down.

He stood up. 'I understand,' he said, and went back to work as she left.

Clooney was waiting in the coffee shop a few doors down. It had changed a lot since the days when Eve had worked there. He had a coffee waiting for her. She told him that Scott had been called home.

'What's he playing at?' Clooney said.

'He's rounding up his troops,' she said.

Adam had called to tell them that Declan had requested a few days off. Lily needed to go to the house and get her clothes. She knew that bringing Clooney with her would give her husband more ammunition to use in front of the kids, but she was too terrified to go by herself.

They pulled up outside the house. They sat in the car for a moment while she braced herself. She opened the door, got out and walked up the path. He followed closely. She put her key in the door and it turned easily. The door swung open and she stepped inside. She could hear him in the kitchen: the radio was on and he was talking to Daisy. When she walked into the room, they were both at the island and Daisy was showing him how to make muffins. There were baking utensils everywhere and they were both covered with flour. Declan was licking icing off his fork. They stared at her as though she was an unwanted intruder. Scott came in through the back door from the garden. He stood staring too. In the thirty-plus hours since the rape, her husband had managed to turn her kids against her. *Always the victim, Declan.*

'What are you doing here, Mum?' Scott asked. He was angry, but when he looked from his mother to his father, his expression changed to concern. *What have you said, Declan?*

Clooney appeared behind her and put his hand on her shoulder.

'What is *he* doing here?' Daisy demanded.

'He's my friend.'

'We know who he is. Dad showed us the pictures,' Scott said.

She looked at Declan. *Did you show them the photos with my blood on them or another copy?* 'You're a scumbag,' she said.

'You have a nerve,' he said, 'bringing him into our children's home.' He was standing behind Daisy holding her shoulder, mirroring Clooney because, as ever, he was the master manipulator. If he hadn't positioned his twelve-year-old in front of him, Clooney might have jumped the counter and beaten him to a pulp. Declan knew exactly what he was doing. Scott fell into line with his dad and his sister, and the battle lines had been drawn.

'You said you had to go the other night, Mum, so you should

go,' Scott said, 'but wherever you end up, we're fine here with our dad.'

Lily looked into her husband's eyes and they were cold, betraying no feeling, but his lip curled slightly to signal his smug satisfaction. Even if she couldn't bear to tell her children their father was a rapist, she could have said that he was a liar and that she was leaving because he was a bully, a manipulator, a paranoid control freak who had mentally abused her for years but she didn't. They had already been led to believe that she was some kind of whore who had chosen to run off with another man. Showing them the pictures – although they were innocent they looked incriminating – was only a small example of what he was capable of. Although her children were staring at her with anger and hatred in their eyes, she refused to fight or plead her case. She would not sink to his level. She would not damage her kids.

This was only the start. He would use the kids, tell them any tale to ensure they stayed by his side. He'd focus all his energy on guaranteeing they felt his pain and pitied him for it, as she had done for so many years. He would try to make it impossible for her to leave him, but she couldn't stay. She was leaving her children with a wolf and there was nothing she could do but wait, bide her time, let them know how much she loved them and that she was sorry for putting herself first but she had to before it was too late. She decided that she would get them back. They had been raised by her to recognize real love, and even if she'd spoilt them a little, they were good kids who would forgive her.

'OK,' she said, 'I understand. I just want you to know that I love you both and I'll always be there for you.'

Clooney stood on guard while she filled three cases with everything she owned. She didn't take the jewellery: she left it all, except a few strings of beads that Daisy had made for her in art class. One case was filled with photo albums and the old shoebox with Eve's letters and photos. She was packed and ready to go within twenty minutes of arriving. The kids stayed in the kitchen with their father and she left without saying goodbye.

She didn't see Declan smashing his cup into the sink and storming upstairs to his room. She didn't see Daisy's tears and Scott reaching for his little sister's hand. She didn't witness her son grow up in that moment: he had instinctively realized that he was his mother's replacement and stepped up to the role she'd vacated. He could rely on all the rainy afternoons when she'd taught him to cook – he'd been young and curious and liked to spend time with his mother. She didn't see him get his sister up in the mornings and make sure his dad's dry-cleaning was dropped off and collected on the way to and from his granddad's garage. She didn't hear Declan venting at his kids when he was feeling so sorry for himself that he had to share his pain. She didn't hear the ugly things he said, blaming them for their mother leaving with another man.

'If you were better kids, brighter . . .'

'If you weren't such smart mouths . . .'

'If you didn't play that stupid piano every night, noon and morning . . .'

'If you weren't such a bloody disappointment . . .'

She lay awake alone in Eve's bedroom, those first few nights, wondering what their lives would be like without her, and how long it would be before they'd allow her to try to make it all better. *I've got to make it all better.*

After that first day and night when she and Clooney had lain together, they separated. He allowed her space to heal mentally and physically. The last thing he wanted to do was hurt, pressure or frighten her. She was experiencing a special kind of anguish reserved for mothers separated from their children. He'd seen it many times before and for many different reasons but the look was always the same. There was resignation and guilt in her eyes. Those first few days she kept to herself, save for mealtimes, when he made sure she sat down at a table and ate. She needed to fight her demons and he stood back, waiting till she'd won.

Eve was not so patient. She had been in hospital for nine weeks and she was more than ready to leave. She was bored and restless and, although she was still weak, the physiotherapists had done a good job at getting her semi-mobile. She walked with great difficulty, her shoulder was still painful, and she suffered muscle wastage on both legs and her left arm, but she could afford to have a physio appointment at home every day. Adam had confirmed that she wouldn't need a second operation on her shoulder, and she had two people waiting to care for her when she got home.

Adam had broken the news to her that Lily had left Declan – Declan had timed his attack for the last day of Lily's working week, so Eve hadn't suspected anything was wrong, even when Clooney hadn't turned up. She'd thought he was taking a day off and maybe helping Paul, who was overwhelmed with the list of wedding tasks Simone had assigned to him before she'd returned to London for an early hen party with her model friends. Paul and she had decided on a small non-religious ceremony in the function room at the Atlantic Coast Hotel and Spa in Westport. The service would be conducted by a woman, and dinner would be served in the Blue Wave restaurant followed by drinks and dancing in the Fishworks Bar and Café. A bus would take hardened drinkers and partygoers to Matt Molloy's Bar for a late-night traditional Irish session.

'Why Westport?' Eve had asked him.

'It'll annoy my mother.'

'The non-religious ceremony?'

'The same reason.'

She was happy that he was pleased to piss his mother off. She had never warmed to the woman. He'd picked that hotel, he told her, because they had spent a weekend there when he'd first started seeing Simone and they had gone back every couple of months since. The spa was run by an ayurvedic doctor, Dr Thomas. He could diagnose and treat conditions with hot oils, massage, individual dietary and lifestyle recommendations to promote healing, balance and good health.

'It's about what you eat and when you eat it,' Paul said. 'It's all about the *vata*, *pitta* and *kapha*.'

'The what, the what and the what?' she asked.

'We're all made up of either *vata*, air and ether, *pitta*, fire and water, or *kapha*, water and earth.'

'Sounds amazing,' she said, shaking her head, pursing her lips and rolling her eyes to signal scepticism.

'It's the mother of all medicine,' he said. 'Give it a go. If anyone needs to rebalance you do.'

She was sitting in a hospital bed at the time, and assured him she'd had her fill of medicine.

'Trust me, the massages are sublime and they'll help you repair.'

She laughed. 'You should work for the tourist board,' she said, then admitted that she was terrified by the notion of anyone massaging her – physiotherapy was still torturous.

'Remember the summer we did our Leaving Cert?' he said.

How could she forget? That summer had come sharply back in focus in recent times.

'The rugby game we played in August?' he went on. 'A friendly with the Dun Laoghaire lads?'

'You dislocated your knee.'

'Well, actually, it was a guy called David Sweeney who dislocated my knee. He did it because I'd met him in a gay club and we kissed and I wanted to kiss again but he was deeper in the closet than I was, if that's even possible. We had words before the game.'

'You went to gay clubs back then? I thought your first gay experience was in college.'

'Not the point of the story.'

'Don't care.'

'He was angry, and when he attacked, he really attacked. He did some damage.'

'OK.'

'And I've been in pain ever since.'

'Is that why you're rubbish at tennis?' she said, with a grin.

'I have arthritis in the knee,' he said. 'And after one session with Dr Thomas, I kid you not, I felt no pain – it'd been years since I'd felt no pain. You have to be careful, Eve. Things could go badly for you if you don't take your long-term recovery seriously. That doctor can help. I mean it.'

'So the wedding is all about me,' she said.

'No, it's all about us but you should capitalize.'

'The new, open, sharing you is unnerving.'

'Don't get used to it,' he said.

'Whatever.'

When Adam arrived into her room that afternoon, after he had left Clooney to look after Lily, he sat by Eve's bed. She was looking forward to hearing the plans that were being laid down to bring her home, but he was quiet and pale, and he didn't smile the way he always did when he saw her.

'What?' she asked. For a moment she thought they had discovered a reason she couldn't be discharged.

'It's Lily,' he said.

'What about her?'

Her heart beat faster because she had heard that tone before, when her mother was sick, her father was sick and Ben had become an organ donor. *Tell me!* her mind screamed, but she didn't say a word, just waited for the worst. Adam was uncomfortable and unsure. He didn't know if he should tell Lily's old friend what had happened, but then again Lily was staying in her penthouse and obviously attached to her brother. Also, he felt bound to Eve, not just as her doctor but as her friend. If he was honest, he was maybe even a little besotted with her. He owed her the truth and the people living in her penthouse owed her the same, plus he wanted her perspective. She was always so clear-headed about everything. He just didn't know how to report it. The words seemed to get caught in his throat and he could read the impatience on her face.

'He . . .'

'He what?' she asked, knowing immediately that Declan had done something.

'He . . .'

'Have you got some sort of speech impediment all of a sudden? What?'

'He raped her.'

Eve blanched. 'How do you know?' She was a little hoarse and her voice shook, not so much that someone who didn't know her would notice, but in the nine intense weeks they had spent together, Adam felt he knew her well.

'He dislocated her shoulder, split her lip, and her face was swollen. He ripped her apart down . . .' He was a doctor but he didn't want to say it because Lily was his friend. Even though she was married, possibly in love with Eve's brother, and he had developed feelings for Eve, he cared deeply for Lily. Thinking about her in pain made him heartsick.

'Where is she now?' Eve said, slipping into business mode.

'Your place.'

'Where are the kids?'

'At home.'

'They can't all stay in the apartment,' she said. 'Where's Clooney?'

'With her.'

'OK,' she said. 'I'll take care of the rest.'

'Aren't you surprised? Aren't you disgusted?'

'Not surprised,' she said, 'and Declan Donovan disgusted me a long time ago. How is she?'

'She says she's OK.'

'She'll be back to herself in no time. If this is what had to happen to get her away from him, fine.'

'He's going to fight her all the way and she won't use the rape to fight back.'

'I understand. He'll be dealt with,' she said.

When Adam had established that she didn't intend to hire a hitman, he left her to make calls and take control. That was Eve's gift. Getting knocked down had taken it from her, and nine weeks was far too long. The bitch was back.

Watch out, Declan, here I come, you fucking prick.

Eve was finally discharged four days after Lily's attack. The neurologist came back and repeated question after question before Adam would finally sign her out. Mostly she spoke the truth, but in some cases she lied. She wanted to go home.

'Do you ever feel dizzy?'

'No.'

'Any double vision?'

'No.'

'Muscle-jerking?'

'No.'

'Changes in sense of smell?'

'No.'

'What about the headaches?'

'Always had the headaches,' she said, fully aware that the entire file was full of her stupid headaches. 'Just let me go.'

Abby wheeled her to the door, and Adam walked with her. Clooney was on her other side and Lily was waiting at home. She was excited. *We're all back together, Clooney. Just like old times.* She was also ready for war. Eve and Clooney were different in so many ways but he and Lily were so similar. *Always taking the high road.* Eve had become a multi-millionaire by being the exact opposite. Money didn't interest her, the game did, and she never lost. Her jewellery was worn by every credible personality and star in the spotlight. Her high-end couture stuff was on every cat-walk in Milan, Paris, New York and London, and that doesn't happen by accident. It had taken years of hard work and a cut-throat attitude. When the economy had started its downturn she had spotted it before anyone else and created a line to be distributed by a major supermarket in the USA. The board had fought her every step of the way, but she had held firm. They had gone from a high-end million-dollar enterprise to a high-and-low-end billion-dollar enterprise. Eve was passionate about her art but she was also a cold and calculating businesswoman: nothing prevented her winning. Declan Donovan had won way back in the summer of 1990 and only because she had been naïve and wouldn't hurt Lily any more than she had to. Now she would finally get one over on him, helping her friend at the same time. *Patience pays.*

The day she left hospital was glorious. The glass doors opened and she rolled out on to the car park she'd spent so much time looking at. Part of her panicked a little that she was leaving the place where Ben had last lived and finally died. She was leaving the place where she had said her goodbyes to him. *I'm getting out, Ben. I promise when the time comes I'll make sure the Ginger Monster is jailed. It's not much but it's all I can do.* Lily was at the apartment. She hadn't seen her since the rape. She missed her, wanted to mind her and make it all go away. When she got to the edge of the pavement she insisted on using the crutches that lay across her lap. She shambled from the path to the waiting car and got in. When she was finally settled she opened the window.

Adam leaned in. 'Don't bully your physiotherapist,' he warned.

'Don't be late for dinner,' she said.

'What dinner?'

'The dinner to welcome me home,' she said, and looked at Clooney. 'You promised me a dinner?'

Clooney smiled. 'Of course there's a dinner. Tomorrow night everyone's coming and of course Adam's invited.'

Adam smiled. 'Looking forward to it.'

'By the way, you're not my doctor any more.'

'There are follow-ups,' he said.

'Screw you. I'm going private.' She waved as Clooney drove off.

As Adam waved back, he wondered what it would be like to sleep with her when she was less fragile. How long it would take, he couldn't say. Everyone healed, mentally and physically, in their own time. *I think we could really be something.*

When Eve finally made it home, Lily had the place full of flowers to add colour. Eve didn't really like flowers but she understood her pal's need to make the place more homely. To Eve the cool blue sea, the green grass, the yellow sun, the streaming rain or grey sky were all features of the apartment, but Lily favoured coloured walls, flowers, fridge magnets, pictures, photos and just enough clutter to suggest that a family lived there but not so much that it appeared messy. Eve liked clean lines, bare surfaces and strong architecture. There were some new cushions on the sofa and a brown-framed, faded picture of her and Lily on the fireplace that separated the kitchen from the sitting room. *That's got to go*, she thought, then took a moment to consider why and where Lily had kept it all this time. When she picked it up and looked at the two of them on the old swing-set, it made her want to cry.

When she looked closer she saw that Clooney was behind Lily, pushing her. Lily and Clooney wore their usual cheesy grins, but Eve was sitting with her arms folded and a face like thunder. Clooney was about seven, she and Lily were five. She remembered the day. Her mother was behind the camera and her dad had been jumping up and down, waving and acting the fool. *Poor Dad*. The memory of him pulling faces made her smile but only for a moment, and then she wanted the picture gone. *Sentimental but hideous.*

She hadn't made a fuss of Lily when the lift door opened and Lily had greeted her – she had just hugged her old friend and told her she was happy they were together again. Lily was sad and still struggling with her new reality. Eve reacted to complex emotions she didn't understand by being practical. She dropped on to her hard white leather sofa and hugged one of Lily's purple furry cushions because her limbs ached and her sofa, a work of art, seemed uncomfortable and unwelcoming.

Lily handed her a cup of freshly brewed coffee and Clooney hovered.

'I love you, Lily Brennan,' Eve said, out of nowhere.

Lily was caught off guard and tears filled her eyes.

'And you're going to be OK,' Eve said. 'I'll make sure of it.'

'You always took care of me,' Lily said, 'but I'm a big girl now.'

'Don't be silly, you're tiny,' Eve said, and grinned.

Lily went to bed early, leaving Eve and Clooney alone. They sat on the balcony, and over a bottle of wine, looking out at a black sea, he told her in great detail what Declan had done.

'Is Danny's house still up for sale?' she asked.

'As soon as the buyers pulled out, the sign went back up.'

'We need to take it down for a while,' she said.

'Lily?' he said.

'Lily and the kids.'

'They think she's the devil,' he said. 'He has completely manipulated them.'

'They'll get sense,' she said, in a tone that suggested that if they didn't, she'd do something about it.

'Eve,' he said, warning her.

'He'll get sense.'

'Eve.'

'Leave it with me.'

'Don't do anything Lily will regret,' he warned.

'I promise I won't.'

They sat together in the cool night air, with a blow-heater, watching the water lap and fold, and when the bottle was finished and Eve was drunk enough to allow Clooney to carry her, they went inside.

'I can walk. It's not sore. I wish I'd got pissed earlier,' she said in her bedroom, shambling around on crutches and pulling a fresh nightdress out of a drawer. 'Mmm, it doesn't smell of hospital but it does smell of cedarwood.'

She headed to her dressing table, Clooney following in case she tripped. She didn't, and waved him away. 'Goodnight, go to bed, I'm fine.'

'It's good to have you home,' he said, closing the door.

Clooney made his bed on the pull-out sofa in Eve's office. Then he turned on her computer and checked Facebook. There were a few messages from people he'd worked with and friends he had made over the years. He left some comments and looked at a few photos that had been recently posted. Mark Grey, a guy he'd worked with on and off over the years, had taken an office job in Geneva. He and Mark had shared a place in Kenya while Clooney was going out with Barbara Cashin. When it became apparent that she was looking for more than just a fling, he had ended it. She had taken it badly and they hadn't spoken for a while. Clooney had left Kenya, Mark and Barbara behind, and the next time he'd met them, in January 2005, when every NGO was in Indonesia in the aftermath of the tsunami, they were in Aceh. By that time Mark and Barbara were living together and engaged. Barbara had softened towards Clooney, and Mark was happy to see his old pal again and they'd been keeping in touch on and off since. Now they were married, with a baby boy, Laurence. They looked happy, and it was nice to see but a little unsettling.

Over the years the majority of the people he had started out with had either gone back to work within the aid organizations in their own countries or in major cities across Europe and America. Few were still in the field, travelling from country to country and job to job. He would be forty in December and he was tired, but not tired enough to envy Mark and his new suburban nine-to-five life. *Good luck but it's just not for me, man.*

He checked his main email account and saw three messages. Two were from Stephanie. In the first one she told him that a British journalist they both knew had been diagnosed with cancer and flown home to London. The second was headed 'Hello from Paris': the final day of her last period had been 18 June – she had remembered the date because she'd run out of tampons in the desert and had had to use her favourite silk scarf. She had returned to the hotel on 2 July. They'd had sex that night and her coil had chosen not to work: she was ten weeks pregnant. She was in France. She had travelled there for an abortion and a break. Abortion was only legal until the twelfth week in pregnancy and she had to be there for a week before the procedure, for mandatory reflection. She had been there two days and her procedure had been scheduled for the following Thursday: if he arrived on the Friday they could spend a long weekend together at the Ritz before she returned to Afghanistan. The email was three days old.

He sat in Eve's swivel-chair, reading the email over and over again. It was so blasé. *An abortion and a break?* The message was short, matter-of-fact and didn't give away any emotion. It was typical of Stephanie. He wasn't judging her – and he didn't want to be a father – but this was a baby, his and hers. Not wanted but there. Even if she did get rid of it in two days' time, it was there now, growing inside her. His mind was racing. He wasn't made for fatherhood. She wasn't maternal. They were rolling stones. They had been careful not to conceive. She had the coil and he'd only stopped using condoms when they'd had blood tests and been declared clean. They were really fond of one another but they weren't in love. She would have been a good mother but war was no place for a child and war was the only thing Stephanie understood. She didn't belong at an American base any more than he belonged in a United Nations city office.

She's ten weeks pregnant. He Googled what a ten-week-old foetus would look like.

Week 10: embryo is now a foetus. The foetus is now the size of a strawberry. The feet are 2mm long (one tenth of an inch). The neck is beginning to take shape. The body muscles are almost developed. Baby has begun movement. While still too small for you to feel, your little one is wriggling and shifting. The jaws are in place. The mouth cavity and the nose are joined. The ears and nose can now be seen clearly. Fingerprints are already evident on the skin. Nipples and hair follicles begin to form.

She'll be eleven weeks pregnant at time of termination. He was almost scared to look but he couldn't help himself.

Week 11: neurons multiply. The fingers and toes have completely separated. The taste buds are starting to develop. Baby has tooth buds, the beginning of the complete set of twenty milk teeth. Baby can swallow and stick out his or her tongue. Whole body except tongue is sensitive to touch. Cartilage is now calcifying to become bone. If it is a boy, the testicles are starting to produce the testosterone hormone.

He read and re-read it. *Whole body except tongue is sensitive to touch.* Will it feel anything? He found a Yahoo answer site in which pro and anti women basically tore lumps out of each other. He looked at medical sites and saw the same arguments. Most in the medical field agreed that pain was more likely to occur in the third trimester. It was too soon for the baby to be aware and feel pain. *Whole body except tongue is sensitive to touch.*

He started his reply on email. She hadn't even left a phone number and she hadn't sent another email since. He had stopped looking at email when Lily had arrived on his doorstep. He had focused on her and nothing else. He wondered if Stephanie was even that bothered. Three days had passed since she'd told him she was pregnant. The subject heading was interesting: 'Hello from Paris'. *Was she having a good time?* He hoped so. *Did she feel heartsick like he did?* It was unlikely.

Hi Stephanie

He deleted it.

Stephanie

He deleted it.

Oh Steph

He deleted it.

I'm so sorry.

He deleted it.

I just picked this email up.

He deleted it.

He sat over the computer, tapping the J key lightly with his finger. *We could spend a long leisurely weekend at the Ritz before I head back to Afghanistan.* Was she at the Ritz? He Googled the website and got the phone number. It was just after two a.m. in Ireland, which made it three a.m. in Paris.

He phoned the hotel. The receptionist picked up after four rings. She sounded bright and breezy, as though it was the middle of the day. In broken French Clooney apologized for calling so late and asked to be connected to Stephanie Banks's room. She took a minute and advised that Stephanie had requested not to be disturbed after ten p.m. He explained it was very important. She considered for a moment and rang the room.

'Hello?' Stephanie sounded sleepy.

'I just picked up your email,' he said.

'I was wondering why you were so quiet.' She yawned.

'Are you all right?'

'I'm fine,' she said. He heard her stretching in the bed, the way she always did when she was half awake, half asleep.

'Are you sure this is what you want?'

'It's what we both want,' she said.

'Thanks for telling me.'

'I hope to see you.'

'Eve just got out of hospital today.'

'Wow. She must have been in a bad way.'

'She was.'

'And now?'

'She'll be OK,' he said. 'Are you scared?'

'They're going to put me out,' she said.

'When and where?'

'Thursday, one p.m. Number ten rue Vivienne.'

'I'll fly in that morning,' he said.

'You don't have to.'

'I want to.'

'I'm really tired,' she said.

'Go back to sleep.'

'And, Clooney . . .'

'Yes?'

'Thanks.'

He hung up and looked for flights that would get him to Paris as early as possible on Thursday morning. He found one leaving at seven a.m. that arrived at nine forty-five. He booked it and emailed to let her know. He asked her if he should meet her in the hotel or if he should go straight to the clinic.

Before he closed the computer he read the last email. It was a job offer to head a food programme in Peru. It had been up and running for four years, managed by a man he was aware of but had never met. The guy was leaving in November but it was hoped that Clooney would be in Peru by 1 October to work with him until the handover. He didn't open the attached file but he answered the email, asking for a week to think about it. He closed down the computer and fell on to his bed. He lay there in the dark with his eyes wide open, his mind and heart racing.

Stephanie needs me but only briefly. I want Lily but she's a mother going through a nasty separation. She's bound to Ireland. What about Peru? No more war. I couldn't be a stepdad to those kids any more than I could be a father to Stephanie's child, even if either of them wanted me to – but then why not? What if Stephanie changes her mind? Could I step up to the plate if I had to? Of course I'd do my best. What about Peru? I could do something in Peru. A fucking baby. If it is a boy, the testicles are starting to produce the testosterone hormone. Eleven weeks. What if Lily and I get together? Would I end up hurting her like last time? Would she want now what she wanted then? What if Stephanie wants me to ask her not to have an abortion? Women change when they get pregnant. My baby is growing inside her. Do I want to ask her not to have an abortion? No. What would it mean for both of us? A completely different life? I don't want a different life. What does that make me? Eve needs me here now but for how much longer? Would I even consider staying in Ireland and settling down? No. Even for Lily? I can't stay here. What about Peru? It would be a fresh start on a project that's actually working and supported by local government. How the hell did we get pregnant? Damn it, Stephanie, if you're so sure and so cool about it, why did you even tell me? Lily, you make me so happy – if only I could be what you need me to be. What about Peru?

The next morning Clooney was tired and quiet. Eve had slept late – it was the first time in a long time that someone wasn't prodding her at a ridiculous hour. He sat at the kitchen counter, drinking coffee and watching the waves splash against the rocks.

Lily appeared in a pair of striped blue-and-white pyjamas. When she passed him she smelt of roses. She looked at him from under her thick chestnut-brown fringe, full of concern. 'You didn't sleep,' she said.

He nodded. 'A lot on my mind.'

'Can I help?'

'No,' he said.

'Please, try me,' she said, pouring coffee from the pot into his mug and into another for herself. She sat opposite him. He looked into her big brown eyes and wondered how much she had been through over the past twenty years. *I'm so sorry, Lily.*

'I have to go to Paris tomorrow,' he said.

'Oh.' She looked disappointed. 'For how long?'

'A few days.'

'Is that all?'

'I'll be back.'

'But not for long,' she said, and she smiled but her smile was just a mask.

'Never here for long.'

'I'll miss you,' she said. She picked up the mug and walked back into Eve's spare room.

It was after eight, and Paul and Simone were the first to arrive to Eve's welcome-home dinner with four bottles of wine and a twenty-four pack of beer.

'Think you have enough booze there, pal?' Clooney said, laughing.

'Better to be safe than sorry,' Paul said, breaking out a beer and handing it to him. He took another for himself and put the rest into the fridge. He'd been buying a wedding suit with his father, who'd read a book called *Bi Any Other Name: Bisexual People Speak Out*. Paul had been answering questions for most of the day.

'If you were stuck on an island would you rather be with a man or woman?'

'I'd rather be with the one I love.'

'So, say Simone drowned, would you rather be with a man or woman?'

'I don't know. It depends on whether the person is attractive, fun, intelligent, sexy, if we have a spark or not.'

'OK, say you have all that, which one?'

'Oh, for God's sake, Dad, I don't know.'

'If I was bisexual I'd pick the man – just in that setting, mind,' his father had said.

Paul had stopped in his tracks. 'Really?'

'Oh, yeah. Given the choice, with just two of us on a remote island and no telly, I wouldn't have to tell him what I'm thinking every five minutes – and I love your mother but it would be a lovely break not to have to beg to get my end away.'

Paul had laughed and put his arm around his dad. He wanted to tell him he loved him and appreciated him, but he stopped short of that. His dad gave him a nudge. 'Best of both worlds, son,' he said.

'She's the one, Dad.'

'I know,' he said, 'but if you're ever stuck on an island . . .' He winked, and they walked on down Grafton Street towards the shop where Gar would meet them to try on suits.

It had been a long day and Paul took a large slug of his beer, then said hello to Lily, who was busy in the kitchen. 'Good to see you, Lily.'

She was wearing a black V-neck dress, and although she was too thin, she looked beautiful. 'You too, Paul,' she said.

'Sorry to hear about your marriage trouble,' he said. Clooney had told everyone bar Adam and Eve that Lily and Declan had split up because they'd grown apart.

'Thanks. Congratulations on your wedding,' she said.

Lily had missed out on Paul's gay years. The last time she'd seen him he was with a beautiful girl and, as far as she was concerned, nothing had changed.

Simone was standing in the middle of the kitchen-cum-dining-room-cum-sitting-room, staring at the view through the glass wall. Balcony lights shone down on the water, highlighting a ship that was passing in the distance. She turned from the window to look at the mezzanine office with its inbuilt bookshelves and beautiful wooden spiral staircase that Eve couldn't climb at the moment. 'This place is amazing,' she said.

'It's very Eve,' Clooney said.

'Speaking of . . . where is she?' Paul asked.

Lily said she'd go and get her. When she was gone Paul looked at Clooney. 'So, are you sleeping together yet?' he asked.

Clooney looked at him with wonder. How the hell . . . He didn't answer and Paul didn't need him to.

Adam arrived before Eve appeared. He brought more wine and a bottle of expensive whiskey but was happy to share the beer. He loved the place too. 'It's very Eve,' he said.

Clooney smiled. He liked Adam and hoped his sister wouldn't chew him up and spit him out like she'd done with everyone except Ben Logan.

Gar and Gina arrived late and hassled: the baby-sitter had told them she couldn't stay past midnight because she was studying for a test. They'd tossed a coin as to who got to stay late. Gina lost.

'Studying, my hole!' Gina said. 'She's probably meeting some young fella. I get out one night in a blue effing moon!'

They had brought more booze to add to the huge stockpile. Gar poured himself a glass of red wine, while Gina and Simone sat down together on Eve's uncomfortable white sofa, talking about how amazing the place was. 'But a deathtrap for young

295

kids,' Gina said, looking from the spiral staircase to the balcony, four storeys up with its low wall, and across the grounds, which seemed to fall off the cliff. 'I mean, a view is all very well but you'd think they'd put up some kind of fence in the gardens. Our youngest would just run off the end of that because he could.'

Simone hoped her kid wouldn't be as simple as Gina's sounded.

In her bedroom Eve was in meltdown because she had nothing to wear. Lily looked in her vast wardrobe. 'You do seem to have a thing for jeans and vest tops,' she said.

'I had a black dress I liked but I wore it the night of the accident with Ben. Clooney had it dry-cleaned but I can't wear it again. Anyway, you're in black.'

'What about the red one?' Lily asked, pulling out one of the only three dresses she could see.

'It's too low-cut.'

'OK, the white.'

'I'm too white for white.'

'How about jeans and one of your beautiful cashmere V-neck jumpers?'

'Adam will think I haven't made any effort.'

'Adam will think you're beautiful.'

Eve considered Lily's comment, then admitted, 'I know he likes you but I told him you'd never go for him.'

'He told me,' Lily said, and smiled.

'Interesting.'

'He said you were a good friend.'

'Yeah, well, he doesn't know me.'

'He's right,' Lily said. 'You're the best possible friend.'

Eve hovered on one crutch to pull out a pair of jeans and a cashmere jumper. 'These will do. It's probably a lost cause anyway, if he's still mooning over you.'

'Oh, I think you've given him something else to think about! He talks about you all the time.' Lily took the jumper and jeans from Eve and followed as she wobbled her way over to the bed on her crutches.

Eve took off her robe and sat in a silk bra and knickers set that Lily imagined had cost more than her own entire wardrobe. The scars on her shoulder and legs were still red and angry. 'What does he say?' Eve asked, looking down at the scars and wishing they'd fade and go away. *I don't have for ever for you to disappear, you know.*

Lily made a mental note to buy some bio-oil for her friend while helping Eve put on her jumper. She still had trouble raising her left arm. Lily worked around the problem easily. 'Well, he asks lots of questions about when we were kids, what you were like, and when he talks about you he grins like a teenager. He repeats the things you say and laughs to himself. He's falling for you.'

'You don't know that!' Eve snorted.

Lily pulled Eve's jeans up and dragged her off the bed into a standing position. Eve held on to her waist while she zipped and buttoned them.

'Yes, I do, because he looks at you the way he used to look at me,' she said, relieved for herself and happy for her friend.

'I don't even know if I can fall in love with someone other than Ben Logan.'

'Only one way to find out. Now, put some makeup on and come outside. I've got to check on the dinner.'

When Eve finally emerged, everyone was sitting at the dining table, drinking, talking and laughing. Lily was being the perfect hostess with Clooney at her side. Music was playing. Gar was taking the piss out of Gina, much to everyone's amusement. She was blushing and saying, 'Stop it,' and Paul was holding Simone's hand and laughing hard. Eve stood back, leaning on her crutches, and watched her friends. The room seemed different filled with people and sound. She realized she wasn't alone any more. *I'm home. Finally I'm home.*

Adam turned, stood up and walked over to her. 'You look stunning,' he said, and kissed her on the mouth.

When he pulled away she grinned. 'You're fast.'

'Not really. I've wanted to do that for a while now.'

She leaned in and kissed him. She only stopped when her legs felt they were going from under her and Clooney shouted at her to get a room. 'This *is* my room,' she said.

The rest of the night they spent eating Lily's gourmet food, drinking wine, telling stories and laughing. Even Paul opened up with a few stories of his own.

When it turned midnight and a drunk, emotional Gina had to go home to relieve the baby-sitter, Eve struggled to the door to say goodbye, with Lily and Simone.

Gina hugged Lily and told her she'd missed her. 'Don't ever go away again,' she said.

Lily promised she wouldn't.

'It's good to have you back,' she said to Eve. 'I was getting a real pain in my arse sitting in that hospital.'

Down the hallway, she leaned out of the lift and shouted, 'Simone, don't go changing!'

Lily helped Eve back to the sitting room where she sat with Adam, Clooney, Gar and Paul. Adam and Paul realized they had dated two of the same girls from Mount Anville School and reminisced about them until Clooney asked if Donald Blair was gay. He wasn't, but it led to a conversation about who was gay in the rugby teams they had played against.

'Martin Walsh,' Clooney said.

'No way!' Gar said.

'Had him,' Paul said.

'Didn't you go out with his sister at one point?' Gar said.

'Yeah.'

'Christ!' Gar said. 'To think I used to wish I was you.' He shook his head. 'Now, don't get me wrong, I wouldn't throw her out of bed for eating peanuts, but Martin Walsh!'

'Wasn't he the guy with the cauliflower ears and the smashed nose?' Eve asked, getting up to join Lily in the kitchen area.

'When we actually got together in college he had two missing teeth as well, but there was something about him.'

Simone laughed. She was sitting on the floor in a yoga position and although she was the only one not drinking she was enjoying herself immensely. 'I'm really going to like it here,' she said, and got up to pee for the eighth time that night. Paul marvelled at how chilled she was about his past. It was as though she was a miracle sent from Heaven, not to save him from damnation, as his mother believed, but to allow him to be comfortable in his own skin. *Thanks, Simone. God, thank you. I love you.*

Adam followed Eve and Lily to the kitchen. Eve was settling herself at the counter and Lily was cleaning it. 'Helluva better night than dinner at Rodney's,' he said to Lily.

'It's a better life,' she said. She wondered how her kids were and if they'd start picking up their phones soon when she called. *Give them time, Lily.*

Adam kissed Eve and told her he was leaving. She wanted him to stay but he was working the next day. 'I'll call you tomorrow,' he promised. A taxi was waiting for him downstairs. He said goodbye to the boys, and to Simone when he met her coming back from the bathroom.

When he was gone, Eve grinned at Lily, who was making coffee in the hope that the boys would at least pretend to drink it. 'Good kisser,' she said, and made a tick in the air.

Simone joined them at the counter. Lily handed her a peppermint tea. 'I've eaten so much I could burst,' she said, then focused on Eve. 'So, are you taking Adam to the wedding?'

'Hadn't thought about it,' Eve said.

'Well, start thinking about it.'

'Do you think he'd come?'

'With bells on,' Lily said.

Simone nodded. 'He's a smitten kitten,' she said.

'I wonder what sex will be like,' Eve said.

'Like it was before, except you won't be as bendy,' Lily said.

'Dr Thomas will sort you out in the spa,' Simone said. 'One Padaghata massage and you'll be circus bendy.'

When the night was over and everyone had gone home, Eve

was exhausted. Lily helped her to bed, and when she'd gone, Eve lay in her bed, talking to Ben about the night. *Paul and Martin pigging Walsh. I've heard it all now.*

Clooney helped Lily finish tidying up. 'The next dinner party we have we'll get a caterer in,' he said, not liking the idea of Lily doing so much work.

'Over my dead body,' she said, happy that he was thinking of staying around at least long enough to have another dinner party. *Live in the moment, Lily.*

When the dishes were done and the counter was cleaned, he said goodnight and told her he'd be gone before she woke. She wished him good luck on his trip. He thanked her and they both hovered, then turned and went their separate ways.

The next day, twenty-four unanswered messages later, Lily turned up in Jack Donovan's garage. Scott was alone – his granddad was out buying parts. He came out of the office smiling, when the bell that signalled a customer rang, but his expression changed when he saw his mother. He asked her what she wanted.

'World peace,' she said.

'Very funny,' he said.

'I have more.'

He was angry, understandably so. She trod gently.

'How are you?' she asked.

'I've been better.'

'And Daisy?'

'She's devastated.'

'Things will get better,' she said. 'I've taken a month's leave from the hospital. I'm going to find a place and when I do you can come and live with me.'

'We're going nowhere,' he said.

'You can think about it.'

'You might have left Dad but we're not going to,' he said, and she heard Declan's voice again.

'I did leave your dad but I will never leave you,' she said.

'Really? Because that's what it looks like, feels like and smells like, so you must be talking shit.'

'I told you, when I find a place –'

'Are you moving in with him?'

'No.'

'He's that woman's brother, isn't he?'

'Yes,' she said, and wondered how much Declan had said about Eve.

'How long have you been sneaking around behind Dad's back?'

'I couldn't tell your father that Eve was in the hospital because I knew he'd try to stop me seeing her –'

'And *him*.'

'And him, yes. His name is Clooney.'

'Stupid name.'

'What I've done has nothing to do with Clooney,' she said.

'Then what?'

'Remember the summer when you were thirteen and you broke your leg on the second day of a month-long stay in France? The other kids would play all day in the pool and you couldn't so you sat far enough away so as not to be splashed but close enough so that you could hear them playing. You were so near to all that fun and freedom but you might as well have been a world away. You were lonely and ignored and you were miserable.'

'What's your point?'

'I've been living that summer for twenty years.'

'You're saying you hated life with us?'

'I'm saying I hated my life with your father.'

'Are you sorry you had us?'

'No. You kids are the one good thing –'

'He's a mess without you.'

'It will get better.'

'You've broken his heart,' he said. He wasn't accusing her so much as stating a fact.

'It will get better.' *You have to have a heart for it to break.*

They stood staring at one another for a few moments.

'I should go,' she said. 'I'll be in touch.' She moved to walk away.

'Mum!'

She turned.

'Daisy misses you,' he said.

'So tell her to answer her phone,' she said. 'And, Scott, don't let your dad tear you down. When he's in pain he does that, so just remember, it's not you, it's him.'

He said nothing, just pursed his lips. He wasn't going to say anything bad about his dad. He might have softened towards his mother momentarily but he was still angry with her and he still blamed her for breaking up his family and destroying his world. *Why do you have to be so selfish? Why can't you just be happy? Why don't you love us enough to stay? How could you leave us?*

When Lily got to the car she felt she needed to walk, so she put her bag in the boot and went up on to the cliff to the spot where she and Eve had spent so much time in their youth. She sat looking out towards Wales and thought about what she was going to do. *I'm so sorry. I made such a mess of everything. It's all my fault. Please forgive me.*

11. *From Paris to Peru*

Eve,

*I'm so, so, so sorry for not writing before now. I just didn't know
what to say. I've started so many letters and they've all ended up
either completely crossed out or blank and crumpled in the bin. A
lot has happened in the past few weeks and I'm not sure how to
tell you or what you'll think of me. I'm not even sure what I think
about myself. I'm so confused. I can't stop crying. You probably
know that I aced my Leaving Cert (I know Clooney phoned
Danny) and it's great news, it really is, but there's a part of me,
and I don't know why, that wishes I'd failed. If I had, I'd have
had to repeat, and it would have given me more time to think
about what I really want. Does that make sense? As you know,
Declan did well enough and he'll definitely get medicine in Cork. I
haven't spoken to him but he's left lots of messages in the restaurant. The boss is beginning to get really annoyed. I know you did
well. Danny told Clooney. I'm thrilled. I also know it doesn't
mean anything to you because you're creative and you're going to
St Martin's based on your portfolio but it's a great result. How
did Paul do? And Gar? I know I should have rung you and I know
you think I don't care but I do. It's just all been so weird here.*

*I wish you were here, and then I think it's probably best you're
not because you'll kill me. You and Clooney are like my family.
There isn't a memory that I have that doesn't include you and
him and Danny. Your dad has been the closest thing I've ever had
to a father. I love you all. You are the family my mum couldn't
ever give me. You know that. You know I love you and you know*

I love Clooney. I've always loved him, and not like a brother, like a boy, like a man, but he was always older and it was never right because he should have been like a brother. I didn't think he felt the same way. I always thought he saw me as the little annoyance who made him laugh or smile every now and again but mostly got under his feet when he was trying to be cool with all the beautiful girls that flocked around him. I never for a moment thought he'd ever think of me like that.

We started spending a lot of time together. At first it was just us messing around together and the only thing missing and out of the ordinary was that you weren't there, and then one night he came back to my place and I made him some quiche and we shared some beers. The stupid electricity went because I'd forgotten to get 50p pieces to feed the meter so I lit some candles and we just sat together and talked, and when it got cold because that flat is so damp (it's a wonder mushrooms don't grow on the walls) we got under a blanket together on the sofa. I don't know what happened because one minute we were laughing and then we were kissing, and I know this is freaking you out but it was amazing, and I was screaming what the hell in my head and I couldn't stop and we slept together and I won't go into it because I know you'll lose it if I do but I think I'm in love with him. For the whole time I didn't even think of Declan once. It was only when he left the next morning that I remembered I had a boyfriend I loved – and I do love Declan. I'm so confused and I feel so bad. I actually feel sick all the time. I can't talk to Declan. I keep ringing and leaving messages with his mother when I know he won't be there, and I know he's probably losing it but I just don't know what to say and I can't lie to him.

Clooney and I have been together every day since. He's left the tent and he's staying here with me. I've had some of the best times of my life with him and there are moments when I think I've died and gone to heaven but then the guilt comes and I want to die because I can't turn my back on Declan and I do love him.

Besides, Clooney and I are just a fantasy. I'm never going to be his girlfriend. He told me he's leaving. He hasn't told Danny yet so please don't say anything. He's bored with his course, and as much as he loves his radio show, he feels he's done all he can do on it. V Kill P is moving to London to be with her girlfriend and he said it just won't work without her. He did an interview in Dublin last month to volunteer building houses in Africa. He's going in a few weeks. He's always been into that stuff and I know he will love it and it will be the adventure he has always craved, but when he told me I actually felt my heart breaking in two. He said it like I should be happy for him and I am, of course, but I can't stop crying because maybe he'll miss me but he won't miss me like I'll miss him. Our family is breaking apart. You're going to London and he's going to Africa and I'm supposed to go to Cork with Declan, and if I don't, and I will and I do love him – but even if I didn't where would I go? What would I do? My passion is Clooney but he's leaving me and so he should. I'm not really even his anyway, I'm with Declan who needs me. He would never walk away. I do love him. I'm so confused and scared because I don't know what I want to do or where I want to go. Am I going to study medicine just because I can? Am I moving to Cork because that's where Declan wants to be? All I know is, I'm losing my family, the people I love, and without you what am I going to be? I can't believe I've done this to Declan. He can never know. It would destroy him. Please never ever tell him. Tell no one. It's just our secret.

Clooney is coming over tonight and I think I'm going to end it. I keep saying that but then I see him and he's only going to be here for another week so . . . I don't know. I've never been so confused. Please write back to me, please don't be annoyed or let down. I love you. Clooney and I being together doesn't change the fact that you are my best friend. Nothing can change that.

Please tell me what to do. I need your clear thinking.

I'm so sorry,

Lily XXXOOOXXX

The plane landed at Charles de Gaulle Airport on time. Clooney hadn't drunk much the night before, despite the quantity of booze on offer. He was clear-headed and focused on getting to Stephanie. She had emailed him back and told him to meet her at the clinic as she would be there from nine o'clock. He got into a taxi, gave the guy the address, then sat back and watched Paris whiz by. Neither man spoke. 'Je Réalise' featuring James Blunt was on the radio. James Blunt was one of Stephanie's favourite artists and Clooney didn't know if it was to do with his music or his background as a soldier. It spilled into the music, the pain and anguish, the loss, the immorality, the focus and importance. Death and destruction, however lamentable, were bigger and more important than an ordinary day spent pottering in your local city picking up the latest fashion or talking about a film you wanted to see. He listened to the song and lost himself in the blue street signs, the bridges and the majestic corner buildings. When they reached 10 rue Vivienne he paid and got out. It was twelve thirty.

He walked inside and asked for Stephanie Banks. He was directed to a room. Stephanie was genuinely glad to see him. She beamed as though they were meeting in a coffee shop or on a sun-soaked beach. Instead she had a hospital gown on and she was lying in a bed with a familiar yellow toggle stuck in her hand – Eve had worn one. They hugged.

'Of course I'd be here,' he said, conscious that they had just twenty minutes before she'd be taken into theatre.

She smiled and kissed his hand as tears built in her eyes. She would not let them fall. She was made of sterner stuff. 'It's for the best,' she said, knowing he was softer than she was.

'Yes,' he said.

'I just wanted to see you, nothing more,' she said.

'You know me so well.'

'Well, you're me without the balls,' she said, and gave a hollow laugh.

It had been a long ten weeks since he'd left. She'd been working solidly. She'd got into some scrapes while he was away but that was nothing unusual. She'd also come upon a story that might make her career if she played it right. If she didn't she'd be sunk, disgraced and maybe even jailed on some trumped-up charge, but she felt she was smart enough to fight whatever was thrown at her and she'd either succeed or fail and become a victim of the man. Either way the message would get out, and although she'd prefer the former, Stephanie Banks didn't care much either way. *That's why I can't be a mother.*

'Tell me your story,' she said, ever the journalist.

'I've been offered a job in Peru.'

'And?'

'My sister nearly died and her lover did die.'

'And?'

'And the girl I loved and walked away from when I was twenty was just raped by her husband.'

'And you think you can save her?'

'No,' he said, because only Lily could save Lily.

'Do you still love her?'

'I think I do but then . . .' He put his hand on her stomach.

'We're not bad people,' she said, and battled tears again. They were never going to win. Her eyes dried and she tilted her head to smile.

'We just want different things,' he said, and took his hand away.

'Exactly,' she said, 'and I choose me.'

'And I do the same.'

'We're not bad people,' she repeated, yet they silently mourned the thickness of her waist and wondered what might have been if they'd been different people who wanted different things in a different time and place.

After she had been taken away, he waited in a corridor watching French TV. She was gone for less than an hour. She was asleep for another two. She woke up with him at her side. She was groggy and had cramps. He stayed for an hour, long enough for a chat and to feed her a little toast. When she was sleepy and visiting hours were over, he made his way back to her room in the hotel. She had let them know he was joining her. The receptionist gave him a card-key to the room that they would share the next evening. He fell on to the bed and phoned Eve's apartment. Lily answered. He asked how she was and Lily said she was fine. They talked for half an hour but in all that time he didn't tell her why he was in Paris and she didn't ask. *I wish you were here with me now, Lily. I'm such an arsehole.*

On the day that her brother had gone to Paris Eve woke up to breakfast made by her best friend Lily. They sat together and it was just like old times. They didn't speak, just enjoyed the silence that comes with knowing someone well. When they had finished, Eve picked up her phone and booked a taxi to the hospital. Lily was confused. 'Are you OK?' she asked.

'Fine.'

'What are you going back there for?'

'I have a meeting.'

'Who with?' Lily asked.

'Does it matter?'

Lily didn't know how to answer but she knew Eve was up to something. 'Do you want me to come with you?'

'No, thanks.'

'OK,' Lily said. 'I'm not going to ask.'

'Best not to.'

After that Eve took a call from the storage company that was holding her family's furniture. She asked them to return it to the house they'd picked it up from. Then she called Lily. 'It's sorted,' she said.

'What's sorted?' Lily asked, coming in from the office, where she'd spent twenty minutes cleaning the skirting boards, which she'd complained were a disgrace. Lily couldn't relax in the presence of dirt and she needed distraction.

What in hell is the cleaner doing? 'The house is off the market, the furniture will be back by the end of the week and Dad refurbished in the late nineties. It's yours for as long as you need it.'

'Your house?' Lily said, mouth agape.

'The house we grew up in.'

'Your house.'

'Our house.'

'And Clooney?'

'He watched two parents die there. He doesn't want the money from it and I don't need it and you're a part of all that was good in it. Danny would be happy and proud.'

'I was never happier than when I was in that house.'

'I know.'

'Are you sure? I'll pay rent as soon as I get back to work.'

Eve didn't care about rent and neither did Clooney, but she knew that Lily needed to feel she was contributing because that was the way Lily was. 'Consider it a trial. If you're happy there, buy it.'

'It'll be a long time before I can afford a house like that,' Lily said.

'We'll do you a good deal, and the divorce settlement will more than cover the cost.'

'That could take years, especially if Declan fights it, which he will.'

'Maybe he will and maybe he won't,' Eve said. 'Either way we can wait.'

'It's charity.'

'It's friendship.'

'It's too much.'

'Bullshit, it's just enough.'

Eve's taxi driver was a Londoner who had left London because he'd fallen in love with a Dublin girl. The money wasn't as good in Ireland but he maintained it was a better life. He lived close to town and made a good living because, he told her, he had the ability to think outside the box. They pulled up to the hospital and he helped her out of the car. When she was upright, had paid him and was facing the doors, she leaned on her crutches for a moment, looking at the hospital's name, before she made her way in.

She stopped at Reception and asked for Dr Declan Donovan's

office. When asked why she was there, she said she had been asked to quote for redecoration. Adam had told her that Declan had wrecked his office, and now all the staff in the hospital knew about it. Redecorating made sense. The woman grinned and gave her directions. She sat in the waiting area in front of his PA, who told her that without an appointment she had no hope of seeing him.

'I disagree,' Eve said.

'He's in surgery so you'll be waiting.'

'That's fine,' she said, and fished out her book.

He appeared two and a half hours later. He strode in, picked up the post from his in-tray and barely acknowledged his PA.

Eve struggled to her feet. He swung round. His face turned from shock to stone in one second. She was prepared. She grinned fiendishly, just enough to put him on edge without verging into panto villain. 'Declan,' she said.

'Eve,' he said. He paled before her eyes.

'Do you have a minute for an old friend?' She appeared cool but internally she was a mess. *Keep it together, Eve. Focus and get this done.*

He smiled at his PA. 'Of course,' he said, through gritted teeth.

Eve made her way slowly into Declan's office. He closed the door behind her, then sat behind his desk and folded his hands under his chin. 'What can I do for you?' he asked.

She laughed. 'This meeting is more about what I can do to you.'

Outside, Declan's PA typed up medical notes, oblivious to the fact that her boss was being blackmailed.

Clooney picked up Stephanie the next morning. She was sore but wanted to stop for coffee in Montmartre, and she made him sit for an artist who drew caricatures of them. They spent a fun and frivolous morning. They enjoyed coffee and croissants and laughed at the drawings, which were destined for a bin. They represented a moment in time, a sad moment at that, in cartoon form. When they got back to the hotel it was late enough to eat and they went into the restaurant. Stephanie was raw and uncomfortable. They had something light, then made their way up to the room. She stripped off and he ran a bath – Stephanie loved her baths. When it was ready she stepped in and he sat beside her, holding her hand.

'Are you coming in?' she asked.

'No,' he said. 'I'll mind you from here.'

'Bullshit,' she said.

He moved to the top of the bath and massaged her head. She rested against his hands.

'My dad says God will judge us if we're wicked.'

'You know I don't believe in God.'

'I do.'

'And it's all relative. Your dad killed countless men and possibly women and children in the name of his country. You just report on it. You let go of a baby not born. Which one of you is wicked?'

'He believes in what he's done.'

'And you don't.'

'I acted selfishly, he didn't.'

'He killed living, breathing, terrified people in the name of war. Our baby didn't know day from night. It had never cried, never experienced grief or sadness. That little one didn't battle and wasn't afraid. The people who die every day in war know what it is to breathe, to pray, to beg, to suffer, to lose, to die and to grieve. If our baby suffered it was for one second. Those people your father has affected are intimate with suffering – they are fighters who clung to life. If anyone knows what I mean, you do.' And she did.

'We're not bad people,' she said.

'No, we're not.'

She didn't cry because she couldn't bring herself to but she let him stroke her hair comfortingly. Eventually he helped her out of the bath, wrapped her in a towel and brought her into the room. She lay on the bed and he presented her with a silk scarf he'd managed to pick up when her back was turned. It wasn't exactly like the one she'd shoved down her knickers but it was close and expensive enough. She hugged it.

'Sometimes I wish I was different,' she said.

'I know how you feel.' He got into bed with her and held her tight. They slept together, and the next day when she battled with the bleeding, he was there to ferry her from toilet to bath to bed. They ate good food, talked and laughed, and in their own way mourned a life that never was.

Clooney waited until Stephanie had left on her flight to Afghanistan. The procedure had taken more out of her than she'd expected, both physically and emotionally. When they said goodbye it was final, and worthy of their relationship. They hugged one another tightly and accepted they wouldn't meet again. It was the parting of two kindred spirits destined not to love one another.

I will miss you, Stephanie Banks.

I will miss you, Clooney Hayes.

When she disappeared into Security, the load he had carried started to lighten. He moved towards his gate, for the plane home and Lily.

When Eve returned home she sat on her high bar stool at the counter and Lily made some coffee.

'I saw Scott on the street today. I called to him but he wouldn't stop,' Lily said.

'He'll get over it.'

'I just want to know how he did in his college exams.'

'I'm sure he did very well, and when he stops acting like a selfish dick he'll tell you.'

'His father has made it clear to the children it's him or me. He's scared, that's all.'

'You'll get them back,' Eve said, savouring the memory of her recent conversation with Declan. *And sooner than you think.*

'He's always got one over me.'

'Those days are gone.'

'Not while he has my kids.'

'Everything will be fine,' Eve said.

Just as she spoke Lily's phone rang and she saw Daisy's name flash on the screen.

'It's Daisy,' she said, beaming. She answered the phone as she walked towards Eve's spare bedroom. 'Daisy,' she said, in a voice full of tears and thanks. She closed the door behind her. When she returned she was happy and confused, and also a little upset.

'Daisy is coming to live with me as soon as I get into the house.' *Happy.*

'How did she know I was moving into a house?' *Confused.*

'Declan phoned her and told her he was too busy to take care of her. She's devastated.' *Upset.*

'Why would he do that?' she asked.

'He's a selfish, hurtful sociopath,' Eve said.

'He is a sociopath,' Lily admitted, for the first time. 'Still, I don't understand. He wouldn't give up his power like that. It's not like him.'

'Maybe he's seen the light,' Eve said. Inside she was dancing.

'Something's going on.'

'Who cares?' Eve said. 'You're getting your baby back. He's out of your life.'

'Do you think Scott will forgive me?' Lily asked.

'Of course.'

'He's old enough to decide where he wants to live.'

'So let him.'

'She could barely speak, she was crying so hard,' Lily said. 'I think I hate him.'

'Good, that's healthy. I'm proud of you.'

Daisy had done exactly as she was told in the aftermath of her mother's departure. She had studiously avoided her calls, just as her father had instructed. She had done all the jobs her father asked of her. She had been on her best behaviour. She was quiet and not at all demanding. She wondered what she had done to make him suddenly call her in the middle of the day and tell her he didn't want her living with him any more. 'Call your mother. Tell her to pick you up.'

'But, Dad?'

'Start packing. You'll be moving out as soon as she moves into that house.'

'But, Dad.'

'*Daisy!*' he roared. 'Do as I tell you! Phone your slut of a mother and tell her you'll be moving in with her and do it now.'

She was stunned. It was like he had punched her in the stomach. She was shaking when she made the call. She hated her mother for leaving but she also missed the joy and lightness she had brought to their house. It was dark and empty without her. Even when Declan wasn't shouting and screaming, when he was trying to be what dads were supposed to be, it was hard work for him. Daisy felt sorry for him but that didn't stop her fantasizing about leaving him. When he ordered her to go, though, she was bereft. He had told the kids he needed and loved them and now he was making her leave. *What did I do to change your mind?* Daisy's mother had abandoned her, and now her father was kicking her out. Lily had tried to soothe her but she couldn't hear her mother over her own sobs – and how could she believe anything she said anyway? She lay on her bed and cried herself to sleep. It was only five o'clock when she drifted off. She didn't wake at seven when her father came home and heated up an M&S dinner in the microwave, or when Scott ran upstairs and changed before running out to get drunk with Josh, Cedric and Ethan. Neither of them checked on her but it didn't matter. She slept until hunger woke her the next morning at eight, when both men had left for work, leaving her with another long day alone and waiting to be thrown out of her home.

Lily was like a cat on a hot tin roof. She just wanted to get into the house and have her daughter back. On the day that the estate agent handed the keys to Eve, Lily insisted on driving to her old house to pick Daisy up so that she could show her their new home. Eve went with her. She parked the car in the driveway.

'It's nice,' said Eve.

Lily wouldn't get out of the car. 'What if he's there?' she said.

'He's never there during the day. Besides, you have me.'

'No offence, but you're currently a cripple.'

'I could beat him to death with my crutches.'

Lily smiled. 'Declan might not be the only sociopath in my life.'

Eve shrugged – which hurt her shoulder. The physiotherapist who came to her apartment was some kind of Nazi hell-bent on making a name for herself by having Eve as good as new in record time. The idea appealed, but the reality was most uncomfortable. Eve was particularly sore. *I could still take him.*

Lily decided to ring Daisy and hope she'd pick up. She did. When Lily said they were outside the house in the car she came to her bedroom window. Eve saw her peering out. Lily asked her to go with them to see the house. She said no: she was busy with Tess and her dad had told her not to leave the house. Lily told her she'd love to show the new place to both of them because, after all, that was where Tess would be visiting her. There was an intense whispered debate between the girls. Daisy hung up and Lily grinned when they appeared in the doorway and walked down the path.

Tess bounded up to Lily where she stood beside the car and hugged her. 'I really missed you, Lily.'

'I missed you too, Tess.'

Daisy took an age to walk down the path. She had no hugs for her mother. She stared at Eve. 'Is that her?' she asked.

'I'm Eve.'

'She's my friend,' Lily said.

'She's a bitch,' Daisy said.

'And your father is still as charming as ever,' Eve said, knowing exactly where the child's attitude was coming from. 'Now, get in the car, we haven't got all day.'

Lily tried to hug her daughter but she pulled away and got into the back seat beside her friend. She was silent on the journey. In contrast, Tess talked all the way. 'You're the jewellery-maker,' she said to Eve.

'Designer,' Eve said.

'My mum says you're loaded and went out with lots of famous people.'

'Your mum's right.'

'Is it true you went out with Robert Downey Junior before he went mental on drugs?'

'Which one is he again?' Eve asked.

'*Chaplin*,' Lily said, immediately engaged. She didn't know a lot of celebrities because she wasn't much interested in magazines but she knew him. *I love him.* Lily would see magazines lying around the hospital but every cover looked the same and all the banner headlines read the same. They were filled with faces she didn't know and with things she couldn't afford. It was depressing. Meanwhile her best pal possibly shagged Robert Downey Junior.

'*Iron Man*,' Tess said.

'Oh, I saw that on the plane,' Eve said. 'No.' She shook her head. 'Never met him. Besides, he's more like Lily's type.'

Tess laughed. 'You're cool,' she said.

Daisy gave Tess a dirty look. Tess didn't care.

'Have you been with any other actors?' Tess asked.

'Loads,' Eve said.

'OK, change the subject,' Lily ordered.

Tess complied. 'Do you live in a mansion?'

'No.'

'Do you have servants?'

'I have a cleaner, but Lily is better than she is so I might have to fire her.'

'Was the guy who died in the car accident your boyfriend?'

'How did you know about that?'

'It was in the paper.'

'Was it?'

'Duh,' Tess said. 'You're famous.'

Lily shrugged. 'There were a few journalists hanging around the hospital in the early days. You were out of it and we got rid of them.'

'Was he your boyfriend?'

'Is that what it said?' Eve asked, clearly panicked.

Lily put her hand on her knee. 'No, it wasn't. It said you were business partners and that you were going to sell your jewellery in his supermarkets. It said you'd gone from high end to low end to no end.'

Eve laughed. She was relieved that the local papers still showed as little concern for the facts as they had when she was last at home. When her father had died, some red-top journalists had come to the funeral to get a photograph of her in black and a comment. She'd told them to go to hell. The line under the photograph had read: *'Eve Hayes's Father's Hell'*. Eve rarely suffered from press intrusion. When she was in America she was one of many *über*-successful people who didn't court the press, and when she was at home she lived under the radar, never attending the many press events or parties filled with important strangers that she'd been invited to in the early days. With every no-show or rejection, the invitations had petered out until there were none. She had no interest in forging some sort of name for herself as a minor celebrity in Ireland. She had retired. She was looking for peace so something relatively newsworthy would have to happen for her to gain media attention. She wasn't famous enough for them to dig for stories. *Thankfully. I'm so sorry, Ben. Where are you today? Here? There? Nowhere?*

They arrived at the house and Lily stopped the car. Her eyes sparkled. Eve handed her the key and she clutched it. It was a beautiful blue-sky day. The tree-lined driveway led to the large house with the pink-flowered creeper that covered most of the white walls. The door was still a beautiful dark blue. The wooden bench still stood under the big oak tree in the centre of the front garden. Lily's heart raced. 'I feel like I'm home,' she said to Eve.

'You are,' Eve said. She wished she could feel the same about the house but, like Clooney, Eve had lost too much in it for her to feel about it the way Lily did.

They got out of the car.

'It's amazing – and you're only a few stops away on the DART!' Tess exclaimed to Daisy, who was subdued and standoffish.

Lily opened the door into the wide hallway and went inside. She held on to the big old mahogany banister that curled at the end and looked at the freshly painted walls – Eve had insisted on getting them done when the furniture had been taken out. There was no evidence of the family pictures that had hung there but in her mind Lily saw them all. The old wooden floors were varnished and gleaming. She went into the large open kitchen, which led to the patio and garden in which she and Eve had spent so much time. She looked out of the glass patio doors and spotted the swing-set. She and Eve had spent so much of their childhood on it. She clapped her hands together. 'I loved that old swing-set!' Then she surveyed the kitchen. It was very different from how it had been when she'd last seen it: all mod cons with an Aga, a separate wall oven and a microwave. 'Your dad did this?' she asked.

'He had a girlfriend who liked to cook,' Eve said. She wondered how Jean McCormack was doing and decided to call her. She was a lovely woman. She had made her father's final years very happy.

She followed Lily out into the garden with Tess and Daisy in tow. Tess sat on a swing and Daisy took the one next to her.

'It's just like yours,' Tess said.

'No, it isn't,' Daisy said.

The trees had grown so tall that Lily could only barely make out Terry the Tourist's old place. She went back inside and headed down the hall into the sitting room, with the big old window that looked out on to the front lawn, the bench and the oak tree. She traced her hand around the fireplace. She opened the white wooden doors that separated the sitting room from the dining room. She'd forgotten how large it was.

She found Eve sitting on the stairs. 'Can I go up?' she said.

'It's your house.'

Lily was taking the stairs two at a time when Tess ran in and followed her. 'Wait for me, Lily!'

Daisy appeared in the doorway.

Eve turned to her. 'So, are you always this miserable and annoying, or is it just because your life has been turned upside down?'

Daisy leaned on the doorway. 'Is my mum having an affair with your brother?'

'No,' Eve said. 'But they do care about each other. They always have. Your mother practically grew up in this house. She was loved here.'

'She was loved at home.'

'No, she wasn't. Daisy, you don't see that now because you're a kid and kids are selfish arseholes who think the world revolves around them. You were happy so she must have been, right?'

Daisy blinked but said nothing.

'Your mother put your dad, Scott and you before herself for nineteen years. She worked, cleaned the house, told stories, cooked all day and night. She had no friends, no spare time and no life. She was on edge, and busy protecting you from your dad's frustration, paranoia and temper. She was lonely and miserable and she couldn't do it any more.'

'You're making my dad sound like he's evil or something.'

'Your dad's a dick, Daisy, but your mother won't say that because she doesn't want to hurt you.'

'But you don't mind hurting me?'

'I'm a stranger to you, and I'll bet what I've said about him is nothing in comparison to what he's said to you about your mother. Does he mind hurting you? Think about it,' she said. She got up slowly and stood with her crutches.

'He's my dad.'

'And she's your mum, so if you're going to stand up for him and his imperfections, the very least you can do is the same for your mum.'

'You think you know it all.'

'No, I don't,' Eve said. 'But I know more than you. Tell your mother I'll be in the car.'

She hobbled outside, leaving Daisy to stare up the stairs after her mother and Tess.

Lily had dropped Eve at the apartment and now she and the girls were in Eddie Rocket's. They had ordered and were sitting in a booth, Lily facing both girls. 'You didn't say what you thought about the house,' she said.

'It's nice,' Daisy said.

'What about your room? Do you like it?'

'Yes.'

'I love it,' Tess said.

'What about Scott?' Daisy said.

'He'll be in the room on the left.'

'Does he know about the house?' Daisy asked.

'I haven't shown it to him yet.'

'So that's it? We're all just going to leave Dad?' Daisy said, and her eyes filled.

Lily tried to take her hand but she pulled it away. 'You'll still see him. You can visit and stay at weekends if you want. He's still your dad.'

'Are you going to move *him* in?'

'Who?'

'The man with the stupid name.'

'No.'

'But you will at some point. After all, it is his house.'

'No. He doesn't live in Ireland. He'll be going soon.'

'When?'

'Soon.'

'Do you love him?'

Lily blushed and stammered. Of course she loved Clooney, but they weren't going to be a couple – as much as she would have liked that. They were never meant to be anything more

320

than they already were. *He was my family first, Daisy.* Daisy picked at her food. She was like her mother – when she was stressed or sad she found it hard to swallow. She had lost weight just as Lily had gained a little. Clooney had insisted on feeding her up and although she was still tiny her bones no longer stuck out. *I'll do the same for you when you're home with me, Daisy.*

Tess was just happy that nothing really had to change. Daisy would still be going to the same secondary school with her and Lily was back in her life. She had missed her kindness and warmth. *You're so lucky, Daisy. Sometimes I close my eyes and I wish I was you.*

When Lily had paid the bill, she drove Tess home. Her mother appeared out of nowhere and practically ran to the car to get the gossip. 'I heard,' she said.

'Everything's fine,' Lily said.

'Tess was devastated and poor Daisy – are you all right, Daisy?'

'I'm fine.'

'I hear you're living with that designer, Eve Hayes. I can only imagine what the place is like.'

'I'll be moving into my own place soon,' Lily said. 'Tess will always be welcome.'

'That's good of you.'

'I should go,' Lily said. She put her foot down and left the woman standing on the street. 'How many years have I dropped that child off and it's the first time she's ever bothered to come to speak to me?'

A few minutes later she parked outside Declan's house.

'Are you coming in?' Daisy said.

'No.'

'Fine,' Daisy said, got out and tramped up the path.

'Daisy!'

She turned. 'I love you and I will make it up to you.'

'How can you?'

'By being happy,' Lily said.

'At least someone is,' Daisy said. She put the key in the door and closed it behind her.

Adam arrived at Eve's with a picnic basket. It was still early enough to eat outside. He insisted that they go down to the grounds and sit on a blanket on the grass looking out at the sea.

When they got there, he helped Eve down on to the blanket and made her comfortable with cushions he took out of the car.

'You think of everything,' she said.

He opened a bottle of wine but neither of them was in the mood for drinking. Instead they just gazed up at the darkening blue sky and started talking. Eve told him about Lily moving into the house and that Declan was letting go of the kids. He propped himself up on an elbow and gazed at her. 'Doesn't sound like him,' he said.

'No, it isn't.'

'Does his decision have anything to do with the medical records you had me pull the other day?'

'Yes,' she said.

'Are you ever going to tell me what happened?'

'Some day,' she said.

He leaned over and kissed her. They kissed for a long time, so long in fact that she was reminded of Ben, and of being a teenager when kissing was king and made the world spin faster. Adam made the world spin faster too, or maybe she was having a dizzy spell, she wasn't quite sure.

They talked about his job and how stressful it was. He was fascinated that she had retired and asked about her plans.

'I have none.'

'Are you scared?'

'No.'

'So you can just walk away from your life's work and your whole identity?'

'Yeah.'

'And you don't miss it?'

'Not one bit,' she said. 'I told you, I'm retired.'

'You'll get bored,' he said.

'Maybe,' she said.

'What about marriage?'

'What about it?'

'Is that something you want?'

'Lily told me you don't do marriage. Is that why you're asking?'

'Partly that and partly I just want to know what you think.'

'I think it's a nice day out but a piece of paper doesn't guarantee anything, which makes it redundant.'

He smiled. 'Always so clear-headed.'

'Some people see that as me being cold.'

'I'm not one of them.'

'Why are you so against marriage?'

He lay down and faced the sky. He told her that when he was seven his father had left his mother for another woman. The woman had become pregnant and wanted to be married. Divorce wasn't allowed so Adam's father had sought an annulment. Although he had been married for seven years, had a seven-year-old son with his wife so there were no grounds, he was granted one on the basis that he had been coerced into marriage because of pregnancy. He went on to marry the other woman and they had four children. Adam's mother had never really recovered. She hadn't allowed herself to get close to another man and had died alone of a massive heart attack at the age of sixty.

'Did you ever see him?' Eve asked.

'No.'

'Did you care?'

'Yes.'

'You shouldn't have. It's better to have no dad than a bad one.'

'How would you know? I hear yours was the greatest dad in the world.'

'It just doesn't make sense to waste time on someone who doesn't want you,' she said, 'especially when there are so many people who do.' She grinned and he kissed her again. 'When are we going to have sex?'

He laughed. 'When you're feeling stronger.'

'I feel strong now,' she said.

'OK, then, soon.'

'You're fobbing me off,' she said.

'No. I'm giving you some time.'

'It's time I don't want.'

'When is the wedding?'

'Two weeks,' she said.

'OK,' he said. 'We'll do it then.'

'I haven't even asked you to the wedding.'

'But you're going to.'

'I'm not waiting two more weeks.'

'Yes, you are.'

'For God's sake!'

'You know, for an atheist you call out to God a lot.'

'You should hear me in the sack.'

'And Jesus Christ and –'

'I say holy shit too, but it doesn't mean I think there's a blessed turd sitting at the right hand of the Lord.'

He laughed. 'Good point.'

They lay together until it got chilly, when he helped her inside. As he was leaving she asked him if she was really going to have to wait another two weeks. He said yes, but he'd make it worth her while.

'Well, you'd better be wearing bells!' she shouted, as the lift doors closed.

Eve was in bed when Clooney got home. Lily was sitting in the lounge area with her feet up, drinking a glass of wine and enjoying one of the many books from Eve's library. She jumped up when he arrived, clearly glad to see him. He looked jaded and was quiet. She poured him a glass of wine and asked if he was hungry. He sat on one of the bar stools at the island and watched her fetch things from the fridge, then chop and cook. She made preparing a meal look so easy. She sat with him while he ate the most delicious pasta dish he had ever tasted.

'You should have been a chef.'

'I should have been a lot of things,' she said.

He lifted the fork to her mouth. She opened it, chewed and swallowed.

'Did you eat today?'

'Yes,' she said.

'Good.'

'I was in the house,' she said. 'Thank you.'

'Don't thank me. I'm just happy you're happy.'

'I am,' she said. 'Declan isn't fighting me for the kids. It's so unlike him.'

Clooney didn't comment. Instead he insisted she take another bite of food.

'How was Paris?'

'Sad,' he said.

'Should I ask why?'

'I'd rather you didn't.'

'OK.'

They talked for a while after dinner, and when it was past midnight Lily made her way into Eve's spare room. Clooney pulled out the sofa in Eve's office. When he went to the hot press to get clean sheets and pillows, he stood briefly outside Lily's room. He leaned on her door and wondered if she was awake or asleep, and if she wanted him like he wanted her. She opened the door and he fell forward. 'Are you all right?' she asked, as he righted himself.

'I missed you,' he said.

'I missed you too.'

She stood on tiptoe and kissed him. When her soft lips touched his, he melted into her, and after that there was no parting them. He lifted her on to his hips, carried her across the room and laid her gently on the bed. He found his place between her legs

325

and was careful to make sure she was comfortable. When they touched there was heat and she wanted him like she'd never wanted anyone before. Later they lay together fizzing, relaxed yet mentally energized. She opened her heart. 'I shouldn't have pushed you away all those years ago,' she said.

He traced her chin with a finger. 'You didn't.'

'I was so scared,' she said.

'I never understood that till now.'

'I did love him.'

'He needed you,' he said. Lily had always yearned to be needed.

'You didn't,' she said, eyes leaking.

'I'm sorry.'

'My fault. We are what we are.'

He brushed away her tears and they lay together in one another's arms. Even though she was still scared about her future and that of her kids, she was happy and she realized she hadn't been happy in a really long time. *I remember now*, she thought, and Clooney asked her why she was smiling.

'I'm happy. I'm actually happy.'

'Good. I'm happy too.'

'Where will you go to next?'

'Let's not talk about that now.'

'Why not? You're the man who leaves,' she said, acknowledging that she had overheard him talking to Adam days before. 'It's OK. I'm not eighteen any more. The life I wanted I got and I didn't like it.'

'I've been offered a job in Peru.'

'I've never been to Peru.'

He grinned. 'Are you thinking of coming to visit me?'

'I might.'

'I'd really like that,' he said. He kissed her and they fell into a deep and peaceful sleep in each other's arms.

12. Where Croagh Patrick meets the shores of Clew Bay

Lily,

I don't know what to say. Your letter finally arrived yesterday. It's, as you say, been a long confusing few weeks. When the results came out and you didn't write or call, Declan and I were really worried. Then Clooney told Danny you did so well and he told me and I told Declan and we really didn't know what to think when we didn't hear from you. Declan kept asking me why you weren't in touch. I felt sorry for him. He was so sad and lonely and I couldn't understand what was keeping you from us. Of course now I know. It was a shock. I knew you and Clooney were close but I never for a moment thought that you'd be together. I suppose that's because I'm emotionally stunted, at least that's probably what you and Clooney are saying. As far as I was concerned he was like your older brother. It was a shock. I think it was mean of you not to write and to leave me hanging. I was worried and thinking all sorts. By leaving me and Declan alone up here worrying about you, I felt like I was put in a spot and had to be there for him or something, I don't know. It was all so frustrating. You just dumped us and I don't want to talk about you and Clooney because it's just stupid. How could you be so mean and stupid? You talk about love and what it means but when it comes down to it you're as clueless as I am.

Ben and I are over. We broke up last night. Paul's parents were away so he held a party at his house and Ben brought Billy along and they were drunk because they'd played an afternoon gig and they'd been drinking since. Ben kept pestering me about London. He told me he didn't want me to go and asked if I could find a college closer to home – he'd even done some research and gave me a list of places that are nowhere near as cool as St Martin's and said that I'd have to apply for next year. It's an argument we've been having on and off since the results came out. He thinks my results are good enough to get me into the National College of Art and Design, but I don't want to go there, I want to go to St Martin's in London. Last night he told me that if I wouldn't apply to NCAD he'd leave his course and come to London with me. Just like that. He was drunk, and Billy was pissed off because he didn't even consider the band, and he said he loved me and if I really loved him I'd stay or at least talk about him coming with me. It was so stupid. He was messy and argumentative and I was already on edge having just read your letter. He called me insensitive and cold and I said he was a stupid boy and I wasn't willing to give up my dream to be with him after just one summer and he was a fool if he was willing to give up his band. Billy was on my side – he threw a beer at Ben and called him names. They got into a fight and I left and went inside.

I met Declan on the stairs. He had a black eye. I asked him what happened and he burst into tears. He was drunk too. We were all drunk. I brought him into the bathroom and cleaned the cut over his eye. It was really deep and I told him he needed stitches but he said it would be fine. It had stopped bleeding but it was a hole in his face. He kept drinking from a bottle of vodka. I asked him how it happened and he said he was mugged. He wasn't because his wallet was in his pocket but he wasn't going to tell me so I didn't push. We went into Paul's room just to talk. Declan was devastated he hadn't heard from you and I was feeling really guilty because I knew you were with my brother. We drank some more and bitched. I told him about Ben just to change the subject from you and suddenly he knew what was what and he put Ben and me down saying we were only a silly summer fling and Ben was an idiot and basically all the things that I'd said to Ben but hearing them from Declan really annoyed me. I told you I was drunk. He said that I'd forget about Ben because as much as I thought I loved him I hadn't a clue what real love was. Of course he meant that he knew, which was annoying, bearing in mind he hadn't heard from you in weeks and you were sleeping with my brother. I flipped. I told him. I said you were probably sleeping with Clooney as we spoke. He got very quiet and the second I said it I regretted it. I tried to talk to him and tell him it meant nothing and that Clooney was going away in September. He looked like I'd ripped his heart out. Even as drunk as I was, I could see the damage I'd done. I didn't mean it, I was just too angry and frustrated, and he has a way of lording it over everyone like he knows best, and I just wanted to hurt him but not that much. He started to shake and to sob and I'd never heard sobs like that before. I sat beside him and hugged him and he hugged me back and cried on my shoulder and then he kissed me and I don't know why but I kissed him back. I've been trying to work out why I did that all day but I can't tell you why because I don't know and I'm not going to blame being drunk because I knew what was happening. He started to take off my top and I let him and then I realized what we were doing and I tried to stop but he didn't listen and he's so strong. He pulled up my skirt and he was kissing me so that I couldn't say stop it. I tried to hold him off but it was like I wasn't even there and then we were actually having sex. That's when Ben came in. He just looked at us and Declan stopped for a moment, then told him to close the door on his way out and I was just shocked. I couldn't speak. I tried but I just couldn't work out what was happening. Ben just ran and I wanted to go after him but I couldn't move. He left the door open but Declan didn't even notice – he just kept going and going, digging into me, and I can't describe the pain. You probably think I deserved it, maybe I did. I couldn't swallow, my ears were ringing and I kept thinking this was a bad dream. Afterwards Declan cried and cried and said that we did to you what you did to him but I didn't want to do anything to you. He hugged me and thanked me for being there for him. I just sat there numb and I didn't know what to say. I was angry at you, yes, of course I was angry, but I didn't want to do *that to you or Clooney or to Ben. I feel sick and today Billy came round and he was shouting, saying I had ruined Ben's life. I reminded him that the last time I saw them they were fighting. He told me that I was a cold bitch and if I didn't want to be with Ben I should have just said something as opposed to fucking the first guy who looked at me. I didn't do that, I swear, Lily, I had no intention of having sex with Declan. I never wanted him and I wouldn't do that to you. I don't know what happened. I know you hate me by now. You don't care that I've spent my whole day in hospital. When Billy stopped shouting he realized that I was bleeding. 'Something is wrong,' I said. He brought me to A&E. They are keeping me in. I'm writing to you from a temporary bed in A&E. You probably think I deserve that and maybe I do. Dad's away on a junket so don't worry, he won't find out. I know I have a nerve asking you but please don't tell Clooney. If I could take it back I wouldn't have said anything. I was just so angry at you and Clooney and Ben and Declan and I know it's no excuse. Billy said he'd post this for me. I told him it was important that it goes today because if I don't send it today I never will and you deserve the truth. I want you to know I'm really sorry. I've never felt worse in my life. Ben is gone. He won't talk to me and I don't blame him. Billy has promised he won't say a word about today, probably for Ben's sake as much as mine or maybe more for his sake. He's still really angry with me but he's here and that's something. I keep thinking, if it was the other way around would I forgive you, and the answer is I don't know. I hope I would but I can't say. Life is confusing at the best of times and I don't know what I can say except that I'm so sorry. Please forgive me, Lily. I don't know what my life would be like without you. I love you and miss you and you can marry my brother if you want.*

Love,
Eve

Lily was desperately upset when Scott refused to leave his father to move in with her. He told her in no uncertain terms on the street outside his grandfather's garage that he was old enough to decide where he wanted to live and he chose his dad. He wanted nothing to do with her, her new house, man and life, and Lily had no option but to accept his stance. *Please forgive me, Scott. I miss you.*

Eve had not been so accepting. *Cheeky little bastard.* She watched Lily tear herself apart and even Clooney couldn't make the pain go away.

'The house will be empty and cold. What will he live on? Doesn't he realize his father is never there? And when he's frustrated, who does Scott think will be on the receiving end of his anger? He'll twist him up and spit him out. He'll spread his poison and make my son hate me. I might lose him for ever.'

Clooney was soothing and sympathetic, Eve less so as she was bored of listening to Lily's anxieties. 'Put a sock in it, Lil, he'll come around.'

'You don't know that.'

'Of course I do,' Eve said, as though she was the oracle and was programmed to explain the human psyche.

Lily argued that business wasn't as complex as people, and although Eve always got it right in business, she was out of her depth when it came to understanding the needs of Lily's children. Eve disagreed, believing that she was perfectly situated to see the world through their eyes. 'They're self-centred and self-righteous,' she said, 'and I'm self-centred and self-righteous so I think I'm the perfect person.'

Eve went to the garage to try to talk to Scott, although she had promised Lily she wouldn't interfere. Jack offered her tea and she politely declined, asking for just a few moments of Scott's time. Jack was happy to let his grandson go for coffee with Eve, asking only that he brought one back when he returned.

They sat together in a coffee shop, staring at one another sullenly.

'You look more like your mum,' she said.

'So they say.'

331

'Lucky for you,' she said.

'What do you want?'

'Did your dad ask you to stay with him?'

'No, and it's none of your business anyway.'

'You're right, it's not. I just want to make sure that staying in that house was your idea.'

'Why do you care?'

'Because when I was your age I thought I had it all figured out and so did your mother, but here's the thing: we didn't have a clue. We hadn't even begun to understand the world and the people around us.'

'Well, I'm not you and this isn't the eighteen-hundreds.'

She laughed a little. 'Funny,' she said.

'I'm staying because he's my dad and it's my home.'

'I feel like I should say something to shine a light but I don't know where to shine it.'

'You sound like the nut-job who passes the garage every morning holding a placard with a picture of a foetus on it and shouting about its hands and feet.'

'She gave me the finger yesterday,' Eve said, and Scott smiled.

He couldn't help liking her. He'd noticed how beautiful she was, and even though she was on crutches, she still had a certain grace.

Eve sighed. She hadn't really thought it through. She hated Declan but his son loved him, and she wasn't the heartless bitch she pretended to be. She needed to make sure that Declan hadn't broken the terms of their agreement and it was clear he hadn't. Scott wanted to stay with him for his own reasons.

'So what's this about shining a light?' he said.

'I did something that really hurt your mother years ago and I lost her and it was incredibly painful and . . .'

'And?'

'Picture your life without her – because if you think that stamping your feet and hiding in a corner is going to change the way things are you're wrong. She's left your dad, there's no going back. Decide whether you love and respect her enough to support her or you don't.'

'She just walked out on him and us.'

'I understand you love your father,' she said, 'but that's not what happened.'

'She's destroyed him,' he said, and he was quiet. His eyes filled.

'She saved herself.'

'You don't understand.'

'I promise I do, and I can see why you'd want to help and protect your father. It's a good thing. But punishing your mother is wrong and you know it. The battle lines that were drawn are gone. You don't need to pick one parent over the other. It's time to move on.'

He sat silently for a moment or two. She wasn't sure if he was going to get up and walk away or if he was actually considering his mother's point of view.

'I'll come once a week for dinner,' he said.

'And two Sundays a month.'

'One Sunday a month.'

She smiled and put out her hand. He shook it. 'That's a good start,' she said, and handed him fifty euro to pay for three coffees and a sandwich. 'Keep the change.' She left him to stand there and watch her make her way to the taxi she had waiting outside. Eve normally didn't interfere in other people's lives, she simply didn't care enough, but Lily had always brought out the lioness in her.

She felt elated and even a little smug as she sat in the back of the taxi. Lily felt too much guilt and loyalty to her children and their father, regardless of his actions, to fight for herself, but Eve wouldn't rest until she had her children back and Declan was as alone and powerless as he deserved to be.

The week before the wedding was busy. Lily spent most days cleaning the house that Eve had paid a team of cleaners to clean less than three months before. When she was alone she'd walk around it, listening to the faint echoes of her childhood. Her heart was so full she felt at times it would burst. Clooney helped her hang curtains and paint walls, and when the furniture finally arrived, he helped her move it in while Eve sat on the sofa and pointed her crutches towards walls and spaces.

When the furniture was in, Lily and Clooney spent a day at IKEA. They came home in two cars filled with vases, pots, pans, china, duvet sets, pictures, picture frames, rugs and plants.

Clooney seemed a little haunted, having lost all sense of time in the shop. 'It's just like Vegas but not fun.'

When the house was pretty as a picture and her daughter's room was ready and waiting, Lily drove up to her old house alone. She insisted that Clooney and Eve didn't come. Although she was nervous of Declan, she felt stronger and she needed to show her daughter that, from now on, they were a team: she was Daisy's mother and Daisy would come first. Clooney and Eve understood, and although they were both concerned about Lily being in Declan's presence without them, they supported her decision.

She rang the doorbell, her hand shaking a little. Adrenalin rushed through her and she was filled with trepidation and excitement.

Declan opened the door. Daisy was sitting on the stairs with a large suitcase beside her. Lily said hello, and Declan glowered at her. She looked past him towards Daisy, whose eyes were red. 'It's time to go, Daisy,' she said.

Daisy stayed on the stairs.

'Daisy, you can see your dad whenever you want,' Lily said, but Daisy didn't move.

It was as though she was glued there.

Declan turned to his daughter. When he spoke his voice was fragile and threatened to break. 'Daisy, do what your mother says.'

She met his stare and their eyes locked. 'Do you really want me to go, Dad?'

He bit the inside of his cheek and nodded once.

Her eyes filled again and chubby tears fell. The sounds she made were of pure pain. She looked at her mother, silently begging her to make everything right. Lily wanted to run to her and hold her, but Declan was between them and an invisible wall prevented her entering. She was an uninvited vampire sucking the life out of her family. She was forced to observe the pain she had caused from a distance. Daisy stood up. When she tried to pick her case up, it was too heavy for her. Declan grabbed it and shoved it roughly at Lily. Daisy moved to walk past her dad and as she did he grasped her and held her tight.

'I love you,' he said, then pushed her away and closed the door, leaving her outside in tears.

In their new home, Daisy lay on her new bed in her bright new room, looking out of the window towards the old swing-set and the rock wall that separated the back garden from Terry the Tourist's old place.

Lily had put Eve's old desk back in the room. She'd spent hours painting it and putting up pictures of Daisy and her brother, Daisy and her dad, Daisy and her friends and Daisy and her mum. She'd covered the bed in a duvet with big flowers and pink cushions – Daisy loved pink. She'd hung a large framed photograph of Justin Bieber over the bed, and Clooney had spent an afternoon putting up a wall of bookshelves, which Lily had filled with all the second-hand copies she could find of books suitable for Daisy's age group and little odds and ends she'd bought in IKEA that added colour and warmth to the room.

Daisy lay frozen despite all Lily's efforts. She was worried about her dad and Scott, and she would miss her room, her piano, her house, her road, her world. She didn't know how to be with her mother, what to say or do. She was still so angry, sad and scared and, no matter what Eve or anyone else said, it had been her mother who had walked out and left them. *How could she just leave us?*

Downstairs Lily spoke in whispers to Clooney on the phone while she cooked, hoping the smell of fresh bread and Daisy's favourite shepherd's pie would coax her down the stairs and back into Lily's life. Clooney counselled patience and waited impatiently for the time when they could be alone together again.

Daisy did come down the stairs that evening, and picked at the food her mother had made for her. She grunted at Eve when she called in to say hello.

'And here was I thinking we were past grunting. Oh, well!' Eve said, and Lily saw her daughter fight to stop the corners of her mouth lifting.

Over the next week it was sometimes easier and sometimes harder. When Daisy spoke to her father on the phone she would be silent and distant afterwards, and on one occasion, when Lily answered Daisy's phone because her daughter was in the shower and Declan had rung three times in a row, she quickly realized he was drunk and wondered how many other calls he'd made in that state. She told him she'd appreciate if he wouldn't call Daisy when he was drunk and hoped he'd make an effort to stay sober when she returned to stay with him the following weekend. He called her a whore.

'Change the record, Declan.'

'What was that you said, whore?'

'Sober up.'

'Don't tell me what to do, bitch,' he said. 'I've had enough of that from your precious Eve.'

'Excuse me?' Lily said.

'Don't pretend you're not in on it, you twisted bitch,' he said, and hung up.

Lily sat on her daughter's bed, dumbfounded. Suddenly the change in his behaviour made sense. He hadn't given Daisy up because it was the right thing to do. He'd given her up because he'd had to. He hadn't aborted his war plan, he had simply lost the battle. She sat on the bed, wondering what Eve could have said to make him do something he didn't want to do. It wasn't long before she guessed what had happened.

*

Eve was getting stronger and steadier by the day, the expensive and intensive physiotherapy and Pilates classes paying off. She was off her crutches and using a walking stick. Adam was very pleased with her recovery, and one evening two nights before the wedding, when Clooney had finally grabbed some time with Lily because Daisy was spending the night with Tess, he came to her apartment with a bottle of wine, a bunch of flowers and a takeaway. It was the first time they had had the place to themselves, and despite his previous stricture, they didn't eat their takeaway, they didn't drink their wine, and the bunch of flowers wilted on the counter as they enjoyed uninhibited and playful sex. They laughed and talked, pushed and prodded, came and came again. They showered and changed the sheets because they both had a weird thing about clean sheets, and they had sex again. Some time between four and five in the morning they heated up a spicy Indian dish and ate it before enjoying another roll in the hay.

'That's the most sex I've had in a very long time,' she said.

'You're not alone.'

'How sad are we?'

'*Watership Down* sad,' he said. He had remembered that she and Lily had watched *Watership Down* eight times.

'That is sad,' she said.

Adam was quirky and funny and kind and interesting, and she liked that he was also a little lost, as she was. He was dispassionate about his career. He was tired of the same old same old, and needed a break or a new focus.

'You can focus on me for a while,' she said.

'Only a while?'

'You could go to hot countries and fix poor broken kids or you could invent a surgical tool that revolutionizes surgery or help discover a cure for bone cancer.'

'All totally doable,' he said, and laughed a little.

She kissed him. 'You can be and do anything you want, Adam. You're an amazing surgeon. You're just a little bored right now.'

He exhaled and raised his hands in the air. 'I am so bored. If I have to replace one more hip . . .' He shook his fist at the ceiling in mock anger. She laughed at him and he turned back to face her. 'What about you? Are you going to take up knitting or painting or bridge? I hear water aerobics is popular with the retired community.'

'Nah, I'm just going to lie here with you.'

'John and Yoko style.'

'I'd like to think we have better hair,' she said.

Eve had realized that she needed to make life changes two weeks after she'd returned from her father's funeral to her home and work in New York. She'd felt homesick, agitated and restless, and a mild collision with a New York taxi had been the last straw. She had been working ridiculous hours, trying to make up for so much time away. She was exhausted, her head was pounding, and when she was standing at the side of the road, with the Irish-Italian taxi driver screaming at her, she remained silent, trying to work out what had happened. She hadn't fallen asleep. She hadn't been talking on the phone and, because she was tired, she had been extra careful to maintain her alertness and watch the road. He had seemed so far ahead. She'd thought there was at least another two car lengths between them. She'd heard the crash and felt the jolt before she'd seen the back of the car. His yelling faded into the background.

Oh, no. Not yet. I haven't lived yet.

That evening she made the decision to stop and look around her, to be present and part of the real world, to engage with people, family and friends. Now that she was doing just that, each moment carried a certain beauty and resonance and it was good enough for her. Eve Hayes was finally fulfilled and content.

'What would you most like to do tomorrow?' Adam asked.

'It's five a.m. – it is tomorrow.'

'OK, what would you most like to do when we wake up?'

'I'd like to take out my dad's old boat and his water-skis –'

'Out of the question. Next.'

'OK. Forget the water-skis.'

'Let's do it,' he said, and kissed her. They fell asleep some time after six.

They didn't hear Clooney return at just before eight. He'd had a long night too. He and Lily hadn't slept a wink. They didn't want to sleep because their time together was so limited that they couldn't afford to miss a minute. Up to that night they had grabbed a coffee here and there and they'd had a drink together while Daisy was in the cinema one Tuesday evening. They had phoned and texted one another but Lily had missed his touch and Clooney had missed hers. He was growing restless. Eve didn't need him any more and Lily was starting a new life, one that he couldn't be a part of, at least for a while. He'd accepted the job in Peru and had two weeks left before he was due to fly out. The contract was for six months.

'Six months is no time,' he said, when they were lying together, gazing into each other's eyes, the way that new lovers do.

'It'll fly by and, besides, I told you I might come and see you,' she said.

'A lot will have changed in six months,' he said.

'Daisy will be settled and Scott, well, hopefully he'll have forgiven me a little.'

'And you might have met someone else.'

'No.' She shook her head. 'I could really do with time off for good behaviour.'

'I don't mind if you do. I just want you to be happy.'

'I know that,' she said.

The next morning he had left early to avoid any collision with Daisy. He kissed her and told her he loved her and would always love her. There was no promise accompanying his words. It was simply a statement of fact.

'I love you too,' she said. She winked at him and grinned. 'Now get out.'

They were both big and bold enough to know that their relationship was not the stuff of legends. He might find an exotic lover and she might fall for one of the many men who would pursue her in his absence. They weren't foolish but they were hopeful that, some day and somehow, they would find their way back to one another. *If it's meant to be it's meant to be.*

Scott promised to stay at home the weekend Daisy returned to her dad's house. He told his mother she needn't worry. He and his dad would take good care of Daisy. 'We've had plenty of practice,' he said, because although he was thawing towards her he was still angry – since she'd left his father had seemed to suffer a lot.

Adam insisted on driving to Westport in his brand new BMW even though there was a perfectly good train service. Eve needed a lot of leg-room up front so Clooney and Lily felt captive in the back, especially when he got lost and it added another hour to the four-hour journey.

It was dark by the time they arrived. Lily was asleep in Clooney's arms. He gently woke her in time to see the light fade from pink to navy blue over the mountains. The Atlantic Coast Hotel was a beautiful building that seemed to be cut out of rock. They walked into Reception and were greeted with smiles. To the right there was a roaring fire, a small library and big cosy chairs, and to the left the Fishworks Bar and Café from which wafted mouth-watering smells, chatter and clinking.

As they checked in, Paul appeared, followed by Simone. He was wearing white towelling slippers and raised his hands in the air. 'You're here,' he said, and hugged them all, prompting Eve to ask if he was drunk already. Simone explained he had spent the last two days having every ayurvedic treatment he could fit into his schedule. 'He's just had a psychic enema.'

'Sounds painful!' Clooney said.

'It's sublime,' Paul said, and hugged Eve again until she threatened to kick him.

He didn't care a jot. He was on cloud nine.

'What's the name of that treatment?' Clooney asked.

'Don't worry about names,' he said. 'I have you all booked in with Dr Thomas.'

'You can shove that,' Eve mumbled, just as Paul's mother came out of the lift.

She ignored Paul's friends. 'You do know they have an actual function room on the fourth floor?' she said.

Paul just smiled at her.

'Yes, he does,' Simone said.

'So why aren't we using that?'

'Because the wedding party is small enough to use the Blue Wave restaurant, which is also on the fourth floor and we love it,' said Simone, smiling sweetly. 'We've very fond memories of it, and it's everything I've ever dreamed of.'

'If you'd used the function room we could have invited some people to this thing,' his mother said.

'By people she means neighbours, and by neighbours she means the people from her church who think I'm a homo.'

'My advice, Mrs Doyle, is to have a psychic enema and get over it,' Eve said.

Paul laughed.

His mother scratched her nose and then her ear. 'You were always a cheeky bitch, Eve Hayes – good to see some things don't change.' She looked at her son. 'At least, *some* things don't change,' she said, barely concealing her grin before she walked into the Fishworks Bar and Café.

'Oh, my God, she can smile!' Simone said. 'It's a miracle.'

Later when they were stuffed with the best fish pie ever made, the girls were on their second bottle of wine and the boys on their third creamy pint of Guinness, Gar and Gina floated in. They, too, were in a trance-like state. Gina ordered salmon and told the girls about a procedure Dr Thomas had recommended.

'He's amazing,' she said. 'Seriously, he's given me dietary advice, he's made me think about how I live and how I feel, and recently it has not been good. He's told me the best times to sleep and wake according to my body type – and the treatments, my God, I haven't felt this relaxed in years!'

'As soon as we've eaten we're going upstairs to make the most of it,' Gar said.

'Yes, we are,' Gina agreed.

'The man's a genius,' Gar said, and clinked his pint glass with the lads'.

Lily had suffered tension headaches and backache for years. She couldn't wait for her consultation. The only doctor Eve wanted in her life was Adam. They stayed up late drinking and listening to the local musicians play. All but Eve danced jigs with the locals and even she was involved in the last dance when four locals insisted on lifting her in her chair and carrying her around the room, much to Adam's horror.

'Easy, easy, easy,' he repeated, trying to keep up with them and steady the chair.

Eve was too merry to feel fear. 'All right, that's enough. Drop the nice lady with the brand-new shoulder!'

Around two o'clock they disappeared into their respective rooms and, consumed by exhaustion, Clooney and Lily fell asleep quickly.

Adam came out of the shower to find Eve looking out at the harbour. She seemed at peace, gazing at the sea and mountains. 'Are you all right?' he asked, resting his hand on the shoulder he had recently reconstructed.

'I'm good,' she said. 'It's beautiful here.'

He agreed, and they went to bed.

Lily was first in with Dr Thomas, followed by an eager and fascinated Adam. Both came away from their consultation with a little more insight into themselves and their bodies. Adam was especially impressed, and keen to read as much as he could on ayurvedic medicine. Dr Thomas gave him a book, which he read in bed after a massage that had left him with an enormous sense of wellbeing.

'You've got to go to him,' he said to Eve, who was reading *Marie Claire* in the bath.

'No.'

'He'll make you feel better.'

'You make me feel better.'

He read from a pamphlet: ' "Ayurveda revives the memory of our immune system, which allows our body to rekindle our intrinsic ability to heal ourselves through treatment and/or prescriptive ayurvedic herbs and oils." '

'Not interested.'

'It can help with post-surgery convalescence.'

'Don't care.'

'Headaches.'

'Really, Adam.'

'It's profoundly relaxing and your body has been through a huge trauma. It's doing a great job healing but this is an opportunity to help it along. What's the worst that could happen? You have an hour-long massage and come out covered in oil? Boohoo. I'm asking you to do this for me.'

'Right, fine. Jesus, I thought all Western doctors were supposed to be anti-alternative medicine.'

'I'm not all Western doctors and ayurveda is the mother of all modern medicine so stop whining.'

She walked into Dr Thomas's small office with her heart beating fast. She couldn't understand why she was so nervous but she was and it was uncomfortable. Dr Thomas was Indian, with a young face and a big smile. There was nothing to fear, and Eve was not the fearful type but still her heart raced, and when he took her hand in his she couldn't control its tremor. Very much like her experience in hospital, he asked her question after question, but this time he did not adhere to a list: one question led to another that was more specific, depending on her previous answer. In some cases it was a question she'd never been asked before. Despite herself, she found that she was opening up and

343

engaging. He examined her tongue, looked into her eyes and took her pulse. He explained pulse diagnosis at great length as he held her wrist between his fingers and thumb. Suddenly she felt the desire to pull away and then she saw the look in his eye: it was too late to pull away.

'You told me that you suffer from headaches but they are not too bad,' he said.

She nodded and her heart raced again. *Here we go.*

'They are bad,' he said.

'I went for tests a few months ago and got the all-clear,' she said.

'It's time for a second opinion.'

'I'm fine.'

'Today I'm going to get rid of the headache you pretend you're not having, and when you go home you need to go for a CT and/ or an MRI scan.'

She sat silently because when the staff of St Martin's Hospital had questioned her about her headaches she hadn't been entirely honest with them. She hadn't mentioned the balance and vision problems she had experienced before the collision with the taxi in New York. The balance problem wasn't an issue when she had been lying in a bed twenty-four hours a day and seven days a week. *I was given the all-clear.* When her vision became blurred after reading for hours on end, she'd told herself it was because she needed glasses. *I was given the all-clear.* She didn't mention the changes she'd experienced in her sense of smell because everything had smelt weird in that hospital. Shit smelt like roses and Chanel No. 5 smelt like baby puke. *I was given the all-clear.* She had reasoned that she was on a lot of drugs and had been locked in that tiny room for so long that it was possible all she needed was fresh air and a fresh perspective. *I was given the all-clear.* If she had told one of the endless interns who had asked endless questions that one of the reasons she had stopped working and sold her shares in her company was because she found it hard to concentrate, her memory was spotty, her spatial awareness was completely out of whack

344

and the smell of cat pee made her crave bacon, they would have kept her in that tiny room and she couldn't have borne it.

'It's time to get to the bottom of it,' he said, and looked at her sympathetically, as though he could read her mind. He went on to prescribe a Talam treatment to alleviate migraine and a Kizchi massage to ease her body's tension and promote healing.

Even though Dr Thomas had basically told her what she had already guessed back in New York, she enjoyed the two treatments and felt decidedly better and more relaxed after them. She wasn't sure if it was the magic of ayurveda or that she no longer had to pretend that there wasn't a problem, but Eve felt calm and ready.

I got the all-clear but they were wrong.

Adam was a happy bunny when she returned. He'd spent the afternoon reading a few more of Dr Thomas's books. 'How would you feel about a trip to India?' he said.

'Great,' she said.

That night they all had an early dinner, and everyone disappeared afterwards to be with the ones they loved and to rest for the busy wedding day ahead. They woke up early and had a leisurely breakfast. Adam stayed in bed reading. Clooney swam lengths of the beautiful azure-blue pool. Lily and Eve sat in the hot tub, watching him glide by under the water.

'He was always like a fish,' Eve said, and Lily nodded.

'Are you going to tell me what's on your mind?' Lily said.

Eve laughed and said that there was nothing.

'Are you going to tell me what you threatened to do to Declan?' Lily asked then.

Eve's smile faded. Lily was looking at her with a mixture of bewilderment and awe. 'I just reasoned with him,' she said.

'Nobody reasons with Declan.'

Eve just shook her head.

'We'll have to talk about it some day,' Lily said.

'I know. Just not today.'

Lily smiled at her friend and hugged her, even though she knew it would make Eve uncomfortable. She pulled away as Clooney

345

appeared, hanging on the side of the pool. He slipped into the tub beside Lily. Eve made her excuses and left them to it. One day in the very near future she would tell her friend about the day that she had gone into Declan's office and sat in front of him for the first time in nearly twenty years. She'd tell Lily that at first Declan had been his usual sneering self but she had soon put a stop to that. She'd tell her that Declan had said she was a very silly woman if she thought that pleading on Lily's behalf would do any good.

'When have I ever pleaded for anything, Declan?' she said.

His eyes narrowed. 'What is it that I can do for you, Eve?'

'You can give Lily her kids back, sell the house with a view to giving her half the proceeds without delay and before the divorce, which you'll agree to as soon as possible.'

He threw back his head and laughed.

You were always theatrical, Declan.

'That bitch is not getting my kids or my money or a divorce. She can live in a rat-infested pit for all I care. She made her flea-bitten bed and now she can rot in it.'

'Or you can do what I say,' Eve said.

Declan leaned forward. 'And why would I do that?'

'Because if you don't, I'll go to the press and say that when I was eighteen years old my best friend's boyfriend raped me at a party. I'll go on record telling them that the boy is now a very important cardiac surgeon here in Dublin. It will take them approximately two minutes to work out who the boy was.'

'You're lying.'

'Try me.'

'It didn't happen like that.'

'It happened exactly like that.'

'No. We kissed and –'

'And you raped me and you hurt me.' She took out the copy of the hospital record that Adam had made for her and threw it on his desk. 'And I have the proof.'

He opened the file and looked through it, then at her. He wasn't so smug any more.

346

'It didn't happen like that. I was drunk. You were into it.'

'I don't care if you believe you're innocent of my rape or justi-fied in raping your wife. I don't care what you think or how you feel, and your employers, patients and the rest of the country won't care either.'

'You'll destroy me,' he said.

'You say that like I should care.'

'You'll destroy my kids,' he said.

She laughed. *That old chestnut, you son of a bitch?* 'I don't give a crap about your kids,' she said, and he believed her. 'By five o'clock this evening I want to see Lily dancing around the kitchen celebrating that you've finally decided to do something decent and you're sharing custody. In two months' time I want the house to go on the market and you will accept the first realistic sum offered. I will be involved in the sale. You will be judicially separ-ated as soon as possible, and the proceeds of the house sale will be divided evenly at that stage. When the time comes you will give her an uncontested quick divorce.'

'You think you have it all worked out,' he said.

She got up. 'Don't cross me, Declan, because I've been waiting twenty years to fuck you up.'

She left him alone to stare at the report on his desk.

Thank you for taking me to the hospital all those years ago, Billy. Wherever you are.

The wedding was beautiful, and it was a dream day. Gar was a handsome best man and his speech started a little rough but in the end it was both funny and touching.

'I wanted to start off light so I went on line and checked out bisexual jokes but there aren't any. I suppose bisexuals are too busy riding all around them to be thinking up jokes.'

Paul's mother's face fell and the room became deathly silent, which meant that everyone could hear her when she muttered, 'For God's sake, do we have to listen to that today of all days?'

Simone broke into a huge grin. She laughed, a real, genuine

laugh, and Paul followed. Like a Mexican wave, that laugh rippled through the crowd. Gar sighed and wiped the sweat from his forehead. He spoke about growing up with Paul and how intimidating it was to be a friend of someone who was a brilliant sportsman, intelligent and, of course, so handsome that every girl in Ireland wanted to be with him. Eve and Lily made coughing and choking sounds.

'Yes, all right, *nearly* every girl, including my wife.'

Gina raised her glass. 'Yeah, you betcha!' she said. Paul's mother seemed happier with that part of the speech.

He talked about how private Paul had been and that, although he understood it and accepted it, this had created a distance between them over the years. Sometimes he had missed his best pal even when he was in the same room. When he looked as if he might cry, he turned to Simone and smiled. 'But then you came along and you took him out of the dark room he'd locked himself into and you brought him out into the light. I've never seen him happier or more content, never freer or more open.'

Simone smiled and tears filled her eyes.

'You complete him,' he said. He winked at the crowd, who groaned at his *faux* sentimentality.

Paul's dad spoke warmly about his son. He didn't mention his sexuality because there was more to Paul than that, and although he agreed his son was private, he was a great man to keep a secret. He was honourable and patient. At that he glanced at his wife. It wasn't conscious but the crowd laughed, and when he realized what he'd done, he laughed too.

Paul's mother raised her glass. *Fine, I'll be the punch-line today but when I'm in Heaven and you're all screaming in a fiery pit then we'll see who's laughing.*

Simone's father wasn't as happy with his daughter's choice of husband as he tried to pretend. He was valiant in his attempt to celebrate but he was no actor. His speech was short and he mostly spoke about how fantastic she was, how open and vulnerable, and how he'd do jail time if anyone ever hurt her. He didn't welcome Paul to the family, as Paul's father had Simone, he simply wished them luck and told his daughter that, no matter what, he would always be there for her. Simone didn't seem to notice his thinly veiled threats to her new husband, and if she did, she was a much better actor than he was. She gave him a big hug and told him she loved him. Paul's mother looked like she was ready to stand up and punch him: she felt entitled to judge her son but no one else, bar God, was eligible to do so. Paul was a gentleman and offered his hand to Simone's dad. When the two men shook, the crowd clapped.

Simone made an excited breathless speech full of thank-yous and warmth as usual. Paul remained silent.

The meal was delicious and far superior to the usual fare provided at weddings. The room looked on to the Croagh Patrick Mountain, which swept down into Clew Bay, and as the hours passed the light changed and the window revealed a series of beautiful landscapes.

Clooney, Lily, Eve, Adam and Gina shared a table, and when the music kicked off, Eve and Adam danced slowly while everyone else threw themselves around at a faster tempo. She put her arms around Adam's neck. 'Thanks for fixing me,' she said.

'Well, I did tell you I'm the best in the business.'

'I didn't mean that.'

It was a perfect day and one that Eve Hayes would remember fondly for the rest of her life.

Eve's benign meningioma tumour was diagnosed in a private clinic. It was a Wednesday afternoon and she was alone. The tumour, although believed to be developing slowly, was inoperable, due to its size and location. It was damaging cells and exerting pressure within her skull.

'You said your mother had a brain tumour,' the doctor said.

'Hers was cancerous,' she said.

'We'll be keeping a close eye on it.'

She didn't ask any questions. She didn't want the answers, not while she was alone and not on a bloody Wednesday. She smiled and shook his hand. *Friday is a much better day for that kind of news.*

'Thanks, Doctor,' she said.

'I'm sorry,' he said.

'Don't be, it was a long time coming,' she said, and walked out, leaving him to stand in his office and comment to himself that it took all sorts.

It was a bright September morning. Daisy was back at school and had made friends with a girl called Willie, which was short for Wilhelmina. They were the same age and her family lived in Terry the Tourist's old place across the wall. She, Tess and Willie had become the local It girls. Daisy smiled more, and although the mother-daughter relationship had altered irrevocably, it had more to do with her growing up and opening her eyes to the world than with any real residual anger. If Daisy was truly honest with herself, and it would be years before she was, she would admit that life was better with her funny, kind, pretty, happy, playful, caring, loving mother, and that in her absence, and after his initial breakdown, her dad seemed more content without her. *Some people bring out the worst in one another, Daisy. Your dad and I are two of those people.*

Scott had come to dinner twice and had even brought dessert the second time. When he told her he was enjoying the bachelor lifestyle with his dad he was telling the truth. They lived on M&S microwave food and the cleaner came three times a week. He and Declan passed each other like ships in the night but when they did spend time together they actually talked. If his dad was in a bad humour Scott just left him to it, and if Scott was entertaining a girl or friends, his dad went out with Rodney or worked late. 'We're fine, Mum,' he said.

Of course, there would be hard times to come and her kids would throw her defection in her face every time they were hurt but, extraordinarily quickly after she'd left home, with the support of the people she loved and who loved her, Lily's life improved a thousand per cent. When she asked herself, *If I knew I was set to leave this earth soon, would I do it all differently?* the honest answer was no. *If it brought me here, I'd do it the same way every time.*

After Lily had dropped her daughter at school, she picked up Clooney and his suitcase. They said goodbye in the airport. Clooney held her tight and kissed the top of her head. She fought tears and gave him a wide, genuine smile. 'Thank you,' she said.

'I love you, Lily Brennan,' he said.

'I love you, Clooney Hayes,' she said, and let him go.

He walked through the gate and disappeared from view. She stood for a minute or two and collected herself.

Time for a new chapter, Lily.

Eve waited until she was strong enough to walk the cliff with Lily before she told her about the tumour. They went up the hill together to their favourite grassy patch. They lay out under a still and warm sky, talking as they had when they were teenagers, Lily resting her head on her arm and Eve staring up at the sky.

Eve told Lily that she'd noticed she was impaired cognitively when she'd returned to New York after her father's death. She was forgetful; numbers and details that had never previously confused her had become difficult to grasp. She was suffering from headaches and had problems with spatial awareness. She had come home because she was tired, bored and wanted a different life, but also because, deep down, she had known that time was running out.

Lily rested on her arm, still and silent, processing the information, but it was hard. She was deeply shocked. 'You survived being hit by a car,' she said.

'Funny old world.'

Lily shook her head from side to side as though somehow that would change Eve's fate. 'Benign tumours are removable. They rarely lead to death,' she said.

'Not this time.'

'How long?' Lily said, sitting up suddenly, anger in her voice, as though Eve was dying just to spite her.

'It's progressing slowly, my symptoms are still relatively minor, it could stall, speed up or slow down further. They don't know.'

'So you could be here for ever?' Lily said, battling tears.

'Yeah,' Eve said, 'for ever and ever.'

On the way back from the cliff they walked slowly hand in hand, until Eve decided it was too sticky, let go and wiped her palm on her jacket. The baby-pink sky was turning red over the harbour.

'Can we finally talk about what happened?' Lily asked, out of nowhere, but Eve knew exactly what she meant.

'Yeah,' she said.

'Declan raped you.'

'Yeah.'

'I must have read that letter a hundred times when I received it and not once did I think of it that way. I thought you were jealous and mean and you wanted to hurt me because I'd crossed the line with Clooney.'

'Is that why you didn't write back?'

'I wrote a lot of letters. Most of them were horrible and I binned them all. Declan had beaten the post. He arrived on my doorstep the day after, telling me he knew about Clooney and that you'd slept together. He begged my forgiveness and asked for a fresh start.'

'I understand.'

'I don't,' Lily said. 'I was so stupid.'

'We both were very, very stupid,' Eve said, and smiled.

'I've kept your letters all these years.'

'I've kept yours too,' Eve said, 'but let's make a pact never to read them. I tried to go back. It didn't work. Let's just stay in the present.'

Lily nodded. 'I want you to know that I began to understand what had really happened after we were married. I should have contacted you but I was married to him.'

'You don't need to explain. I love you, Lily.' She shrugged her newly built shoulder. They walked on for a while in silence.

'A brain tumour?' Lily said. '*Really? A fudging brain tumour?*' she shouted at the red sky. '*Well, you'll have to do better than that, do you hear me?*'

Eve laughed at her friend. 'Yeah, screw you, sky, universe, gods, aliens, nothingness, screw you all!' she said, shaking her fist.

Then Lily turned to her friend, tears raining down her face. 'Fuck you, Eve Hayes,' she said.

'Fuck you too, Lily Brennan.' She took her friend in her arms and kissed her head, the way she'd seen her brother do. 'Think about it this way. Whatever happens, we found our way back to one another to right our wrongs and that's worth something.'

Lily agreed and held her tightly. 'And we'll fight it to the end.'

'Yes, we will.'

Eve told Adam next. He was angry and shouted at her for hiding the truth. He pointed his finger at her and walked across the floor, then back again. When he finally stopped shouting, he stormed out red-faced, only to return an hour later to hold her in his arms on her ridiculously uncomfortable sofa. She explained that she had come home to die and it had taken a car crash to make her want to live. She apologized – she'd always known the all-clear was a mistake. She asked his forgiveness and wondered if he could fall in love with a woman on Death Row. 'I only ask because if the situation was reversed I'd still fall in love with you,' she said, 'and I'm selfish, self-centred and truly believe the world revolves around me.'

He kissed her. 'Don't forget that you're a bitch.'

She grinned. 'To the very end.'

He insisted on more and more tests, and she obliged him because it was the least she could do, having made him a part of her life when she should have known better. The Hayes family just weren't long for this world. *Good luck, Clooney. You'll be the last of us.* The results didn't change, no matter how much Adam wanted them to. The outlook was uncertain. Eve might live for one year or ten, depending on whether the tumour continued to grow or stalled. Two days after she'd told him of the diagnosis, he arrived with two cases.

'What's this?'

'I'm moving in.'

'Who asked you?'

'Life's too short to wait to be asked,' he said. He put his suitcases in Eve's room and after that it was their room and their apartment, and the first thing Adam did was order a new sofa. Every night he'd read about alternative medicines into the early hours. He kept coming back to ayurveda.

He woke her late one night.

'What?'

'Remember when I asked you to go to India?'

'Hmm.'

'You said yes.'

'Hmm.'

'So we're going to Kerala, OK?'

'Hmm.'

'Say yes.'

'Yes.'

He leaned over and kissed her lips. 'I'll book it tomorrow,' he said, and she turned over and fell back to sleep.

She told Clooney via Skype, because she wanted him to see that she was well and happy and, despite the brain tumour, as healthy as she could be. He was the hardest to tell because he had received this kind of news too many times. She was bright and breezy and told him that the outlook was not as bad as he might think. She warned him not to come home.

'I'm coming home.'

'So that you can sit around for the next ten or twenty years and wait for me to die? Because that's how long I intend to live,' she said.

'Eve,' he said.

'Live your life, Clooney, because I'm living mine. OK?'

'If you get any sicker . . .'

'If I get any sicker, Lily will be on to you before I even think about lifting the phone.'

The rest were easy. Gina cried every time she saw her for the first few weeks but after that she settled down: Eve was going nowhere fast. Gar told her she was a trouper and Paul sat down and put his head in his hands. When his face reappeared he told her he and Simone and their little one would be there for her: she wasn't to go anywhere till the kid was born because they wanted her to be godmother.

'Is that because I'm rich and dying?' she asked.

'It was because you're rich – the dying bit is a bonus,' he said.

She laughed. 'I'd be honoured.'

'Good.'

The evening before she and Adam flew to India for a month's stay in Kerala, Eve waited for Lily in the kitchen she had grown up in. Lily had run down the road to get coffee and, without really thinking about it, she started to roam around. She went up the stairs and passed the wall that had once held the pictures of her and her family, which had been replaced with a painting of a sunset. Daisy and Scott's faces greeted her on the wall at the top of the stairs. She walked into the room her mother and father had died in. One wall was painted pale lavender, and it smelt of fresh linen and Lily. In Daisy's room she sat at her old desk and traced the carving of BGML. *Where are you now, Ben? Will I see you again? Are you waiting for me? Unlikely, but it's a nice dream.*

She made her way downstairs, went outside and sat on the swing-set she and Lily had played on.

Daisy appeared with her schoolbag on her back. She dropped it and sat beside Eve. 'Mum told me,' she said.

'Oh,' Eve said.

'Are you scared?'

'No.'

'Why not?'

'What's to be scared of?'

Daisy thought about it for a long time. 'I don't know,' she said.

'I bought you a piano,' Eve said. 'They'll deliver it any day now.'

'Really?' Daisy said. She was pleased and surprised. 'I thought you didn't like me.'

'I like you as much as you like me.'

'Well, then, that's a lot,' Daisy said, grinning.

'It is, now that I've bought you a baby grand.'

'A *baby grand*, holy crap!' She jumped off the swing.

'Where are you going?'

She pointed to Terry the Tourist's. 'To tell Willie.'

'You're welcome!' Eve shouted after her.

Daisy stopped, turned and walked back to her. Eve stopped swinging and Daisy hugged her. 'Thanks, Eve,' she said, and ran off, leaving Eve alone again on the swing.

'You're welcome, Miss Daisy,' she said, and her eyes welled. She wondered if she'd live to see the girl grow up, follow her dreams and fall in love.

When Lily returned with coffee she found her contemplative friend swinging so she joined her. They swung slowly at first, then faster and faster and higher and higher until their feet were touching the sky.

'The one who swings highest gets a wish,' Eve said.

'I know what my wish is,' Lily said. 'I love you, Eve Hayes.'

'I love you, Lily Brennan.'

They screamed at one another just as they had when they were little girls. When they both felt sick and the swing-set jerked a little ominously, they stopped, walked back inside and got busy with living.

Eve's Bucket List
- One month with Adam in Kerala at an ayurvedic spa. ✓ FANTASTIC, I feel amazing.
- Be there for the birth of Paul's baby. ✓ Aaaah, it's a little girl called Lisa.

- Oversee the sale of Lily's house and the transfer of Lily's half. ✓ No gloating – time to let go.
- Be at Lisa's christening. ✓ Priest didn't even ask if I was a Catholic. What an odd ceremony.
- Take Adam, Lily and Daisy to Peru for two weeks. ✓ I miss Clooney.
- Buy the apartment. ✓ Finally I'm home.
- Get to know Scott. ✓ Ongoing.
- Live unwedded and happily ever after with Adam. ✓ Ongoing.
- Sell the house to Lily for €100. ✓
- Lodge €50 into Clooney's account. ✓
- See the Ginger Monster go to prison.
- Be there for Lisa's first steps.
- Be there for Scott's graduation.
- Be there for Daisy's wedding.
- Live long enough to see Clooney and Lily reunited.
- Screw it, hang on till I'm seventy.

Eve's Funeral Plan

Lily,

Make sure they don't lay me out for people to look at and touch me. The number of neighbours and strangers who touched Danny's face was outrageous.

Regarding the (closed) casket, I'd prefer a dark one to light. Light wood just looks cheaper. And unvarnished, if possible.

I've no problem with flowers, as long as they are not carnations or lilies (no offence).

Obviously it won't be a religious ceremony, it will simply be a gathering to remember me and send me on my way to a full stop or a new beginning wherever that may be. I'd like you to speak, and Clooney and Adam, of course. I've got quite close to Daisy in the recent months, and if she wanted to say something that would be cool, if not I understand. Paul won't speak, but Gar and Gina might, and that's fine too.

NB I do not want the speeches to be sappy and/or boring. Please let nobody talk about me like I was something special and the best person they ever knew (well, maybe you can but no one else). I hate watching the news when someone is killed and their friends and family say that they were the most amazing person who ever lived and there has never been or never will be a person like them. I've yet to hear someone say: 'Ah, he was all right, a bit of a dick with drink on him, but to be fair, he didn't deserve to be stabbed.' I want people to be real and say how they feel. I'm not perfect. I want that reflected.

Music is very important. Make sure wherever you hold the memorial service it's wired for sound. Keanan's was dreadful so don't lay me out there. I'd like 'Tower Of Song' by Leonard Cohen and I want the full song played – don't turn it off halfway. That's all eight verses. After that I'd like 'Grapefruit Moon' by Tom Waits, and just for fun and for Adam, Ray LaMontagne's 'Trouble'. I'd love Daisy to play keyboard if she wants, she's such a beautiful player. The piece she does from The Piano soundtrack is amazing but again I don't want to push her. Having said that, if I live till she's over twenty I'll be really pissed off if she doesn't.

There will be a large fund put aside for the after party and I want it to be a party. Leave me in the box in the funeral home and head to the Killiney Hotel. They will put on a four-course meal and I want you all to drink and dance till dawn. When I'm ashes, and no matter what time of the year it is, wait until it's a sunny day, then take Danny's old boat out: you, Clooney, Adam, Daisy and Scott, if he wants to come. Gar, Gina, Paul, Simone and my goddaughter are also welcome. Bring a picnic and throw me into the sea with the fishes and Danny, and don't be sad. Be happy we found one another again and we were lucky enough to live the lives we've lived, and when Adam is sad and lonely *remind him that he was loved and will love again, even if he makes his annoyed face.*

I love you, Lily Brennan.

Eve XXX

PS Very important, make sure to check the direction of the wind before you pour me into the sea. Wind direction is key.

To whom it may concern

As of today Eve Hayes still lives.

Love

Lily

Acknowledgements

I was knocked down when I was twenty and I've always wanted to tell that story, but instead of a simple car-hit-pedestrian scenario, I wanted to write about an incredible accident, one that the reader would question as to whether or not it was possible. I wasn't having much luck until one day in the TV3 dressing room I asked producer Tom Fabozzi if he knew of anyone who would have a story to share. He proceeded to tell me about the accident he and his girlfriend had been involved in one late night in Sligo in the early nineties. It was incredible. In fact, so incredible that every aspect of the accident has been re-created here, including, unbelievably, some of the dialogue. I replaced Tom with my character Eve, and wrote it exactly as he told it. He shared X-rays and reports with me, talked me through every detail of his recovery, and we both reminisced about hospital life and the monotony that comes with being broken and bed-bound. Tom's kindness, patience, and his ability to recall the most horrific night of his life with such clarity and humour have been invaluable, and I am so grateful to him because the rest of the story and its tone came from there. Thanks so much, Tom. We'll all miss you in the halls of TV3 and wish you every success in your new role with Fine Gael.

Speaking of TV3, I'd like to thank all the team and the ladies I've met through *The Midday Show* – it's been an honour and a pleasure working with you all.

Thank you to Dr Thomas in the ayurvedic spa at the Carlton Atlantic Coast Hotel in Westport for his invaluable advice.

To all my pals and family – after five books you know who you are. I love you all.

To my husband Donal, for always being there and taking care of me so well. I'm grateful for you every day.

And sincerest apologies to the people who went hungry when I locked myself away for months on end: Hallie, Jo, John, Enda, Tracy, Lainey C, Eimear, The D'Oracle, Gamo . . . loosen up your belt buckles because the feeder is back.